Praise for JF Ridgley

Red Fury Revolt

"A positively great read! Once again, Ms. Ridgley has a winner. Her character development and attention to detail make it nearly impossible to put the book down after just a few pages!"
—Casey Gemeny

"A well-researched and extremely readable account of the Boudicca rebellion. I read a lot of historical fiction on the Roman army. This is the third such novel I've read on the Boudicca revolt and it's certainly on a par with *The Year of Ravens* and *The Eagle and the Raven*, which is saying something since the latter is a classic. The Agricola character is well drawn as is Suetonius and Boudicca, of course. I will certainly buy the following books in the series."

Vows of Revenge

"The best book I've read all year! The literary world needs JF Ridgley! I knew this book would probably be good after reading a few short stories from Ridgley, but I didn't know just how good. How good? Damn good! Get it now, good. This book is like a feast. I would LOVE to see it adapted for the big screen. Epic, epic, epic. Can't wait for the author's next novel."

"A great read beginning to end. I couldn't put it down. Villains that you hate and hero's that you can't help loving."

Threatened Loyalties

"Ridgley has woven a wonderful tale. Love, identity, rebellion, intrigue, and adventure in ancient Rome. Well-executed plot and engaging prose. Very infrequent, minor editing quirks that are easily overlooked and forgotten."

"I love the way this author melds romance of her characters and real-life events in Ancient Rome. This book had me hooked from the beginning."

For the Family

"JF Ridgley is a bold, gritty, new author. Her words grab you by the throat and don't let you go. Viciria is a fantastic historical character. If you like Spartacus, Ridgley is the writer for you! Give this book a shot and let a Rome expert open a door to the past and show you things you never knew happened in Rome."

"Again, she got me on page one. She is one awesome writer who has a lot of ideas in her head. Can't wait to read everything she writes."

Other books by JF Ridgley

Historical Fiction
Red Fury Rage
A Roman Affair
Red Fury Rebellion
Games Romans Play
Vows of Revenge
Birth of a Bully
Threatened Loyalties
For the Family
Mirrored Reflections

Contemporary Romance
18 Wheeler
Love Backwards

Praise for Red Fury Revolt

I feel that Ms. Ridgley has done very well at telling her story, while being respectful to the events that devastated Britannia, and even shook the Roman Empire itself, in A.D. 60 to 61.

This book would have made an excellent stand-alone novel; however, I am glad to see that Ms. Ridgley intends to make it into a series. Those familiar with Roman history in Britannia will recognize some of the names; names of individuals whose place in history would culminate over twenty years after the end of this book. I look forward to reading them.

James Mace
Author of *Soldier of Rome: The Artorian Chronicles*

BOOK ONE OF THE AGRICOLA SERIES

RED FURY REVOLT

JF RIDGLEY

Paperback ISBN 978-1-951269-42-5

JF Ridgley: http://www.jfridgley.com
Cover art: Cathy Helms www.AvalonGraphics.org
Editing: Nathan Barnes http://www.SharperQuill.com

Rpridepublishing

To Joe,

Thank you for believing in my dreams.

Foreword

By James Mace

WHENEVER WE HEAR about known historical persons, in this case Gnaeus Julius Agricola, historians tend to focus on the more sensational events, rather than the persons themselves. We are left to decide for ourselves what type of man he was. Was he a loving husband and father, was he a kind and just person, or was he prone to vices such as avarice and cruelty? We do not know. The most detailed accounts we have of his life come from the historian, Tacitus, who was Agricola's son-in-law. Because of this, it is often assumed that anything written about Julius Agricola would be prone to bias and flattery. Strangely enough, though, Tacitus says little about the man himself, but rather he focuses strictly on his achievements. And like every case of when an author attempts to pen a novel based around actual events wherever the histories are vacant, one must use conjecture and no small amount of literary license.

So, when JF Ridgley asked me to write the forward for her first book, I confess I was honored, with a bit of trepidation. As an author of historical novels set in Ancient Rome, it is extremely difficult for me to enjoy reading similar works. This is true of many authors, who will often find themselves inadvertently comparing the book they are reading to their own works. Many of us view this as a great tragedy; that we often lose the joy in reading a genre we love. That being said, what drew me into this novel was that it was quite different from my own Roman works, which tend to be very battle-centric, and more focused on the military aspects of the story. Ms. Ridgley provides here a very compelling and highly emotional human-interest story about two very different people joined together, and subsequently torn apart by the violent events surrounding Boudica's rebellion.

When she came to me asking for advice as well as some good source material, she made it clear that, while the characteristics of Julius and the other protagonists were entirely of her own making, she wanted to make certain she got the actual historical events reasonably correct. Too often, an author will blatantly twist, or outright change known historical fact, in order for it to melt with their story; so, I admired that she was willing to put in the extra effort to avoid this as much as possible. One book that I strongly recommended for her was George Shipway's *Imperial Governor*, which I feel is one of the most underrated historical novels out there. It is a delicate balance that historical novelists attempt to maintain: the telling of the stories that are in their minds and in their hearts, while maintaining a sense of historical accuracy and believability.

Character LIST

Romans

Nero - emperor of Rome

Decianus Catus - procurator/tax collector Suetonius Paulinus - consul/governor of Britannia

Gnaeus Julius Agricola - tribune and tribune laticlavius; second-in-command

Essex - Julius' first personal slave

Lugh - Julius' second personal slave

Valerius - Julius' uncle and first centurion

Primus Pilius- first centurion of the Ist cohort

Valeria Procilla - Julius' mother and Valerius' sister

Domitia Decidiana - Julius' betrothed

Marcus - Julius' friend and decurion/officer in charge of cavalry and the official guard

Centurio Felix - first centurion to Julius

Demetrius - retired centurion who cares for wounded.

Prasutagus - dead leader, husband of Boudica, father of Morrigan and Rhianna

Boudica - wife of Prasutagus, mother of Morrigan and Rhianna, leader of the revolt and the Iceni tribe

Morrigan - Boudica's elder daughter

Mergith - warrior and Morrigan's betrothed Rhianna - Boudica's younger daughter

Myrradin - druid priest

Neeca - slave rescued and adopted by Rhianna

Trinovantes

Diras - leader, father of Calgacus

Marleth - wife of Diras, mother of Calgacus

Calgacus - son of Diras, Rhianna's intended

Tancorix - friend of Calgacus, warrior

Iceni – Britanni

Glossary

Auxiliary - non-Roman soldiers from various provinces

Ballistae - any manned weapon such as a scorpion, or catapult

Carnu - upright horn of the Britanni

Cavalry - auxiliary soldiers on horseback under the command of a Roman officer/decurio

Century - ten groups of less than a hundred soldiers who make up one cohort

Centurion (referred to as centurio) - most experienced soldier on the field. Carries a vitus stick as a symbol of authority. . . and he can use it

Consul - commander of the province

Cornicen - plays the circular horn 'carnu' to sound the consul's orders

Cohort - ten divisions within the legion

Decurion (referred to as decurio) - cavalry officer in charge of the auxiliary cavalry

Fortress - main housing for a legion

Fort - outside housing for a legion

Javelin - narrow-throated spear that bends upon impact. Soldiers carry two

Laticlavius - second-in-command to the consul or legate/highest tribune (usually a young officer with no experience)

Legate - commander of a legion

Legion - army unit of Roman soldiers

Marching Camp - mobile housing dug in each night, filled in each day

Optio - carries the unit's eagle, second-in-command to the centurion

Principia - main headquarters of the highest officer

Praetoria - consul's living quarters

Signifier - carries the unit's signum/banner and relays orders to the centurion during battle

Tribune - lieutenant in charge of two cohorts each. Five tribunes to a legion

Tubicen - plays the 'J'-shaped horn of the cavalry and sounds the decurion's orders

Centurions of the Cohorts

Centurions of the Centuries match the centurion of the cohort All wear red capes ,red tunics ,greaves on calves, carries a *Vitis stick*/oak staff

Primus Pilus
First Cohort
Call: Long

Second Centurio
Call: Long

Third Centurio
Call: Long /Short

Fourth Centurio
Call: Long/Long/ Short

Fifth Centurio
Call: Short/Short/ Short

Sixth Centurio
Call: Short/ Short /Long

Seventh Centurio
Call: Short /Long/ Short

Eighth Centurio
Call:Short /long / Long

Ninth Centurio
Call: Long/ Long /Long

Tenth Centurio
Call: Long /Short / Short

All legionaries/soldiers - Red capes- Red crests- Red Tunics

Legion Officers

Emperor of the Empire of Rome
Purple/ gold Cape
Purple or gold tunic or whatever he wants to wear

Praetorian Guard -protects the Emperor
Purple Cape
White tunic w/ 2 narrow vertical stripes

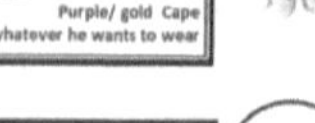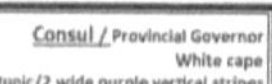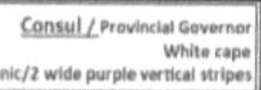

Consul / Provincial Governor
White cape
White tunic/2 wide purple vertical stripes

Tribune Laticlavius -Second in Command
White cape
White tunic/2 wide purple vertical stripes

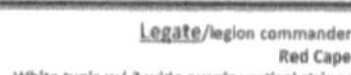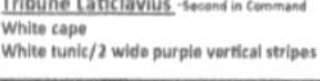

Legate/legion commander
Red Cape
White tunic w/ 2 wide purple vertical stripes

Legion Tribunes

Red Cape   White tunic w/ 2 narrow vertical stripes
in charge of two cohorts

| 1st/2nd | 3rd/4th | 5th/6th | 7th/8th | 9th/10th |

Decurio
In charge of Cavalry
Red Cape White tunic w/ 2 narrow vertical purple

Praefecti/Admiral
In charge of Navy
Blue cape White tunic w/ 2 narrow purple stripes

Prologue

"TRIBUNE GNAEUS JULIUS AGRICOLA, you finally found us." An arrogant smirk grew on Decianus Catus' round face as he lounged his thick body back in his chair. The stink of greed pulsed around Julius as he stood before the tax collector's desk. Gold dangled from the man's neck, wrapped both wrists, and encircled each finger of his hands. Even his blue tunic was embroidered with gold threads.

"My apologies, procurator. I had hoped that by now, you had received the report that storms delayed my arrival."

"I did."

Decianus fingered the scroll lying on the cluttered desk. A scheming spark danced in the man's beady eyes. He leaned forward and laced his fingers in front of him. "I received Suetonius' orders temporarily appointing you as my tribune. At your uncle's request, I am sure." The corner of his narrow lips lifted. "So, I am certain, you are well-trained to kiss ass."

Julius bit his lip to quell a rebuttal. This, being his first assignment as tribune, he could not piss off Nero's appointed procurator to Britannia. "Hopefully, my abilities will benefit Rome."

Decianus chuckled softly and then flicked his finger as if dismissing Julius like a slave. "Get your things in order. We attend the Iceni chief's funeral tomorrow."

Prasutagus had died? The Iceni chieftain was one of Rome's best allies in Britannia, deserving of Rome's highest regard, especially at his funeral. Yet something about Decianus' words did not set right in Julius' gut.

However, that was not his concern now. This was his first assignment with the legion, and this detachment from the XXth Valeria needed his fullest attention.

"Yes, procurator." Julius saluted then realized he was saluting a civilian. Decianus was an equestrian—not an officer. Feeling stupid, Julius evacuated the suffocating tent.

The site of Decianus' Germanic guards lounging before the procurator's tent bothered Julius like a rash. They were big brutes who reminded him of dumb oxen with long hair, flowing mustaches, and a sneering arrogance that pulsed from their flesh as greed had from Decianus.

His personal slave, Essex, unfortunately had to direct the camp slaves to raise his tent next to Decianus. All across Rome's empire, the official tents were placed side-by-side in the fort's center, leaving Julius no choice in the matter of where his lodgings were to be put up.

Julius rolled his shoulders and scanned the marching camp that stretched before him like a busy quilt. Horses grazed in the wide ring of grass encircling perfect rows of tan leather tents of the two centuries from the XXth Valeria. Soldiers drilled near the gates, enduring the stern scrutiny of their centurions. Guards strolled the top of an encircling berm of fresh earth, as they scanned the distant trees beyond the rain-filled ditch outside the perimeter of the dirt wall. Those soldiers, who were off-duty, stirred their food rations in pots over small, snapping fires before their tents, sharpened swords, or polished armor and shields. Bursts of laughter punctuated the evening air.

At last. This was what Julius had always wanted, the chance to be with the real men of Rome—the legions. Fortunately, his assignment with Decianus was only temporary. Whatever else awaited him had to be left to the gods.

Fragrant herbs hanging from rafters of the thatched roof scented the main hall where Boudica's heart lay dead in her chest. Her husband's body awaited his warriors to carry him to his funeral stanchion.

She needed to hear him laugh and to drown in his smile. She needed to see his blue gaze that could challenge the clearest day. But the gods had taken him from her without warning.

She brushed aside his golden mustache, remembering how his hands, his mouth, and his body had feasted on hers through the many years.

A sob cut through her. Her knees crumbled, and she dropped to the bench beside him. He is gone! So suddenly! Why? Why had the mother goddess taken him? Why?

Prasutagus had balanced her. She couldn't deal with the Romans without him because she despised every one that stepped onto Iceni lands. Even now, would the Iceni people even accept her as their leader? No assurance came.

Boudica covered her face and let tears pour into her hands. A soft hand slid across her shoulders. "Mother."

Their youngest daughter sat on the bench beside her. Rhianna's long, golden hair—hair the same color as her father's—brushed across Boudica's knees. "Mother, I want him back," seeped from her lips.

"As I do, Rhianna." Boudica clutched her daughter's hand. "As do I."

Her daughter's large, blue eyes pleaded for what could never be—Prasutagus' return. "Father seemed so healthy when he returned from the hunt."

"I know. I know." If she had known her husband was ill, she would never have argued with him about granting Nero half of the Iceni lands should he die. It was an old, bitter argument that she could never agree to. This was their land. Not Rome's. The old fury resumed its burn.

Their eldest daughter strode into the hall and melted onto the bench. Rarely did anything crack the shell that surrounded Morrigan, yet tears streamed silently from the girl's gray eyes.

Boudica hugged both—Rhianna, her father's gentle daughter, and Morrigan, the daughter who matched her own looks as well as her hatred for Rome.

Both daughters were betrothed to warriors who would stand with her, an assurance she would need now. Morrigan had Mergith, son of the Iceni. Their union would keep the Iceni blood pure. Rhianna had Calgacus, Diras' son of the Trinovante, whose hatred of Rome remained strong.

Long ago, Romans had claimed Diras' city and renamed it Camulodunum. Like all the other tribes in Britannia, Rome had demanded the Trinovantes' absolute submission. Many hated this Roman yoke as much as she did.

Myrradin stepped into the hall. The druid priest was a sliver of a man and always dressed as a shadow. "Your people await their new leader," he said. The sound of his voice held no compassion.

"Has Diras arrived?" Boudica asked.

"No."

With a weary sigh, she stood, bringing her daughters up with her. "Then it is time. We go now. We must see your father to his people."

Chapter 1

"CRONE MAIDEN. MOTHER." "Destroyer. Beginner. Increaser." "Death. Birth. Fruitfulness." The druid's chants commanded the air, as warriors lifted her father to his funeral stanchion. Rhianna clutched the pendant, embossed with a racing Iceni horse that her father had given her for her bonding day with Calgacus. It matched Morrigan's pendant that now pierced the drape of wool at Mergith's shoulder.

This same horse image also crowned her father's helmet, shadowing his face, and his round shield, lying atop the seven-colored cloak blanketing his body.

Only days ago, her father had burst into the main hall, his boisterous laugh lifting to the rafters. He had swept her up in his arms and swung her in circles. "Ah, my beautiful Rhianna. News. Where is your mother?"

During another argument over Rome, he had collapsed in Boudica's arms. She and Morrigan had bolted to his side, only to hear his dying wish, something Rhianna failed to understand. But her mother had promised she would honor it with her life.

Now, her mother stood alone, beside his stanchion, stalwart as any warrior, knowing the Iceni now looked to her to protect them from Rome's greed.

Her mother couldn't do that alone. She needed the Trinovantes' respect, so all tribes would recognize her as the Iceni leader. Otherwise, the gold torc around her neck meant nothing.

Her mother's sharp features, her iron-gray gaze, and long, auburn hair radiated that strength. Even though Rhianna stood with Morrigan at the opposite end of the burial mound, there was no doubt her mother felt as alone and abandoned as she did. Neither she nor her mother had anyone to stand at their sides this day. Yet, Morrigan had Mergith.

Unlike Morrigan and Mergith, whose souls had already joined, hers and Calgacus' had not. His constant attention suffocated her. Yet, for the first time, she wished he were there.

She scanned the distant trees as the Iceni continued to lay their parting gifts in the pit beneath the burial stanchion. Each person nodded to her mother and then passed to rejoin the others chanting to honor her father. Bronze trinkets, silver bowls, flasks of ale, colorful blankets, and more created mounds of gifts that would see him home. Proof of their love and respect.

Like a winter wind, the air seemed to freeze at the sound of distant drumbeats and the clank of metal from the nearby valley. People's attention shifted to the hide of a silver wolf concealing a Roman soldier carrying a wooden staff that displayed the standard of Rome's tax collector.

Behind that standard rode a Roman officer wearing a black-crested helmet. His red cape draped the rear haunches of his horse ornamented with silver trappings. Behind him glided a column of soldiers like a long, metal-scaled snake. Every soldier carried a large, red, rectangular shield with a yellow-winged pattern and wore a gladius banging against his thigh. Their long, red capes swayed with each measured step.

Cavalry soldiers riding silver-decorated horses escorted the cloth-covered box carried in the middle of the column. Following them strode a guard of bare-chested men whose long hair draped like capes down their well-muscled backs. The black-crested officer raised a hand and barked, "Halt!"

A circular trumpet sounded, and the serpent's body stopped. A man wearing a white tunic with two, narrow purple stripes, appeared from the cloth box. The odd-looking guards accompanied this Roman as he strode up the rise toward her father's stanchion. His gaze fastened on the piles of funeral gifts.

Her mother's sharp glower followed each step until the Roman halted before her. "Who are you, Roman, to intrude this day?"

The man tore his attention from the gifts to focus on her mother.

"Decianus Catus. Procurator of Rome."

"If you come to honor my husband, you are welcome. If not, I demand you leave."

"Demand?" A glimmer of mirth lit in his eyes. "And you are?"

"I am the queen of the Iceni. You will deal with me now." The procurator lifted a hand, a finger pointing skyward.

It flicked. "Tribune."

The black-crested officer dismounted and motioned to a soldier with the white crest stretching across his helmet.

"Centurio. With me."

Both strode through the guards and joined the procurator on the rise. The man glanced back at the officer. "Circle the stanchion."

Stunned, the tribune hesitated. Even the centurion shifted with uncertainty.

"You heard me, tribune. Give the order."

The tribune jerked to life. "Centurio, circle as ordered." The centurion raised the first two fingers of each hand and pointed between the stanchion and her people. One hand circled to the left and the other to the right.

Rhianna's heart clambered in her chest the moment the serpent split and separated her, her mother, Morrigan, and Mergith from the rest of the Iceni.

Outside the silver ring, her people stirred. Men reached for weapons. Churl, her father's first warrior, jerked his sword arm across his chest. "Wait."

The women restrained the men with a gentle touch while children hid in their mothers' skirts. Mergith caught her sister's wrist, stopping her from going to their mother. "Churl said to wait."

"I regret to find the leader of the Iceni dead," the procurator said loud enough for the gods to hear. "Still, I have orders from Rome to collect payments on loans granted to the Iceni."

"We owe nothing to anyone," Boudica announced. "Not even to Rome."

"Records show your people owe much for the loans that built Camulodunum."

"Camulodunum?" Her mother shrieked with laughter. "We owe nothing to your designs, except for what my husband granted your emperor."

The procurator relaxed back on one leg. "What has the leader of the Iceni granted Rome?"

Rhianna could only wonder what thoughts were searing through her mother's mind. Finally, Boudica spoke. "Prasutagus grants half of the Iceni wealth and no more to this Nero." Her hand flicked as if throwing a tidbit at this man.

"And you have papers proving this agreement?"

Those who could hear gasped at such an insult. "Proof?" Boudica huffed loudly. "We have no need for proof. Our word is law. Is not Rome's word equal?"

"No papers?" Laughter bellowed from the Roman's lips. "Tribune, they expect us to accept the word of a woman who calls herself their leader."

The tribune stared at the fool and then said, "The Iceni have never proven false before, procurator."

"And how would you know that, tribune?" The man's gaze locked on Morrigan's glare. "See that they don't interfere."

The tribune nodded to the centurion, who pointed to six soldiers to stand beside Rhianna, Morrigan, and Mergith.

Somehow, the druid had escaped. Rhianna found him lingering in the shadows of the distant trees.

Like a tightening noose, she couldn't breathe until the tribune's worried gaze found hers. *Please stop this. Whatever is happening, please make him stop.* She willed her message to him and gasped when he jerked away his attention.

The procurator raised a hand. "Agreed! Half of the Iceni wealth now belongs to Rome, as well as the payments owed." Fury exploded on her mother's face. She scooped a handful of dirt at her feet and flung it into the Roman's face. "How dare you insult my husband's dying wish with your greed?"

He backhanded her, twisting her mother aside like a bent tree.

"By word of Rome, I dare."

Pain seared through Rhianna as if she had been the one slapped. She cried out and staggered backward. The nearest soldier grabbed her by the waist before she could race to her mother.

In that same instant, the ring of soldiers braced behind their shields, their swords appearing like metal teeth.

"Curse you! Curse Rome!" Boudica screamed and then coated the procurator's face with spit. Cheers and laughter roared through the Iceni.

The procurator simply lifted the edge of his red cape and wiped his face. The cape dropped, and his finger pointed at Boudica. "Flog her."

Churl's arm shot forward, releasing her father's warriors into the soldiers like a stampede, only they began to fall beneath the locked shields and stabbing swords. The air filled with metal striking metal and cries of pain.

Soldiers barely restrained her and Morrigan, while the Roman's guards strung their mother to Prasutagus' stanchion like an animal hide.

"Mergith!"

Morrigan's scream tore Rhianna's attention to her sister, where two soldiers jerked their blades from her man's belly. Wrenching free, Morrigan fell to the ground, clutching Mergith's body to her chest. Screams and tears exploded from her as the man she loved wilted lifeless in her arms.

Rhianna thrashed against the arm wrapping her waist and searched for someone to end this. *The tribune.* "Do something! For the sake of my father, the gods. Stop this. Please!" The tribune looked skyward as if beseeching the gods, his fists clinching. Meanwhile, the procurator began removing her mother's silver bracelets, even the comb in her hair and lifted the royal torc for all to see. "Rome's first payment." Then he ripped her mother's gown away and nodded at the centurion. "Begin."

The centurion glanced at the tribune. While glaring at the procurator, he nodded.

The lash fell and then fell again, continuing to destroy her mother's flesh while the remaining Iceni people watched, helplessly confined by soldiers.

Rhianna's insides twisted as Morrigan's sobs cut through her, and the lashes sliced the entirety of her mother's body. Lurching free from the soldier's grip, Rhianna bolted for the stanchion to protect her mother. She had to stop this, to do whatever she had to, to stop this horror.

Barely two strides away, an arm clamped her against the leather cuirass of the tribune. His worried expression radiating in his gaze was her only hope.

"Please, don't let him kill my mother. Please."

He thrust her back to another soldier. "Take her. And keep her this time."

The soldier dragged her back to Morrigan. Another soldier had stretched her sister's throat to the sun as she spewed curses on every Roman soul present.

Rhianna glared at the tribune as lash after lash continued until her mother's body sagged against the ropes. As if called, his gaze found her and his jerked away as if stung. "Halt!" barked from his lips, and the whip wilted to the ground.

The procurator wheeled, livid at the order. "What in Hades are you doing, tribune, giving that order?"

"You want her dead?"

"Do I care if she is?"

Not only had the tribune stopped the flogging, but he also seemed to welcome the procurator's wrath with a direct glare.

Relief barely had time to melt through Rhianna as her mother struggled to her feet. "You filthy pieces of shit," spewed from Boudica's lacerated lips.

The procurator stormed to the stanchion and then jerked her mother's face up to his. "No one insults Rom—" Again, she covered his face with bloody spit.

Again, he cleansed his flesh of the insult with his cape, but this time he smiled. "Take them all prisoner!"

When his friend Tancorix stumbled through the trees, Calgacus released the axle of the broken wagon to the ground.

"It's. . . insane!" Tancorix gasped. He bent over to breathe. "They've taken them. . . all but the dead. . . to the fort. The Iceni. Everyone."

Calgacus and his father rushed toward the warrior. The rest of the Trinovante gathered around them. "What? They what?" his father asked.

Tancorix shook his head and shrugged. "The Romans. . . also flogged Boudica."

"No." Diras ran a hand through his long hair. "They flogged Boudica?"

The warrior nodded. "Yes."

Fear hotter than fire seared through Calgacus. "What about Rhianna?"

His friend's gaze hit him like a fist. "They took her and all the others."

"They better not touch her. Rhianna is mine, and I'll kill any Roman who does." He scanned the bristling warriors ready to kill every Roman who had crossed their lands. "Enough of Rome's insults. Let's go."

Before he stepped away, his father slammed him against the nearest tree trunk. "Don't be a fool, son. You know how many Romans are here." Pain and rage flooded his father's face. "And you know we don't have the weapons to fight. Not yet."

Calgacus didn't care about weapons. He didn't care about how many Romans he had to face. "It's Rhianna. You know what they'll do to her. . . and all the other women."

His father's grip eased slightly. However, his determined, blue gaze grew hotter. "I assure you, Calgacus. . . and all of you." Diras scanned those surrounding him. "The Romans will pay for this and for more. For everything. But not today. This, I promise."

Chapter 2

JULIUS BRISTLED AS HE RODE alongside the Iceni prisoners as they stumbled toward the marching camp, their hatred intensifying with each step. And why not? After all, Decianus had claimed the king's burial wealth and the Iceni plunder—all carried back to camp in the soldiers' capes. Did the insult stop there? By the gods, no.

The greedy fool had demanded the Iceni be taken prisoner to be sold as slaves for insulting him, gloating that he would have Boudica sent to Nero as a prize.

Obviously, it never mattered to Decianus that recent reports had warned that Britanni tribes were growing restless of Rome's demand for taxes as well as submission to its laws.

Regardless of what Rome did for them, which amounted to stopping their continual warring, financing the building of roads and temples, and establishing sensible laws that increased trade with the Empire.

What was more, this insult to the Iceni could easily become something that the Senate could not afford right now. Everyone knew Nero was depleting the treasury at an alarming rate with his self-serving greed.

Julius sagged under the weight of Decianus' matching imperial arrogance. He could not stop the flogging, nor could he stop Decianus from bringing the women into camp. And since Nero's imperial procurator knew that, he could do as he damn well pleased. His orders were only to protect the fool's ass. *Sons of Dis and Jupiter, help me stop this man.*

Felix strode alongside Julius' horse. The centurion's red cape paled to the rage burning on his face. "Jupiter's balls, tribune, you cannot allow the procurator to do this. You well know, women are not to be in any camp. There will be nothing but fights and disorder. More men will be out of commission before dawn than from any battle."

Julius almost laughed. And just how was he to stop the bastard from dragging whomever he pleased into the camp? The centurion pounded his palm with the polished grapevine—or *vitus*—that all centurions used to enforce an order. And right now, it appeared Felix wanted something to pound.

Julius almost pitied the men. "See that the men are too exhausted to do any more than fall asleep, centurio. I do not care how you see this done."

Felix almost smiled.

Julius' thoughts shifted to the golden-haired daughter walking beside her mother carried by her warriors. He could not erase the image of her deep, blue gaze pleading for him to stop Decianus. If she only knew how he truly wanted to stop this disrespect to her father. Prasutagus never deserved what was happening, nor did her people.

Yet there she stood so innocent, so alone. When she bolted toward her mother, he had to stop her before the lash touched her as well. Such horror should never ruin such perfection.

If he found a way to protect her, would the gods recognize his meager attempt? Would it appease their wrath and redirect it toward the true source of this contempt—Decianus Catus? An idea came to him: a pathetic and meager one.

Julius turned his horse toward his friend wearing the red and black crest indicating his authority over the cavalry riding outside the column.

"Decurio, to me," Julius said, and then wheeled away from the formation. He stopped a safe distance away to wait for Marcus to join him. "The blonde daughter. I want you to get her to my tent before anyone touches her."

Marcus stared at him in shock. "You? Of all people."

Julius glared at the decurion. "To appease the gods for what that idiot started back there. By the gods, Marcus, it was the man's funeral."

"Right, Julius. Certainly. Come morning, the entire camp will be saying the same. They only fucked the women to appease the gods."

Julius' horse felt his frustration and danced restlessly. "Just see this done, decurio."

"Tribune, send wagons back to collect what was left," Decianus said the minute Julius drew his horse to a walk beside the man's litter.

"The mother bitch, keep her alive. Oh, and burn everything."

Julius slid from the horse so he could talk as privately as possible with the fool. "Procurator, women are not to be inside the camp. I thought you knew that."

"I do," Decianus shrugged, "but as prisoners; they are prisoners—to be sold to pay taxes they owe Rome. And tell me, just where am I to keep them if not inside the camp? As I see it, the camp is your responsibility, tribune. So, see that your centurions keep order."

"If I am to keep order in the camp, then I expect to see that the women are kept with the rest of the prisoners and nowhere else."

"Oh, I think not, tribune. I want them brought to our tent area. My guards and I will see they are well taken care of there."

Julius could barely swallow the mounting bile strangling him.

Decianus chuckled from inside the curtains where he lay sprawled like a puddle of old mush. "What? Are you afraid of their gods, tribune?"

"No. Of ours." Julius vaulted onto his horse and returned to the front of the column.

Smoke from the braziers cooking the evening meal lingered over the marching camp as he rode through the gates. He dismounted, handing the reins to the attending soldier, and faced Felix. "Call order."

The cornicens sounded. The soldiers on duty scurried into formation before a centurion.

Julius met the gaze of the short, defiant centurion. "Take the Iceni queen to the medic's tent."

"Yes, tribune. The women?" Felix asked.

"Take them the procurator's tent in the praetoria. Post guards to see no one leaves. Is that clear, centurio?"

"Gladly, tribune."

"And be sure the male prisoners are well secured, where they see little. They will hear enough. Keep the children there."

By the time the Iceni prisoners were shoved through the gate, the camp had jolted to life like an excited beehive. Already, the off-duty soldiers had encircled the Iceni women like hungry wolves, their hands fondling flesh.

Every nerve in Julius' body felt raked. "Centurio, take the men back to the Iceni village for the rest of Decianus' plunder. Leave nothing of value and burn everything. Then double the guard."

A vicious smile beneath the white crest. "Consider that done, Tribune. The more men kept away and busy, the fewer to flog tomorrow."

Now, all he could do was to try to protect the golden- haired daughter from the horror about to explode. Then deal with whatever came at sunrise.

As wives were torn from their husbands and mothers and daughters yanked apart and fondled like livestock, they fought the assault like the Furies. As Decianus' guards forced the women through the camp, lascivious glee mixed with ignored campfires and smells of burning food.

Julius' stomach fully collapsed with no sign of the golden-haired daughter anywhere. "Venus, I beg you, help Marcus get her to my tent untouched," whispered from his lips. "And I will do what I can to see she remains so."

"Be brave, little sister. Don't let them break you," were Morrigan's last words before rough hands tore Rhianna from her sister.

Panic crippled Rhianna's body as the soldier with a red and black crest dragged her toward the camp's center ahead of the others. She fought his grip every step of the way until he tossed her inside one of the larger tents.

The moment he released her, she charged for the tent flaps where two smirking soldiers stood guard. The soldier grabbed her and tossed her back inside.

"Stay here. Do not go out there. Understand?" he ordered.

She understood well enough. Her father had made sure that she and Morrigan knew the Romans' tongue. "No. Let me go."

A small man wearing a slave's necklace appeared in the tent. The soldier immediately barked an order, "Essex, tell her to stay here. That she will be safe in here if she does. Tell her. Make sure she understands."

Safe? She couldn't breathe. Sweat broke on her skin. How could she be safe? Just beyond the leather walls, shrieks were already erupting with sounds of ripping cloth and coarse male laughter.

"Do not leave this tent or that will happen to you as well," the slave said in Iceni.

"Liar!"

When Morrigan screamed, Rhianna started for the open tent flaps. The soldier grabbed her by the waist again and threw her deeper into the tent. "Listen to Essex."

She stumbled between two large storage chests and braced, ready to claw at either man if they came close.

This Essex stepped in front of her. "Daughter of the Iceni, if Marcus says you are safe here, believe him. He does not lie."

She studied the little man pointing outside toward the terror rising like a firestorm.

"Do not go out there," he said, "unless you choose to be beaten senseless like all the rest of your women. Understand?"

Chapter 3

Julius strode across the walkway of the guard station, above the main gate, while off-duty soldiers swarmed with envy before Decianus' tent. As a centurion approached, they scattered, only to return like flies to a manure pile.

He hoped Marcus managed to get the girl to his tent. He hated to think what would have happened to her if she were not . . . or to any woman during the night.

Unfortunately, he could not do anything for them. They were Decianus' property tax payments. All of them, including the blonde-haired daughter. This was all he was able to do to protect her from the ensuing nightmare—hide her for as long as possible.

He needed to check with Felix to be sure the men knew not to touch the prisoners and that enough guards were stationed outside Decianus' tent in case a few escaped. However, the idea of facing the centurion's fury again was not a welcome thought.

Two months back, he had joyously received his first appointment with the legions. While his mother's brother had shared much of what to expect as a tribune, his uncle failed to tell him about feeling powerless with such men as Decianus.

Julius' thoughts were disrupted as Marcus and his cavalry drove the herd of Iceni horses through the main gate into the grassy areas just inside the dirt wall. Two stallions, a black and a bay, reared and screamed defiance while the mares dropped their heads to graze with their foals at their sides. Then the wagons loaded with the remainder of the Iceni goods lumbered in behind the herd.

Julius welcomed the intrusion and hurried down the ladder as Marcus dismounted by the gate. "All went well?" he asked.

"Nothing is left if that is what you mean. But Prasutagus' body was gone before we got back to the gravesite."

"I cannot say I am surprised." Maybe that would appease their gods. Julius could only hope so.

Marcus slid off his helmet and then tucked it under his arm. "Dealt with the guest in your tent yet?"

"You got her there before Decianus could touch her?" he asked with relief.

"I left her there, but I cannot guarantee she stayed." Marcus smirked. "Bet you cannot wait to enjoy her tonight?"

Julius sagged with frustration. "Like I said, she is in my tent for her protection, nothing more."

Marcus shrugged. "But Decianus will sell them all as slaves. So, what are you going to do with her, then?"

The question was direct and true. Yes, the Iceni captives would be sold as slaves. What was he going to do with the blonde daughter? Maybe having her taken to his tent had been irrational. However, he could not bear the idea of knowing men were touching her flesh and using her.

"Nice horses," he said to change the topic.

Marcus nodded toward the herd. "They are. The Iceni are well known for fine horses. I cannot wait to try the bay one." He looked at Julius, his gaze more intent. "I was wondering. What does Decianus plan to do with the stallions?" "Line his pockets with more gold than Nero will never see."

"Will he sell the bay?"

Julius met Marcus' curious gaze. "For the right price, I believe Decianus would sell his soul to Hades."

Marcus slid his helmet over his head. "I think I will see if the bay is worth Hades' price."

Julius' attention returned to the stallions. The black one moved like an agile wind while the bay appeared more substantial. Good breeding either way. He toyed with the idea of riding the black to keep his mind from the beautiful blonde goddess hidden in his tent.

While tying his cheek guards, Marcus nodded at Felix storming toward them. "Glad you have to deal with him and not me."

"Tribune, the Iceni goods have been delivered into this madness."

"Excellent, centurio. How is the queen?"

"Living." The centurion's face softened slightly. "So ya know, I went easy on her, as best I could."

"Praise the gods for that." Julius scanned the soldiers milling before the brutal insanity exploding inside the canvased praetoria. "Find something for those fools to do. Clean the latrine or something."

"Consider it done." Felix stepped away.

"And centurio, at dawn, see that the women are taken to the medics and kept out of sight. I want the tent guarded as well."

"If any of 'em live to see the sun rise." The soldier hesitated and then met Julius' gaze. "You know their men should be killed."

"Probably." If this happened to his mother, Julius knew he would find a way to kill the prick who did it. "But Decianus sees them as tax revenue."

"Likely sold as gladiators if they make it back to Rome," Felix retorted. The stocky soldier saluted and wheeled about. "Get off your lazy asses and do something, you horny bastards. Pay attention out there, you pieces of shit."

Morrigan? Rhianna? Boudica's brain raged. Rome's insults had cut deeper than the lashes ever could. Yet, that paled to the hell that was happening to her daughters. To the Iceni women. Her anger returned, coiling like a snake.

If the Romans could disrespect Prasutagus' death and his people this way, what would stop them from disrespecting all the remaining tribes as well? Maybe now the other tribes would fear becoming Rome's next victim and join her in ridding their lands of all things Roman.

But, somehow, the Romans would pay for what they did to the Iceni, she promised the canvas wall before her.

The tent flaps rustled behind her as someone entered. "How is she?"

"She lives."

Words of the Roman tongue sharpened her hearing. "Good. I want all the women brought here at dawn."

"Have you lost your mind, tribune? This tent is not big enough for that many."

"Then get a bigger tent, and see they are dressed and cared for. Understood?"

"By the gods, tribune. They are prisoners."

"Orders, medic, and keep them out of sight. Is that clear?"

"Yes, tribune."

Boudica's gratitude opened to the goddess Andraste for bringing the women to her.

> *I thank you, Andraste, warrior goddess of victory. I beg to you, you who have never fallen, see and hear my plea to lead us to victory over those who insult your people. I ask you to send us your wisdom that we may destroy those who know nothing but greed. Help us return our hearts and lands to you, the invincible, and help us rid our lives of this*

Roman filth.

I ask that I may be your instrument of Rome's destruction. I ask this for my people and for those who know your might and power. Lead us, Andraste, to victory!

Boudica's eyes opened. Her heart closed. "So, it begins."

Chapter 4

ALREADY, HE WAS DREADING the morning report. If any of the women escaped and got among the men during the night, they would be met with an unparalleled horror. Soldiers were glaring at him as he strode toward his tent, angry from not being able to participate in the orgy going on in the officers' quarters. Frightened screams and lascivious laughter already poured from the overly guarded area where his tent had to remain.

For the last few hours, he had avoided returning there by riding the black stallion. Like Marcus, he wanted to purchase the black stallion for himself now. As well as the girl because if he did, she would be his property and no one could touch her, including Decianus. If he did not. . . she was doomed to the horrors breaking out.

It was not only a matter of Decianus and his guards raping her, but Silvius and his thugs, and whoever ultimately bought her. She would be a prize for any brothel. That realization had made him sick.

But could he afford Hades' price? Not likely, not with Decianus lining his pockets.

Sons of Dis. All he could do was pray that Jupiter noticed his meager attempt to respect her father's death and protect her. However, did the gods really care?

The girl's fragrance of violets assaulted Julius the instant he stepped into his tent. The top of her golden head was like a beacon as she jerked her legs tighter to her body to hide deeper between his storage trunks.

He tore his attention away from her to set his helmet on the desk. Essex appeared from the sleeping area and reached to remove his cape. The absence of its weight was a reward. "I hope your day was good, dominus."

"Hardly." Julius turned his back toward his guest, whose gaze prickled his skin like invisible needles. "I cannot believe Decianus could lower himself to disrespect Prasutagus' funeral like he did."

Essex removed the leather cuirass and set it on the armor stanchion, folding the cape over one shoulder. "I heard he did much to disrespect him, dominus."

Julius nodded toward the screams piercing the leather walls. "I did what I could to stop him. I truly did." He shot a questioning glance toward the girl, hoping she understood him.

Essex lifted the under-tunic from Julius' body, another blessed relief. "I have said as much to Rhianna, dominus. However, she does not believe me."

Rhianna. That was her name? He liked the sound of it. "What did you do for my people?" Rhianna asked in fluent Latin.

She understood. Good. Julius sat on the corner of his desk to confront her scrutiny. "I had you brought here to protect you from what is happening to the others." He nodded toward Decianus' tent.

"You. . . you aren't going to—"

"No. I am not going to harm you in any way, Rhianna. If I could have stopped all this from ever happening to your people, I would have. Your father was a good man. Rome knows that."

Tears blossomed in her eyes. "My father did all you ever asked. He worked with you. Why would Rome allow this?" "Rome did not, Rhianna." Julius clasped his hands on his thigh. "Decianus did. And I will see that those in Rome know about it as well."

A tear trailed down her cheek and sank into his heart. "My mother?"

He coughed into his fist to clear the effects of her tear. "She is in the medic's tent and being cared for."

"My sister?"

Julius looked up at the peak of his tent, not wanting to answer. "With the other women." He looked at her and met her glare. "They will be taken to your mother when. . . this is over."

Rhianna's gaze raked him from his head to his foot dangling off the desk. "Is it just his men doing this?"

"I have given orders not to touch your women unless they escape." However, if any did get away from Decianus, he was not sure any would remember the order. Not with all the brutality flooding the camp.

Her gaze dropped as sobs tore through her body. He wanted to go to her, hold her, comfort her, and let her grief pour into him. He knew that was impossible. She would turn on him.

Julius rose from the desk to let Essex the horse sweat from his body and massage the tense muscles. He stopped before the trunks. "Rhianna, I will not stop you if you choose to leave. Nor will I stop what awaits you if you do. But, as long as you stay inside my tent, you are safe from that torture."

Should she believe the words of this Roman? *I am not going to harm you in any way, Rhianna. If I could have stopped all this from ever happening to your people, I would have. Your father was a good man. Rome knows that.*

She stared at the vacated spot on the desk before her. This Roman had appeared to dislike the tax collector's orders after the Romans arrived. And when she pleaded for him to stop the flogging, he had, and then he had endured the tax collector's fury as a result.

Rhianna swiped tears from her face and looked at the closed flaps. He said he wouldn't stop her if she fled, and every muscle begged her to flee. If she did, there was no doubt of what awaited her out there. Something far worse than staying inside the Roman's tent. Or would it be worse? She desperately wanted to believe this Roman.

An insane sense of guilt washed over her. Was it fair if she went untouched? Would the others choose to flee this Roman's tent if they were promised such protection?

Doubts raced through her mind as she watched Essex peel away the soldier and the Roman became a man. Her gaze drifted to the perfection of his backside. So different from Calgacus, who bulged with strength. Yet every muscle on this Roman was rock hard from his shoulders down to his narrow ankles. She watched how the metal stick glided so smoothly over every ounce of flesh, dipping into each muscle crevice, and gliding over the next.

She jerked her gaze away. He was Roman. Regardless of what he said, he had participated in destroying her father's final journey, having her mother flogged, and what was happening to her people. Her hand rose to clasp the only piece of sanity she still possessed—her father's pendant hanging around her neck.

Rhianna bolted awake at the sound of a trumpet. During the night, when the Roman had laid a blanket over her, she had started to fling the wool aside. But the warmth drew her deeper into its folds.

Stirring beneath his covers, the Roman sat up, combing his hand through his hair as he released a long groan. He saw her staring at him. "Rhianna, good morning," he said with a sleepy smile.

She knew his name now. Julius Agricola. While he had eaten dinner the night before, he'd told her his name and that he was from Cemenelum. He had asked her to eat with him. How could she when she knew no one else had anything to eat?

He also had Essex place the food and wine onto one of the trunks sometime during the night. And despite her determination not to eat it, obviously, her hunger won.

A rooster crowed, stirring the early dawn with the sounds of men grumbling to life as men did even in every village or camp, coughing, groaning, and insulting each other. A sense of routine settled in the air until a woman screamed and a man laughed.

This Julius closed his eyes as if in disbelief, freezing the air in the tent until his slave stepped through the tent flaps with a tray of cheese, bread, and water. "Felix is frothing mad," this slave stated.

The Roman stood on the plush rug beside his bed. "Still?" he remarked.

Dark hair curled across his chest and narrowed over his tight stomach muscles like an arrow pointing beneath his loincloth. Then he walked to the desk as if she weren't there and sat to let Essex shave his face.

His face was a sculpture of regal perfection, not hidden behind any facial hair as men in most tribes enjoyed. He had a pleasant mouth that smiled easily. His eyes were a soft brown that matched the color of the waves in his hair. The only possible flaw was a small cut left behind after Essex shaved his jaw—a meager imperfection.

The thought played in her mind of how confusing these Romans were. Scraping their skin clean with metal sticks, cutting their hair short, and shaving all hair from their faces, all of which seemed so ridiculous. Nevertheless, that was what Romans did.

"I imagine Felix will be merciless at morning report," Essex said as he wiped this Julius' face clean and drew a white, padded tunic over him, letting the long leather strips flap around his hips. Shorter ones dangled over the muscles of his upper arms.

"You can count on that," Julius assured as he tied a red scarf around his neck. Essex buckled the leather cuirass, knotted a strip of purple cloth about his waist, and then attached the red cape. In a breath, this Julius became the Roman.

As he claimed his helmet from Essex, the reality of everything that had happened returned. Tears blurred Rhianna's vision. Her father's funeral ruined, her mother flogged, her sister and the rest of the women brutally raped and beaten. She hated all those who had destroyed her people. But how could she hate this one who had done nothing more than attempt to protect her?

He turned toward her. "Rhianna?"

Air halted in her lungs as her gaze lifted from his leather sandals to the gold-tipped, leather strips that dangled to his knees, over the leather cuirass that blazed with the eagle emblem of Rome, along the red cape flowing over one arm, and then at the Roman whose face was shadowed by his black-crested helmet.

"I have to go. If you need anything, tell Essex." He started to leave.

"My sister. My mother. The women. . . I need to see them." She had to know if they still lived.

He stopped before the tent flaps but failed to turn. "I will check on them."

"No, please. I need to see for myself. Julius, please."

Chapter 5

THE MOMENT HE ESCAPED THE TENT, Julius looked up at the sky filled with fat rain clouds. Somehow, he had endured the one long night of Decianus raping the Iceni lands like he had the women. It had been equally merciless.

Even though the screams and laughter had faded into silence, he was forced to endure each and every move Rhianna made, every sob and every breath. Each time he moved inside the tent, she pleaded for him to take her to her mother.

Sons of Dis and Jupiter, he did not want to do that. He did not want anyone to know she was still existed until it was too late to do anything.

Do what with her? He still had not figured that out.

So, he simply had to avoid her pleas.

The sound of her saying his name was melting his resolve not to at least hold her. It constantly drew his attention to her beautiful eyes—fragments of the sky—and to her hair, golden rays from Sol. His hands ached to touch the porcelain of her skin, so soft, so smooth, and so perfect. He shoved his helmet over his head, feeling the black crest's tail shift over his back. The moment that he emerged from his tent, the cornicens announced his arrival. Men came to attention. There was a thrill to that moment, but it was followed with a heavy sense of responsibility for each life before him.

"Gods be blessed, centurio," Julius said as he joined Felix, who glared at the nearest row of soldiers.

"If they wish, tribune."

Julius scanned the restless rows of soldiers again. Not very pristine; more like last night's leftovers. "Password: 'Venus in all her glory'," he said.

"Yes, tribune. Venus in all her glory." Felix glanced at the clerk logging the words for the day.

"Reports?"

"The women are in the medic's tent. Two Gauls are dead. One stabbed. One dances without his cock."

Julius smirked. "Well then, Decianus has his very own eunuch."

A hint of a smile crossed Felix's face, a major achievement for even the gods to create. The strange expression dissipated like summer dew. "Five of our men disobeyed orders when three female prisoners."

"Then see they are adequately punished."

"I will see that these fuckers wish they had never seen any women—even their own mothers."

Julius inhaled the delicious morning air and then released it. "See to it, centurio."

Felix and the other centurions faced him and recited their daily oath. "Tribune, we will do whatever may be ordered and be ready at every command." They saluted and burst forth with their own orders that brought the men to life like an agitated beehive.

Julius knew he should return to his tent to read any incoming reports or orders that had arrived that morning and write necessary replies. However, he walked the camp, observed the centurions drilling the men, rode the black stallion, worked out with Marcus, and lastly, checked on the women, who were battered and bruised beyond recognition but remained alive. He did just about anything to stay away from his tent . . . and Rhianna.

"Tribune!" Decianus called out as he stepped from his tent.

Julius froze, dreading to face the man.

"I want the prisoners cleaned up and prepared to leave. Silvius the slaver will be coming tomorrow to relieve me of their stink."

The slaver! Rhianna! Julius turned. "About that. I need to talk to you."

A smirk mixed with the greedy expression on the procurator's face. Julius could almost see him adding up denarii. "The other daughter. You want her?" he asked.

"Yes. And the stallion."

"We can discuss this after I read the results of the latest inventory of Iceni goods. After my bath. Good day, tribune."

If he actually could manage to purchase Rhianna, how could he deny her this last chance to see her mother and sister before they were taken away? She would never forgive him if he did that. He had to find a way to take her to the medic's tent.

Julius pulled the hood of his leather cape further over Rhianna's head and gripped both of her arms as gratitude blazed from her eyes. Every torturous thought of seeing her grew more elegant than the sunrise. He only wished to hear her laugh and knew that when he did, it would stir more than his soul. "Remember, stay in the medic's tent until I come for you."

"I will. . . Julius. I will."

He would never tire of hearing his name fall from her lips, nor her name floating from his. Rhianna's voice was more beautiful than the sound of a songbird.

The moment he appeared outside his tent with her at his side, men stopped stirring pots, sharpening weapons, cleaning leather, or chopping wood. They had forgotten about her . . . until now.

Keeping his full attention straight ahead and a possessive hand holding her cape-covered elbow as if she were already his property, he led her toward the medic's tent.

Chapter 6

R HIANNA FELT EVERY STARE from the men watching them walk away from Julius' tent. Hard, cold gazes followed them like wolves on the hunt. She understood now why Julius wanted her to remain in his tent. Had Morrigan and the others faced this each night? Julius had assured her it was the procurator's guards who had assaulted them. He had given his men orders to not touch any of the Iceni women. She wondered if they obeyed. She blocked her mind to what surrounded her as they drew closer to a large, white tent near the rear of the camp.

Guards at each corner stood at attention as he led her closer and pulled back the tent flaps so they could enter.

Blinded by both the sun's glare and the leather cape, Rhianna saw nothing inside until Julius turned her to him. A worried expression tainted his face.

"Remember what I told you, Rhianna. Stay here until I return for you," he said and waited for an answer.

"I will, Julius."

He left, and Rhianna found her mother barely moving on the cot at the rear of the tent. Morrigan sat beside her with her knees drawn up to support her forehead.

They live! Relief melted over Rhianna until she saw the ocean of destroyed faces separating her from her sister and mother. Clumps of hair had been ripped out. Bruises covered all exposed flesh. No one moved with ease. Yet through swollen eyes, their glares came with cold fury.

Morrigan's gaze hit her like a fist. "Well, Rhianna, don't you look lovely this morning? So fresh and even wearing the same gown."

"Yeah, mine was ripped off me," a woman added. "I have only this filthy tunic now."

"Yeah, like the rest of us," another said.

Rhianna couldn't move as insults exploded at her. "This is my second one. Gave this one to me this morning after using me all night. Still can't pee."

"Didn't need tunics where I was."

"And look, you still have Father's pendant," Morrigan announced.

"Save your anger . . ." Boudica rose on her arm, but pain dropped her back to the cot.

Rhianna stepped toward her mother. She had to do something, but there was no pathway through this wall of fury.

"Did you hear her? She calls him Julius. The Roman has a name."

"Piece of shit is what I call him."

"We noticed how he touched you—all kind and sweet. Not the way they touched me. Beat me is more like it."

They hate her. But it wasn't her fault Julius never touched her. What had she done?

"So, what did you do to stay so sweet for him, Rhianna? Suck his cock?"

"Bet she did or he'da beat her like they did us."

"She's one of us," Boudica snapped and then cried out in pain from the effort.

The tent silenced as Morrigan jumped up to help her, her voice melting with concern. "Mother, don't move. You'll break open the scabs."

Rhianna stepped forward, but women crowded closer.

There was no way past them.

"What would Calgacus think if he knew she was a Roman lover and liked Roman cock now?"

"Julius is not my lover. He tried to protect you," exploded from Rhianna's lips.

Sick laughter filled the tent.

"You're saying your Roman tribune couldn't stop them from raping us?"

"Guess he couldn't."

Someone spat on her. "Well, you ain't one of us now."

"Yeah. Go back to his tent. You ain't welcome here."

The wall of hatred grew thicker. The words sharper. Spit peppered her feet like bee stings. Wheeling about, she fled the insults amid a cacophony of victorious laughter. Tears blinded her path. She didn't know where she ran except away. Away.

Julius stepped into the procurator's tent.

"Greetings, tribune. How was your night?" Decianus asked with a knowing smirk.

"I have had better."

Decianus rolled his eyes. "I cannot imagine that by any means. I suppose you are here to purchase this girl?"

"I am. How much for the golden-haired daughter and the black stallion?" Julius asked.

"The horse goes for sixty denarii." A smile slithered across Decianus' lips. "The girl, maybe I should let Silvius decide her price."

By every god on Mount Olympus, Julius wanted to wipe that smirk off the man's face.

"She is not his right now."

"True. So, I will say—"

Decianus met Julius' gaze.

Greed danced with pleasure. "Two thousand denarii or Silvius will decide her price . . . if he sells her at all."

Two thousand sixty denarii! Sons of Dis. I cannot afford that, and the bastard knows it. But what choice did he have? He had to protect Rhianna.

"Agreed," Julius chocked.

Decianus motioned for a clerk to approach and shoved the bill of sale toward him for his signature.

The moment he stepped back from the desk, he wondered if he had just signed away half of his salary. However, Rhianna was his now. His and no one could touch her. "I want this recorded in Camulodunum."

"Oh, it will be," Decianus assured him as he handed the parchment to the clerk.

Julius vacated the tent and heard a scream. He bolted with men racing behind the tents to hear someone say, "Hold the little bitch. She is meaner than her sister."

Julius slung body after body aside until he found the two men holding Rhianna to the ground. The lush flesh of her thighs and breasts flashed while she clawed at the man climbing between her legs.

Someone yelled, "Tribune!" The crowd scattered like frightened mice, just as Felix roared into view.

"Get those men back on duty. Now, centurio!" Julius yelled as he snatched Rhianna to his side.

She wheeled, her hand clawing down his cheek guard. He dragged her, thrashing, to his tent where he released her. She stumbled back toward his trunks as he tossed his helmet to Essex. "I told you to wait for me."

"You . . . you took them from me." She came at him with the fury of a banshee. "They hate me. Everyone hates me now." She yanked his dagger from its sheath and slashed across his cuirass, leaving a scratch across one eagle's wing.

He grabbed for her hand and missed. "Took what? What, Rhianna?"

The blade glistened between them, and then something solidified in her searing gaze so hard it chilled his bones.

"What do you think, Roman? You take. You . . . you . . . destroy. You . . ."

Julius lashed out, knocking the weapon from her grip. The knife flew across the desk, knocking the inkwell to the rug. Ink poured out like black blood.

The guards bolted into the tent. "Tribune?"

He grabbed her wrist and yanked her to him, letting her thrash. "Leave. All of you."

Everyone evacuated the tent as her fists pounded against his shoulder. Each blow slowed until her fury melted into sobs, and she wilted into his arms. "I couldn't stay there. They all despise me. Even Morrigan and my mother."

Chapter 7

A CORNICEN SOUNDED. By the gods, he did not want to deal with evening formations, passwords, and orders. Rhianna needed him. Yet, his men gathered outside while Felix fretted over the reports. They would simply have wait until he appeared and dealt with the evening routine.

"Essex!"

The slave raced into the tent.

Julius pulled Rhianna away from him and handed her to Essex. "Watch her with your life."

"Yes, dominus, I will."

He scanned the tent for any place where she could escape. Nothing. She stood beside Essex like a stone statue of Venus. The men outside were getting impatient. He heard them coughing and shifting armor about.

He lifted her chin with his finger. Her blue gaze was deeper than Neptune's sea. "Rhianna, you are safe here. I will be back as soon as I can."

She tore her chin from his touch and looked away.

The cornicens started to announce his appearance when he stepped outside but stopped when he came back inside for his helmet. They inhaled once again to announce him and halted when he stopped by the guards.

"Watch her. See she is here when I return." The guards saluted.

Julius jammed his helmet onto his head, leaving the cheek guards loose. The horns trumpeted as he joined Felix in glaring at the line of restless men.

"Trouble in the tent, tribune?" the centurion snarled. He ignored the insubordinate remark.

"Evening password is 'Britanni.'"

The clerk beside Felix wrote. "Reports?"

"Found the two fools responsible for disobeying orders by attacking the Iceni prisoner."

"Were they insubordinate?"

"Yes, tribune. They are under guard waiting for you to witness their punishment for disregarding the order to not touch the prisoners unless they were escaping."

Rhianna had escaped the medic's tent. The men had stopped her. However, flashing images of her beneath one sent cold fury through Julius' veins again. His order was to only stop them, not rape them.

"Recommendations on how to deal with the fools?"

"Five lashes each. All watch."

Rhianna's mother had endured at least ten lashes before he had stopped Decianus' assault on her. Julius thought of making the numbers equal, but that would only take longer, and he needed to get back to Rhianna.

"Arrange it."

"It will be done, tribune."

"Then let us get this over with."

Felix and the other centurions faced him and recited their daily oath. "Tribune, we will do whatever may be ordered and be ready at every command."

Onlookers' ridicule rippled from the off-duty soldiers as Julius stepped up on the riser. He sat in the cross-legged chair placed before two soldiers stripped down to their loincloths and lifted a hand. All fell silent. "Centurio, read the accusation."

"Mario Dectius Liberus, you were ordered to drill the IIIrd Vexillation. Instead, you attempted to rape an Iceni prisoner against orders. Miles Septimus Argos, you were ordered to drill with the VIIIth

vexillation and also assaulted the Iceni prisoner. You both have been found guilty of neglecting duties to Rome and this camp by disregarding the standing order. You are to receive the punishment of five lashes. So ordered by Nero Augustus and Tribunus Gnaeus Julius Agricola. Do you understand these charges?"

Both soldiers glanced at each other and then nodded. Remarks and jests rang in the air while the first was stretched to the lashing pole. Julius slumped in the chair. "Get on with it!"

During the second flogging, his attention drifted to the gates where the guards permitted entry to a colorfully dressed, native Britanni. Since he strode directly toward Decianus' tent, the man was no stranger to Roman forts.

Julius refocused on the soldier's punishment and stood the moment the final lash fell. "Five! Take both to the medic. Dismiss the men," he ordered.

He had barely stepped off the riser before Decianus' personal slave approached. "Tribune, Procurator Decianus Catus wishes you to join him for dinner."

Julius' thoughts collapsed. He wanted to be with Rhianna, not that fat fool. However, he had no choice but to join the greedy bastard and his strange guest. Matters dealing with his marching camp and Rome had to come before all else.

Snarling, he stormed toward his tent and barged through the dropped flaps. Both Essex and Rhianna jolted upright at his sudden intrusion.

Essex stood almost to attention. Rhianna remained seated on one of his trunks. She wore one of his longer tunics, a brown one that made her hair appear more like spun gold.

Julius slammed his helmet on the desk. "I am called to the procurator's tent for dinner," he said as he ripped off his armor. While his body relished the relief, he studied Rhianna. She remained on the trunk while running her thumb over her father's pendant, resting in her palm.

He slid into a clean tunic and then glanced at Essex. "I will be back as soon as possible."

"All will be well when you return, dominus."

Julius entered Decianus' dining area of the massive tent where three couches surrounded a small walnut table. Pieces of roasted rabbit, buttered beets, boiled eggs, dried figs, chunks of fresh, and rye bread filled the area with their fragrances.

"Androitux of the Regni has brought news from Camulodunum," Decianus said and waved for Julius to take the vacant couch. "But first, we dine."

As Decianus speared a beet, he continued the introductions. "Androitux, this is the tribune I was telling you about, Gnaeus Julius Agricola."

Julius forced his mind to the moment. However, it was more like trying to tame a wild tiger to do so. All he could think about was how Rhianna might react to the news that her people were leaving with the slaver in the morning. Not only that—how would she deal with the fact that she belonged to him now?

Accepting a silver goblet of wine from a male slave, Julius reclined opposite the Regni guest. Everything about the man was lean and hard from his black hair, held back in a braid, to the sinister mustache that drooped beyond the edges of his mouth. A menacing scrutiny filled the man's green gaze. "How are things with the Regni?" Julius asked the man.

Androitux toasted Julius. "Most excellent, tribune."

"Any news from Suetonius?"

The Regni leaned forward to consider his next morsel. "The consul will be attacking the druid encampment on the Isle of Mona soon enough. That is the rumor, I hear. And the tribes are snarling during the consul's absence again."

Julius swirled his wine. No doubt, the news of the Iceni had traveled faster than a wildfire in a windstorm. With Suetonius hidden behind the western mountains, the threat of an uprising presented more reasons to be concerned. "Are the IXth Hispana aware of this?" Julius asked.

The man smirked and then answered, "Most definitely. Yet, all I have heard is that Cerialis enjoys a very pleasant visit with the Brigante queen."

Decianus grinned as he dipped a hunk of bread in oil. "And quite satisfied, I am sure, if I know Cerialis."

Julius was well acquainted with the legate of the Hispana. Petilius Cerialis enjoyed women wherever he could. It was well known that Brigante Queen Cartimandua enjoyed all the pleasures Rome offered, down to any Roman who graced her tent, while her husband and his men snarled like caged dogs.

"If I know Nero," Decianus announced, "and I do know him, Cerialis will definitely gain the appointment of consul one day."

Androitux stretched his lanky body along the couch. "You, tribune, wish to be legate some day?"

A baited question. Of course, he wanted such an appointment. The point here was—did he want Decianus' patronage? Julius ate another beet. "I serve Rome."

"I expected to hear that." Androitux shrugged. "Me? I wish for nothing more than a good woman and a warm bed. Thanks to my good friend Decianus, my simple wish will be answered tonight."

The procurator lounged back in the cushions. "Pick as many as you wish to warm your bed, but be careful, my friend. They are a vicious bunch. You may want a few of my guards there as well in case one chooses to cut off more than your ear." Decianus pointed to the bandaged wound where one of the women had almost bit off his ear lobe.

Impatience gnawed at every nerve in Julius' body. He would take a flogging rather than continue to sit here and listen to such banter. He faked a yawn and asked, "Do you have any more news? I have matters in my tent to attend to."

Decianus snorted into his wine. "I bet you do, and I can just imagine what they are."

The Regni shrugged. "I do, tribune. You have been recalled to Camulodunum. To leave immediately."

Camulodunum? He had just been assigned to Decianus' ass barely a month ago. So why so soon? Julius studied the two men.

"No need to wait for your relief." Decianus handed him an official scroll. "Take the Ist and one of the supply wagons back with you. I plan to join the IXth Hispana." As Julius broke the consul's wax insignia on the scroll and scanned the words, his mind began a rapid whirl of what he needed to do, starting with Rhianna.

What should he do with her? Find a place in Camulodunum for her? He preferred keeping her with him. However, if he were ever assigned to a proper legion, she would have to stay in the village where she could flee back to her people.

Since he would be home in approximately two years, he could send her back to his mother. However, the issue of his betrothal with Domitia complicated that option. Maybe Rhianna could stay in Suetonius' villa in Camulodunum that his uncle had mentioned once before. He could pay some retired soldiers to see that she was safe and remained there. He rolled the parchment and set it beside him. "Does Silvius still plan to leave with the Iceni in the morning?"

Decianus reached for a piece of meat. "He does, at sunrise."

"How many guards does he want to escort him back to Camulodunum?"

Decianus waved a spoon at Julius as if to dismiss him. "Said he has his own."

"Then I need to see to the arrangements." Julius swung up from the couch, placing his goblet on the table. "I wish you both a pleasant evening."

He crossed to his tent, hidden in the shadows. Pale moonlight spilled over the simmering coals of extinguished campfires. Sounds of soft snores filled the air. Nothing seemed amiss.

The guards saluted when he approached and dipped in between the drawn flaps. He stood for a moment until his eyes adjusted to the dark so he could see Rhianna asleep between his two trunks. Essex rose from the back of his tent to help him undress.

He waved the groggy man back to his pallet and sat at the desk to read the orders again. A letter he had received from his uncle had said his present duty would be only temporary. "Until they find a role better suited to you." Still, something itched about all this.

However, he thanked the gods for the reprieve from Decianus. Any reason to not be a part of the fool's greed was a blessing.

The frogs and owls sang amid the brisk wind blustering against his tent. The day crept over him like a fog. Suddenly, every muscle felt exhausted. He rose and walked through the sweet fragrance of violets to his bed.

Chapter 8

A WOMAN'S SWOLLEN FACE resembling a bloated carcass floated in Rhianna's sleep. "What would Calgacus think if he knew she liked Roman cock?" "Bet she did, or he'da beat her like they did us." The young girl's eyes stabbed Rhianna as sharp as any knife plunged into her breast.

"Yeah. Go back to his tent. You ain't welcome here."

"Well, you ain't one of us now."

"Be strong, little sister. Don't let them break you . . . break you. . . break . . ."

Rhianna gasped awake. She was standing between the trunks, trembling. The Romans hadn't broken her. The women had. Even as she rubbed her arms, their spit seared her skin where it had landed.

She started toward the tent flaps, but fear cut through her. She froze. Soldiers were out there, waiting, watching. The walls of the tent were closing in around her, and she had nowhere to go. No one to—

"Rhianna." Strong, gentle hands glided down her arms, soothing the burning particles of spit. "You are safe here with me."

The familiar fragrance of sandalwood and sage turned her to the only source of kindness that kept her from dying. His face was filled with concern and compassion—the very things she needed. "I will take care of you," he whispered.

The Roman! She jerked away. "You did this. The women hate me because of you."

"No, Rhianna, they hate because of what happened to them. However, it does not matter now. You are safe with me."

No threat pulsed from the image standing in the shadows that were holding her so gently. A soft, warm gaze pleaded for her to understand. "It doesn't matter. You are safe with me," echoed in her brain.

"H-hold me," eked from her lips.

Strong arms enfolded her and kept her from shattering. A luring masculine fragrance soothed her senses. She felt her head pressed against the expanse of his chest and heard a steady heartbeat that quieted her own. She drew back to see who was doing this. The Roman.

Julius. She ran her hand along the sharp stubble of his jawline to the bare flesh where a mustache should be, over his soft lips that kissed her fingertips. He was so different from anyone she had ever known.

"You are so beautiful," he whispered.

Her father's voice echoed in her brain. "Ah, my beautiful Rhianna."

She blinked, expecting to see his golden hair and laughing blue eyes. Instead, she saw this man, gazing down with soft brown eyes. His brown hair stood at odd angles in the dim light, making him less Roman. More human. More ordinary.

"Even my mother," whispered from her lips, like puss oozing from a festering wound, "hates me."

A small smile appeared. "None of that matters now, my love." He drew her head back to his heart.

She clung to him, feasting on the security surrounding her. To let go was to sink back into that black abyss of hatred.

Julius lifted her in his arms and carried her to his cot, warm with his fragrance. He eased alongside her, brushing his hand along her neck, combing her hair over his pillows. "Let me take care of you," he whispered. He cupped her face and kissed her forehead. So soft. So gentle.

Her heart, cringing in her chest, unfolded like a flower, opening to the hope that he offered.

He ran his fingers through her hair until she relaxed as if basking in warm waters where rays of sunshine danced through a thick lace of green leaves. She started to breathe again.

A strange new hunger stirred through her when his lips kissed her, when his mouth caressed her skin, and when his hands soothed her. A delicious world began with a slow spiral that carried her away from everything.

Julius listened to the rain pattering on the tent like tiny pebbles. Again, the desire to join with Rhianna surged through him. It was too soon. He remembered her virginal cry the moment he entered her, claiming her as his. Together they had climbed to the skies only to fall as one.

He brushed a finger along her silken cheek and sank his hand into the wealth of golden silk lying between her breasts.

She stirred awake and turned, imprinting his mind with her wide-eyed innocence and beautiful gaze.

"Good morning." He tucked his chin to taste her lips yet again. When her lips failed to respond, he drew back. Confusion radiated on her face.

"Julius, I . . . where am I?"

"With me, my love. With me." Julius chuckled softly.

He never wanted her anywhere else.

She lifted her head to scan the tent as if she had never been here before. Her gaze returned. "I . . . we . . . did we . . .?" She sounded frightened. Was it because she had given herself to him? "Yes, my love. You are mine and I am yours." "Oh." She shifted beside him as pleasure drifted over her face and a small smile appeared. Her hand grazed over his chest, combing through his hair.

The determination not to join with her again melted. He could not help himself and delved into the cream of her neck, basking in her delicate scent of violets. Her head tilted back, allowing him even more access. Lazy moans played in his ears as she responded to his touch.

He found her again, hearing a whimper, welcoming him. Their bodies danced to the skies once again. She arched beneath him, crying out, "Julius!"

At the sound of his name on her lips, he released his soul into her, a soul he no longer owned. She had claimed it completely.

Julius melted, spent completely, languishing in the creamy flesh and silken hair until the morning trumpet interrupted with its call, reminding him of his duties.

Essex ventured into the tent. "Dominus, oh. Excuse me, dominus." The man whipped around to leave.

"Essex." Julius moved from Rhianna, pulling his blanket over her.

The man halted but did not turn about. "Shall I tell the centurio you are ill, dominus?"

"No." Julius kissed Rhianna's forehead, nose, and mouth and wished there were some way he could remain. An eternity would never be long enough. "I wish I could stay with you, my love, but I must go."

Rhianna moved so he could stand. Her virgin blood, smeared over his thighs, appeared like a sacrifice. It was in that moment he knew the gods had given him a new life. A new direction. A new reason to live. Rhianna.

Joy bubbled through him as he dressed. He picked up his helmet. At the tent flaps, he halted and looked at Essex. "Get things ready. We leave in two days."

Chapter 9

"*G*ET THINGS READY. *We leave in two days.*" Panic flooded cold through Rhianna, destroying the delicious feelings curling through her like a warm kitten.

"My mother? Morrigan? The women?" She drew the blanket over herself and sat up. "What will happen to them? To me? To us?"

"Rhianna." Julius returned and squatted beside the bed. "You stay with me, but they leave—"

"Without me?" She clutched his arms. Did they hate her so much they would leave without her?

He grimaced. "No, Rhianna. They go with Silvius." "Silvius? Who…?" She didn't know anyone named Silvius. "A slaver. He purchased them."

"No! They . . . they would rather be dead than slaves." She scrambled from the cot, and they stood, facing each other. "Father was loyal to Rome. He . . . he paid your taxes. He gave you whatever you wanted. Julius, you can't let this happen to them. You have to stop this . . . this Silvius."

His gaze became dark and serious—Roman. "Rhianna, it is done. I can do nothing now but protect you."

How could he protect her if her people had been sold as slaves? Mother Goddess! "That means I'm . . . I'm . . ." Her legs crumbled.

Julius caught her by the arms and held her. "It was the only way, Rhianna. But you will never be a slave to me."

His touch stung like a slap. She jerked away and stumbled and wheeled to face this Roman. "Then I truly am your slave now?"

"Yes, however, as my slave no one can touch you. No one."

"No one but you."

"True. But only if you want me to."

Outside, the trumpet sounded again. Felix started yelling insults at the gathering men. Essex fretted like a hen. "Dominus, the men have—"

"They can wait." The Roman rose to his full-commanding stature. "Rhianna, you will be my slave only until we return to Rome. Once there, I will free you and marry you. I promise."

Rhianna cradled her father's pendant, studying the identical image of the horse that had raced across his helmet and shield an eternity ago.

Essex joined her on the cot and handed her his slave necklace. "Best they see you wearing this. They know me."

She looked up at his round, gentle face. "Where did you learn Iceni?"

He played with the chain on the slave necklace. "My mother. She was from here when the Romans came the first time. My father was a Roman. He bought her. When he was called back, we went with him. She died aboard the galley, so he sold me to the young dominus' mother."

"Will he sell me to someone?"

Essex shook his head. "I don't think so. The young dominus is a man of his word. I know that much."

"What about my people?"

The question didn't settle well on his face. "The women and children will be sold in Rome or to someone on the mainland. The men will be sent to the mines or the Ludus to school as gladiators. Your mother . . . I don't know."

Her insides caved. "Why?"

"It is the way of things. Rome has little tolerance for those who refuse to submit to her rule." He smiled bravely. "You are lucky. The young dominus truly cares for you." He stood. "Wear this slave necklace if you leave the tent. It protects you." He left, leaving her to stare at the tin bar with the name "Agricola" pressed into the metal. The tin was light, but the realization that her people would never be allowed to see their homes again made it heavy in her palm. They would be taken to this land Julius had tried to tell her about, this place called Rome. Everything her people knew was destroyed. Nothing would ever be the same again.

She forced the new chain over her head and let the tin rest against her heart. She was the property of the man she had given herself to. She lifted the slave necklace. How was being Julius' slave any different from what her people would experience?

She gripped her father's pendant as his voice echoed in her memory. "This is for the man you give your soul to, Rhianna, daughter of the Iceni."

She had given herself to this Roman, and she had no one but him now. Not even Calgacus. When the women told him their lies, even he would despise her.

The days passed long and slow. Essex brought her a new gown, water to wash with, and a comb. Outside the tent, the camp bustled with new energy. Inside the tent, her world was dissolving into oblivion.

She continued to comb her hair, hearing the pendant scratch against the slave necklace. Noise outside drew her attention. Then Julius stepped through the tent flaps.

"Dominus." That was what Essex had called him.

Julius rushed to her, kneeling beside the cot where she sat. His helmet shadowed his face. His cape pooled over his feet. The smell of his leather cuirass filled her nose. "Never call me dominus." He lifted her hand to his lips. "Julius. Only Julius."

He removed the slave necklace, tangling the chain in her hair, and set it beside her. "Wear this only when you go outside. Not in here. Never around me. Ever."

He set his helmet beside her. However, he failed to relax. "We have to leave tomorrow for Camulodunum."

"What happens then?"

He forced a reassuring smile. "I will find us a place until I return to Rome."

"Until then, I am your slave?"

"It is for your protection, Rhianna. No one will touch you."

Essex appeared with a tray of food. Julius rose and let the man remove all that was Roman, then cleanse him with the metal stick.

Even as he ate and described buildings that were beyond her imagination and told her about his mother and uncle who lived in a place called a villa. She sat there numb, void of life. Silent. A slave.

"Have they left?" she asked, even though she already knew the answer. Beyond the tent, campfires crackled. Men taunted. Owls hooted. The guards shifted. No screams or slaps. There was nothing but a camp settling for the night and the huge void left behind by those who no longer wanted her among them.

"Rhianna, I promise—"

She reached across his plate and pressed her fingers to his lips to stop the coming words. She looked down at the pendant. She lifted it in her palm to gaze at it—her last memory of her father. The only good memory left of her people. She was to give it to Calgacus on their bonding day. That would never happen now.

She rose from the bench and circled the desk. Julius' warm gaze watched with concern. This man owned her. She was his now. He had claimed her. Even now, she wanted to feel him caress her and make her body sing and her soul fly. She had felt more with this Roman than she ever dreamed possible. Something she had never felt with Calgacus.

When she came close, Julius rose. He was slightly taller than she was, so her chin rose, and their lips met for a moment. She drew back, lifting the silver chain from around her neck, and slid it over his waves of soft brown hair. The pendant settled against his heart.

"As long as you wear this, my soul will be yours," whispered from her lips.

A soft smile slid across his face. "Then I will never take it off."

Chapter 10

EVERY SOLDIER'S ATTENTION FOCUSED directly on the three blue-black ravens swooping across the dismantled marching camp and disappearing into the distant tree line, glimmering from the morning rains. Julius also watched, but he was not sharing their alarm. Frustration attacked.

The daily offerings to Mars and Jupiter had favored the march to Camulodunum. Felix and the rest of the centurions agreed they had the gods' favor.

Julius curbed the urge to yell to the men, "The damn roosters ate all the grain. All of it!" He needed to get the men moving, so they would forget the harbingers of death. He vaulted onto his new stallion.

Once in the saddle, he pulled his red cape from beneath him and scanned the line of soldiers who appeared more like farmers than Rome's lethal force. Brown leather capes draped each man and protected the polished helmets bulging against their chests like misplaced pregnancies. A pack pole of meager belongings rested on one shoulder and a leather-covered shield dangled off the other like market baggage. Capes had been shoved back to reveal heads with every color of short hair and every variety of face possible—young, old, scarred, and fresh. They chatted and laughed now—the ravens all but forgotten.

Julius released his breath and scanned the three supply wagons overloaded with tents, gear, and Decianus' plunder. Rhianna rode on his personal wagon in the center of it all. Her golden hair gleamed like a beacon in the morning sunlight.

If only he had more time to convince her of how much she meant to him. However, everything was happening too fast. His replacement had arrived. He had to hand over his reports to the new tribune. Deal with preparations to leave. Inspect the men. It was an endless mess of details, reports, and protocol.

There could never be enough rosy dawns or moonlit nights to prove to Rhianna that she was his life's focus now. He drew her silver pendant from beneath his leather cuirass. *As long as you wear this, my soul will be yours.* Her whispered words played in his mind like a caress. He meant it when he said it would never leave his neck.

He kissed the silver pendant and then dropped it beneath his cuirass as Felix approached. "So, centurio," Julius said, grinning. "I am sure I can find you a horse to ride today, if you would like one. I would rather ride the boat with the Ferryman than be on one of those monsters." Felix glared at the restless stallion. "Unpredictable fools."

Julius laughed. His new stallion pawed the ground, ready to move. Rhianna said the horse's name was Aerie. He liked that name. He looked to Marcus, riding his new bay stallion, and his unit of guards gathering behind him.

"Ready, decurio?"

"Yes, tribune."

After years of hearing his uncle's stories of the legion, Julius had dreamed of such moments as when the men left the dismantled marching camp and started out. He cantered toward the first section of men and then halted to ask the traditional question that began every march.

"Are you ready?"

"We are ready!" the men answered.

Relishing the hearty sound, he galloped toward the middle of the column and supply wagons where Rhianna sat beside Essex. Her smile ignited his soul. He drew to a rearing halt. "Are you ready?"

"We are ready!"

He rode toward the rear section, where he halted for the third and final time. "Are you ready?"

"We! Are! Ready!"

The thunderous answer fired through his veins. He wheeled Aerie and released the stallion into a ground-eating gallop toward the front. His flapping cape yanked at his shoulders. The tail of his black crest whipped his back like a lash. He slid to a halt at the front of the column and then nodded to Felix.

"Move!" the centurion yelled and motioned to the two cornicens. Their horns blared, filling the brisk air with their clarion command. The first signifier lifted his standard and tilted it forward. All along the column, the remaining standards copied the motion. The soldiers adjusted their belongings and stepped forward.

Aside from slapping at biting flies, all was placid and pleasant for most of the morning. Then, thunderclouds rose in the sky like a large gray wall. Dread flowed over Julius. Rain.

It never seemed to stop in Britannia. Back home, people constantly prayed for rain to fill cisterns, grow crops, and water stock. There was never enough. Here, in Britannia, it was a constant blessing—if being constantly wet was a blessing.

The column moved to the soft sound of drums setting stride. Ditties peppered the air as men marched, laughed, and sang. Everyone was silenced when they noticed the vultures circling beyond the thick tree line at the bend in the road.

Julius' heart lunged into his throat, shattering the blissful thoughts of making love with Rhianna. Something horrible had happened beyond those trees, and every nerve screamed that he did not want to witness what had attracted Hades' birds. "Centurio, halt and rest the men. Have them uncover."

He shifted to face Marcus. "Decurio, with me."

"Yes, tribune." Marcus motioned to his men.

The stallions relished the freedom to gallop ahead. When they rounded the turn, the stench of blood and death hit Julius like a fist. Hundreds of vultures scattered from where they feasted on a slaughter more horrific than any battlefield. Aerie slid to a halt and fought every step closer to the gory feast. Headless bodies sprawled in pools of blood and urine as if a half century of warriors had trampled them into the mud.

"Check the perimeter." Julius pointed at the surrounding tree line.

Marcus motioned to five guards who saluted and left.

Julius forced the stallion closer to the mutilated body of Silvius lying among the empty chains that once had held the Iceni prisoners. Beside him lay a warrior covered with swirls of blue paint, his intestines bulging like large worms from a long gash across his stomach.

"He is a Trinovante," Marcus said. His bay stallion pawed restlessly in the mud, splashing blood onto its hoofs. Julius scanned the trees. By the gods and Jupiter, he had to get Rhianna and the men to the capital city as fast as possible—before there was another attack. "Send a messenger to report this in Camulodunum."

The five guards returned and stopped before Julius. "What did you find out there?"

"Nothing, tribune," the nearest guard said and pointed toward the darkening clouds. "They went north and west. Moving fast."

A tingle of relief drifted through Julius. However, more could still be waiting for them at any turn. "We need to get back."

Julius wheeled Aerie and charged away from the butchery. The distance back to the men seemed to have doubled. At last, the silver armor, red capes, and uncovered shields appeared. In his absence, the farmers had become Roman soldiers. He found Rhianna's golden hair and sighed with relief.

Felix jogged toward him, worry blatant on his face. The expression deepened at the sight of blood on the horses' legs. "What was it, Tribune?"

"Ambush. Trinovante." The guards surrounded Julius and the centurion. "Apparently, they came for the Iceni prisoners. They are gone, and Silvius and his men were mutilated."

The centurion beat his vitus stick against his leg. "Any sign of where they went?"

"North and west."

"A diversion?"

Julius shrugged. "Possibly."

He had reviewed the map with the centurion the night before. They were two days from Camulodunum, which meant they had to make camp for the night. He had prayed for more nights with Rhianna, knowing that once in the capital city, there would be few nights if any. If they moved fast enough, he could get everyone to the nearest fort. Combretovium.

The stallion reared. Julius leaned forward and brought the horse back to the ground. "We move toward the fort Combretovium." He looked at Marcus. "Send a messenger to report our arrival."

Marcus gathered his men. One rider saluted, wheeled his horse away, and left at a gallop.

Felix saluted and then turned to the signifier of the Ist. "Move!"

The signifier waved the standard. Horns blared. All down the column, the banners motioned and sounds echoed. Men picked up shields and pila and prepared to march. Had the roosters lied?

Calgacus studied the gathering clouds for the sun's position. It had been glorious killing the Roman filth even as he watched the riders galloping toward the Roman fort. Now, more would fall. And he would have Rhianna back where she belonged . . . with him.

The column should march into view by high sun as Seric had predicted the gods would release their storm.

The eight-year-old boy was never wrong about the weather, which was why they had brought him.

Now, it was a matter of waiting. Calgacus' greater concern was that the coals stayed hot enough in their buried pots to fire the arrows when needed. He studied the narrow valley. Nothing but a circling hawk graced the sky. A busy wind bent the leaves and grass along either side of the empty road that cut like a brown ribbon in the middle of the two thick tree lines.

Tancorix had returned with the news that the tribune rode at the head of the column and that Rhianna rode on a wagon in the middle. Every muscle in Calgacus' body wanted to be the one to kill the bastard who had taken what was his. But Rhianna was more important.

He crouched tighter behind the thick bush as Roman scouts appeared on the road. The riders halted their horses and sniffed the air. One broke from the group and loped closer to the trees that hid his warriors. Everyone had washed off the smell of blood and filthy gore in the nearby stream, so it would not carry on the wind and alert the Romans of another strike on them. Still, the air coiled with tense anticipation. He knew his men would only move when he gave the signal.

"Now?" Orvic whispered.

"No. We wait for the column. Then, kill all the Romans you want."

The brush behind Calgacus rustled. Tancorix appeared, dragging the eight-year-old boy fighting the grip on his tunic. "Little shit found us."

Calgacus' stomach fell. "Seric, I told you to stay in the cave," he whispered bitterly. He motioned at Tancorix. "Take him back."

"No!"

Tancorix clamped a hand over Seric's mouth and slammed him face down on the ground.

The boy's wail halted the Roman scouts. One looked directly at the brush that hid them.

"Did you hear anything?" the scout asked.

The Romans' horses milled about while the scouts listened intently. Only bird song and wind filled the air.

"Not worth checking," one scout finally said.

"Yeah. Musta been some animal or something," another said.

"Best we get our asses back to the column."

Sons of Dis, it is hot! Julius studied the pressing clouds and untied the cheek guards to let them flap, creating the only possible relief to be granted. The morning breezes had stopped, and the air had grown thick like a mattress. It was going to storm. No gentle pit-pat of rain. Not this time.

The scouts appeared, returning without any urgency— a good sign. Julius lifted a hand to stop the column. The men needed a rest after Felix's unrelenting pace all morning. "Centurio, call rest."

"Halt!"

The command sounded down the line. Standards relayed the order and the column eased to a stop. Immediately, men lifted water bags to their thirsty mouths. The scouts saluted. "Greetings, tribune. Hail, Venus in all her glory."

Password complete, Julius nodded.

"Anything to report?"

"Nothing, tribune. All clear."

The hairs on Julius' neck rose while the scouts moved their horses to the side of the dirt road. Still, nothing felt right. Was it the coming storm that itched? Because the clouds were thickening while the air failed to move.

"Centurio, light march."

"Yes, tribune." Felix saluted and motioned to the cornicens. Again, the clarion call sounded, the standards waved, and drumbeats began.

A smile blossomed inside Rhianna as she watched Julius ride Aerie as if he belonged on the animal. Only Calgacus could handle the stallion. Her father had planned to give both stallions to Calgacus on their bonding day.

Distracted by grief and fear, she'd lost track of time since her capture, but it seemed just days ago that she was attending her father's last day with all the Iceni who had respected her. Now, they despised her, even though her fate mirrored their own. She, too, was a slave.

Yet, being Julius' slave wasn't the same as what the others had endured. Julius respected her, protected her. He even promised to make her his life mate, and that promise had settled nicely inside her.

His gaze traveled over the heads of the column and found her. Only her. He lifted her pendant and kissed it before dropping it beneath his cuirass again. A blush tinted her cheeks as her body warmed.

She had given herself—body and soul—to this Roman whom she should hate with every breath. But she could not. Being with him had been like the druids' magical rocks that pulled together with an invisible power.

Everything suddenly changed along the column, like a touched nerve, when everyone again noticed vultures circling beyond the trees, something she didn't understand.

Worry niggled at her nerves when Julius rode off with his guard, and the men, who reminded her of peasants, became Roman soldiers.

Relief sighed from her when Julius returned alive and then ordered the column to change direction to a different roadway from the Roman's capital city they called Camulodunum.

The column moved faster and in silence, as if worried. Angry thunder rumbled in the distance. A restless wind followed, clipping through the trees. The looming clouds lowered like a blanket, cooling the air. Rhianna sniffed at. the first hint of rain. She loved the scent of—

Flaming arrows burst from the trees and rained down like fiery hail, sinking into mule-packs, wagons, and soldiers, setting everything ablaze.

All along the column, red shields mushroomed into a small village of red huts. A mule broke free and bolted through the line, shattering the neat little coverings. Three burning arrows sank into Julius' wagon, setting his trunks on fire.

A long, familiar whistle pierced the air and brought Rhianna to her feet in time to see Julius fighting Aerie as the stallion reared and thrashed angrily beneath him. Two spears sliced the air and yanked him from the horse and from her view.

The bay stallion also fought its rider until the man disappeared into the void that had swallowed Julius. The two stallions bolted away toward the source of the piercing call.

Julius! He was hurt! Rhianna jumped from the wagon and started toward the front of the column. Essex caught her arm and yanked her against the wagon wheel. "Stay. Here."

She jerked free and had started toward the front of the column when a warrior appeared, slitting Essex's throat. The spurting blood blinded her. The warrior lifted her in his arms and charged toward the trees. A familiar war cry reverberated through her brain.

Calgacus.

Chapter 11

A DELUGE OF RAIN EXPLODED from the black clouds as Calgacus raced into the trees, carrying her farther and farther from the column. Farther from Julius. Images of the two spears taking him from Aerie seared Rhianna's brain. *I need to go to him. He is hurt.* Her heart thundered against her ribs.

A Roman javelin slammed into a nearby tree and jerked her from her thoughts. Another sank into the ground. Calgacus never missed a stride, even though limbs struck her legs like whips. He charged into a frothing creek, splashing water onto her blood-soaked tunic, climbed past a screen of evergreen boughs, and then ducked inside a narrow cave. Gasping for breath, Calgacus placed her on her feet. "Rhianna, you're free of their stink." He bent over, supporting his massive body with his hands on his knees. "And you're back with us."

Wet, golden hair straggled over his mouth and shoulders like bronze snakes. Even in the dim light of the cave, his square, un-shaven face glistened victorious until he saw the slave necklace and yanked it from her neck, breaking the chain. He tossed it into one of the black crevices. "Rhianna, you're no man's slave, now."

His warriors clambered through the cave's entrance, one by one, collapsing to the dusty floor, exhausted, but jubilant. Some were wounded, yet others wore the Roman blood like a banner.

"Don't worry. The bastards won't come this far. Not in this storm." Calgacus brushed her cheek with his hand again. "And your mother and sister are safe. They're fine. So is everyone else."

Brutal visions of the women flooded over her. Their venomous insults rang in her brain, which explained the cold glares from some of the warriors. She wanted to bolt from the cave and race back to the column.

Then memories of the soldiers flashed in her mind. Julius couldn't protect her if she went back. He could be dead. A vice closed around her. She couldn't breathe.

"You're shivering." Calgacus led her to the rear of the cave, grabbing a blanket from somewhere, and wrapped it around her. "Here, I don't need it," he said gently. The fragrance that surrounded her wasn't sandalwood and sage, but horse sweat and dirt.

Warmth radiated from Calgacus' massive body like a heated rock. Instead of drawing closer, Rhianna drew the blanket tighter and sat on the nearest stone, seeing it all happening again in the black ribbon of water trickling through the cave floor.

It all came back like lightning. Her father's piercing whistle that called the horses. The fire arrows. The yells. The spears and Julius disappearing. The feel of blood spattering her face and arms, and then Calgacus plucking her from the wagon. Then, the storm's wrath exploded. Even in the back of the cave, she heard the bursts of thunder outside.

Calgacus sat beside her. "Rhianna, this was the first chance we had to get you away from them. Seric—"

"Seric was with you?" Fear jerked her face to Calgacus. "Not Seric. He's too young for this."

"We needed him to tell us when it was going to storm. He said at high sun, and praise be to Brig, it did." He dug in a pouch at his waist. "This is all there is to eat . . . a hard biscuit. We can't light a fire. Not yet anyway."

She shook her head at the offering. "You shouldn't have brought Seric. He is no more than eight years."

Tancorix appeared with a gourd. He knelt at the underground stream to fill it.

"How many made it back?" Calgacus asked.

Water gurgled into the gourd. "Three wounded. Five or so killed," Calgacus' friend said as he stood.

"Where's Seric?" Rhianna asked. Desperation filled her words. Seric had always been her shadow.

"Javelin got him."

Tancorix left with the water.

Calgacus jerked to his feet and turned in circles before her, sliding his hands along his temples. "Why didn't the little shit stay here as I told him? Why?" He knelt before her, clasping her hands in his. "I'm sorry, Rhianna. I didn't mean for this to happen to the boy."

She pulled from his touch—not only because of the child—but because she belonged to another. "Your warriors need you. I'm fine."

Lies. She wasn't fine. None of this should have happened. She could already hear Seric's mother screaming, "You killed my son! He died because of you and your Roman lover!" Dread penetrated deeper than any cave shadow. She couldn't face their accusations again.

She wanted the safety of Julius' tent, his arms surrounding her, his hands caressing her. She wanted to hear him say, "You are safe, Rhianna." She needed Julius.

But he could be dead. So, who would protect her if she went back to the Romans? The soldiers? The shadows around her grew thicker and deeper.

Calgacus returned and settled beside her again. "Rhianna, I'm worried about you. You seem different. Whatever it is, I'll take care of it. Just tell me what to do." She looked into the deep concern in his blue gaze and knew she should love this man for no other reason than he risked his life to save her people from slavery. She wanted to, but she couldn't. Sobs tore through her. "Calgacus, tell me this isn't real. Tell me I can go home."

"It's real, Rhianna, as are the lashes covering your mother's body." He scooped cave pebbles into one hand. "A wagon got stuck in the mud, or we would have been there with you at your father's funeral." One pebble plunked into water. "Tancorix told us what happened. After the Romans took everyone away, we buried the dead with your father and Mergith."

A sense of relief whispered through her. Their souls were with their ancestors. Maybe if she went home, she could start over and forget about Julius.

"I need to go home. Please, Calgacus. I need to see where Father is buried."

"Son, you all right?" a deep voice beyond Julius' closed eyes asked. A cold rag settled on his forehead.

A groan crawled through his throat, and as he tried to shift, his brain splintered. His cheek throbbed like an angry drum. His neck and arm warred with every other sane part of his body. His insides twisted, and vomit spewed into a bucket that suddenly appeared at his side.

"Your father was right; you do have a hard head."

His father was dead. At least he knew that was real, which meant his brain could function. Gasping for air, Julius fell back onto the cot. Jupiter's cock, he hurt.

"Where am I?"

The blurred image sitting beside him cleared somewhat to the image of a strange man, weathered like a retired centurion. "In the Combretovium. Name's Demetrius." The soldier rinsed the rag out and swabbed cool water over Julius' forehead again. "You are one lucky son-of-a-bitch is all I can say."

"And you are?"

"Like I said, name's Demetrius. Retired from the IInd Augusta, I[st] Cohort, a year ago. Centurio. Remember who you are, son?"

"Agricola. Tribune to Decianus . . . no, Sueton . . . no . . . orders to . . ." He quit. "How long have I been here?"

"Goin' on about seven days." Demetrius bent forward, resting both elbows on his thighs, hands dangling. "Spear cut past your jaw and planted in your upper shoulder. The other spear cut your left arm near to the bone. Not to mention the fall you took. Guards about gave you up to the Ferryman."

A heavy sigh escaped Demetrius' chest. "Why in Hades were your face guards loose anyway? Shoulda kept 'em tied, boy. That woulda saved you from some of this misery."

Julius looked for something familiar, anything to establish where he was. He recognized his burned trunks by the plastered wall. Images of Rhianna riding on his wagon came as well.

"Rhianna?"

He grabbed around his neck for her pendant. Pain shot with each attempt until the chain tangled with his fingers and the Iceni pendant bit into his palm. "Where is she?"

"Be still. You will break open your wounds." The firm hand kept him from rising. "Must be the one you been talkin' to." Demetrius shook his head. "Made no sense to me. Women are not allowed in camp."

A piercing whistle screeched in Julius' mind. It mixed with the vision of fire arrows. Two spears. The stallions. The memories came roaring back to him, the blue-black ravens, the scout's report, the flood of Britanni, and then everything going wrong. Never again would he trust the omen of roosters eating all the grain. Never again.

Rhianna could be anywhere now. He started from the bed, releasing a thousand knives through his brain.

"I have to find her."

The soldier put a hand on his chest and pressed him back against the pillow. "You are not fit to move, at least not yet. Besides, scouts are out looking for her."

Julius knocked the hand away and forced himself from the cot.

The room spun, and then everything went black.

Chapter 12

Tᴀᴇ ʙʟᴀᴄᴋ sᴋᴇʟᴇᴛᴀʟ ʀᴇᴍᴀɪɴs of her village chilled Rhianna as she walked through the scarred earth where she once played and laughed with Morrigan. The fire pits that once cooked meals and warmed flesh now looked like white blisters in the burnt dirt. She scooped soil into her palm, hoping to feel life flow back into her.

Nothing.

Calgacus pointed at the distant tree line bathed in early morning shadows. "Tancorix witnessed it all from over there." He stopped beside Rhianna and looked back at the burned funeral mound. "I wish we had been here to stop them."

"No." Images of her people falling beneath the Roman shields returned. "Because you weren't, you were able to save my people from becoming Roman slaves." If they were still her people. "Otherwise, you would have joined them." He grumbled and then led her into a nearby glen encircled by burnt oak trees. A blanket of black grass infested with dirt hills encircled a larger mound—her father's grave.

The Romans had returned to burn that, too.

Calgacus stopped beside her and rested on one leg. He jerked his chin toward the site. "We buried your father there in the middle and the others around him before the bastards returned," he said gently.

She studied him. His brilliant blue gaze floated over the graves and his effort to respect all those he could. Calgacus was like that.

She smiled and continued her examination. His hair gleamed like currants of gold pouring over his shoulders. Nothing like the soft brown waves that had curled about her fingers.

Rhianna clenched her hands into fists with the memory and found her way to the largest mound. She slumped to the grass to press her hand into the warm dirt. There was no doubt now. Her father was gone. He was with his ancestors. Tears flooded from her eyes. "I miss you, Papa. You were all I had. I need you. I want you back."

Something fed into her and surrounded her heart like a message that said he was there, with her, and still loved her. Rhianna collapsed over her father's grave, sobbing, until a whistle sounded in the distance. Tancorix's warning call. Roman scouts had been seen.

"We have to go, Rhianna."

She couldn't move. She didn't want to go. She knew what awaited her once she left the gravesite. For the last week, Calgacus and his warriors had hidden by day and moved by night. She slept, ate, and helped care for his men . . . when they let her.

Anger and doubt burned in many gazes. Even in odd moments, Calgacus felt distant. She wondered just how many more would share the same thoughts when she returned to the Trinovante hill fort. It would be better just to let the Romans have her.

Rhianna lay beside him in his tent, smiling. He heard her moan with pleasure as his fingers traced every inch of her silken skin. She caressed his flesh with a soothing touch. Suddenly, she began to fade, her face twisting with fear.

Julius sat upright, fighting to keep Rhianna, but the room spun. His burned trunks floated slowly along the wall. Sweat poured from his skin. Once again, she was gone. He slumped back onto the cot, feeling the tear in his soul. Rhianna was out there. He had to find her. At least Marcus had assured him that he had ordered his scouts to search for her and to bring her back unharmed.

The scouts had reported spotting groups of Britanni fleeing through the trees and bogs. However, they knew how to disappear from view as quickly as lemurs, ghosts that moved through the villas at night.

Whatever it took, he knew he would find her. Rhianna was his life now—all that mattered to him. But how?

Plans began to form. First, he needed to get to Camulodunum and make certain Decianus had recorded the sale. Since he was not under orders to the legion now, he would hire men who would go with him who knew the land and the people, and men who knew Iceni.

The city was filled with retired soldiers looking for pay. It did not matter that it would cost him more than he should spend. He needed to find Rhianna.

Venus. Bring her to me. I beg you. Yet the goddess' ears were deaf to his constant plea. He dragged himself from the cot and staggered to stand. "Essex!"

An attending slave, carrying fresh bandages, stopped at the foot of the cot. "Dominus, your slave is no longer with you."

Julius scoured the man with his gaze, knowing the slave had nothing to do with Essex's death. During the week that he had lain here helpless as a babe, Demetrius had told him all that had happened. One of the Britanni had slit Essex's throat.

"Help me dress," he ordered.

Chapter 13

ULIUS DRAGGED HIMSELF FROM THE WAGON SEAT and leaned against its wheel. His head split with pain. The deep cut in his shoulder burned like the fires of Hades, punishing him with the thought of so much as moving. Yet, he had made it to Camulodunum, even though it meant riding in a wagon. Felix's replacement, a tough man much younger than Felix, stepped beside Julius. "Release the men, centurio," he ordered.

"Yes, tribune."

The fact that Felix had caught an arrow in the eye still tortured him. Earlier that week, his woman and two sons had arrived in Combretovium to claim the centurion's ashes. Julius managed to comfort the woman even as he staggered on his feet. Felix's death only added to his vow to kill the fool who had taken Rhianna and had killed Essex. That red fury drove him to live another day until that oath was honored.

His new centurion spouted the order, and his meager column of soldiers spread into the streets like a broken water pot. Marcus lingered by the wagon.

"Go with them, Marcus. I will be fine."

"Nothing else to do. Besides, I am curious why you were ordered here so soon."

Why indeed. Julius scanned the surrounding portico filled with the legal offices of the fort's headquarters, the Principia.

The sun-filled court bustled with retired soldiers who expected Nero to grant them Britanni land for their service. Men he would need to help him find Rhianna. Not too far away, Emperor Claudius' new temple was in the final stages of completion, rising as radiant as a white jewel set in a barnyard of buildings.

Julius shoved off the wagon wheel and cradled his helmet under his arm because there was no way his brain was going to allow him to wear it. He walked toward the records office. Marcus followed him, past banners hanging on the walls that displayed the four legions stationed in Britannia. The IInd Augusta was keeping the western tribes quiet, while the IXth Hispana controlled the northern area. The XIVth Gemini and most of the XXth Valeria now fought the druids on the Isle of Mona with the consul, minus the two cohorts of the XXth Valeria who had been ordered to protect Decianus' ass. The official standards remained with the legion and its eagle.

Julius continued into a white plastered room marked for a future mural to be painted. A clerk sitting at a massive oak desk in the center of the room looked up from his chair. "What can I do for you, tribune?"

Julius set his helmet on the desktop and supported himself on the desk with his good arm. "I am Gnaeus Julius Agricola. I came to report an attack on a supply delivery." He closed his eyes to keep the room from spinning.

The clerk nodded. "That has already been reported, tribune."

"And to make certain of my purchase of a slave." The room started a slow spin again. "Iceni princess, daughter of Prasutagus, name Rhian—" The walls shifted. His stomach roiled.

"Water!" the clerk shouted to the nearby attendant.

Julius managed to take the cup handed to him and started to lift it to his lips when Marcus coughed beside him. Then his name exploded in the room.

"Julius! There you are! Marcus! It's about time you got here."

The bellowing voice of his uncle shattered in Julius' brain. He released the cup, spilling water over the desk.

"In the name of Caesar, what took you two so long getting here? Oh, never mind that." His uncle halted beside the desk. "Demetrius told me you were near dead when the men brought you in. What in Hades happened? Oh, tell me later."

The clerk handed Julius a slip of parchment. "The slave purchase is confirmed, tribune."

Julius sat on the corner of the desk and managed to fold the receipt. Why was his mother's brother, Valerius, in Camulodunum when he should be in the west country with Suetonius?

"Bought a slave, did you?" Valerius grinned as he looked at the receipt. "Is it a female? Of course, it is. Been practicing on her? Well, of course you have." A hard elbow jabbed Julius' rib cage.

Pain shot through his chest as his uncle winked at Marcus. "He will be glad he did." The centurion propped both hands on his hips as if ready to make a grand announcement. "Got a surprise for you. However, I have to wait to tell you. Your mother will be furious if I say anything more."

"Mother? She is here?" Why would his mother be in Britannia? She should be home, tending her flowers.

"That she is, son. However, I will not take you to her until you have gone to the baths. I could use another visit myself. Only thing better than bathing once a day is bathing twice." Valerius chuckled at his humor. "That way you can tell me about this slave of yours."

Julius slumped onto the long wooden bench in the changing room and dropped his head in his hand. Maybe he should not have come to the city so soon.

Marcus sat beside him. "You going to make it?" Julius shrugged and let a Britanni slave remove his tunic and sandals. By the gods, he missed Essex. When he stood from the bench, Rhianna's necklace swung away from his chest.

"Where did you get that?" his uncle asked as his personal slave removed his tunic.

"Rhianna." He whispered her name like a precious secret.

"Huh," was his uncle's response.

After pouring cool water over his head, Julius followed his uncle into the steam room and sat on the warm bench. His uncle tossed a cup of water over hot rocks piled in the center of the room. The rocks sizzled and released a cloud of white steam.

The moment Julius rested against the heated wall images of the attack drifted in his mind. He should have done so many things differently . . . formed the men around the wagons, not changed his route, and killed the man who took Rhianna. Who was he? What did he look like?

To avoid any further questions about Rhianna, Julius asked, "How is Suetonius doing with the druids?" He knew that his uncle's first love was the legions, and nothing pleased him more than talking about them.

"Druids are one nasty bunch. Got them trapped on the island. Sons of Dis and Jupiter, those fool priests chant and bellow endlessly on their horns. Our men have learned not to pay attention to their damn noise, even though it drives their warriors and their bitches into mad frenzies. By Jupiter, we will calm that area if we have to . . ." His uncle's voice droned on.

Julius' thoughts settled on Rhianna. He could taste the honey of her lips and smell the fragrance of violets that lingered on her creamy flesh. He clutched her pendant and heard her whispering, *As long as you wear this, my soul is yours.*

His soul wanted to climb out of his skin with the sweat. He wanted to drift away with it and find her, be with her wherever she was. Breathing became thick and heavy. His uncle pulled on his arm. "Better get you in cooler water before you pass out."

The instant Julius stood, the room swirled. Marcus gripped his elbow and helped walk him into the next room where murals of elephants and Roman soldiers trampling local tribesmen covered the plastered walls. The cool air slowed the spinning room where the men were lounging on a submerged bench in the massive pool.

Julius followed his uncle down the steps into the water and sat alongside him. Things began to right themselves until a voice spoke.

"Well, you did make it after all."

Julius' eyes snapped open. Decianus Catus. What the fuck was he doing here?

"I heard you had arrived. Has your uncle seen your slave yet?" Decianus winked at his uncle. "You will like her." The desire to pummel the man soared through Julius' veins. However, the short, fat fool stood and climbed out of the water, letting a slave wrap him in a towel.

Julius' fists opened and closed on his thighs as he watched the procurator leave. "That son of a fucking whoremonger."

"What did he do to piss you off?" Valerius asked after dousing his own head with water.

"Flogged the Iceni queen at her husband's funeral, killed some tribal members, took the rest of the Iceni prisoner, let his guards rape the women, and then sold the lot to Silvius."

"Silvius? Heard he was dead, killed in a raid of some sort."

The image of the slaver's headless body itched Julius' skin. "Same ones that attacked us."

Silence followed as his uncle stared at the rippling waves created by the procurator's departure. "Suetonius does not need complications from the local tribes right now, not before we finish off with the druids anyway. We—"

Julius slid beneath the tepid water and swam to the other side of the pool.

Although the cool water and massage helped rid much of the pain from Julius' body, his brain still throbbed. He had intentionally kept the pace slow to Suetonius' villa. The pace did little to stave his uncle's continued oration about how the consul had granted him permission to use his new villa in Camulodunum.

"Well, since Essex was killed, you will need a new personal slave." Valerius looked back at his own slave, following discreetly behind them. "Torus, go to the slave market and see if you can find a suitable slave for the young dominus."

The tall man bowed. "Yes, dominus."

No one could replace Essex, but he did need assistance. Julius thought of Rhianna doing that. Once he found her, would she not be shocked if he had learned some of her language, which would help when questioning the locals during his search for her.

"Mind going with Torus?" Julius asked Marcus. "And find one that speaks Iceni."

"Not at all." His friend grinned and dropped a reassuring hand on Julius' good shoulder. "And I think I know why."

Memories of his home in Cemenelum flashed before him as they walked through the front court of Suetonius' stucco villa burrowed behind high, protective walls. An array of containers filled with fragrant plantings of sage, rosemary, and other herbs and flowers sat by the front doorway.

More than anything, he wanted to see Rhianna standing in his doorway to greet him. However, if he did not find her before he returned home, he had no choice but to sell his mother's villa in order to return. Of course, there was hope the scouts would find her.

Julius followed Valerius across the gold wings of a massive mosaic eagle filling the entry floor and dropped a bit of dried basil onto the flame burning on the small altar at the end of the vestibule. "Help me find her," he asked and then passed into the heart of the villa—the atrium.

A blue-and-white bowl was the only object sitting on an oak table that stretched before a rectangular pool full of glistening water. Julius walked to the nearest red couch and sat before his legs gave way. Another familiar voice burst into the room.

"Julius! Oh, Julius. You are here. Praise be to Juno and all her mercy. We were so worried about you."

He watched as his mother, Procilla Valeria, hurried toward him with outstretched hands. White streaked her walnut brown hair now, but the same gentle, patient face beamed at him.

His mother remained the one person capable of erasing any problem with her smile. However, there would be no smile once she learned he intended to marry Rhianna and would sell the villa to find her if necessary. All that could wait.

Pain stabbed as she caressed the thick scab along Julius' jawline. "Oh dear, we must keep that from scarring."

He pulled from her touch. "Mother, why are you here instead of back with your gardens?"

She sat beside him. "You, of course." She cast a warning glance at her brother. "Procillius Valerius?"

"I said nothing, Procilla." His uncle sat on the facing red couch. "I admit it was hard. I would rather fight druids any day."

Her soft hazel eyes batted over a clever grin. "We have a surprise for you, dear. One that is long overdue."

The enchanting look on his mother's face and then his uncle's crafty expression fell in Julius' stomach like a load of bricks. He studied both until Valerius shifted his attention to one of the side rooms and motioned someone forward. "Come here, girl."

Julius stared at the image of the goddess Venus appearing from the shadows. She wore a light blue tunica over a gold undertunic. A simple, gold tiara lifted a wealth of rich, brown hair back from her angelic face. The rest cascaded down her back in long, lush curls. Dark blue sapphires dangled from both ears, and a delicate string of pearls and sapphires encircled her slender neck and wrist. A thick gold cuff wrapped her other wrist. A blush tinted her flesh as she smiled beneath ever-long eyelashes.

"D-Domitia?"

Chapter 14

CALGACUS FOUND HIS WAY to the front of the cave where the men sprawled, muttering the rumors from the Iceni women that Rhianna had given herself to the tribune. That she was a Roman lover.

The slurs burned in his brain. Maybe the Roman hadn't beaten Rhianna, but it was obvious the fool had somehow destroyed her. She wasn't herself. She was distant and withdrawn. There was no doubt in his mind that she had resisted that piece of Roman filth.

Calgacus slid down beside his friend, who poured vinegar over the wound in his thigh. Tancorix's lips drew back tight from the searing pain and then asked, "How is she?"

"I swear to Andraste and Tranis," Calgacus said, "I'll kill that Roman for what he did to her."

"We will kill all of them . . . in time." Tancorix slumped back against the cave wall. "For now, though, we best wait until their scouts quit crawling around here like lice. I'm tired of their stink." He closed his eyes and joined the other men already snoring.

Calgacus shifted to a more comfortable position against the cave wall and closed his eyes, but sleep failed to come.

Once again, he remembered sounding his whistle and the two boys leaping onto the stallions and racing away. Then, the two spears arching through the sky toward the tribune. The cascade of fire arrows plummeting into shields and the wagons. The men racing into the burning chaos. It all blazed in his memory.

He wished it had been the tribune's throat that he'd slit instead of the slave's. Nevertheless, he still relished the feel of Rhianna filling his arms.

He and Rhianna would have been joined by now if her father had not suddenly died. Their bonding day had been set two years ago when he was eighteen winters, and Rhianna was fifteen. The sun gleamed in her hair the day their parents spoke the words uniting the strengths of their tribes.

Soon after, Romans demanded more of the Trinovante men to either fill the levies for the legions or build their temple to their god Claudius. The Romans took his brothers to the mainland where they died fighting one of Rome's battles. For those same two years, he had lifted and cut stone for this Claudian temple and swallowed Rome's damned superior attitudes. He had just returned home to learn that Prasutagus had died. Then the world tilted into this insanity.

Now Boudica pleaded with all the tribes to rid themselves of Rome's yoke and regain everything they had lost: their lands, their homes, their lives, and their gods. If not, Rome would do to them as they had the Iceni. Many leaders agreed with her. But not all.

After what they had done to his family and now Rhianna's, he agreed with the queen, especially if it meant killing every last arrogant Roman who set foot in Britannia.

"Domitia's father allowed her to come here so you two can finally join our families," Julius' mother said. "Much longer and we would have lost her."

"Well, it is time you were about getting sons for Rome anyway." Valerius waved toward Domitia to join them. "Not little Britanni shits. Not that they are not necessary, of course. But Rome needs sons—loyal, true sons."

Julius stared at his uncle, his mother, and then Domitia still standing where she had stopped. Was this why he had been ordered to Camulodunum? To get married? The room began a slow spin.

"Neeca, get a cup of water." His mother sent a tiny slave girl fleeing to the kitchen. "Val, maybe we should not have surprised him like this."

"Nonsense, Procilla. He is a man now. He has taken a lot worse. The way I figure, it would be best to get right to the wedding. How about tomorrow? Well, it has to be." Disregarding the pain screeching through his brain, Julius jerked his gaze to his uncle. "Tomorrow? What do you mean, tomorrow?"

His mother patted his hand. "I know it is a lot to fathom right now, but after what happened, we want you two to have as much time together as possible before we have to return home."

Her expression pleaded for him to understand. However, all comprehension instantly evaporated from his brain. Surely, they did not bring the girl standing before him with the intention of him just marrying her here of all places.

Well, he could not. He fingered Rhianna's pendant, hearing her words whisper in his memory. *As long as you* . . . Well, his soul belonged to Rhianna. Not that it mattered to those around him.

Valerius waved to his sister. "Come, Procilla, let us leave these two. I am hungry. Is there anything to eat?"

As his uncle and mother headed toward a back garden, Domitia settled in his mother's place on the couch, folding her hands neatly in her lap. "Julius, I cannot believe I am here."

He thought he was about to hear a giggle, but she took the cup of water from the slave girl and handed it to him. It remained in his dead hands.

"It took me a while to get used to being at sea, but I never got sick. Not once." She looked so proud. Julius realized in that moment that nothing ever existed between him and this stranger. It never had. Of course, love was never a consideration in marriage. All that did matter were the benefits gleaned from the arrangement. Her family profited from his family's political prestige, and his family gleaned her father's financial support. Nothing else.

Rhianna had given him something beyond just living for Rome and family. Herself. He realized this had happened the instant he had set eyes on her and knew he needed to protect her even if it meant his life. Nothing like that had ever happened with Domitia.

"I am so glad to see you," Domitia whispered. "We were all worried when we heard you were terribly injured."

Her fragrance of roses began to suffocate him. "I . . . I think I would like something to eat."

She rose, waiting for him to get to his feet. She took his good arm and lead him to the garden triclinium. Potted palms waved in corners next to unlit oil lamps dangling from bronze candelabras. The air was fresh and quiet as he reclined next to his uncle on the head couch.

A female slave appeared with a tray of cheese and bread slices and placed it on the center table. She looked like an older version of the young girl, the one called Neeca, who had brought the glass of water. Both of them had golden hair like Rhianna.

His uncle reached for a slice of cheese. "It will not take long before you forget that slave girl."

"Slave girl?" his mother asked and munched curiously on a slice of honeyed bread.

Valerius lifted his cup for a refill. "Seems he bought an Iceni girl. Should not have cost too much."

Julius choked on his chilled wine. Only two thousand denarii and maybe the entire villa to find the bastard who took her.

Domitia stiffened and rested her wine cup on the table in front of her, silent to the point of frigid. Anger choked in his throat. This was not necessary in front of her.

"Then, where is she?" his mother asked. "She was taken captive," Julius answered.

"Well, with Domitia here you can forget this slave girl," his uncle announced. "I know I am looking forward to nephews. Her mother birthed five sons, you know."

Procilla tossed a piece of cheese at her brother. "Val, not here, not now, of all places."

Marcus and his uncle's slave strode into the garden with a lanky, red-haired man in tow and another, who appeared to be a slaver. Julius motioned for Marcus to recline.

Torus cleared his throat. "I found one that speaks Iceni, dominus."

"That he does," the slaver announced and shoved the red-haired man forward. "Prove it."

Anger flashed in the slave's green eyes. "There's not a tongue around 'ere I dunna know," he said in Latin.

Julius studied the gangly man: short, freckled throughout, and well worn. "Your name, slave?"

The man straightened tall. "Lugh mac Mhordha of Hibernia. Call me Lugh."

"We will call you shit if we want to," Valerius snapped. He looked to the slaver. "What brought him to Britannia?"

"Says his pa was a trader here," the slaver answered.

Lugh ran a large hand through his wiry, red hair that refused the caress. "That he was." He easily met Valerius' glare, something few men could manage. "Being as how I tagged along with my pa for most of my young years, I came to know all this land you Romans call Britannia."

"Do you speak Iceni?" Julius asked, using the little Rhianna had taught him.

Lugh's green eyes sparkled. "I do, but I dunna sing it as you asked."

Grinning, Julius ate a strawberry. "Then why are you a slave and not a trader?"

Lugh grimaced. "Well, there be a centurion's woman I left quite happy, but her man wasna', seein' as how he caught us together, ya see." He gave Domitia a teasing sidelong gleam. "Now if 'n I be singin' to ya in my native language of Hibernia, I'd be havin' these ladies cooing in no time." He winked at Julius' mother.

Julius could not believe it. His mother actually blushed and tried not to smile. Valerius nearly bolted from his couch, but Procilla placed a hand on his forearm, holding him down.

"Get rid of this ass before I skin him alive!" his uncle bellowed.

"Skinnin' my arse, will ya be tryin'?" Lugh asked. "That's like a Roman. Now where I come from, we be thinkin' of more clever ways to torture a man. We'da pulled his tongue outta his arse, we would."

"I can have that—"

"I want him." Julius ignored his uncle's glare and Marcus' chuckles. "How much?"

"I'll sell him cheap to get rid of the fool. Twenty-five denarii."

"Not a denarius more than ten," Valerius countered.

Julius studied Marcus. The sparkle in his friend's gaze said enough. "Twenty."

"Twenty, it is."

"Have you lost your mind?" Valerius flipped on the couch to confront Julius. "There is no reason to trust this fool."

Julius looked at his new slave. "Can I trust you?"

"I dunna lie to any man. I give as I get. If 'n you're wonderin' if I like Romans. Not particularly. The natives here killed my family. So, I dunna have reason to prefer them to you."

"You are a fool, Julius. He is an irreverent shit if ever there was one." Valerius shifted his attention back to Lugh. "You know anything about being a personal slave, do you?"

"Not a damn thing."

Chapter 15

B IRDS GREETED THE ROSY DAWN as Rhianna stumbled over a small twig and sagged against an ash sapling. Calgacus scrambled through the dense underbrush behind her. With him came a rush of his warriors, who ventured on without them.

"Come on. Cave's not far. Rhianna, come on," Calgacus ordered in a hushed voice.

"I can't keep up. I can't." Her stomach lurched and then heaved again. "Do you have any water?"

He ripped a near-empty water pouch from his side. "Here. We have to go."

A Roman trumpet sounded morning revelry behind the distant ridge. She dropped the water pouch as her heart slammed against her ribs. *Julius!* He had come for her.

Before she could think further, Calgacus swept her into his arms and bolted through the forest. They splashed through a frothing creek bed and then halted inside another small cave where five of his men had already collapsed about the stone floor like worn rugs. Once they were inside, Tancorix covered the entry with brush.

Rhianna's eyes adjusted quickly to the shadows. "Where are the rest of the men?"

"In other caves along the creek," Calgacus answered and set her on her feet and drew her toward the rear of the cavern. They passed the men tugging at blankets for warmth and sleep.

"You'd better get some rest," he said. His voice sounded curt and tired. He slid down against the rocks and closed his eyes. In a breath, the soft sounds of slumber claimed him.

A crevice drew her attention. She worked her way into its dark consuming shadows where the sound of slow trick- ling water greeted her. A large rock brushed her leg like an offering. She slid down beside it and closed her eyes.

Once again, she felt Julius brush aside her hair. She licked her lips, remembering how his kisses fed her, reassured her that all would be well. "Be patient, my love. It has to be this way until we get back to Rome. I love you." Could he really love her? Did she love him? Should she have ever given herself to this Roman? Had she become a Roman lover because her people no longer wanted her? Was Julius even alive? She didn't know anything anymore. Tears welled in her eyes. She wanted answers. She wanted the safety of his arms, his tent. She was tired of running and living in caves and bogs, existing in a world that didn't want her. Even the men following Calgacus did so for no other reason than loyalty, which had nothing to do with her. She wanted a home where things were ordinary and safe.

"Rhianna? What are you doing back here?" Calgacus' deep, husky voice jerked her from the vision of Julius' leather tent, from the warmth of his cot, and from him.

"I just wanted to be alone, I mean, away from the rest of the men."

His large shadow sat at her feet and gazed through the dark distance of the small cavern. A long silence drifted between them. He shifted restlessly against her leg.

"Your mother says the Romans must be sent back to their Caesar or be destroyed."

It was no shock that her mother was spreading her venom again. "And your father, does he agree?" Rhianna asked. Warmth from Calgacus' body taunted her to draw closer. But she couldn't.

He shrugged. "Agrees, like most of the other tribal chiefs. We want our land and levies back, as well as destroying what the Romans have forced us to build. But starting a war with them leaves some, like the Regni and Brigante, uncertain."

"What do you want?"

Even in the shadows, she saw the depth of his gaze. "You, Rhianna. I want things as they once were." He brushed her hair from her cheek.

A sense of violation seeped beneath her skin, drawing her from his cold touch. His fingers curled into a fist, and he drew away to study his arms laying over his knees.

A heavy guilt washed over her. He didn't deserve this. Not after risking his life for her. "Calgacus, I'm sorry. I —"

He shook his head and drew in a deep breath. He let it out and then cleared his throat. "If you're hungry, here's some food for you." He sat a small pouch at her feet. "We'll be at the hill fort soon." He rose and left.

The hill fort. The women. Their hatred. Panic, as real as if she still stood in their midst again, returned with its venom. "At least we fought . . . didn't let them break us . . . or turn us into their pets." Her skin stung with memories of the women's spit, while their horrid laughter had driven her into the hands of the soldiers.

Julius had washed all those moments away with his touch, with his presence. She wanted to be with him, not here in a cold cave. Yet, she knew she should be loyal to the Iceni people—her people, even if they were wrong about her. Were they wrong? She wasn't a Roman lover. Or was she?

So much had changed since her father died. However, one thing he had always assured her was that everything changes. *The seasons, the days, even the moon. It was life. And you moved with it. Fighting it broke you like a tree in a storm.* His words were clear in her mind.

Her heart halted. Her throat closed. When he died, the moon was whole. Last night it was, once again, a full, white spot in the black sky. Her flow always came just before that, as regular as the tides. She had missed her flow. *Mother Goddess, I can't be . . . I can't be carrying Julius' child. A Roman's child.* No, she couldn't be.

But she could be. Julius had spilled his seed inside her many times. That explained why she had been sick, why her breasts were hot. She was carrying his child!

The flood of joy dissolved instantly into absolute fear. If she were carrying a Roman's child, who would accept it, love it besides Julius? No one.

No. No. This child was hers. No one else's. Hers. It belonged to her. It was part of her. She would die before anyone took it from her.

Julius' body lay silent, without pain, and promised to remain so if he did not move. Breathing was enough, thinking forgiven.

He needed to hear Rhianna sigh, laugh, whisper his name. He should have been more alert, placed more guards around her, or listened to Felix. This constant guilt was endless and useless. The familiar slow ache grew inside his gut but had nothing to do with his wounds.

He closed his eyes to feel her gliding her hand across his face, whispering his name. He all but had her in the room with him, crying out with passion, her hands driving him deeper into her body until their souls touched.

Then the image of Domitia intruded. She stood before him, innocent, sparkling with wealth, expecting to become his wife. Why did they have to bring Domitia to Camulodunum, expecting him to marry her?

His uncle's voice echoed in his brain. How about tomorrow? Well, it has to be.

"No, Uncle, it does not need to be." Julius' hand fisted in the covers, sending a punishing threat up his arm. "It does not have to be at all."

His mother scurried into the small room. "Put those there and go," she ordered, pointing at the nearby chair. Lugh followed and laid a blue tunic and matching toga over a corner chair. He started to leave.

"Lugh, stay."

As his new slave hesitated and then retreated to the wall, his mother sat on the bed next to him, smiling. "Julius, darling, you must get up."

"Why?"

"For the wedding, of course."

"I want no part in this."

An expression of agitation slid over her face. "Of course, you do, dear."

"Mother, why did you come to Britannia?"

"To see you." She stroked his forearm. "Domitia's father said his galley was bringing supplies to Britannia, and this was a perfect time of year to come. It was Domitia's idea to come with me. I do so enjoy her company. She is a delightful girl. It was not an easy journey for me by any means, but Domitia was there every moment that I needed her. As she will be for you, my dear."

Her face turned serious. "Her father wanted me to assure you that he has already started arranging for your election the moment you are back in Rome." She ran her fingers over the wound running from his jaw down to his neck. "We must see that this is treated so it will not leave a scar."

He pulled away. "Oh, the election, of course."

Procilla Valeria had been a powerful force in his life after his father's execution by Gaius Caligula. Since then, his mother, Suetonius, and uncle had directed every moment of his life in Rome: teaching him about the legions, honoring the gods, and driving home the fact that he would one day enter the Senate. Julius had welcomed it all, until now.

He suddenly realized that neither his nor Domitia's feelings had ever mattered. Now, they did. So, regardless of what his mother or uncle wanted, he was marrying Rhianna. "I cannot go through with this, Mother. I will not marry Domitia."

Her face paled. "Oh, Julius, w-why? I mean, it is all planned. Domitia is a wonderful girl. She will make you such a wonderful wife." Tears welled. "I know you may not care for her right now. It takes time. That is why it has to be soon. You can share what time you have here in Britannia."

He covered his forehead with his bad arm, gritting his teeth against the pain that jolted through him. "Not now, Mother."

She pulled his arm away. "Julius, it must be now. Her father considered dissolving the betrothal because you failed to marry before you left. Domitia and I explained that it could not be helped. You were ordered to Britannia so quickly."

She reached to stroke his cheek again, but he flinched from her touch. "Please, darling. Imagine what will be said if the wedding is cancelled."

"Yes, of course. And both of us are expected to participate regardless of what either of us want."

His mother's hand stifled the gasp that escaped her lips. "Domitia has always adored you." Her hand dropped limp in her lap. "She begged me to let her come."

"I intend to marry someone else."

His mother's back jolted straight. "Not that slave girl!"

"I have decided."

"Julius!" Procilla stood quickly and began pacing circles before the bed. "She . . . she will bring nothing but embarrassment and trouble." His mother stopped and looked at him. "And was she not taken back by her people?"

His glare and silence answered her question.

She lifted her chin. "Darling, it is better that this girl returned to her own kind, where she will marry someone from her tribe. Her people expect her to, I am sure same as we expect of you."

The pendant shifted across his chest. Rhianna would never marry someone else. She was out there waiting for him to find her.

"Besides, whatever you spent on her cannot have been that much anyway."

"Two thousand denarii, Mother."

Aghast, she staggered to a chair. "You have lost your mind. Think of your future. We will not be able to afford your election."

"In that case, I will remain a farmer in Cemenelum."

"No. Your father will scream from his tomb if you do."

"I doubt that."

"You are hurt. Still delirious from all that has happened."

He failed to answer.

His mother stormed toward the doorway and halted. "Now, do not be long, Julius. Val expects to see you soon." She hustled away, flashing a triumphant smile.

Lugh stepped from the shadows and poured water in the washbowl. "Ya know, your ma, she be right."

"Did I ask for your comment? Slaves speak when spoken to."

"The lass be wedded and bedded by now anyway."

Julius' hand clutched Rhianna's pendant. "That does not mean I have to go through with this charade."

Lugh set the pitcher on the table. "Truer words never be spoken. Dumb, but ever so true."

Julius sat up, ignoring his body's argument and his slave's insolence. "Dumb? Why?"

"Ah yes, dominus," Lugh said. "This be the slave girl ya bought like me, and ya believin' the lass loves ya. Because I'm supposin' she be givin' ya that pendant. Iceni?"

Julius scowled at the brazen fool.

"Thought so. Nice. But it be given to the lass for her betrothed, given to her before the bonding day. Likely, the lad she be promised to will be wantin' her back and I be bettin' he be the one nearly killin' ya.

"Now the lass is not knowin' that you survived will be thinkin' you be dead, would be my guess. Womenfolk—I know them to be sure—be fickler than the weather."

Lugh chuckled and shook his head. "I hate to be sayin' this, but the lass already be forgettin' ya. Given ya up for dead, she has."

Gathering fury spun in Julius' pain-filled brain like a storm. Yet he could not block out the slave's words.

"Now that lass out there loves ya." Lugh motioned toward the bedroom door. "As clear as the midday sun. I be figurin' she's dreamed of nothin' else but givin' herself to ya. She be a lovely little thing to be havin' to warm your bed for sure. Wed and bed the lass, I say." He shrugged his bony shoulders. "And if the gods be givin' the other'n back to ya, you can be decidin' then what to be doin' with the both of them."

The insolent slave supported himself with one arm on the table and waited for a response.

Thoughts of having Lugh beaten played in Julius' mind. Or should he listen? No matter how he fought it, the truth came.

Rhianna did not know he lived. She was now free, no longer a slave. No longer his slave. The warrior who took her back to her people did live, so they could be most likely married by now.

The facts hurt like a gut punch. He groaned and fell back into the pillows. "You know what a eunuch is, Lugh?"

"Heard they can't be pleasurin' a woman much." Julius nodded.

"You touch my mother or Domitia, and I will see that you find out."

"Yes, dominus."

Chapter 16

JULIUS LOUNGED IN THE LARGE TUB set in the back alcove of the kitchen. The hot water soothed the cramped muscles in his body.

Lugh sat on a bench in the room and watched each slave scurry about their work.

"Out!" His uncle's order boomed against the white-washed walls. All vacated instantly, except for Lugh, who nonchalantly met his uncle's glower.

Julius sat up in the warm water, sloshing some onto the limestone floor. "Lugh, stay."

His uncle shrugged and started pacing. "Tell me you are not stupid enough to have paid two thousand denarii for that bitch slave of yours." He halted at the foot of the tub and waited for the answer.

"I did."

"We drown dogs for less stupidity."

Julius rose from the water and accepted the towel from Lugh. "I would not suggest trying to do that."

"Who is going to stop me?"

"Me." Every nerve itched. His uncle had done far worse to runaway slaves. "And the fact that you would not risk hurting Mother by killing her son."

"Then explain yourself. For a Britanni bitch? After all your mother has sacrificed for you, you would ruin your future?"

"As for Mother, once she meets Rhianna, she will love her as I do. She will have our children to keep her delighted. Do not call Rhianna a bitch."

"Two thousand denarii for nothing more than a litter of Iceni puppies." His uncle flung his arms to the ceiling and continued pacing. "At least Domitia brings a dowry that will keep your mother safe as well as pay for your election. And she will have children to be proud of."

"I could care less about all that now."

"You are a fool. Domitia is perfect. Surely you see all that she offers you. This . . . this bitch brings you nothing but sweet cunny. She has no loyalty to Rome."

"I said, do not call Rhianna a bitch again. She is my slave, and her name is Rhianna."

"I do not give a rat's ass what her name is!" His uncle stopped. "In fact, I do not give a fuck that she is your slave. I do care about your mother, your future, and this family. Bringing this . . . slave of yours back to Rome will only disgrace your father's name."

"Hardly."

"That assault damaged more than your shoulder." Valerius resumed pacing. "Well, the . . . slave girl is not here anyway. You will likely never see her again. It was wasted money. But I expect you to repay every denarius you spent on her."

"You can expect whatever." Julius squared his shoulders even though pain sliced down his back. "I am the head of my house, and I will determine that. Not you. You are no longer my guardian."

His uncle jerked to a halt. "By the gods, Julius. What has gotten into you?" Valerius walked toward him, hands on hips and ready for battle. "How are you going to explain all this to that lovely girl out there who expects to marry you today?"

"Magnificent piece of work," Valerius said. "Don't you agree, Marcus?" Ignoring his uncle's continual banter, Julius followed his uncle as the man strolled through a gathering of Britanni women attempting to appear Roman by wearing stolas. Nearby their husbands paraded about in their new togas of various colors—but not the senatorial white. They looked pitiful in comparison to the citizens back home.

Julius had once dreamed of wearing his father's senatorial toga—fine, white wool hemmed with a broad, purple stripe. That did not matter any longer. Any other color of a proper toga would suffice now.

They walked past Claudius' equestrian statue set outside the wide, marble steps of the new temple. He leaned close to Marcus and asked, "Remind me again—why I am going through with this farce?"

"To keep peace with your family until you find Rhianna," Marcus said as they climbed the temple steps. "The patrols I sent out reported that there was a small skirmish with scouts near the Trinovante territory," he said, "but no news of Rhianna. Not yet. We are looking for her." Julius nodded and forced himself to follow his uncle.

He hated to admit it, but Lugh had made sense. If he did not find Rhianna, he would have lost all that mattered to him. So, in order to keep peace, he had decided to, as Lugh said, "wed and bed" Domitia.

Hopefully, the scouts would find Rhianna before the women returned to Rome, and then this charade could be annulled without embarrassing Domitia. Her father could easily arrange another betrothal for her with little scandal.

Julius' mother bustled about Domitia's bedroom. "I do not know what has come over Julius. A slave girl of all things," Procilla muttered. She reached for the red-orange veil and swished it through the air like a fan. "He will come to his senses once this wedding is over. You will see, my dear."

Domitia studied Julius' mother in the mirror. "Will he?" she asked.

Procilla's face flooded with questionable certainty. "Of course, he will." She hurried over to the bench and gripped Domitia by the shoulders. "All men are weak. He is simply blinded by the Britanni slave is all. Once he holds you in his arms, he will realize you are the right woman for him." Domitia pulled away. "How can you be certain of that?"

"Because my son cares about you. He always has and he knows you. The slave is nothing but an . . . an infatuation . . . and gone."

Domitia turned from the woman and looked into the mirror. When she saw Julius for the first time, he had failed to see her watching from the staircase shadows. He had come into her father's atrium for their betrothal, laughing with his friends, who taunted him for being the first of them to lose their freedom. He was handsome and looked kind. Adonis paled against him.

Then, while his friends had hurried out to the gardens ignoring the lararium, she saw him nod to the altar of her family gods, and her heart melted. In that moment, she had fallen in love with Gnaeus Julius Agricola.

Her slave woman Excelia had caught her gazing at her future husband and pulled her back up the stairs. "Domina, it is bad luck to see your betrothed before the ceremony."

Domitia remembered refusing to wash her hands or face for a week after Julius slipped the betrothal ring on her finger and kissed her cheek so carefully that day.

She believed that her world was perfect until her father considered breaking the betrothal because Julius was "dragging his feet." Her father had begun thinking of Claudius Meander, a man older by ten years and hairy, as a replacement.

Procilla had fortunately agreed with the idea of getting married in Britannia, knowing it would be a wonderful surprise for her father. He only believed they had come there to visit.

Then Suetonius and Valerius had arranged for Julius to come to Camulodunum so they could at last be wed. Now, because of this Iceni slave girl, Julius did not want any part of marrying her.

The small, handheld mirror reflected the obvious reason why. Domitia saw nothing in the reflection but an ugly creature staring back at her. "Why should Julius even want to touch me?" She dropped the mirror to the table and turned away to hide her tears.

"Oh, darling girl, he is in pain." Procilla drew her into her arms. "He is not himself."

The tears fell, ruining Excelia's efforts to make her beautiful. Sobs followed. "Julius wants her, not me!"

Procilla clasped her chin and lifted it to look directly into her eyes. "He will, my dear. I promise. Tonight, you will make him think of nothing but you."

Domitia reeled at the thought. With five older brothers, she knew what the men expected, but nothing about how to accomplish it. "How do I do that?"

Procilla sighed. "My dear. All you must do is . . ."

Chapter 17

VALERIUS USHERED HIM AND MARCUS through the temple doorway. All three men drew their togas over their heads to honor the gods and nodded piously to the statues of Jupiter Optimus Maximus and Claudius Caesar, which stood in the center of the temple. Sunlight blazing through the opening in the ceiling gleamed on both as well as the murals donning the walls of elephants parading through streets filled with dancing people who resembled Romans more than the Britanni.

They knelt. Julius pressed his palm forward in Roman tribute and then rose—another well-schooled observance. "The statues were shipped over from Rome," his uncle blustered. "Who would expect the Britanni to be able to accomplish that sort of art? In fact, I am surprised they accomplished building something like this temple at all."

An elderly priest appeared from the inner sanctum of the temple at the same moment that his uncle touched Julius' shoulder and motioned toward the doorway.

A small covey of women appeared, and he saw Domitia wearing the traditional red-orange veil that draped entirely over her, blinding even her steps forward.

The original mothers of Rome, the Sabine women, had been stolen from their homes and married off to Romulus' men. These women had blindly submitted to this act in order to save and honor their families.

The fact that Domitia was blinded by the veil was in tribute to these daughters. The willingness to marry him was her act of submission to the man that her father had chosen for her.

Julius' insides froze. Rome had granted him the perfect Roman wife who would give him wonderful Roman children. Yet, all he wanted to do was bolt out the back door. Only there was no back door, and the entry to the sanctuary was blocked with onlookers. The sides of this trap closed around him.

The squeal of a sacrificial piglet echoed from the shadows. The sound cut into him as if he were the sacrifice. The priest chanted to the gods. He and Domitia shared grain cakes. He recited the rote words that every Roman child knew by heart, and then Domitia answered with the bride's traditional words, "Where you are, Julius, there I shall be." A gold cord bound his and Domitia's wrists. The priest faced the crowd and in a clarion voice announced, "I present to you all Gnaeus Julius Agricola and his wife, Domitia Decidiana."

Wedding chants exploded along with applause. People poured around them and ushered them back through the streets to Suetonius' villa for the awaiting feast. Once there, the villa's doors opened, and a slave handed Domitia the traditional grease to coat the doorway to attach unspun wool to the sills.

When she turned to Julius, her short puffs of breath rippled the veil, making it flicker like a flame. All waited expectantly for him to lift and carry his wife into her new home. How was he to do that with only one good arm?

However, Marcus lifted Domitia and placed her in his arms. "Don't drop her." His friend smirked as he stepped back.

Regardless of the screeching pain, he managed to step into the vestibule with his new wife and then almost dropped her on the eagle mosaic. He took a deep breath before leading her into the atrium where her scowling slave woman presented the traditional candle—the symbol of fire, and a bowl of water—the symbols of life.

Domitia ceremoniously touched them, making the home her own. She then stood there, waiting for him to lift the veil and present her to everyone as his wife.

Rhianna studied the clouds drifting across the azure sky, allowing the sun to bask over a multitude of spring flowers blanketing the distant field. Streams rippled down their beds and fresh breezes danced through the trees. Every living thing rejoiced in being alive, except her.

Constant nightmares haunted her. Visions of her mother's iron-sharp gaze cut into her pregnant belly. The druid's greedy hands tried to grab the child from her. Morrigan's victorious laugh echoed, while she thrashed in birthing pains.

Each morning Rhianna woke, praying that she wasn't pregnant, that her breasts weren't tender and swollen. That she wouldn't be sick again. But she was.

After she lingered against another tree, Calgacus stopped beside her. "I'll carry you if you're tired."

She was exhausted. Dread weighted each footstep that brought her closer to her mother, her people, and their scorn. "Why are we still moving? The sun has been up for hours." Calgacus chuckled. "We're on Trinovante lands now. Can't you tell? The air is cleaner."

Rhianna looked away. A large, flat rock jutted into a wide, bubbling stream. Willows, heavy with new leaves, swayed overhead, creating a whisper in the air. She slumped to the damp grass, scooped water into her hand to drink, and splashed the cool liquid over her face, letting it drizzle down between her hot breasts.

Calgacus sat down on the slate slab beside her and then pulled one knee up to his chest. "It's over, Rhianna. You'll never see another Roman. Not if I can help it."

She studied the man who knew well that Romans were everywhere and went wherever they wanted. "Is that possible?"

He began skipping pebbles across the gurgling stream like a boy. A pebble bounced five times, lifting sparkles to dance in the tiny waves. "I'll do all I can to make it so." The pebbles stopped. He looked at her. "Beltane is over."

She brushed her hand through the violets, sprouting through the cracks in the rocks, enjoying her favorite scent drifting to her nose. She and Calgacus should have joined during Beltane, the spring festival.

A pebble skipped twice over the water and disappeared. "Do you still want to be my woman?"

"Do you still want me?"

The pebbles dropped from his palm. "It doesn't matter what happened with the Roman. I want you, Rhianna. I always have. I always will. Will you be my woman?"

Sunlight caught in his golden brows arching over sky-blue eyes. His perfect nose led to lean, firm lips hidden beneath a full mustache that could never hide his broad smile.

Tears filled her eyes. He still wanted her. Would he if he knew she carried the Roman's child? No. It was her child.

And, if he could accept her child as his own, then she would do anything to be a good woman. "Yes, Calgacus. I still wish to be . . . your woman."

Chapter 18

"M AY I PRESENT—" The announcement lay like rocks in Julius' mouth. "My . . . wife, Domitia Decidiana." The bustling atrium burst into applause. He and Domitia were directed like trophies to a bench, while the crowd smiled, nodded, offered gifts or congratulations, and moved toward the food tables. Marcus shoved a goblet of wine into his good hand, and everything became unreal.

The smirking face of Decianus appeared in the line of guests. Just seeing him pushed Julius beyond endurance when the procurator leaned in close. "I am sure you will enjoy your new wife more than that slave girl." With a burst of laughter, he moved on to ingratiate himself with Domitia. Instead of smashing the gloat on the man's face, Julius lifted his goblet for more wine. A cold knot solidified in his gut, allowing him to meet each remaining guest until he excused himself and found the latrine. Lugh followed, close on his heels.

Once alone, the slave came to life. "Well done, lad. Well done."

"Nothing is well done." Julius relieved himself into one of the piss holes.

Lugh pulled up his tunic and relieved himself right alongside. "I'd say it was. Everyone couldna' be happier." He brushed down his tunic. "By the way, who be it that be tellin' ya somethin' private?"

Julius slumped onto the latrine bench. "Decianus Catus. Rome's procurator to Britannia and a fool."

"I didna' think he be one of your favorites by the way you be lookin' at him."

Valerius appeared in the doorway. "What are you doing in here? Guests want to see you."

"Dominus, his shoulder be flarin' again. He shouldna be up and about much longer be my way of figurin'." Lugh motioned to Julius. "Like I be tellin' ya, ya shouldna be carrying that girl."

His uncle glowered at the slave and then Julius. "Your arm is bothering you?"

"Yes. How long will this go on?"

His uncle leaned against the doorway and crossed his arms. "It will last until you bed your wife."

Jupiter's cock, no part of him wanted anything to do with this night. Yes, Domitia appeared ever so lovely, but he was in no mood to appreciate that. "How soon can that be?"

"Given your arm is bothering you, no more than an hour. At least mingle a bit more."

"Then get Decianus Catus out of here."

Valerius looked at Lugh. "Can you get him out without causing a scene?"

"Most definitely."

"See to it."

Lugh left, and his uncle sat on the latrine bench. "I must tell you that everyone is very concerned about this Iceni bitch of yours. Your mother is right, you know. No proper Roman wife should compete with such filth."

Julius' fists coiled, wanting to strike the man. "Do not call Rhianna a bitch—or filth again."

Valerius released a sigh then propped both hands on his knees. "My advice, if you want it, is to leave your wife full of your seed and get back to the men."

Getting back to the men was a peace offering. "When are you leaving to go back with Suetonius?"

"Next few days. You could come when you can and bring your men with you."

"Can you wait until I get the needed supplies?"

Valerius nodded.

They left the latrine, and his mother approached. She handed him a goblet of strange-tasting wine. "Lugh said you are not feeling well, my dear. Drink this. It will help." She shifted her attention to her brother. "Val, that new slave of Julius' spoke with one of our guests and escorted him to the door. Do you know anything about that?"

His uncle grinned. "Does not wait around much, does he?"

With Decianus out of the villa, Julius could breathe. All he had to do now was make Domitia content and get back with the legion, which may provide a way to find Rhianna.

Rhianna stopped on a slow rise before the hill fort. Round, thatched huts had recently been built outside the rock fences. Herds of cows and horses grazed near new stone dykes that resembled long ropes curving through the various hills. Men plowed the north slopes.

Breezes carried the pungent aroma of rich, fresh dirt, plowed like long, brown scars in the earth. People moved about at chores, laughing, and waving to one another, as children raced about with dogs snapping at their heels.

"Why so many new huts?"

"Families came here, asking to join us because the Romans have given their lands to Roman soldiers." Calgacus helped her over a log. "Come on. Your mother wants to see you."

Fear coursed through Rhianna's veins. Would her mother ever want to see her again? Would anyone in her tribe want her among them?

Calgacus led her toward the hill fort where the ringing sounds of blacksmiths' anvils surrounded her. The Romans controlled all metal shipments, yet a thousand hammers seemed to be striking anvils. Bitter sulfur and smoke scented the air, filling it with the sizzling sound of cooling metal.

"Why are so many working on metal? Where has it come from?" she asked as she forced yet another step toward the hill fort.

"The mainland. We traded cattle to make weapons. We will no longer bow to Rome's demands."

A dog covered with a long black coat and a white band around his chest, saw them and charged toward them.

"Faolan's grown," Rhianna said. He'd been a puppy the last time she'd seen him. With white-tipped ears alert, the dog bounded toward them, his large brown eyes gleaming over his pointed muzzle.

Calgacus squatted to greet his dog and ruffled the hair of a boy who had followed. "Kill any Romans?" the boy asked.

After wrestling Faolan to the ground and sending the dog into a joyous run, Calgacus stood. "Thousands."

Faolan came to walk beside Rhianna and licked her hand. At least the dog was glad to see her. She rested her hand on the familiar, furry head.

"Didn't you leave any for me?" the boy asked, skipping backward while leading them deeper into the village.

Calgacus laughed. "You couldn't kick even one of their knee-caps."

"Could to. See?" The boy's foot lashed out.

Locking his foot under the boy's heel, Calgacus tossed him onto his back like a turtle. Two lanky boys standing near the one of the huts burst into laughter. The young boy flew at them in a fury. A fight exploded, something that constantly happened back home . . . when there had been a home.

Rhianna's heart thundered harder in her chest with each step closer to the square, thatched hut surrounded by wooden pillars. Every part of her wanted her father to come out to greet her, but Tancorix appeared, motioning them inside.

The meeting hall loomed empty except for a simmering flame cooking rabbits in the center fire pit. All along one wall, women sat on benches before looms as they worked the strands of wool. They stopped the instant she stepped into the dim light. Since the attack on the slaver and his men, the women's faces had healed. But not their gazes. They remained as hard and sharp as knives.

The air chilled like a winter wind as Rhianna turned to study the large cloth of blue wool emblazoned with an endless swirl of silver embroidery. It hung behind a carved, wooden throne where Calgacus' father sat.

Silver bracelets covered his wrists, and the silver insignia of a tribal leader, a torc, encircled his thick neck. His tanned face appeared clean except for the thick, golden mustache drooping well past his chin. His multi-colored shirt brightened the room while his dirt-covered breeches made him appear as if he had arrived from the fields. And he may well have.

Standing stiff, her mother rested her hand on the back of Diras' throne. A silver torc also encircled the red lash marks around her neck. A new, multicolored robe blazed under Boudica's auburn hair.

As Calgacus led Rhianna closer to his father's platform, her mother's iron gaze pierced her. Every step was like walking on hot coals. Fear reared its claws, ready to cut down her backside at the first hated remark.

Rhianna drew upright, defiant. Something new and strange steeled inside her. Never before had she needed to defy anyone. Now she had something to protect. Her child. The remaining figure on the platform, the druid, drew back into the shadows. Myrradin's black hair hung over his black robes. Although her father had kept a strong respect for the gods, he never liked this druid priest. He said Myrradin was more devious and manipulative than any Roman ever could be. Rhianna shared that feeling.

Diras stood. A comforting smile appeared beneath his mustache. "Rhianna, daughter of the Iceni, you are returned to us."

Chapter 19

BOUDICA WATCHED AS HER DAUGHTER approached with shoulders straight and her eyes challenging. There was something different about her. Was it possible that Rhianna now saw that these Roman invaders were arrogant, selfish, irreverent, and heartless creatures?

The clatter of the looms ceased, and hatred ignited in the women's eyes as they had the day Rhianna entered the medic's tent. Boudica had forgotten about that day in the tent when the women had tormented Rhianna until she ran from them. How they had gloated at their victory!

However, Rhianna remained her daughter and deserved the same respect as Morrigan. The gods must have found some reason to protect her and not the others. Until the reason was known, she had to deal with this situation before the hatred exploded again.

Her own hatred toward Rome would never change. Other than seeing all Romans dead or purged from their lands, nothing could ever rectify what they had done to her and to her husband. As a result, warriors and families from every tribe had come, wanting to rid their lands of the invaders and return to the old ways known since the beginning of time.

Myrradin leaned close to whisper. "She carries a Roman's child for the goddess Andraste."

A protective surge plunged through Boudica's hatred of all things Roman. This included any Roman's child. If Rhianna carried such a child, then she alone must decide its fate. Not the druid.

"And maybe she does not."

"We are glad you are out of the hands of the Romans, Rhianna," Diras announced. "Modron be praised for returning you both to us."

"And I thank you, Diras, for all you've done for my family and my people." Rhianna's attention shifted. "Mother." Never had her daughter's gaze battled with such intensity. Boudica welcomed it. "It is good you are with us again, daughter of the Iceni. I hope you are pleased to be here."

"It is good to be free, is it not?"

Boudica almost smiled. Rhianna had grown sharp words. "We heard you have been rather ill since leaving the Roman."

"I was. The journey was exhausting."

"Yes, as it has been for all of us. Some more so than others." Boudica's strength was fading into pain. Yet she had to ask, "Do you carry the Roman's child?"

The bluntness of the question struck Rhianna like a slap. The question now was, would she admit to carrying his child or deny such? Boudica braced for the answer.

Rhianna's chin rose. "I do not carry a Roman's child. This insult to our people has been a nightmare for me as well."

An unborn child can create such protective strength. However, Rhianna was right in that this had been a nightmare for everyone.

"Absolutely."

"I ask to speak."

All attention shifted to Calgacus. In the meeting hall of the Trinovante, it was Diras' place to answer, not hers.

Boudica submitted to the leader.

"Yes, Calgacus, son of the Trinovante, you may speak."

"I ask your approval to join with this woman."

Diras looked to Boudica with questions lurking in his gaze. "Do you waver on the matter of uniting our tribes with this joining, Boudica?"

She met his curious gaze. "Is this what the daughter of the Iceni still wishes?"

Attention shifted for Rhianna's answer. "It is, Mother."

Boudica controlled her smile and said, "Calgacus, son of the Trinovante, my daughter no longer brings a bounty." A joyful gleam lit his face. "All that I request is your daughter's hand in this joining. But I submit to my father's answer if he feels the Trinovante needs such bounty."

"If my son is content, I am content," Diras said with a broad smile.

"Then, as queen of the Iceni, I say we are also satisfied with this joining of our people, with my daughter and your son."

"It is an honor to unite our loyalties." Diras stepped forward, wide-legged and fists on hips. "What say you, Calgacus, tomorrow?"

"It would much please me."

Boudica noted that Rhianna stiffly accepted Calgacus' arm around her waist. Doubts stirred. Had the girl lied? Time would tell. Until then, more important matters needed to be dealt with.

"Then tomorrow it is!" Diras stamped his foot and bounded from the platform.

Boudica led Rhianna through the side doorway in rigid silence. All around them children dashed. Dogs barked at unseen objects. Cats lazed in the sun. Two young men were busy tattooing their arms with blue dye called woad. Women looked up from their weaving or wheat grinding. This was as it should always be, Boudica thought.

She headed toward a solitary hut at the back edge of the village. "Many doubt your loyalty now, Rhianna. They had to know if you carried his child."

Her daughter's curious gaze belonged to her father.

Boudica blocked the pain of that memory.

"Doubted my loyalty, simply because of the lies the women told?" her daughter asked.

"Yes."

Rhianna stopped. "Are they now convinced?"

"Possibly."

"Are you, Mother . . . convinced?"

"Time will tell." To change the direction of their words, Boudica said, "It is most fortunate that Calgacus still wishes you as his woman."

"And why shouldn't he still wish this?" Rhianna touched her arm, igniting the memory of a lash cutting flesh. Boudica jerked away.

The reaction to her daughter's touch was ill received, making her words even more bitter. "We have nothing to offer his tribe but our loyalty."

"Is our loyalty not enough, Mother?"

"It is more than enough—if what you say is true." Hard, cold silence rose between them like a wall. "Then Calgacus and his people will have no regrets. Nor will our people," Rhianna assured her mother with a tilting smile.

Morrigan appeared from the hut carrying a long sword and wearing on her shoulder Mergith's betrothal pendant, identical to the one worn by Julius.

"Rhianna, you are with us again. I hope you are pleased to be away from your Roman master."

Rhianna wheeled to face her sister as if she were about to be attacked. "Why would you think otherwise?"

Morrigan smirked. "I would think you would prefer—"

"Morrigan, there is your sister's joining to prepare for," Boudica blurted.

"A joining? Rhianna? With whom?" Morrigan rested on the weapon like a cane. "There is no Roman filth here, so with whom and when?"

Without her usual melting from her sister's scrutiny, Rhianna stated, "Tomorrow. Calgacus and I will join our lives and our tribes as Father wished."

Morrigan smiled. "Then you managed to keep your senses after all."

In that moment, Boudica knew Morrigan recognized the change in her sister as well.

Chapter 20

A FTER WHAT SEEMED AN ETERNITY of men relishing the idea of escorting Julius to the bridal suite, he now lay alone with Domitia. Wives had abandoned their husbands to prepare her for her wedding night, having left him to endure a litany of ribald jokes about how to fuck her. The men then hoisted him onto their shoulders, mindless of his arm, and dumped him into bed with his new wife, lying there ever so innocent.

"Julius?" Domitia's hand glided across his chest. "Are you well?"

Her touch made his skin crawl. "I am fine." A lie. He wanted no part in claiming what should be for another man to enjoy. Not him. Domitia deserved that. He rolled toward the side table for the wine goblet.

Yet, she snuggled against him, pressing her voluptuous breasts into his back and her stomach against his buttocks. One leg slid along his. "I was worried you were too tired." She nuzzled her cheek between his shoulder blades.

Memories of Rhianna roared through his brain. "I . . . I am . . . just really tired."

"Too tired?"

He gulped the wine and managed to lie back in the pillows.

She slowly began rubbing his chest, his belly, and then glided lower.

His body responded against his will. He started to make some stupid excuse for her to stop, but before he could, her tongue began to play over his nipple.

"Domitia!" He pushed her away, stunned. He had thought her a virgin, not some cheap prostitute.

She jerked back into her pillows and clutched the sheet tight beneath her chin. "I am sorry. Did I hurt you?"

"No. No." He studied the frightened girl beside him. If Lugh had anything to do with this, the man would be executed. "Did someone tell you to act like this?"

She glanced away as her face turned scarlet. "Your . . . your mother said—"

His mother! "My . . . mother? How did she know . . . why did she even—"

"Julius, I just want to please you. I really do. I know nothing about . . . how. Your mother said . . . if I . . . I mean if you—"

He touched her lips with a finger to silence her, faked a smile, and forced another lie. "You do, Domitia, you do." He reached for his wine goblet again and realized it was empty.

"You hate me." Sobs shook her body, and she curled away into a ball. "You h-hate me."

By the gods, he did not want her enduring this humiliation. "Domitia. Domitia!" He ran a hand over the silken skin of her shoulder. "I could never hate you."

She rolled to him. "Then why can I not please you? Why? Is it because you prefer the slave over me?"

Yes. "No, Domitia.

Adoration radiated from her sweet, innocent gaze, too rich to enjoy. "Julius, there is nothing I want more than to be your wife. I loved you the first day I saw you."

Her words became a blur. He blinked and saw Rhianna laying there. Golden hair. Blue eyes. Sweet smile. His hand sank into that wealth of blonde hair as if starved. He rolled on top of Rhianna's lush body. Her legs parted, and he plunged into her, pouring himself into her yet again. A flood of contentment washed through him as the sweet depths of Rhianna swept around him.

"Julius?"

In an instant, everything shifted to a shocked brown gaze—not blue. Brown hair—not golden—spread across the pillows. The suffocating fragrances of roses—not delicate violets—clogged his head.

By the gods and Jupiter, what in Hades have I just done?

The fragrance of roasting pork floated into her mother's hut along with constant laughter. Although Beltane had happened months ago, the Trinovante village immediately burst into the infectious joys of a bonding celebration. The pounding iron had stopped almost instantly, and men raced off to hunt meat for the wedding feast.

All morning, women brought small gifts for good luck: vases filled with spring flowers, water pots, plates, and cups. Even a stranger had given Rhianna a wedding gift of a metal griddle for honeyed cakes. Their generosity was overwhelming.

The warmth of the bathwater filled with violet flower petals, saturated her body, reaching her soul that Julius held . . . if he lived. She could never wish him dead like the others.

She wanted him to live and to find her. But that might never happen now. Not if her mother had her way and the tribes agreed to run Rome off their lands. Julius' child might be all she would ever have of the man who had made her heart sing with joy.

Would Calgacus see the babe as a hated Roman or simply an innocent child begging for life? As her child?

If he would, whatever it took, she would be a good woman to him. She would honor him and give him children if he would just allow her to keep her child.

Please, Deae Matres, help me be a good woman. Help me keep my baby.

She drew her hand through the petals and closed her eyes. Julius appeared. He was there, his lips drawing her close, almost touching hers. She lifted her face to the caress.

"No!"

Her fist smashed into the water, spraying petals onto the floor. Whatever it took, she would be loyal to Calgacus, and someday . . . someday, she would give him the love he deserved. She would will it with her loyalty . . . if he accepted her child.

She curled into a tight ball, resting her forehead on her knees, and rocked back and forth, the petals sloshing over the edge of the tub. "He will accept it. He will."

Morrigan entered the hut with a comb in hand and stood there, stiff. The air around her would have chilled the coldest of nights. "Rhianna, will you let me arrange your hair?"

"Are you sure you want to?"

Morrigan nodded.

Rhianna rose from the water and accepted her sister's hand from the washtub. Wrapping wool around herself, she sat on the nearby bench. Morrigan stepped behind her and eased the comb into her hair.

It caught in a tangle. Her sister's fingers faltered to work the mass loose. Another tug. Another pull. Each harder. Each desperate.

"I miss him, Rhianna. I miss everything." Morrigan's hands covered her face, while her body quivered into sobs. "Rhianna, he's gone. Mergith. Father. Gone. They're all gone."

She reached for her sister, but Morrigan stepped back and threw the comb against the wall. A vase followed. Another.

"I hate them! Hate them all! They didn't need to kill him!" She wheeled, facing Rhianna. "You never knew the horror of their filthy hands . . . their filthy bodies." Her hands scraped over her arms. "I hate them for what they did to me. To all of us. To Father. To Mergith. I'll kill them, Rhianna. I will. I won't care who the Roman is. If I see one, I will kill him."

"You're right, Morrigan. It was horrible. It was wrong. But I don't want to lose you, too. I've lost enough."

Morrigan scoured her face with her hands. "All I see are the Romans killing him. All I hear is Mergith calling my name." Her sister melted into Rhianna's embrace. Sobs tore through both of them.

"Never forget his love for you," Rhianna whispered. "No one can destroy that. No one. Not even Rome. He will always love you."

Morrigan sagged to the nearby bench, letting tears fall one after the other. One hand swiped at her cheeks, spreading the sadness across her high cheekbones. She took a long deep breath, let it out, and then motioned Rhianna to the bench.

"Tancorix got my pendant off Mergith before the Romans could take it. He . . . he gave it to me. I'm sorry for all I—"

"Don't be sorry, Morrigan. None of this should have happened."

A brave smile appeared on her sister's lips. "I . . . I can sweep your hair up, Rhianna. Like old times. Will you let me?"

"I want you to."

Her sister's fingers ceased trembling the longer she worked. The longer she braided, the longer they talked of how Tancorix was teaching her to fight and how hard it was. They shared a laugh over how many times he had made her vault onto a horse until she simply slid to the ground.

Morrigan handed her a silver mirror, polished to reflect the braided crown of violets, blue forget-me-nots, and yellow flowers. "You're beautiful."

Calgacus' mother, Marleth, peeked through the doorway. "Rhianna, daughter-to-be, I bring you a gift."

The woman then came in, holding a blue wool gown embroidered with a rainbow of colors swirling around the neck and sleeves. "Will you honor me and wear this?"

It was elegant and rich. Beautiful. Rhianna slid into the gown and caressed the soft wool over her stomach. "Thank you, Mother. I will cherish this always."

A young boy burst into the hut. "They're ready! Come on."

Morrigan walked beside Rhianna to the back entrance of the meeting hall where Calgacus paced a new path in the dirt. His hair was stiffly limed back like a flaxen mane frozen in the wind. His mustache poured over the corners of his mouth like fluid gold. His blue tunic and trousers matched what she wore.

When he saw her, his eyes caressed her face, her hair, her gown. His long fingers curled about her hand. "Rhianna."

The sound of her name brought tears. Every part of her melted with guilt as he pulled her to his side and led her into the hall where Diras, Marleth, her mother, and Myrradin waited by the cold fire pit. Once again, only his parents' smiles granted warmth.

"This is a good day for our people, for our lands," Diras announced and motioned to the front doorway where nervous excitement mingled through the gathered crowd.

Everyone silenced the moment she and Calgacus stepped into the setting sunlight. They allowed him to lead her into the center circle of the gathering, where Tancorix held ropes tied to a haltered bull and cow, both adorned with spring flowers.

Diras stood with Marleth. Boudica joined Morrigan, leaving them alone before the eyes of both tribes. Myrradin stepped forward, lifted his arms, and called to the gods to witness this joining. His raven cawed from the thatched roof. Calgacus spoke. "Rhianna, daughter of Prasutagus, daughter of Boudica, daughter of the Iceni, I ask you to share my life."

"I will share your life, Calgacus, son of Diras, son of Marleth, son of the Trinovante."

Tancorix handed the lead ropes of the bull and cow to Calgacus.

"I give to you, Rhianna, this bull and cow as a promise to care for you."

He offered the ropes to her. She took them. Morrigan handed her a sheath of hay. Rhianna turned to Calgacus. "I give to you this grass to care for them as I shall care for you."

He dropped the grass before the cattle. They dropped their heads to eat the offering. People nodded.

Diras handed him a strung bow that Calgacus offered to her. "I give to you this bow as a promise to protect you."

Morrigan handed her three arrows. "And I give you these arrows to aid you as I will with my life."

He accepted the arrows and placed one in the bow, raised it skyward, and then released it into the air.

The arrow soared straight and true. Another sign of promise. He handed Tancorix the bow and remaining two arrows, and then poured a handful of grain into Rhianna's hand. "I give to you this grain to feed you."

She ate three grains and stopped. She had nothing to offer to clothe him. Nothing. Julius had the only thing she had left to offer, her pendant—and it too was gone. A restless silence stirred the crowd.

Morrigan stepped forward with a length of the dark blue plaid threaded with red and yellow that she had woven for Mergith. Diamond tears lingered in her eyes as she placed the soft wool in Rhianna's hands. "Take it, sister. I have no use for it now."

Blinded by tears, she faced Calgacus and forced the words from her lips. "I give you this wool to clothe you."

She let the cloth unfold before everyone who were awed by its beauty. She, then, draped it over Calgacus' chest, drawing it together at his shoulder, held together by only her fingers. She had nothing to hold the wool because her pendant rested on Julius' chest.

"Nor do I have a pendant."

Rhianna turned to Morrigan whose hand opened to display Mergith's pendant in her palm. She took it with a tight but grateful smile and somehow managed to pierce the sharp end through the fabric. She stepped back.

"Calgacus, son of the Trinovante, as long as you wear this, my soul . . . will be yours." The words burned through her heart like fire.

"And I give mine to you Rhianna, daughter of the Iceni." He kissed her.

They were joined. Their tribes' loyalties were merged. It was done. Complete. All except for her heart that was dead in her soul.

Chapter 21

Lugh stopped translating Iceni for Julius and stepped back into the shade of the portico the moment Domitia strolled into the garden. Now that she was married, she could appear in a domina's stola bordered with embroidery around its hem and sleeves—not the tunica of a virgin.

It was green like the emeralds sparkling around her neck, wrists, and in her hair, which Excelia had parted in the middle since Domitia was a wife now. "Good morning, husband." She said as she joined him on his bench.

"Good morning, wife," Julius said with relief. He must not have cried out Rhianna's name last night. "You look"—'rich' blasted through his brain—"very nice this morning."

"Thank you, Julius." Domitia's attention fell on Rhianna's pendant lying on his tan-colored tunic. "What a lovely pendant." She reached for it.

He withdrew from her touch. The pendant was the only possession he had of Rhianna's. By her intense gaze, it was clear Domitia was enchanted by it.

"It is nothing . . . nothing compared to your jewelry," he assured her, hoping to detour his wife's interest.

"But it is quite lovely. May I see it?"

"Seriously, Domitia. It is too plain . . . for you."

"Is it really?" Domitia sat back and studied his face. "I can only imagine why you will not allow me to even touch it." She sprang from the bench and went to the nearby table. Lifting a silver pitcher, she tipped over a silver goblet.

When nothing came out, she banged it down and wheeled on the young slave girl. "Neeca, water!"

Resting her hand on the table, Domitia gazed beyond the garden walls as she asked, "Did . . . your slave girl give that . . . to you?"

It had to come out eventually. Julius swallowed and answered, "Yes."

Domitia's gaze dropped as she slowly turned to him. "Then you must value her over me."

"I do not." His biggest lie yet. He did care about her. However, it was just that she should never have been brought to Britannia in the first place.

Domitia caressed the white petals of one of the roses filling a vase on the table. "I wonder."

"Domitia, I do care for you." Dropping the pendant under his tunic, Julius stood from the bench and reached for her arm. "Please understand. I—"

She jerked away. "Understand what, husband? That you care more for a Britanni slave girl than me?"

"Domitia, I want you to be happy, but—"

"Then tell me!" Tears glistened in her burning gaze. "Is she more beautiful? A better lover? Is she—?"

"Domitia, stop this. You are wrong." He grabbed her shoulders before she could bolt back into the villa.

She jerked free, her hand, once again, securing her to the table. A lone tear trickled down her cheek. "Are you sure of that, Julius? Are you certain I am wrong about this slave girl?"

Julius' hand cradled the back of his neck. "Rhianna is not a threat to you. I—"

Domitia raised her hand, commanding him to cease. "I will hold you to those words, husband."

His mother breezed into the garden as the slave girl set a new pitcher of water on the table. "Oh, Domitia, how perfect you look in emeralds."

She poured water into Julius' cup, drank, and then set the cup back down. "Julius dear, you look absolutely pale. Are you well? Is something wrong?"

He sat on the bench. "I am fine, Mother. Just tired." His mother glanced at Domitia for her confirmation.

Domitia managed a meager smile. "Well, it has been a lot to deal with, my darlings. But all will get better now that you two are married."

She waved for Neeca. "Tell your mother to prepare a light breakfast." The girl left. Procilla settled on one of the dining couches in the triclinium. "Join me. Val will be back soon." Neeca brought strawberries and cheese to a small dining table encircled by the couches. Domitia reclined beside his mother who reached for a piece of the fruit. He reclined across from his new wife and ignored the vast void that now separated them.

"Val is worried, Julius," his mother said heavily. "This morning, he heard rumors that the Britanni are restless. Could they be planning something?"

"I would not be surprised." Domitia reached for a glass of water. "Do you not remember hearing strange howling in the theater during that play, Mother?"

"Oh, yes! I forgot how horribly frightening that was. It certainly had nothing to do with the play." Procilla nibbled on a berry. "Honestly, I am starting to miss the warmth of my gardens."

Valerius strode into the triclinium, clean-shaven and combed. "You two are up early for newlyweds." He reclined on the one remaining couch. "I would have thought you would be busy making sons for Rome."

"Val, not this morning."

"Okay, Procilla, I will mind my tongue." His uncle lifted his cup for water. Neeca poured. "Heard the strangest thing at the baths this morning," he said. "The statue of Victory in the forum fell face down last night."

Julius reached for a piece of cheese. The statue face down was an omen to retreat. Knowing all that had happened lately made the morsel taste like dread and sand.

"Could not believe it, myself. Had to go see," Valerius said with a sigh. "It was insane. Women were screeching and running all over the place. Their husbands were huddled like fretting chickens. Idiots. My guess is that some slave intentionally knocked the statue over to create this insanity."

"Possibly, but why?" Procilla asked, fear hiding behind her gaze. "Well, regardless of why," she asked and turned to Domitia. "When is your father's galley leaving?"

"Day after tomorrow."

"Well, with the rumors as this, maybe I should leave on it." His mother turned her attention to her brother. "What do you think?"

"It is probably nothing. However, I think Suetonius should know about these occurrences. I will send a messenger to him. Best get back there myself."

Julius reached for a strawberry. "What does Suetonius intend for me to do now? Go to back with the Hispana or go with you?"

"Not sure." His uncle shrugged. "If you want, Julius, you can stay here until you get his orders."

Everyone's attention fell on Julius, especially that of his new wife. If the Britanni did have plans to revolt, he wanted both women gone from there. "Domitia, for your sake and safety, it may be best if you leave with Mother."

"Oh, Julius. Not so soon," his mother fretted. "You two need more time together."

"Mother, I agree with my husband." Domitia's glare flashed at him like a spear. "It may be best for everyone."

Procilla sighed. "Well, Julius will be coming home after the first of next year." She looked at him. "And then you and Domitia will have all the time you need together. I can see that this has been a shock to both of you." She smiled bravely. "Right, Val?"

"Absolutely, Procilla," Valerius said. "Gods be blessed." He lifted his goblet in a toast and then drank. "And Julius, do you think that fool slave of yours could possibly arrange what you need before we leave?"

Chapter 22

NO BUGLE CALL AROUSED ANYONE. Only a rooster crowing outside the small hut woke Rhianna from a restless sleep. A few cows lowed; sheep bleated. A dog barked. Calgacus' arm wrapped her waist, pulling her against his massive body. A grumble of satisfaction vibrated in his chest. He snuggled closer and went back to sleep.

She thought of pulling away, but the warmth of his body penetrated through her, luring her to stay. Memories of Diras' voice booming the night before replayed through her mind.

"For all present, I honor this joining of our tribes as a father and chief of the Trinovante." He had waved toward the doorway where four warriors appeared, carrying a roasted pig. It was placed before him to make the first carving for her and Calgacus, and then carve fat slices for Boudica and Morrigan. Then the work went to the serving women to feed everyone.

Fighting, boasting, toasting, and cursing erupted. Men bargained for weapons and goods along with cattle and horses.

A huge warrior had silenced everyone with a sudden outburst. "I bet my life that no man can bend the arm of Thorg!" He propped his fists on each hip and waited for a challenger.

Rhianna had expected Calgacus to accept, but he rested back in his chair with a smirk until his father stood and announced, "I will accept this challenge!"

A collective gasp echoed through the silent hall because if Diras lost, Thorg would become their new chief. Calgacus sat up, his gaze as sharp as a hunting dog's as all eyes focused on the two men stretched out on their bellies in front of the honored table.

Both men looked like matching rugs of hard muscle. They clasped hands, and Myrradin thumped the butt end of his staff on the wooden riser. Rigid tendons burst down both men's arms and their backs rippled with strength. Determination turned the two men's faces scarlet.

The fate of the tribe swayed like the tide while the crowd fretted like nervous birds. As Diras' hand lowered toward the ground, Thorg smirked into the Trinovante chief's eyes. Then, Diras slowly pressed Thorg's hand the other way. The smirk melted, and Thorg's hand kissed dirt. An explosion of cheers roared with victory the instant

Myrradin's staff thumped and the druid announced, "Diras!"

Thorg bolted to his feet. "I am your—"

"Stop! Before you speak your oath, Thorg." Diras dusted his trousers free of dirt. "I had your loyalty before, so keep your life and your freedom. Just be at my side when we face our destiny."

The huge man hoisted him off the ground with a hug. "My loyalty is yours, Diras!"

Released and coughing for air, Diras swept his hand toward the door. His personal warriors reappeared, carrying new spears heaped on blankets. Curiosity and excitement mixed the moment he reached for a spear and lifted it over his head.

"This lance represents our resistance to Roman tyranny. I present this to Boudica, queen of the Iceni, who has suffered most from Rome's oppression."

She took it. The sharp tip matched the gleam in her mother's eyes. "I accept your gift, Diras, Chief of the Trinovante, and I swear that we, the Iceni, will honor it."

The Iceni men roared, and the women nodded with smiles. A few doubtful gazes found Rhianna as her mother continued, "We will honor the bond between our tribes and all others who join us as we purge our land of this vermin." Boudica jabbed the lance into the air. "This will lead us! This will strike fear in the hearts of those who doubt our strength!" Deafening cheers exploded. Dagger butts pounded on low, wooden tables and benches. Feet thudded the dirt floor. When Diras handed Calgacus the second spear, it all calmed. "I grant you this gift that you may be the symbol of our future . . . of our traditions."

Smiling broadly, Calgacus stood and raised it over his head. "With this I will honor our tribes as brothers and sisters. May the skies fall on my head and the earth swallow me if I fail."

The druid stepped forward. His eyes were like black stars caught in the pits of his shallow, rutted face. His chin seemed sharper than the spear Diras had handed him. The weapon rested on the druid's palms as he began to speak slowly, but his words were clear.

"Andraste, goddess of war, Camulos, god of our city, supreme god of all things." The sleeves of his black robe slid down his scrawny arms as he lifted the lance to the thatch roof. His voice rose. "Hear us! We give back to you all things taken without respect to you! We give back all that you deserve! Help us!"

His raven answered from the back corner as if the gods had spoken and the onlookers hooted and cheered.

The remaining weapons were presented to each man. Goblets were lifted, toasts were made to seal oaths, setting servers scurrying to refill them. A determined happiness filled the hall.

Rhianna had noticed Calgacus had lifted his goblet for each toast but drank little. Then, his gaze trailed softly over her like a restless breeze . . . over her face, into her hair, resting on her eyes.

That same look had accompanied them to their hut where he had removed each flower from the braids until her hair cascaded down her back.

His touch, his lips, and then his body brought her from a dark pit into a glorious place with misty fields. With it came a sense of security, safety, a future at his side, but her body had not come to life as . . .

Calgacus sucked her earlobe between his teeth, jolting her back to the present. He nibbled down her neck, tingling every nerve in her body until she cringed and twisted in his arms to face an impish boy ready to laugh.

She brushed his face with her hand. "Calgacus, I promise to be a good woman for you."

"You already are," he whispered.

Calgacus stretched his naked length across the bed mats, pulled the blanket over his midsection, and then propped his head on one hand.

Feeling his sparkling gaze, Rhianna drew on a robe and forced her mind into the preparations of making her first meal for her husband.

"Wild honey cakes and fresh milk." He sat up, delight sparkling in his gaze. "You haven't forgotten."

She lifted the cakes from the new griddle and drizzled honey over each one. "How could I forget how much you love these?"

Satisfaction from the smile on his face was interrupted with the thought of what Julius would think of the honey cakes. She blocked the thought, as if stomping on a bug, and placed the platter on the bed mats.

Calgacus ate and then sat the platter on the supply box by the bed. His hand slid into her hair, warm and strong, to draw her lips to his. She let herself be absorbed and let the kiss edge toward the dark depths of her soul.

Pounding drums jolted them apart. "Calgacus! Calgacus!" a voice bellowed outside their door. "A meeting in the hall! Calgacus!"

"We're coming!" He rose from the mats. "We've got to go."

Rhianna stood and pulled his mother's blue wedding dress over her head. Calgacus did the same with his shirt and leggings, and then opened the door for her, his eyes tight with worry.

The paths between huts were filled with people racing to the meeting hall. Nothing joyous gleamed in their faces. Fear, fury, and anger hung breathless in the thick crowd.

Her mother motioned them to the platform at the front where Morrigan whispered, "Roman scouts were seen not far from here."

Just before returning to the hill fort, Rhianna had learned that Morrigan had killed two scouts and was now accepted as one of the warriors, which explained the transformation in her sister.

Rhianna remembered her father's words about change as she gazed across the hall now brimming with anger instead of joy. She drew closer to Calgacus' side and welcomed his arm around her as the meeting hall exploded into slurs and insults. Fury spewed with its venom.

"I say we stand our ground. If they come, we kill them. Leave us alone; they live."

"Fool, kill one of them and you bring all the legions down on us. I say kill 'em all now. Run their asses back to Rome. I've had enough of their insults."

"If something isn't done, we'll lose everything like the Iceni."

A short man stepped before the platform with his hands spread wide. "Couldn't we be like the Regni and join Rome? At least we'd own our lives."

Her mother's scrutiny pierced the man like an arrow, and then the hall settled under her command as Boudica began to speak, her voice clear and distinct.

"Why be moderate like the Regni, hoping for empty titles of freedom? You all understand how freedom differs from Roman slavery. You know how much better poverty is without a master, than wealth as a slave. Rome takes our lands and seeks to enslave us. Have you not seen the abuses we, the Iceni, have suffered?"

She released the shoulders of her gown, letting it fall to the floor, and turned slowly. She pulled aside her hair so all could fully view her backside.

The crowd gasped at the web of red scars wrapping her nude body. At last, she faced them, covered herself, and then looked into their stunned faces.

"We were raped by Rome and stripped of our belongings to pay their taxes . . . to pay their loans. And who is to be blamed for these insults?" Curiosity lurked in her voice. She offered the answer with an open palm. "The Romans?" "Yes!" People yelled. Heads nodded. Voices spewed even more accusations toward Rome.

"No!" she yelled back. Her hand coiled into a fist and jerked back. "We are to blame!"

The stunned crowd drew back with a gasp.

"If we leave a plate on the floor, will not the dogs come to clean it?" Her hand swept before her as the image settled on each gaze. "Let us do now what needs to be done, while we can still bequeath honor and integrity to our children. For if we forget our past, we give our children to slavery!" Angry faces confronted angry faces. Hands coiled into fists and thrust toward the roof. Red fury rose from their throats.

Boudica basked in the fervor, her face like an ivory statue until all quieted.

"Should we fear the Romans? Are they more numerous? More courageous? Is this not our land, given to us by our gods? Land known to us and that is our ally?" Her voice climbed. "Then, let us go against Rome, confident of good fortune. Let us show Rome that they are but hares and foxes trying to rule over dogs and wolves!" She grasped her lance and shoved it into the air. "Andraste! Lead us to victory!"

Chapter 23

Julius, Marcus, and his uncle followed the women's litter, which was carried by slaves, through the cluttered streets of Camulodunum. Days had passed like weeks since Domitia noticed Rhianna's pendant. In the presence of his mother and uncle, Domitia was the proper attentive wife. Alone in bed, she was as distant as Rome itself. He had followed suit.

His uncle's continued to drone about Suetonius' intentions in the west country, which amounted to finally wiping out the druid population, because the priests persisted in stirring up trouble wherever they could. After all, Rome recognized all the Britanni gods and, in return, simply expected the Britanni to pay homage to Rome's gods. They refused even the most meager tribute.

Julius had heard enough from his uncle and observed the burgeoning city as they strolled through the streets. The old Trinovante hill fort reminded him of the filthy Subura back in Rome. Here, thatched roofs, not clay shingles, covered most structures, making the city a tinderbox.

Furthermore, if there was a revolt, the decrepit ramparts surrounding the city left it vulnerable to even an assault from children. This was another reason he had decided that Domitia needed to join his mother and return to Rome as soon as possible.

Procilla motioned to stop in front of a shop bursting with newly painted pots and vases. "Wait. I want to take some of their pottery back home. It is quite lovely."

The slaves set the litter on the road, letting the women step from the cushioned mattress and disappear inside the small workshop.

Marcus cleared his throat. "When should I tell the men to be ready to leave?"

"Day after tomorrow is soon enough for me," Valerius said and shifted his attention. "Julius?"

"Domitia's father's galley leaves tomorrow. Perfect timing, actually. Like you said, Suetonius needs us." He faced Marcus. "Send a message for the men to meet us at the Principia in two days."

"Marcus." His uncle stopped the decurion in his tracks. "Have a messenger sent to the Hispana with a report to Cerialis about what is going on here."

"Yes, centurio." Marcus disappeared into the crowd. Julius' mother appeared in the shop's doorway. "Lugh, come here. I simply cannot understand these people."

His new slave, lounging behind them with the litter bearers, grinned. When he started toward Procilla, Julius met his sparkling gaze with a warning, and the expression faded.

"I do not trust that fool slave you bought," Valerius grumbled while chewing a worn cuticle.

"If Lugh is as smart as he thinks he is, he will behave," Julius retorted.

"The little shit is too smart, if you ask me."

Julius watched Lugh banter with the shop owner. "I intend to learn as much of the local languages as I can from him."

Valerius scowled. "So you can find that Iceni . . . girl you bought, right?"

"Yes."

Demetrius approached like sunshine bursting from behind a dark cloud. "Greetings, citizens! Marriage suits you, tribune. You look better. How is the arm?"

"Improving."

"Good." The retired centurion planted himself beside them. "Thought you both should know that bodies of Rome's newest citizens floated in with the tide this morning. Would not have wanted to be any one of those men. Mutilated beyond recognition."

"Sons of Dis and Jupiter." Valerius scrubbed his hand over his face. "This is not good. Not good at all."

"As I thought you would say," Demetrius said, "and was the reason why I found you."

"I will send a report to the consul." Valerius scowled. "I have been meaning to talk to you about the ramparts around this city. What happened to them?"

Demetrius shook his head. "Left to rot as I see it." "You realize that if there is an attack, it will never protect anyone."

The centurion shrugged. "I totally agree. I have told the magistrate."

Valerius' jaw clenched and unclenched. "By the gods, man, something has to be done about it."

The retired soldier sighed and scanned the busy streets. "I can try again."

Her mother's chariot lurched over another muddy rut, tossing Rhianna against Morrigan, who stood in a wide-legged stance to drive the chariot and ponies toward the old Trinovante capital now called Camulodunum.

Her mother rode with them, her attention focused on the road as if she could already see the city. The same city Julius had been taking her to.

Rhianna blocked her mind from his memory and instead studied her mother and sister who were alike in so many ways. Sunlight ignited their auburn hair like flames streaming down their backs, while their matching grey eyes could flash like lightening.

Both shared a common hatred of Rome that Rhianna found difficult to comprehend, even though she knew she should share their feelings just as Calgacus did. As did everyone following behind Boudica's chariot.

However, her father's ideas still echoed in Rhianna's conscience. He had said that all the resistance the tribes had accomplished with Rome had amounted to nothing but pain and suffering. He had thought it was better to work alongside them and gain what could be achieved.

Considering her father's beliefs, he would have sided with the Regni rather than the rest of the leaders riding in their chariots alongside her mother.

Overnight, her mother had become the symbol of Rome's injustice: Boudica—the insulted. Boudica—the defiant, the bold, the rebellious. Boudica—the blessed of Andraste, Modron, and Etaine. The chants were endless.

Rhianna turned back to see the masses following them. One moment the throng constricted in a tight band and then expanded like lungs for a deep breath.

Over the last few weeks, people from all over Britannia, intent on destroying Rome, had joined her mother. The Dobunni, the Catuvellauni, and many unknown tribes came to fight. Even warriors from the Regni tribe and the Brigante, defying their chiefs' loyalties, had come, adding their bloodlust.

Tribal colors were displayed on horses, flagged on chariots, gleamed on painted shields, or topped elaborate helmets.

As different as the tribes were, they all breathed one anger and existed only for revenge against what Rome had claimed from them. Land. Family. Temples. Taxes. Gods. Or just for the glory of battle. But they came, and the angry mass grew in numbers each day.

One color remained missing. Roman red. No one dared wear such a color. Yet Rhianna still felt the warmth of that red wool surrounding her and the arms that came with it. The chariot lurched, shattering the memory like hot metal thrust into cold water. She had to think of his child. No. Her child. The child she prayed Calgacus would accept.

She couldn't tell him and destroy the glowing happiness in his face. Now was not the time. Her bones said so.

Myrradin's chariot, driven by his accolades from the holy isle of Mona where the consul planned his destruction, pulled alongside. Like warriors drawn to her mother's hatred of Rome, young accolades came to the robed priest, who radiated a vulture's greed. His sharp gaze fell on her belly and then cut upward to meet hers.

She returned it without blinking, knowing that Myrradin would search for any way to sacrifice her child to Andraste, whether the goddess wanted it or not.

Terror stirred deep. Her world was evaporating like a mist, revealing a murky darkness full of monsters forcing her to survive among the growing hatred and fury.

Rhianna stepped off the slow-moving chariot to get away. Her only hope was the man riding Aerie. A silver helmet with a golden boar snarling from its crown barely shadowed the impudent sparkle in Calgacus' eyes. She barely took two steps before he plucked her like a flower from the dirt and set her before him.

She settled against his chest draped with Morrigan's cloth and held with Morrigan's pendant. She remembered pressing hers to Julius' chest and feeling his heartbeat. She remembered his words, *Then I will never take it off.*

She still wanted to be with Julius, but she had sworn loyalty to the man whose arm held her firmly against his body, who had risked his life for her, who still wanted her as his woman.

Calgacus was strong, kind, good, and willing to risk his life for his tribe to protect those he loved. And he loved her as she should love him. In time, she knew she could, if she knew her child was safe as well.

"Boudica!" a rider shouted. A lathered horse broke through the crowd and raced toward the lead chariots.

Aerie shifted to avoid the horse and rider drawing to a sliding stop. Boudica lifted her hand, halting the other leaders' chariots. The rest closed in around, trapping even the air.

The rider jumped to the ground and tossed the reins of the worn horse to one of the men. "The Hispana leaves for Camulodunum."

Boudica stepped from her chariot, her face cold and immobile. "How far away are they?"

"Two nights," the man said.

"How many?"

"Half the legion."

She stepped back onto her chariot and viewed the restless mass. "Calgacus, son of the Trinovante!"

His body flinched against Rhianna. Aerie reared slightly. "Yes, Boudica!"

"Gather the warriors to meet among those trees." Her mother pointed the black lance toward the distant grove at the foot of a stone outcropping near the River Gipping. "Families, prepare camp until they return . . . victorious!"

Cheers roared. Her mother's words traveled from mouth to mouth, spreading excitement like a field fire.

Calgacus gathered the reins in one hand. A new face, a stern expression, replaced his smile. He started to lower her to the ground.

"Stay here."

She clutched the fabric covering him with both hands. "No! I'm going with you."

Calgacus smiled and kicked Aerie into a canter toward the trees as Morrigan drove her mother's chariot for the large, flat rock jutting out of the ground. Boudica, his father, and the priest gathered on the rock's ledge, whispering quietly until the warriors had gathered around. Boudica waited for silence. It came.

"The Hispana marches to save Camulodunum. They must not arrive!" The warm spring breeze carried her words. "It is you who must destroy them!"

She pointed the lance at Calgacus, piercing his soul, but not flesh. "Calgacus, son of the Trinovante, can you lead them to victory?"

Hearing his name rattled every nerve in his body. Aerie reared, ready to bolt. "Yes, queen of the Iceni. I can!"

Aerie circled beneath Boudica's smile. The queen thrust the lance skyward. "Then do so. Destroy them! And may Andraste take you to victory!"

Eyes turned to him, gleaming like hungry dogs panting for a signal to move.

"Victory to Andraste!" Calgacus yelled, thrusting his lance skyward.

Fists and long swords thrust into the air. "Destroy the Romans! Destroy the Hispana! Andraste! Andraste! Andraste!" Their chants filled the air.

His body thrilled with the challenge. He would make them all proud, starting with Rhianna. He would make a future for her, their children, and for their people.

"Our future begins now. Tonight, we seek the gods' favor," he yelled. "Tomorrow, we honor them with Roman lives. Follow me!"

Chapter 24

JULIUS AND HIS UNCLE LED THE WAY through the high pass that sloped down to a flat plain with mountains to the south and east.

A panorama of pine trees, blue skies, and white clouds hemmed the view like a thick cloak. Before them yawned the massive fort of two legions, the XIVth Gemina and the XXth Valeria. A ditch, sparkling with fresh rainwater, encircled the fresh, timber-cut walls. The four closed gates proved a threat lurked in the air heavy with smoke and the fragrance of roasting rabbit. "Smells like we are in time for dinner," his uncle said and glanced back at the men who had accompanied them from Camulodunum.

Although their enlistments had expired, some of the men had signed up again, either out of frustration at not receiving the land Rome had promised or simply to escape their women.

Julius understood the latter. With the legions, he had a greater chance of finding Rhianna than if he stayed with a woman colder than any snow. Besides, Camulodunum was an agitated hornets' nest. His uncle's spies had reported on whispers in the taverns that the Britanni were planning something.

"They would not be that crazy," his uncle had huffed on hearing this.

Let him think what he wanted; the reports made the hairs on the back of Julius' neck bristle. If Boudica had been defiant enough to spit in Decianus' face after nearly being flogged to death, she could not be trusted to remain passive.

The horses worked their way into the valley. "I do miss a good meal," Valerius said. "Not that a woman's tastes fail to be pleasant. Just too complicated. Too many spices and sauces. Plain food settles better and keeps a man healthier."

His uncle straightened, sucked in his belly, and jerked his head toward the men, his white crest swishing with the sudden movement. "I figure they are as hungry for rabbit as I am."

Julius sniffed the alluring aroma. "Apparently, they have trapped enough for all five thousand men."

"No doubt." His uncle chuckled.

Their horses adjusted to the downgrade that led directly to the fort, jerking to either side while they searched for footing. The guards on the main gate pointed and talked to one another. One soldier disappeared from view. Suetonius would know of their arrival before the guards demanded they identify themselves.

When the screech of an eagle pierced the air, the twangs of firing catapults and ballistae, men drilling, and the hammering of metal silenced. The glorious bird circled the fort, drawing all to a halt.

The men behind him pointed. Excitement filled their whispers as the eagle soared over the strait to the island of Mona.

"Did you see that, Julius?" Valerius asked in an awed tone. "An eagle. Jupiter Optimus Maximus is with us." A smile beamed beneath his cheek guards. "The gods are with us!" He twisted around in the saddle. "We bring victory!"

"Mars Victorious!" the men yelled back.

The following morning sun peaked over the top of the distant trees when Calgacus rode Aerie toward his father's tent where Rhianna appeared with a food pack hanging from her shoulder. Nothing could ever be more beautiful, except to hear her laugh again. Whatever it took to wash the horrors of the Roman from her mind, he would do it. Calgacus dismounted and drew her close, feeling the stiffness in her body slightly soften, but not disappear. With a heavy sigh, he stepped back and tried to smile. "Rhianna, I want you to stay with your mother."

"No." She jerked away.

"Rhianna, please."

"I'm going with you, Calgacus, even if I have to walk." Pride warmed through him. "Fine then."

Faolan galloped toward them and licked his hand. He ruffled the dog's head as his parents appeared from their tent.

"I told you she'd go with him," his mother said to the man chuckling at her side. She looked at Rhianna. "Are you sure you want to be a part of this, daughter?"

"Yes. They will need help with the wounded."

"I pray there are few," his mother said and then turned to Calgacus. "Take care of her, son. Bring Rhianna—and your large carcass—home to us."

He kissed his mother on the cheek. "I will bring her home, Ma. And many heads for you, Da. Better keep Faolan here with you."

"The gods be with you both." Diras held out the ancestral sword of his fathers. "Here, take Cadaryn with you."

Calgacus accepted the sword as if it were a gift from the gods and slid the weapon into the scabbard on his back, the metal weighing heavy from the many generations who had wielded it.

It was both an honor and a responsibility that drew him and his father into each other's arms.

They broke apart. "And remember, son, the Romans are but lambs awaiting slaughter, and that Andraste will give you strength and wisdom. Look to her."

Calgacus' throat closed. He looked at the dog eagerly panting beside him. "Stay, Guard." Faolan lay down beside Diras' feet.

Before Calgacus crumbled from everything coming at him, he turned and swung onto the stallion. He lifted Rhianna up behind him and then rode from the main camp. His father's words rang in his ears. *The Romans are but lambs for slaughter . . . Andraste will give you strength and wisdom. Look to her.*

He silently prayed the goddess wanted this victory. The sacrifices, chants, and blue warrior paint itching his skin failed to offer the needed assurance.

He lowered Rhianna into the wagon with the other women who also had decided to go and then lifted his lance skyward. His war cry filled the air as he leaned back, letting Aerie rear. Tancorix and the other warriors answered him.

This was for Rhianna and their children. This was for his parents and his people. Whatever it took, it would be done.

Finally, the wide field the Romans would have to travel through opened before Calgacus. The sight of the white gravel road cutting through Trinovante land tore through him.

He listened to hear the soldiers' marching drums. All was still. Not even a bird chirped. Danger loomed in the air like a filthy disease. "Tancorix, find the Hispana and report back tonight. I want to know how many and how fast they are moving."

His friend wheeled his horse to leave, but Morrigan urged her stallion in front of the man, blocking the warrior's departure. "I'll go with him."

Calgacus studied Rhianna's sister. Ever since her return, she had practiced with any warrior who would show her how to fight, ending up with Tancorix honing her vengeance. Even though she had killed two Roman scouts and had garnered the warriors' oath to protect her back, Calgacus still wondered if she was ready for battle.

"Morrigan, stay with the wagons and the women. We'll do the rest," Calgacus ordered.

Fury flashed from Morrigan's eyes. "Don't protect me, Calgacus. I will fight. I will do my share to destroy anything that stinks of Rome."

He turned to Tancorix. "Want her with you?"

"I don't know." His friend rested his hand on his thigh and stewed over the offer. "She's a woman. Can she keep her mouth shut?"

Morrigan frowned at the taunting warrior. "You ass, I know more about quiet than you ever will."

"I'll take her along and see." Tancorix bolted away at a gallop, leaving her racing to catch him.

Calgacus motioned to the nearest warrior, a youth from the Brigante tribe who was giddy with his first attack. "Tonight, I want all the leaders to my fire," he ordered. "See they all know."

"Yes, Calgacus."

Warriors chosen from the various tribes squatted, sat, stood, or leaned against the surrounding trees draped in the deep shadows of night. Waiting for their news, all attention focused on Tancorix and Morrigan.

"What did you learn?" Calgacus asked his friend.

"They're moving fast and will pass through the valley by mid-morning."

Logs crumbled into the flames. Sparks flew and died. "How many?"

"Half a legion, maybe more." Attention shifted to Morrigan's response. "Including their leader and horse guard."

Calgacus nodded and was about to speak when words came from the shadows. "High sun will be a good time to attack. If you kill the scouts first."

Hands flew to swords at the stranger's words. Calgacus raised his palm, halting everyone. "Show yourself, stranger."

A man concealed beneath a leather cloak stepped into the firelight. "The Romans will have been at a quick march since they left the fort. They will be tired at high sun." He tossed off his hood, exposing a thick mane of white hair. "This will make them less ready

. . . if that is ever the case. But, if they are warned by their scouts, you will lose."

"They will lose." Morrigan stepped toward the stranger. "We double their number."

The albino laughed. "Then you know nothing of their legions."

Her hands rested on her sword.

Calgacus waved the men down. "And you do?" he asked. "I do." The stranger opened his cape to reveal his gladius, dangling along his thigh. Roman armor covered his shoulders and chest, a dirty, white tunic covered the rest of the man. He even wore the same Roman sandals with their bits of metal poking into the sole. Hobnails they were called. Calgacus knew well how they felt when kicked.

The albino easily endured the scrutiny with a smile. "I know these forced marches as well as any in their legions." While his warriors murmured, Calgacus studied this man's scarred face. Had this stranger been sent by the goddess to help them gain victory? Or was he a traitor? A spy?

"What's your name, albino?"

"Guntar of Germania. Son of Olaf."

"Then Guntar of Germania, son of Olaf, how do you know Rome's legions?"

"I was in the Hispana's auxiliary and fought with them until the Roman leader raped and killed my woman." Guntar spit into the fire. Stones sizzled. "Now, I wish to kill them all."

"What else do you know about the Romans?" Morrigan asked.

Guntar smirked. "I know I had no problem finding you, so they won't either. Smelled your smoke. Walked right past your watch. Mistakes." He shrugged. "The valley over this ridge is bordered on both sides by thick forests. A perfect place for an ambush. They'll know that, too.

"Wait on either side of the valley pass and do nothing until signaled. Once the scouts pass, the legate will determine all is clear. Then, attack."

Exactly his plan. Calgacus smiled. But he hadn't thought of the scouts. "I agree."

"Just one mistake, my friend. One arrow shot too soon. One snap of a twig. It's over. We lose." Guntar shrugged.

"What if one of their scouts returns?" Tancorix asked.

"They won't. They'll be dead. I'll see to it."

Chapter 25

CALGACUS SCANNED THE OTHER SIDE of the verdant valley where half of his warriors hid. During the night, they had moved behind the opposite hills without breaking one blade of grass in the valley or leaving one track to be read by the scouts, who had passed through the valley long ago. Minutes stretched like hours even though the day was bright with cloudless, blue skies where hawks circled. A perfect day to kill Romans.

He stroked the neck of the blindfolded stallion, its ears shifting nervously to all sounds. "Shh, my friend," he whispered to quiet the animal. "Soon, we will kill the fool who thought he could claim you."

Brush rustled softly behind him, and Tancorix and Guntar appeared, bloodied and smiling. "Legions are close," Tancorix said.

Guntar stepped onto the back of a nearby chariot harnessed to two ponies, each blindfolded and held still by warriors. He leaned over the chariot's side. "Remember. Kill the centurions before they can spout orders, or I might follow the order."

Calgacus chuckled softly. "Then, my friend, I'll have to kill you."

The albino straightened behind his driver. "I pray you would."

Drumbeats thundered across the valley. The sound led a long column of silver squares swaying in unison with each step. Soldiers, wearing various white and black crests on their helmets, marched outside the column as if they owned the world.

A red standard blazing with the letters 'HSPA' above the image of a bull led the column of silver squares marching along the road.

The warriors' eagerness pulsed across the valley like a wave. Every nerve wanted to explode. Tension coiled in the air. *Andraste, make them wait, wait for the perfect moment.*

Calgacus stretched his back against the weight of Cadaryn between his shoulder blades. He tightened his grip around the black lance.

Romans finally stretched across the valley floor from end to end like a long, silver ribbon. The legate, riding in the middle of his guards, raised an arm. Horns sounded, and the column sagged to a halt. Tired laughter carried across the valley. Many lifted water bags to their mouths.

"I don't believe this." Guntar nodded to Calgacus. "Now!"

Calgacus pointed his lance at Orvic, who held the long battle horn. The man lifted the instrument to his lips. The horn's hollow sound echoed across the valley, releasing thousands of screeching arrows from both sides.

Soldiers twisted in all directions as warriors and chariots flooded into the valley like two avalanches. More arrows darkened the sky, drawing Roman shields up into strange square formations.

Calgacus yanked the blind off Aerie and swung up on the stallion's back, letting the horse bolt down the hillside with Guntar's chariot driver racing toward the middle of the Roman line. The taste of its first blood gleaned by his hand. The albino's lance shot toward the red-crested officer.

However, the Roman's stallion wheeled, and the lance sank into the nearest guard. Calgacus drew Cadaryn and sliced the sword into another guard.

The shield squares shifted into circles, surrounded by a shield barrier punctured with gladii points like silver thorns. War cries mixed with barked orders. Roman pila crossed paths with the falling arrows.

He lifted his shield and felt one of the pila plunge into the wood, shifting its weight and making it awkward to hold. He tossed aside his shield, and then brought Cadaryn's blade down on another guard.

"Who goes?" the soldier bellowed from the guard station over the fort's main gate.

"Centurio Procillius Valerius and Tribune Gnaeus Julius Agricola. We bring the recruits the consul ordered."

"You will have to wait, centurio."

"You asshole, let me in. I am the primus pilus for the consul. Now open the damn gates."

"Primus pissant to me, you fool. Now wait . . . as ordered."

His uncle snarled beside Julius. "I will see that fool eats shit when those gates let us in."

Julius steadied his horse, shifting sideways. "The gates are closed for a reason, uncle. The soldier is doing his job, I would say."

"The whore spawn should know who I am."

A different centurion leaned over the guard's railing and nodded. "I know the motherfucker. Let them pass."

Julius followed his uncle into the fort where they both dismounted. His uncle's fury dissipated the moment they handed over the reins to a recruit and started through row after perfect row of tents set in exact squares.

Mouth-watering aromas of roasted rabbit accompanied them along with fragrances of leather, oil, manure, and sweat. Orders, clanking metal, and male laughter added to a common existence shared by all forts everywhere. Always exact. Always the same.

As they drew closer to the heart of the fort, the praetoria, Suetonius Paulinus stepped from his tent. His white tunic displayed two wide, purple stripes, granting him the rank of patrician as well as consul. Yet there was nothing soft about this man, not even his face.

"Be that the bloke your uncle's been tellin' us about?" Lugh asked quickly and in Iceni.

Julius nodded with a scowl to silence the slave. The sight of the man who had acted more like a father to him than a soldier while he was growing up, felt assuring. But as a consul, Julius knew he had to attend to proper respect demanded before the men.

During their hurried ride into the Dobunni territory, he had endured his uncle telling him of the consul's many successes in mountain warfare. This man had been drawn from retirement by Caesar Nero for that reason alone and had been ordered to use his expertise to quell the Britanni once and for all.

The instant Suetonius saw them, his dark brown eyes flashed with a youthful eagerness. "Valerius, praise Jupiter, you are back earlier than expected. And with the men we need for tomorrow's assault. Julius, I am surprised to see you so soon."

The consul motioned to the younger tribune standing nearby, his second-in-command who wore the black and white crest of a laticlavius. "See these men are housed and rested with the men."

The laticlavius saluted and left, motioning the recruits to follow. Suetonius waved toward his tent. "Both of you, join me for dinner."

Julius followed his uncle into Suetonius' tent where stale aromas of prayer incense and warm leather lingered in the musky air. Lugh followed as they all strolled across the wood flooring that displayed an identical mosaic of the Roman eagle that had filled the consul's vestibule in Camulodunum.

Acknowledging the small busts of Caesar Nero, Jupiter, and Mars, Suetonius continued deeper into the largest area of his tent where a desk, map table, scroll cabinet, chairs, and three couches awaited use. Slaves stood before the remaining two private sections.

After the slaves removed everyone's armor and helmets, Suetonius sighed and settled onto one couch. He motioned to have the wine poured as Valerius plopped his carcass on the couch to his right and took a proffered wine cup.

"Glad we made it in time for the assault. Oh, by the way, I managed to bring Julius as well, to assist as needed."

"Yes, Julius, it is good to see you. But were you not married to your betrothed?" Suetonius asked.

"I was, consul. The women have left for Rome, and I felt you may need me."

Years had passed since Caligula had executed Julius' father. Followed by the fact that Procilla had spurned his offers of marriage and chose to raise the boy alone, still needled beneath Suetonius' skin. Even though he had invested a great deal of time to charm her, after many years of so-called friendship, she still remained unclaimed by another.

Her son, however, did not wear the usual arrogance of most patricians' sons as he stood like a statue waiting for orders to join them.

Julius had obviously been well disciplined in protocol. Why wouldn't he be? Valerius was the best centurion any consul could possibly have. In addition, his friendship was valued beyond measure.

"Julius, join us." Suetonius motioned to recline.

The statue shattered into a living being, who reclined on the remaining couch and accepted a wine cup. He reached for a slice of cheese on the center table.

Suetonius reached for a boiled egg and asked, "I hope my villa was to your liking."

"Exceptional and appreciated." Valerius emptied his cup and lifted it for a refill. "The wedding was a grand success. We thank you for your generosity." He glanced at his nephew. "Do we not, Julius?"

"Yes. Thank you."

None of the pleasures of wedded bliss showed on Julius' face.

"I figured you would prefer to stay and enjoy your new bride, tribune." Suetonius sipped wine.

"Respectfully, I truly consider this opportunity to fight for Rome of more importance."

A politically correct response from boy he had watched grow up, of which Valerius obviously approved.

Suetonius hid his budding smirk. Julius was fleeing his new bride, something he remembered doing as well.

"You are most welcome," Suetonius said, lifting his wine as a toast. "Yet, I am glad you chose to come with your uncle because we can well use you. Tribune Albinus tore his leg in a fall this morning, so I will assign you to take his place with the IXth and Xth cohorts. Their centurions are strong enough, and I am sure you know the value of listening to them. Is that acceptable?"

Julius swallowed the smile emerging on his face. "It would be an honor, consul."

"Good then." Suetonius stood and handed his wine to the nearest slave. "Now, you both need to know how we will rid this island of this druid filth once and for all." He walked to the map table.

"We cross here." He pointed to the narrow junction between the mainland and the Isle of Mona. "Boats launch from here at dawn the moment the tide begins to change."

It isn't Julius. His crest is black. Not red. Rhianna clutched the nearest sapling, her insides twisting as the Roman soldiers scrambled into formation.

Calgacus and the warriors had flooded from either side of the valley. She saw Calgacus burst from the underbrush, his boar helmet flashing like a beacon. Their battle cries collided over the heads of the soldiers. It was like watching tidal waves crashing into each other.

"Rhianna, come. We're gathering to pray to Andraste to protect them," the woman beside her said. "Come."

The woman waited for Rhianna, but she couldn't move. She had to watch what she didn't want to watch, men attacking and killing each other. It was horrible, yet it held her to the tree.

"Leave her. She's worthless," another woman spat.

The disgruntled women moved deeper into the woods to join the others, kneeling with hands raised skyward and already chanting to the goddess.

Her knees melted beneath her, sliding her down to the moist earth. If they lost . . . if they lost, Calgacus would not be able to protect her or her child.

"Mother goddess, please protect him. He is all I have. Please, don't take him from me."

Guntar's chariot charged into a circle of soldiers, breaking it into silver fragments before bolting out on the other side. Calgacus followed, gutting soldiers like helpless pigs. He drove Aerie through a gap between the red shields, slashing Cadaryn through necks and arms before the soldiers could strike.

The sword took on a life of its own, cutting through flesh like a scythe. He sliced through another Roman's arm and then stabbed another's face. Aerie reared and planted both front hooves on a chain-mailed chest, crushing yet another Roman.

Three Roman cavalry charged him. He swung Aerie around and bolted away from the slaughtering confusion. When the first Roman reached him, he wheeled back around and sliced under the horse's neck. Another strike sliced the soldier's neck. The second Roman raced close enough for Calgacus to draw back and plunge his blade deep into the rider.

A black lance sank into the third guard's back, freezing the soldier's gladius midair before it could come down on him. Morrigan halted Skye. She was blood-covered and gleaming with victory. "Thought you were running away."

He laughed at her insult. "From what? Romans?" Skye danced beneath her in a pool of blood.

"Possibly."

"Hardly. Are there any left?"

"Enough for us, I think."

"Then, we have more to do."

They raced the stallions back into the melee, their war cries filling the air.

The blare of a trumpet managed to penetrate the thunderous chaos as the Roman officer and his remaining guards bolted from the destruction.

Chapter 26

CALGACUS DREW AERIE TO A REARING HALT and then waved Cadaryn, releasing a victory cry so loud his father's fathers should hear it. Warriors everywhere answered. The roar sounded over the valley floor as the soldiers who remained were slaughtered.

Armor, helmets, pila, and gladii became prizes while warriors danced among the dead. Roman heads became trophies tied to belts or hung on war chariots until the warriors' arms could plunder no more. Women raced from the trees ready to care for the wounded warriors and claim prizes of their own.

He found Rhianna carrying a bucket of water and rags. When he grabbed her from behind, she screamed. Joy flickered in her face and then died, her expression worried. "Mother Modron, you're alive! Are you hurt?"

He had hoped to see the same triumph that hummed through his body. "We won, Rhianna. Can you believe it? They can die. We can destroy their hold on us. We can regain what we once had. We can!"

"Yes, Calgacus. They can die."

When he showed her his collection of Roman heads held by a leather strip strung through the eye sockets, she gasped, dropping the bucket of water.

"Calgacus, you . . . you strung them on ropes!" Confused, he studied the leather strips to find the flaw. He saw none. "I had to. Their hair is too short."

It was a horror beyond anything Rhianna had ever imagined. The dead were sprawled everywhere and in every manner. Eyes wide, frozen in fear—Roman and Britanni alike. Fly-covered mouths gaped in screams.

When she found yet another dead Roman with wavy brown hair laying in the bloody muck, every nerve cringed. So far, Julius wasn't among them.

With Calgacus' help, they found a warrior alive in need of more care than she could give. He carried the man over to the other women, leaving her to search for more, or to search for Julius.

Andraste had answered her prayer. Calgacus lived. She knew she should be overjoyed, but that wellspring had gone dry. She hated death, yet many, like her mother and all the other leaders wishing to destroy all things Roman, glorified in it. The killing and the justification for such acts failed to bring what everyone wanted. Peace. Security. Those seemed impossible now.

She scanned the bloody field filled with death and misery, knowing so many would now be joining their ancestors, instead of growing old with loved ones.

Would her child ever have the chance to grow up in a world that her father had wanted? So often he had explained how, while the Romans had demanded taxes, they had also brought peace by stopping the fighting between tribes.

He might have been right about bringing peace, but that came at a cost. Taxes, crops, slavery, and land. Even with that demand, the tribes had flourished, and many had grown in numbers because fewer sons were buried.

Calgacus' trophies were another thing that affected her more than she expected. Even though she had grown up seeing heads of the dead adorning doorways or dangling by their hair on the sides of chariots, she never expected to see those strands threaded through eye sockets. Normally, they were carried about by the long hair. But Calgacus was right. Romans cut their hair too short for that, and she now wondered if that was the reason.

Julius' gaze flashed before her, warm, soft, and so full of life. The thought of his eyes gouged out sickened her. A single tear broke free and ran down her cheek.

She shouldered her cheek dry, and then touched a warrior's neck for a pulse. "He's alive!" She began washing his face with water, until other warriors appeared and carried him to the healers.

Morrigan limped toward her. She was covered with gore but smiled as if adorned in the finest fabric. A wound on her thigh had clotted dry even though it was deep.

"Let me wash that." Rhianna knelt to begin washing the dried blood from her sister's leg with the vinegar water and a small, well-used bar of comfrey soap.

"I killed four today." Her sister beamed and winced from the stinging pain. "F-four."

Rhianna glanced up from her work. "You look as if you killed all of them."

"I wish I had, but I killed the fool who did this." Morrigan seethed through her teeth. "Ouch! That hurts."

Rhianna tied a bandage around the wound and stood. "You need stitches, but this will have to do for now." She draped her arm around Morrigan's waist and helped her sister hobble to the growing shadows by the tree line.

"It was glorious. I know Mergith was with me. I felt him. Ahhhh!" Her sister slumped onto a tree trunk. Her gaze became serious. "I would have killed him if he were here. Your Roman."

Rhianna cringed. Julius was no longer her Roman, even though she still wanted the safety of his tent and to feel the joy she had known there.

"Do you still care for him?" Morrigan asked.

"No." It wasn't a total lie. She didn't want any of this to happen to anyone.

She left Morrigan and continued her hunt for more wounded. She found Calgacus digging the albino's trampled body from under his chariot.

He laid the man on his cloak and then pressed a hand to the man's chest. "Andraste sent you to us, dear friend. We honor you for your sacrifice." He knelt, kissed the hilt of the dead man's sword, and touched Guntar's forehead. "I will kill many more for you. This I swear."

She waited for him to notice her and then asked, "Do you need me to . . . tend to . . . anything?"

A small smile quirked on his lips. "Yes, I need you, Rhianna. Tonight, when we are alone, and you can take care of that pain." He drew her into his arms and kissed her, leaving his own tracks of blood around her shoulders.

She stepped back and glanced deeper into the darkening forest. Women were gathering wood for the funeral pyres of the fallen warriors. "I . . . I should go help find wood."

He released her and turned back to Guntar's dead body. The search for wood took her deeper into the forest, into the solitude only the verdant bushes and trees offered.

Silence that only the animals knew. She sat on an old stump and let her tears plummet.

Pulling away from Calgacus as she had had torn a fragment from his heart. He deserved her total love. She wanted to give herself totally to him. But she couldn't. Her soul still belonged to another. Julius.

Chapter 27

J ULIUS FOLLOWED HIS UNCLE TO SUETONIUS' DESK to see a
parchment displaying the markings of the fort, the measured distance to the Menai Strait, and where the catapults and onagers had
been placed. Arrows were drawn across the strait like fish, pointing
to where the boats were to land.

His IXth and X[th] would move almost straight across the water
for their landing. Julius memorized what lay before him. The IXth
cohort. The Xth cohort. His men . . . his responsibility. His heart
danced with his childhood dream of leading men.

"Do the men know what to expect once they land?" his uncle
asked while handing his wine to the nearest slave.

"Definitely. I have had the centurions talking of little else but
the maneuver."

Suetonius pointed to the last arrow on the map. "Julius, this will
be a unique opportunity for you. I want you and the rest of the tribunes to take the beach all along here. Expect a rather loud welcoming party. But I think the majority of the fools will be here where the
I[st] will land, where I will be."

"Ballistae?" Valerius pointed at a line of squares with dots along
the shoreline opposite the island.

"Yes. There will be a constant barrage while the cohorts land,
moving down the beach until all the men have landed. They will stop
when we are ready to move inland."

Suetonius looked up from the map. "This fucking island has
been the center of resistance long enough." He straightened up from
the desk, his gaze almost venomous. "I want this spawn extermi-
nated once and for all."

Julius read the map again. The plan involved floating men down the strait while the catapults hammered at anything that moved on the beach, shifting down as men disembarked and formed on the beachhead. Not too difficult since the land appeared flat. He saw marshes behind the trees covering a rise where he was to land and then villages behind that.

"I cannot tell you how good it is having you back, Val." Suetonius stretched his shoulders. "Guard." A guard stepped into view. "Call for a general assembly."

The guard saluted and left. A cornicen sounded soon after he left, summoning the officers.

The consul looked at his uncle. "What do you think, Val?" His uncle stepped back from the desk with a lurid grin.

"Consider it done, my friend."

Julius joined the other four tribunes positioned behind Suetonius and the two legates. Off to the side, Marcus stood with the decurions, holding their red and black crested helmets. The centurions, with their various black and white crests that indicted their cohort, gathered behind his uncle. Curious glances scanned Julius, but nothing was said.

"As you know, we take Mona at dawn." Suetonius propped his hands on either side of the map and looked at the sea of faces. "And finally deal with this rabble of crazy, chanting fools. I want the men on the boats quickly while we have the slack water. See they remember to go down on one knee, or they will be swimming with Neptune. The catapults and ballistae will hammer the beach until everyone is offloaded. Remain covered even on the beach. "The boats will release five at a time. The first wave will discharge here."

The map was held up by two slaves while Suetonius pointed at each of the dots that related to the landing area. "The next will offload here. The last will offload here. Form and wait for my signal. I am sure we will not be welcomed."

Dangerous chuckles and vicious smirks rippled through the tent while the consul cleared his throat. The tent silenced. Suetonius motioned to Julius. "Tribune Agricola will be taking the place of Albinus. Are there any questions?" The centurions' questions erupted like an assault itself.

While listening to Suetonius calmly address each one, Julius recited the plans in his mind. The pressure of it all closed in on him. His throat went dry as his brain spun with concern and excitement.

Suetonius thrust a fist forward. "Mars Victorious!" All saluted. "Mars Victorious!"

The tent emptied, and his uncle dropped a heavy arm across Julius' shoulders. "Fortune smiles at you today, Julius, with an outstanding field of soldiers. Your centurions are well qualified and have the men working well. Trust them and keep visible. But stay in the rear."

"No problem," Julius assured him. However, more doubt coursed through him than blood.

His uncle leaned in close enough to whisper, "And watch out for Petronius, tribune in charge of the VIIth and VIIIth. He is a pompous little ass and a bit of a showoff." As if summoned, the short tribune with dark hair and eyes met Julius outside the tent. "Petronius. VIIth and VIIIth cohorts." He waved to Suetonius' laticlavius.

"Titus, I will cover for you."

"You do that, tribune." The officer laughed and disappeared in Suetonius' tent.

Too short to drape an arm over Julius' shoulder, the tribune moved closer. "Agricola, is it? You are in time for glory. Tomorrow is going to be a rout. I cannot wait to see the looks on their faces."

Julius glanced behind the soldier at two restless centurios scowling at the tribune. They were his centurions. The Xth's centurion wore a black crest, while the other had nine sections of black and white peppering his crest. They turned to leave.

"Centurios!"

The centurions wheeled about, came to attention, and saluted. "Tribune."

"Thanks for your help, Petronius. I can handle this from here," Julius assured him with a placating smile. "Get some rest. Tomorrow is going to be a big day for all of us."

"I love you, Julius." Julius reached out to draw Rhianna's soft, lush lips to his, but only swiped through air. Gasping, he clutched the Iceni pendant . . . but not Rhianna. He swung around on his cot, dropping his bare feet to the rug.

Dampness curled around his ankles like a cat as images of Domitia flashed in his mind. His new wife stood there like the goddess Juno, shifting from pain to fury. Why had he gone through with this farce of a marriage? By the gods, why? No answers.

Thoughts of Essex accompanied him as he walked to the piss pot and relieved himself. The old slave would have been awake by now, fussing over him like a mother hen.

He looked across the tent where Lugh slept, filling the tent with his snoring. Like an insult, the slave rolled to his side and jerked the coverlet over his shoulders.

Julius drove both hands through his hair, then over his raspy jaw line to remove the last remnants of sleep that would not be returning. He walked to the desk and poured wine into a cup.

When he appeared through the tent flaps, both guards jerked to attention. "Tribune? All is well?" one guard asked.

"As can be."

He drank while gazing at the long lines of leather tents bathed in moonlight and the smoldering campfires outside each one. Shields propped against pila created images of small pyramids before the tents. Soft thuds of distant drums drifted on the night air. Druids and warriors preparing for tomorrow.

The assault had already begun between doubt and excitement. The battleground was inside him. He should be making love to Rhianna now as if for the last time. It could be his last time, from what his centurions had told him about what he would face tomorrow.

"The fools yell curses day and night. Constant drums," one told him. "Eventually, it gets to some of the men."

"The fools race chariots over the beach and curse us continuously."

"Women, with blue swirls over their entire naked bodies, screech and curse like possessed Furies."

"It never ends with these people."

One centurion growled as they walked back to the units, "I would not have my mouth on any one of their tits. Likely poisoned. The little fools are weaned on it."

After all they had said, it made Julius wonder what the warriors were like. Maybe their bows could throw lightning or something.

He grinned and tossed back the last of his wine. When he walked inside, he found Lugh sitting on a bench, stretching his back.

"You be restless tonight." Lugh rose and lifted the cup from Julius. "Will ya be hav'n more?"

Julius nodded and sat in the desk chair.

Lugh poured two cups of wine and sat back down on a nearby bench. "Pa and I were here once. I wasna' more than a sprite. We vowed never to go back to that island of fools. Aye, never regretted that."

"You never went back?" Julius leaned forward, cupping the wine in his hands. "Why?"

Lugh stared off into the shadows. "Ever seen someone sacrificed?"

Julius shook his head.

"Ain't nothin' to forget or ever see again." Lugh shifted on the bench. "We went tradin' wool for grain to get us through the winter. If 'n I remember, it was the night when the dead souls walk. Not far from where we pitched our things, a group of those black-draped priests dragged a poor man out of the trees. They came chantin' and wavin' arms like trees in the wind." Lugh shook his head.

"The man was shittin' his pants, beggin' them to let him go. Before he knew it, he was pole axed upside the head. Another priest flung a rope around his neck and tightened it until the man was barely breathin'. Musta come to, 'cause he fought like a fiend. When he quit, they dropped him face down in a pool to drown his soul. Pa said it was so he could see where he was goin'."

Silence pooled in the tent as the images of that poor man ate into Julius' imagination.

"Next day, when Pa was dealin' with their leader, a priest came forward carryin' the man's bloody intestines in his hands. He told the leader to make the trade and that it was a good sign."

Lugh took in a deep breath. "Pa and me left that same day, but we sold the grain quicker than a star falls, because we didna want the man's spirit invadin' the grain. They're a crazy lot to be sure."

Julius nodded, and then, again, silence reigned. "About killed us gettin' back here though." Lugh met his gaze. "You do know about the pits of quicksand all about the beach, don't ya?"

Julius nearly dropped his wine. "Quicksand?" Suetonius had said nothing about quicksand.

Lugh nodded. "I fell into one pit and like to never got out. Two of the lunatics helped Pa save my arse. None too easy I might say. Said to be more careful next time."

"Where are these pits?"

Lugh smirked. "All over where your benevolent consul is plannin' to offload. Pockets of the shit lurk all along the beach. Many deep enough to suck in a man or horse in an instant."

Julius sank back in the chair. He pictured the battle line

formation, saw it start forward, and men disappearing into these pits. It would freeze the entire line. By the gods, I need to tell Suetonius.

"Lugh, have my things ready when I get back."

Chapter 28

WITH RHIANNA BESIDE HIM, Calgacus harnessed the ponies to Guntar's chariot. Their victory was proof that Romans could die or be driven back across the great water. Joy thrilled through his veins as he brought conquest back to her people, to their people, those whose lands one day would be theirs again.

He glanced back at his warriors, walking taller and with greater confidence. Their jubilant smiles mirrored the brightness of the sun. Many danced and cavorted. He wished he could join them.

There had been moments when he had doubted if Rhianna wanted to be with him and share in this victory over Rome. However, last night had renewed his belief that she would never go back to the Roman who had nearly destroyed her. She had lingered in his arms, responded to his caress.

Tears gleamed in her eyes as she bravely smiled. "Praise Andraste you weren't hurt." Her words sang in his ears still. Smoke from the campfires appeared in the midday sky.

People at the edge of the camp gathered, eager for the news. Calgacus could see their emerging smiles.

A boy raced away toward the leaders' area. Soon Boudica and the rest of the leaders drove their chariots through the throng, slicing it in half like a warm knife through butter.

Calgacus thrust his arm skyward. "We bring you their destruction! We bring you victory!"

Cheers, both behind and before him, answered. The throng raced toward them, blocking the leaders' chariots.

"Orvic, you and the rest, bring the trophies from the wagon," Calgacus said to the warrior striding alongside the chariot. Roman blood still coated him as he smiled and bolted back for the leather-wrapped bundles on the wagon. The lead chariots drew closer and, at Calgacus' signal, his men unveiled their prizes—Roman standards, weapons, armor, helmets, blankets, all that the Romans once possessed. The crowd swarmed around to watch the leaders examine the trophies.

Boudica pulled a silver wolf fur from beneath the plunder and walked toward him. A smile emerged on her scarred face as she held out the pelt. "Well done, husband of my daughter. Protector of your people," she announced in a full voice. "Take this. It has been well earned."

A mix of joy, pride, and relief sang through him. He waved the pelt like a flag and released another victorious yell. It seemed that the world answered.

Morrigan pressed Skye alongside his chariot. "Mother, I bring you trophies of their deaths." She lifted her string of Roman heads for all to see.

Admiration added to Boudica's smile. "Well done, daughter of the Iceni. Andraste be praised for your return, Morrigan." She glanced at Rhianna, standing beside him, and then walked back to her chariot.

His father's voice jolted Calgacus back from Boudica's insult to Rhianna that had hit like a fist in his gut.

"Well done, son of the Trinovante. You have been returned to us."

"Da, praise to Andraste!" Excitement returned, bringing Calgacus back to life. After he handed the reins to a stiff Rhianna, he stepped into his father's arms and then his mother's. All his men cheered as he gave Marleth the fur.

"Come, Calgacus and Rhianna, come with us that we may celebrate this victory," his mother said with tear-filled eyes. His parents climbed back in their chariot and left with the rest of the leaders.

When Calgacus stepped back beside Rhianna and reclaimed the reins, she touched his arm. "I will be with the grain wagons."

He held the eager ponies from moving and slouched against the chariot's side. "Rhianna, all you eat is dust back here."

Her gaze turned as hard as the metal in Cadaryn. "Better dust than bitterness."

"Rhianna, please, everyone expects us to be with the leaders."

"Of course. It is where you should be. But I will no longer be even near her camp."

Between the restless ponies jolting the chariot to move and the swarm of people moving past them, he couldn't stop her from stepping from the chariot and walking back to the wagon now empty of trophies. She took hold of the lead rope, sent the young boy away, and turned the team of oxen toward the herds of goats and sheep.

Chapter 29

ALONG WITH THE OTHER OFFICERS, Julius knelt on one knee and held one palm outward with his head bowed. The fragrance of grain flooded the consul's tent along with a thick heat warring with the early morning chill. Sweat broke beneath his cuirass.

Suetonius began his invocation to the gods. "Jupiter Optimus Maximus, may you find our sacrifice favorable. We call upon you to help us destroy your adversaries. Janus, we now open the gate to your temple so you may lead us in battle."

He opened the lararium doors of the small replica of the gods' temple. "Mars Victorious, we offer these sacrifices to your glory today." He tossed more grain onto the small flames, which flickered in the incense burner.

"Venus, Victoria Augusta, we plead for your blessings this day that we may purge those who fail to recognize your greatness and that our virtue and piety are pleasing to you that you will grant us victory over those who deny your greatness." The consul stepped back from the lararium and knelt, palm out, his head bowed.

The waiting priest broke the neck of a hawk, drained its blood onto a candle, and inspected the bird's entrails. "Omens are good. The gods hear your prayers."

Forearms clapped across cuirasses in one thump. Neither Julius nor the other tribunes moved until Suetonius stood and faced everyone. "The day is ours, comrades! Now, go and prepare for victory. Give no quarter this day!"

They rose, saluted, and evacuated the tent as if it were on fire. Petronius closed in. "Did you hear about pits of quicksand all along the beachhead?"

"I heard." Julius lengthened his stride toward his cohorts, in hopes of losing his new companion.

Petronius kept up, huffing and talking. "Did your centurios explain how the boats were getting over? The current can be swift and tricky. We will be boarding when the tide begins to reverse course. Keep the men down and covered. No telling what the cocksuckers are going to throw at us other than—"

"Tribune Agricola!" Valerius marched toward Julius, his all-white crest gleaming in the dawn shadows. The centurion's scale-mail glinted like captured stars in the gleaming dawn. His red cape battled the white, gold-tipped linen strips, swaying from the waist of his under tunic, with each urgent stride. The man stopped and glared down on Petronius like a stinkbug he was not allowed to squash.

Petronius wilted. "Excuse me, centurio. I best see to my men."

"Good thinking, tribune."

His uncle waited until Petronius sauntered off and then transferred the same glare onto Julius. "That little pissant of a slave of yours had better be right about the quicksand."

Valerius propped both hands on his hips. "If not and that slave of yours is lying, I will pull his tongue out his ass even if he does belong to you."

"If Lugh is lying, I will help you," Julius answered. A calm had seeped into his flesh as he confronted the centurion. The man's expression melted into concern. "Well, watch where you are going and make the bastards come to you. Stay in the rear. Understand, tribune?" "Yes, centurio."

"Good. After morning formation, the onagers and ballistae will begin firing. Be sure to order the men to ignore the fools' curses when they reach land."

"Yes, centurio."

His uncle started to leave and halted. "If he is lying, I swear, I'll—"

Julius walked away, leaving his uncle with his curse.

Tension drifted in the air while the IXth cohort helped each other don armor before their tents. Once covered, they shifted beneath the weight of the metal and adjusted weapons until everything felt like familiar flesh. Some appeared intent and somber while others threw insults toward the druids.

Julius joined his centurions watching the men prepare. The cohorts' cornicens sat by the tent flaps, wiping down circular horns that would sound his orders to the cohorts.

"How are they?" Julius asked.

Fabricus shrugged. "The recruits are fretting. Would not expect much else, though."

One centurion turned to Julius. "Quicksand, huh?"

"Lots of it, I guess."

"Shit."

Everyone appeared ready. As the men began picking up pila, Julius coughed into his fist to clear his throat, which had been closing with the mounting tension. He had to do this right.

He had dreamed of this when visions of victory were simple.

There was nothing imaginary about this now. Lives rested on his conscience, lives like those of Essex and Felix. He could not fail, not this time.

"Centurio, assemble the men."

"Yes, tribune."

Fabricus nodded to the cornicens, who rose and sounded the command to muster. Clusters of men moved instantly into lines of polished armor, holding shields to their sides and pila to their right. Eyes looked blindly forward.

Julius could easily separate the experienced from the inexperienced by the worry creasing their faces. Could they see the same concern reflected back at them? He prayed not. "Comrades, you have heard those cursing Rome, promising death, threatening to destroy all that is Rome, even our mothers! You have heard of the sand pits along the beach."

Eyes glanced left and right, allowing him to know he was not the only one worried about being sucked into the ground.

He forced a confident smile across his lips as he continued. "We will fill those pits with their asses, not ours. Because our gods have promised victory!" He shoved his arm skyward. "The gods are with us! We are Rome! Are you with me?"

"We are with you!"

He asked again and then again.

Their answers surged through his veins.

"Stand ready for victory!" He signaled dismissal. The cornicens sounded the order and the centurions took over. The Tenth received the same message with the same roar. Again, their answers exhilarated him, made him proud to be among them. These men were Rome. They were one.

Together they would be victorious.

The consul's cornicens sounded orders to muster on the main field for his last words before battle. Julius returned to the Ninth and stepped before the standard-bearers.

"Prepare!" The order echoed down his part of the column. Shields lifted. Fabricus looked to Julius the moment the VIIIth cohort moved in behind the VIIth.

"Forward. Move!"

Taking his place beside Petronius on the official platform, Julius stood with feet apart and hands clasped behind his back like the other tribunes.

Every ounce of what he wore felt heavier. The red cape pulled on his shoulders like a boulder. The officer's purple sash, double knotted around his midsection, seemed to cut him in half. His helmet felt like a vice covering his head and the black crest-tail lay like a long whip between his shoulder blades. Although he stood as still as the other tribunes, the linen strips of his undertunic teased his legs and arms with every twitch.

He did not want to stand there, waiting. He wanted to move. To discover what the Fates had in store. Instead, he blankly watched the white cape shift around Suetonius' legs and against the white, gold-tipped strips of his under tunic. Under one tanned arm, Suetonius held his white- crested helmet. Morning gleamed on his golden cuirass like trapped bits of sunlight tied across his midsection with the same official, purple sash.

Before Julius stood thousands of Rome's most lethal forces, ready to do battle and destroy any and all who threatened her. Line after perfect line, still as steel, hard as oak, and ready.

"Comrades!" Suetonius yelled from the center of the platform. "We have endured enough curses, threats, and insults from those we will silence today! We will bring glory to Rome. We will bring honor to our families. For this day belongs to Rome. To you!

"Give no quarter to these savages who are determined to humiliate us before our ancestors and before our gods. We will be victorious! Are. You. Ready?"

Hungry roars resounded three times. "We! Are! Ready!"

Chapter 30

BLUSTERY MORNING WINDS BUFFETED Julius' face and the fog-shrouded waters of the Menai Strait. The water moved in tidal transition that would last about an hour before fully changing direction.

Most of the continuous line of flat-bottomed boats had already crossed, each filled with soldiers hovering beneath their shields in a testudo formation along the shores of Mona. The firestorm of ballistae shifted their aim down the shoreline with the arrival of approaching boats until only the IXth and X[th] remained, ready to ferry across to the island.

Individual groups of naked warriors painted with swirls of blue waved weapons and welcomed them to come meet death. Behind them, druid priests waved arms and chanted to the billowy clouds that housed their gods to rain down their destruction on Rome.

The piercing screeches of flaming ballistae scattered them like disturbed flies on cow dung, and like flies, they returned to the sand dune behind the beachhead.

Suetonius' laticlavius motioned the IXth to board. The men filled the space, squirming closer on one knee, and lifted their shields over their heads. The moment the IXth floated off, more boats appeared for the Xth and Julius.

He carefully stepped onto the rocking platform and knelt with the rest of his men. His guards' shields locked over him the instant the boat was released. He found Marcus' red and black crest riding at the back of his boat as his cavalry drove horses into the strait.

A barrage of arrows and sling-stones greeted them. Curses carried in the air at the same moment the boat ground ashore. The ballistae continued peppering the sand dune until they had disembarked, and the warriors fled. Any pause in the assault and another rain of arrows, spears, and stones began firing from the sand dune. A fire arrow stuck into the rear of the boat, setting it ablaze.

"Sons of bitches!" growled one of the soldiers. He splashed water over the flames even as the boat beached and was evacuated and set adrift.

A horse bolted loose from the VIIth and raced off toward the I[st] cohort, fragmenting the formations like broken boxes. Then, the animal sailed hooves-over-head into a pit and was left to thrash to its destruction.

"Testudo! Testudo! Now!" Julius yelled. His cornicens sounded, and every soldier disappeared beneath a shield as feet searched for that one mysterious sand trap, the one that would suck him in and never let go.

Fabricus appeared beside Julius. "Men are ready, tribune." He fed off the calm gaze of the centurion.

"Find the pits."

"Yes, tribune."

Little red boxes began breaking away from the formation and poking sticks into the sand, marking a safe pathway to the sand dune.

"Our gods will devour your gods this day!" Priests chanted to the heavens. A continuous rain of arrows fell, and warriors yelled their war cries while bare-breasted women screeched along the dune like angry locusts.

Marcus and his unit of guards approached behind the lines, waterlogged from the crossing. Occasionally, horses stopped to shake water off like dogs. "Hope you are ready for this," he said with a grin.

"As I'll ever be," Julius said, even as his guard blocked an incoming arrow. "First line! Pila!" he yelled to his cornicens who sounded the order.

The first line of spears flew into the air and dropped onto the surge of warriors, driving them off the dune.

They returned and yelled insults. "You will disappear! No one will find even your shit!" Shields blocked another deluge of arrows.

Marcus handed Julius the dripping reins to a grey horse. "Here, in case you really wish to ride through this shit."

No part of him really wanted to vault into that wet saddle, but he needed to see what was happening to be able to direct his men. He vaulted onto the restless mare, blocking his mind to the memory of Aerie rearing and the lances cutting into his flesh. "But can you keep up?"

"We can." Marcus swung onto his horse and then wheeled back to his guard lurching onto their horses.

"Curses on your fucking mothers!" "Fuck you and your whore sisters!"

Julius rode the mare down the rear line of his IXth and X[th] cohorts. "Forward!"

His cornicens, positioned intermittently along the rear, sounded his orders. Centurios echoed it, and the red line drew up like a drawn red rope. Inch by slow inch, the men began maneuvering around the markers and into a hail of spears and arrows. More pila crossed through the air and sank into warriors scrambling backward. His soldiers climbed up the sand dune like fire ants, killing any who resisted until the warriors fled for safety.

Or, so it appeared.

He had read about this ploy of the Britanni—retreat and lure the line into a surprise attack. His soldiers now feasted on the apparent victory as they crested the hill and started to pour down the other side.

Julius halted on the rise and saw the awaiting trap hidden in the nearest marsh. "Halt! Halt, damn you!"

His cornicens replayed the order again and again. The signifiers, standing in the center of the rows, frantically waved the order with their banners. At last, the centurions' whistles sounded, and the men halted.

A breath later, a melee of screaming warriors exploded out of the marsh grass, and the dance of death began again. It was like harvesting wheat. His soldiers continued forward, cutting down warriors, and stepping over the dead.

The rear line in Petronius' VIIIth cohort broke and started back toward the dune, threatening his IXth's flank.

Where in Hades was the little shit?

Julius bolted toward the VIIIth's optio, clambering to stay behind the retreating line. "Where is your tribune?" he yelled at the man.

"Dead!"

Petronius? Dead? Shit. "Close with the IXth! Signal the same to the VIIth. Now!"

"Yes, tribune."

The call sounded, and the VIIIth shifted, throttling the imminent threat. The VIIth followed.

Warriors and druids were once again racing away into a dense clump of oak trees near a village filled with conical huts and a lace of rock fences. Another perfect trap for his now four cohorts surging forward in pursuit.

"Halt!"

The order echoed through the air, bringing all to a breathless stop. He raced to the cornicens of the Xth. "Burn the village." He rode back to the IXth. "Guard the Xth."

"Yes, tribune," each optio answered and then relayed the orders to the centurions directing the forward movements. He sagged on the exhausted grey, letting the guards sweep around him. He scanned the movements of the VIIth and VIIIth. They were still engaged with an attack that was melting like snow on a hot day.

Marcus presented a fresh horse. "You are one hard tribune to keep up with."

"And it is not over." Julius slid off the stumbling mare and then barely managed to throw himself onto the fresh horse.

A horde of warriors raced from the sand dune toward the rear of the VIIth and VIIIth. No centurions could see this assault.

"Rear reverse! Rear reverse now!"

The cornicens sounded, the banners waved, and the rear lines of the VIIth and VIIIth wheeled about. The centurions continued the frontal assault, while the optio ordered the rear to form and attack.

Julius rode to his IXth and ordered them to cover their flank.

As if hitting a wall, the approaching warriors staggered to a halt, and like any trapped animal, looked for an escape. There was none. The remaining six cohorts flooded into view and surrounded them, killing all who failed to drop their weapons and sink to their knees.

A thick cloud of black smoke from the blazing stacks of hay and burning huts created by his X[th] swirled around Julius.

"Decurio, close this end!"

Marcus saluted and called the order to his tubicen. The rider lifted a straight, wide-mouthed horn and sounded the order to his cavalry. The cavalry wheeled their horses about and swept into the melee, closing off all means of escape from this side.

Suetonius appeared on the sand dune, raising a hand, and his cornicen sounded victory. The sound echoed from all cornicens on the field.

"Mars Victoria!" Julius yelled.

A delicious roar exploded from his men. "Mars Victoria!"

Chapter 31

THE THRILL OF VICTORY COOLED in Calgacus' veins with each turn of the iron bar filled with two rabbits sizzling over the licking flames. Rhianna sat in the fire glow, pushing a bone needle through a rip in another pair of his breeches. She untied a knot in the wool thread and then continued her mending.

Who would mend the gash that Boudica had delivered earlier, he wondered? It made no sense. Even though she wasn't a warrioress like her sister, Rhianna should be with the rest of the Iceni because she was the daughter of the Iceni leader.

However, when he tried to change her mind about staying up with the leaders, she pulled even farther away from him than she already was. He couldn't deal with that anymore.

Morrigan appeared from the shadows, startling him from his thoughts, and squatted by the fire. "I can't wait until tomorrow," she told the flames.

Rhianna stabbed the needle into the fabric and disappeared in the underbrush.

"What's with her?" Morrigan asked. Confusion riddled her face. "And why are you camping back here and not up with the others?"

Calgacus gave the rabbits another turn. "She prefers being back here and doesn't want any part of being up with your mother or the leaders."

Morrigan slumped to the ground. "Because of what Mother said today, right?"

"You're as smart as any druid."

She sneered at him and then grew serious. "Like the other leaders, all Mother thinks about are dead Romans or how to make certain they become that way. Rhianna knows that."

He turned the rabbits. "She does, but why Boudica shunned her is beyond me."

Morrigan stretched her shoulders. "Like Father, Rhianna prefers a peaceful way through any mess. Not destruction in any form. Right now, Mother only sees Rome's destruction and can't stand the reminder that there is any other way."

One rabbit leg caught fire. Calgacus put it out with a quick brush of his hand. "She's the gentlest girl I know. I love her for that."

"I love her for that, too. Three warrior women in one family could be deadly." She leaned forward and poked at the flames. "May I eat with you?"

"There's enough."

"Maybe Rhianna can mend my tunic, too."

He grinned up at her. "Watch out for the needle. She's lethal with it."

Though victorious cheers echoed through the darkness, the night stretched as if nothing had happened. With Faolan lying beside him, Calgacus could hear the night creatures and breathed cleaner air. The true music was the sound of the sisters talking and laughing, and he began to see why Rhianna preferred being back here.

"I'm going for water." Rhianna retrieved a bucket sitting before Faolan. The dog stopped licking his paws and disappeared with her.

The moment she left, Calgacus faced Morrigan. "Who's meeting in your camp tonight?"

"All the chiefs and their leaders. You know you should be there."

He glanced to the distant camp where thick shadows moved around fires. Rhianna stepped from the night shadows. "I agree. You need to be there. Both of you. Now, go," she said.

He dropped to a squat and faced the fire. "I'll find out in the mornin—"

"Calgacus, you are the son of Diras. You should be at your father's side." She dropped the bucket and faced her sister. "And Morrigan, you should be with Mother. Now go. Both of you."

Calgacus and Morrigan wormed their way closer to his father and Boudica, listening to the three strangers facing the tribal leaders.

"The plan is working better than expected," said one messenger. A fresh whiplash stretched across his cheek when he smiled. "They grow more restless as more of their statues fall face down in the dirt."

"And the river now runs red with Roman blood," another added with equal pride.

"More continue to wash up on the shore of the estuary each day at dawn," the one with the gash along his arm said. He chuckled. Vindictive laughter rippled through the listeners.

"The citizens grow restless and fear they are trapped," the third messenger added. He straightened up with the same air of assurance as the other two who nodded. "But we swear to each of them that they have nothing to fear. Surely, who would dare go against the might of Rome? Just now they begin to build defenses."

The pleased look on Boudica's face vanished. "Defenses?"

"Yes, dear queen. They force us to remove their filth from the trenches." The gashed messenger pointed to his wound. "And we do try to move faster; truly we do, under lash and all. It is such slow work."

She studied the smirking man. "Do you know which slaves are with us?"

All three nodded. "A few remain who have taken the Roman laws to heart. We know them and will see they are taken care of." He rubbed the butt of his sheathed knife to make his point ever clearer.

Boudica gazed into the hungry fire. "At daybreak we surround the city and attack only when the trumpets sound, not before." She straightened and scanned everyone gathered. They waited like trained dogs. "And tomorrow we begin the destruction. Destroy everything Roman. Tomorrow we take back what is ours."

Myrradin stepped into the fire glow, his gaze hungry for revenge. "I have asked Andraste to lead us to victory. And I know now that she is with us as she was with Calgacus." He pointed at Calgacus, chilling his blood with a crooked finger. Cheers hooted. "May Camulos be honored with her gift!" Myrradin yelled.

His raven cawed from his shoulder, confirming the statement, as did the explosion of war cries.

Chapter 32

THE ENTIRE ISLAND APPEARED TO BE COVERED with smoke from the burning oak groves, villages, and marshes. Suetonius wanted it all black, but the island was bigger than he had expected, so it would take far more time than he wanted.

Still, he smiled, leaned forward, and stroked Imperious' white neck. "Once the men are done, the bastards will not be holding their filthy sacrifices any longer."

Valerius smiled. "You can be sure of that. Scouting parties are out looking for any survivors."

"Have them counted and prepared to send back to Rome with the rest of the stock."

The horses nipped at each other, jingling the ornaments on their bridles. "I do not care if Rome wants nothing more than their damn dogs, slaves, wool, and little else from this province." Suetonius snarled. "I want nothing left of this island. Nothing. These fools have caused enough trouble." Valerius' attention drifted across the slate grey water.

"That is about all Rome can expect from this shit hole."

Valerius looked tired, too tired. They all were, Suetonius thought. The stresses of the legions every morning drained them both more each day. However, he knew he would never be ready to retire to his villa outside Rome, not with Marcia. "What was the real reason your nephew came with you?"

Valerius slowly shook his head. "Fool boy found an Iceni bitch and let himself fall for her. Bought her, or so I hear. You did get the report about the assault?"

Suetonius watched the sun drop behind the smoke and turn blood red. "Something about a slaver being killed and the captives being released."

"That's the one." Valerius swatted at a fly settling on his arm. "Seems they came for the girl, too. She is Prasutagus' daughter, I think."

"His daughter? Why were any of them taken as slaves?"

"Something about payment on taxes or loans."

Imperious snorted from the smell of smoke. Suetonius remembered the greedy face of the procurator that Rome had dealt him. "Not that little pissant Catus again?"

"I believe so. Julius was there. You could ask him. He was acting tribune to his guard until Procilla got to Camulodunum with Dom—"

The surrounding guards stopped the messenger racing toward them. The rider drew to a halt and saluted. "Express permission to speak to the consul."

Suetonius raised a hand. "Let him pass."

"Consul, the IXth . . . the IXth Hispana was nearly destroyed on its way to Camulodunum."

Suetonius stared at the soldier. "Destroyed? The IXth? Cerialis?"

"The legate lives. Here is his report." The rider presented a rolled parchment.

Valerius took it and then handed it to Suetonius. He broke the official seal. It was Cerialis' handwriting stating that a horde of Britanni had assaulted the Hispana, killing nearly half of the legion. He insisted that he could keep the remaining area secure, but he could do nothing for the capital city.

Suetonius dropped the parchment, letting a slave pluck it from the dirt. "I want Julius in my tent . . . now."

"Too bad about Petronius," one of the tribunes said while feasting at the tribunes' mess table.

Julius dipped a bread chunk into gravy. "I was wondering. What happened?"

The man next to him lifted his cup to be filled. "Rode his horse to one of those pits."

"It stopped. He did not," another said with a smirk and then bit into a roasted leg of rabbit.

"Smart horse," the tribune across the table added. "From what I heard, Petronius went in headfirst. His guards tried to haul his ass out and were almost pulled in with him."

The rest laughed even as cups rose to Petronius. "May Neptune relish his company."

Everyone drank and then resumed eating. Julius spilled wine to the ground to honor Petronius. No man deserved to die that way.

The Ist's tribune slammed his drinking cup on the table, startling everyone. "I could not believe it. We lost three men to those damn pits."

The tribune beside Julius added, "Any wonder why the men refused to advance? Hades have me, but even I was scared to move forward."

The talk changed to the day, the crossing, the rout, burning villages, and destroying what remained of the druids' bloody oak groves.

Julius' thoughts went to the image of soldiers dragging a blonde-haired girl from of one of the huts, raping, and then killing her. It ended before he got to her.

The tent flap swept back, flooding the area with cool air. A guard stepped into view. "Tribune Agricola. Consul wants you. Now."

Suetonius flipped his stylus end over end on the desk and glared at Julius. There was another time that he remembered Procilla's son this nervous. He was ten and had taken a horse out instead of doing as his teacher had ordered. He almost grinned but asked, "How familiar are you with the Iceni?" Julius cleared his throat. "I was assigned to guard the procurator Decianus Catus when he was in their territory. Little more."

"It is true that you own a daughter of Prasutagus?"

"I do."

"Why?"

Julius stretched his neck and obviously wanted to move. However, he did not. "For her protection."

"From?" The stylus picked up speed in Suetonius' hand.

"Being raped and beaten like the rest of her women."

"Tribune, I thought you knew women are not allowed in camp."

"The procurator ordered it."

The stylus hung above the desk. "But you allowed it."

Julius closed his eyes. "My mistake, consul. I was not aware I could refuse an imperial order."

A mistake often made by inexperienced officers. The stylus began again. "Regardless of that, what happened?"

"We arrived at the funeral of the Iceni leader. When the procurator demanded payment for taxes, Prasutagus' woman refused, and spit in his face for not honoring her husband's will—"

The stylus slapped down on the desk. "Will? What will?"

"Prasutagus willed half of his property to Nero. It was not written or recorded, yet his widow expected Decianus to accept their word."

"That son of a bitch. Any intelligent official knows the tribes value their word as law. As Catus should have."

"The procurator did not and chose to claim all of the property as payment, as well as any who defied him."

Suetonius leaned forward on the desk. "And I understand the same warriors who took your slave were presumed to be the ones who slaughtered Silvius and freed the Iceni. Am I correct?"

"To my knowledge, you are correct."

He flicked the report on the IXth Hispana toward Julius. "We just received a report from Cerialis that a rebel force nearly decimated his legion and now heads toward Camulodunum."

Picking up the stylus, he began stabbing the end into the pile of letters. "Do you believe this Boudica is capable of ordering such an assault?"

"Definitely, consul."

Suetonius exploded to his feet, kicking the chair against the leather wall. Driving his hand through his hair, he paced the confines of his tent, feeling trapped.

"A woman! A fucking woman leading a revolt against Rome . . . against me. No one defies Rome and no one makes a mockery of me. No one. I will kill that bitch if she does!" Swallowing hot bile from his throat, Suetonius leaned on the desk with both arms and tried to breathe.

"I am leaving the laticlavius here to finish things. I want you with me as acting laticlavius. Prepare to leave at dawn."

Chapter 33

"WILL THE ATTACK BE TOMORROW?" Rhianna asked as Calgacus and her sister appeared in her small camp. Ever since they left, thoughts had plagued her that Julius might still be in the city. If he were, she wasn't sure what she would do. She wasn't his slave now. She was free and joined with Calgacus. Then again, the child she carried was Julius', whose arms she still dreamed of surrounding her.

Calgacus squatted down and drank from the gourd in the water bucket, letting water run from the corners of his mouth. He wiped his lips with the back of his hand. "Are the rabbits ready?"

"Of course." She removed the iron shaft with the edge of her dark green cloak and laid them on a wooden platter sitting on the nearby rocks.

"Then, let's eat."

An owl hooted and another answered. Morrigan took the platter that Calgacus offered to her. Rhianna took hers and then sat back on the wool blanket. "You didn't answer my question."

"Yes. We will take our city back tomorrow," he answered without looking at her.

Her stomach closed; she couldn't eat the small portion remaining on her plate and handed it to him. "You need this more than I do."

"I don't want it." He pushed away the offering.

"I'll eat it," Morrigan said and claimed the morsel like a greedy urchin.

The flames popped and crackled, lighting their somber gazes. "I'll be with the men tonight. I need to keep them sober." He climbed to his feet. "Morrigan, what are you going to do?"

She rubbed Faolan's ears. "I'll stay. I don't want to be with a bunch of drunks anyway."

"Don't stay on my account." Rhianna tossed a small branch on the flames. "I'm no child."

Rhianna stared into the shadow where Calgacus had disappeared. Night breezes rustled the leaves over the makeshift tent stretching from the side of the wagon. A log fell into the flames, sending sparks shooting up to the stars. Nearby, the goats and cattle grazed in the dark.

Morrigan began sharpening the Roman gladius she claimed from the assault on the Hispana. "I really don't want to be with the men tonight."

Rhianna sighed, letting her discontent join with the darkness. She had seen how drunk the men were before they went on a raid. Now, with the druids' blessings, it would be worse than ever.

However, if her father hadn't died, none of this would be happening. She would never have known Julius, and she would not she be carrying his child. That fact sent a sadness over her like a disease.

Morrigan oiled the whetstone. "Don't worry about Calgacus. He's the best fighter among us."

"I know." He was. Yet, if something happened to him, there was no doubt that the people would turn on her, and her mother wouldn't stop them. Only Calgacus stood between her and their wrath. Only he protected her life and her child.

A long silence lingered, cut only by the grinding whet- stone and boisterous laughter in the main camp.

"The priests say the omens are good for tomorrow," Morrigan muttered as she sharpened the blade.

Rhianna stopped stroking Faolan's fur. "Would they say anything else?"

"Yes, they would." Her sister set down the weapon. "Rhianna, don't you think we should be taking back what is ours?"

She resumed running her hand over the soft black fur. "Father wouldn't want this."

"Right now, if Father tried to stop the leaders, he would be out voted."

"Even if the leaders do run Rome off our land, it will never be the same. We aren't the same." She studied her sister's face, luminous from the fire. "Just look at you. You're a warrioress now. Even if Mergith or Father could come back, you would never change back to what you were before."

Morrigan poked the flames. "I'll never go back to that helpless creature. And after what they did, I never want to see another Roman alive."

"What happened to us was done by the procurator. The tribune—" Rhianna wanted to say Julius, but his name caught in her throat "—he never wanted this to happen."

Morrigan's gaze shot over the campfire. "But it did."

"Yes, it did."

"Are you sorry that Calgacus came for you?"

"No, Morrigan. I'm not . . . sorry." Part of that was a lie. Even if Julius did hold her soul, she willed her loyalty to Calgacus. If the people would accept her and her child, she would be content.

Morrigan shifted and set the gladius beside her. "What has this Roman taken from you, Rhianna?"

"Nothing." Only her soul. "I just don't want anything more to happen to our people, to us, to Calgacus." Rhianna forced her hand to glide over the dog's fur, to sooth the dog as well as her nerves. "You know, Mother is right. You are like her . . . a fighter. I am like Father. I want peace."

"One day, there will be peace again." Morrigan started sharpening the blade again. "Once the Romans are gone and we take back what is ours, we will have peace."

As the dawn pushed the darkness aside, Calgacus placed a hand on a Roman sword that rested opposite Cadaryn. The view before him revealed a massive, angry ring of warriors surrounding the old Trinovante capital claimed by the Catuvellauni who lost it to the Romans.

During the rituals the night before, the priests had proclaimed that the god Camulos demanded his city cleansed of all Roman filth, and that the goddesses Andraste and Epona promised death to all Romans.

And it begins now, today. When the horns sound.

Aerie shifted beside him. He stroked the elegant, black neck to calm the horse and then adjusted the silver Roman disk gleaming on the horse's forehead. Six more jingled from the chest strap. Calgacus' round shield hung from the Roman saddle that he had grown to like. With the four leather-covered pegs around his hips and thighs, he was kept secure when he used his swords now.

The night before, the same messengers had arrived again at Boudica's campfire with more news. The city still expected the Hispana to arrive, not knowing that all the Roman couriers had been killed before they reached the city.

The messengers assured everyone that panic increased daily. Only now were the Romans assisting in repairing the surrounding rock wall, which reached no higher than a man's waist, one that ponies could leap over.

Aerie suddenly shifted as Faolan bounded through the trampled underbrush with Rhianna following. What was she doing coming this far forward? He'd left her with the other women and their wagons to await the signal to come into the city.

He wished she shared the joy of ending Rome's rule over their lives. To him, she was the rising sun, the flowers of the earth. She was his soul. All he wanted was to make her right again, as she was before the Roman destroyed her. Two full cycles of the moon had passed since he had taken her from that Roman. Even if it took him an eternity, he would find a way to see her smile again. It was a promise that sank deep in his own soul, a promise that would keep him alive.

"Rhianna, you should be with the wagons, not here. The horns will be sounding any minute."

"I had to see you. I——"

He would kill every Roman out there just to hear her say she loved him. His heart thundered in his chest, hoping to hear those words.

"I pray," she attempted a meager smile, "the gods watch over you and bring you back. I need you."

Calgacus released his disappointment in a breath and cupped her cheek in his palm, feeling her rest in it. She closed her eyes as if soaking up something from his touch. "And I need you, too, Rhianna. I will return. This is our day. I promise."

Tears drizzled down her cheeks as she pulled from his touch. His hand clinched as if abandoned. Anger welled. It would be released on the Romans. He pulled his dagger free of his belt. "Rhianna, keep this, in case——"

"I don't want it. I have Faolan. He'll take care of me."

"Rhianna, Faolan may not be enough." He slid the weapon under her belt.

Drums thundered in the distance, and Morrigan raced Boudica's chariot before the mass of warriors. Roars followed in waves. Boudica shoved her black lance skyward and yelled, "Until our lands are cleansed of this Roman disease! Until then, nothing will be as it should be . . . " Her voice faded as her chariot raced away.

Rhianna clutched his arms, returning his attention to her. "Just come back to me, Calgacus. Don't let anything happen to you."

"I will, my love." He brushed the tears away from her cheek. "Wait for the signal and then come with the rest of the women." He looked at Faolan. "Stay. Protect." The dog wilted to the ground.

Morrigan stopped Boudica's chariot beside a warrior holding an upright horn that bore the face of an open-mouthed serpent. The queen nodded, and he blew into the instrument.

A long, mellow sound issued from it. Other horns echoed the same melodic blast around the city, releasing a deluge of chariots and horses to flood across the plain toward Camulodunum.

At the sound of the horn, Calgacus sprang onto Aerie's back and joined his father's men. His war cry blended with the human flood spreading toward the city like angry wolves. Tancorix, Cyric, Orvic, and Edan, with at least fifty more, swarmed around him, eyes bright with bloodlust. Another war cry burst from his lips, and his men answered. He would see Romans die today, maybe even the one he sought.

The closer they rode toward the short stone wall, shields appeared like red spots, and a volley of pila cut through the sky. Calgacus lifted his shield as a javelin glanced away. Lances and arrows launched from the war chariots riding over the undulating trenches. The boys of various tribes kept a constant barrage of sling-stones and arrows in the air, keeping the shields up and the Romans down.

Calgacus headed toward an open section of the wall for Aerie to leap like a gazelle into a nest of soldiers. The harvest of Roman flesh began as he sliced with both swords and kicked soldiers away from Aerie, the Roman saddle holding him on the stallion's back.

Cyric and Tancorix appeared beside him, and together they feasted on Roman blood, their screams, and their destruction. Pain, grunts, and cries sang in the air with the thunderous clash of metal and wood, flesh, and bone. A glorious dance of death exploded around him until his swords fed on nothing but air.

The hot, coppery stench of death assaulted Calgacus' nostrils the moment he halted the gore-covered stallion and looked for yet another Roman to kill, but only bodies of Romans lay before him, squirming like maggots. Those living had fled deeper into the city.

He jabbed the Roman gladius back into its sheath and raised Cadaryn to the gods witnessing the start of the cleansing from a cloudless sky. A yell roared from his lips. Victorious cries sang from around the distant walls. Soon, the city rang with the sound of triumph.

Chapter 34

THE INSTANT THREE FIRE ARROWS lifted from the city walls, children twirled about while their mothers exploded into cheers and songs of praise to the gods and goddesses. Wagons began racing toward the captured city. Even Faolan pounced off the sides and seat of the wagon, barking with excitement.

The jubilance swirled around Rhianna like a whirlwind, yet she remained numb in the midst of it all. This was where Julius had been ordered to come. This was where he had been taking her. Would he be lying dead in the street? What if she found people torturing him? What would she do? Save him, or would she have to watch?

Her hand rested on his child that grew closer to her heart each day. She would do what she must to save her child. That alone was all that mattered now. She had to save her child.

What if she found Calgacus lying dead among the Roman bodies? Her insides froze with each step closer to Camulodunum.

The horrid smell of death assaulted her the moment she passed through the opened gateway. Gagging, she tried to look away from the sight of citizens of the city—men, women, children, and Roman soldiers—sprawled in the streets in their own putrid pools of death. Yet, the women drove their wagons over the bodies as if they were mere dirt hills.

A red fury welled inside Rhianna. What she saw wasn't the Roman soldiers pillaging this time. It was the ecstatic horde rejoicing over the victims and laying claim to anything inside homes. Chests, cloth, anything metal, anything moveable, and anything not latched down was loaded into whatever could be found—carts, wagons, satchels, and blankets. This was her own people raping the city, as the Romans had her home.

"Move on or get out of my way!" someone yelled from behind her wagon. "Get over!"

Two blood-covered warriors burst from a doorway, dragging a simple citizen wearing a slave's tunic, and slaughtered him in the street like a cow.

She couldn't be part of this.

Rhianna jerked the bawling animals into yet another street where brutality thrived like a malicious beast.

A grain cart lay overturned and ignored. It wasn't gold. It wasn't anything but grain. People would need grain to survive the winter because no one was planting crops. But they were too busy massacring and feasting on the death of Romans.

She started tossing the bags of grain into her wagon until arms grabbed her from behind, lifting her into the air. Her scream blended with his bold laughter. "It's ours, Rhianna. Camulodunum is ours!" Calgacus yelled.

He is alive! Joy shot through her as his blue eyes danced in the late afternoon sun. She clung to his blood-spattered neck and felt his arms sweep around her.

Beaming, he set her down. "Let's see what we can find."

"I won't be a part of this!" She motioned at the busy street filling with Roman goods. "I . . . I won't take what isn't ours."

All sense of victory drained from his face. "Rhianna, we only take back what was ours to begin with."

"No, we're not. I won't be like them." She pointed at two women fighting over a vase. "I will take only what is necessary to survive all this insanity. Help me with this grain."

Chapter 35

WITH THE WAGON FILLED with the grain from the broken cart, Rhianna let Calgacus drive the wagon beyond the chaos to a villa that remained untouched. After he broke open the gates, they drove into a courtyard lined with colorful pots of herbs and flowers.

"Let's see what we find—need in here." Calgacus kicked open the doors to the main house. Scowling, she followed him across a black marble floor inlaid with a golden eagle. They entered a large space with a small pool in the middle of the room, where two red couches invited them to recline. An opening in the ceiling allowed rainfall to fall into a pool filled with trickling water. A beautiful, blue-and-white pottery bowl sitting on an oak table tempted her to claim it. *It does not feed people.*

She walked past flowing curtains, her hand lingering on the soft fabric, and then followed a covered walkway sur- rounding a garden filled with blooming roses and phlox. Bushes surrounded small areas filled with a group of loungers facing a large table. It was so beautiful and peaceful here.

A doorway not far away drew her. She entered a small cooking space filled with pots and plain pottery bowls stacked on a wooden table. Knives, wooden bowls, cups, and two braziers lined the wall beside a space where a fire had burned. Thoughts of taking all of it crossed her mind. Well, maybe not everything or she would be no better than everyone else or the Romans.

A side door opened onto an outside alleyway where three rooms, closed by rough-hewn doors, faced a high, outer wall. She opened the first to a small chamber filled with bunk beds along the wall. A cracked pot, emitting a stench of urine, sat by the door. Two chipped cups sat on a square, rough-hewn table placed on a filthy, ragged rug in the center of the dirt floor.

Slave chambers. Would Julius have let her to stay in such a place? Or would he have kept her with him, inside where everything was spotless and clean?

By one of the beds lay a tattered comb with the familiar swirling designs of her people. Some of the wooden teeth were missing and the remaining ones held long, golden strands.

Something lay beneath a pile of blankets on the bed above the comb. She lifted the wool to reveal a blonde- haired woman with her throat slit. Her death glare drove Rhianna outside, where her insides heaved what little her stomach contained.

Faolan bolted through the kitchen doorway and started scratching on the second door. When she carefully opened it, the dog bolted past her to a young girl, squirming across a pile of grain sacks in the corner of the room. She couldn't be more than ten summers and could be the daughter of the murdered woman.

Rhianna stopped inside the doorway. "I won't hurt you, little one. I promise."

Pushing Faolan aside, the girl glanced around the dusty room for some escape. The dog stood before her, waiting expectantly for her to come play with him.

"Faolan, down," Rhianna said.

The dog dropped, but his tail swept the floor as he waited. She walked to the dog and knelt beside him, resting an arm over his shoulders. "My name is Rhianna. His name is Faolan. He won't hurt you, either. I won't let him. What's your name?"

The blue eyes glanced at Faolan and then returned to Rhianna. "N-N-N-Nee...ca."

"Neeca, we won't let anyone hurt you."

The girl looked to the wall where the dead woman lay beyond. "But my . . . my mama's d-dead." Tears swelled in her innocent gaze.

Rhianna moved to a closer grain sack. "I saw her. I'm sorry. But you're safe, Neeca. You're among your people now."

"NO!" The girl bolted back to the wall. "They k-killed her."

Rhianna swallowed her red fury. "I won't, Neeca. I'm not like them. Faolan and I will not let anyone hurt you. I promise." She stood and glanced around the room. "I was looking for grain. Will you help me find more?"

Rhianna leaned against the wagon while Calgacus' warriors disappeared back inside the villa for the last of the grain bags. Neeca sat beside Faolan on the wagon seat, swinging her legs back and forth over baskets filled with the knives, a brazier, and more that Calgacus had talked Rhianna into keeping. He had used every reason conceivable to keep other items that included the blue-and-white pot.

She had agreed simply because the wagon was filled with sacks of grain while his plunder only filled the space beneath the seat. She truly dreaded the moment when they had to leave.

Tancorix had arrived with orders from her mother and the druid to burn everything. Rhianna sent the warrior back to the leaders to look for grain before their destruction began and wondered if any would listen.

They were to gather at the temple courtyard by order of her mother. Thoughts of what lay between here and there now consumed her. More dead bodies of innocents like Neeca's mother, bodies of Roman merchants, and bodies of soldiers like Julius.

"How old are you, Neeca?" Rhianna asked to block the thoughts.

"Nine summers." The girl continued on, telling her story to the panting dog beside her. "We owned a shop before the Romans took it from Papa. We couldn't pay their taxes. Ma said they made us slaves after they killed Papa."

Faolan started licking the random tears falling from Neeca's eyes. Climbing onto the wagon seat, Rhianna drew the small, trembling body to her.

"M-ma says they're not all b-bad. Like the man who owns us and the villa. He . . . he was nice. He always brought me a g-gift when he came back."

How strange to hear someone else say a Roman could be nice. "Who was he?"

"The consul. Momma and me took c-care of everything, and the people who came here." Neeca shrugged her tiny shoulders. "Like the family who came to meet their son. He had been hurt and didn't feel good. They brought him a bride, and they got married." The heavy sigh slumped the girl's shoulders. "He wore a pendant that she wanted, but he wouldn't give it to her."

Julius? Rhianna's heart lurched to a stop. "Did . . . did you see it?"

"Uh-huh." Pulling away, Neeca nodded and plucked a chicken feather from Faolan's fur and played it back and forth across her hand. "It had a horse on it. Like the one that man with you wears."

The world swirled around Rhianna. "N-Name? Do . . . you know . . . his, this Roman's, name?" *By all the gods, don't let it be Julius.*

Neeca stopped to think. "His uncle called him . . . Julius or something. Her name was Domitia." The girl returned to her chicken feather.

Rhianna's insides twisted like a wet rag. Vomit surged into her throat. If Calgacus hadn't come for her, she would have been dead like Neeca's mother—just another dead slave.

Blind to everything around her, Rhianna let Calgacus take the wagon deeper into the growing insanity. Every street, every corner, every garden was filled with drunken delight that failed to penetrate the dead stupor that consumed her. All she could think of was the filthy slave quarters that would have been hers and the rich rooms inside where Julius would have stayed with his new bride.

His voice echoed in her brain. *Rhianna . . . You will never be a slave to me . . . Never call me dominus again . . . I love you. Only you . . . You will never be a slave to me.*

The wagon came to a halt, jerking her from her shock. They had arrived at the temple plaza filled with throngs of people dancing, singing, and cheering, already drunk in their jubilance.

A stone sculpture of a statue of a man riding a horse had fallen, and people were beating it with anything. The statue's head broke free and was lifted to the darkening sky. "Death to Rome! Death to Claudius!" It was dropped, then urinated on, kicked about like a toy, and laughed at.

Calgacus motioned toward the two rows of columns surrounding a massive, white limestone building in the center of the chaos. "We had to build that for their Roman god, Claudius. See those columns? I know each one personally." A cluster of bloody warriors stood under the portico that surrounded the plaza like wide arms. Many of the men were busy bringing in horses, oxen, and chains.

"What's going on?" Calgacus asked the nearest man leaning against a wooden support pole.

"The rest of the Romans and the Roman lovers hid in their temple, thinking their gods will send their legions to come and protect them."

Silence filled the air so suddenly that Rhianna looked to see the afternoon sun beaming down on her mother, who had appeared near a corner column of the temple mound.

"Bring a team and a chain!" Boudica yelled.

Oxen were led through the crowd, and she began wrapping a chain around the base of the nearest column. She nodded to the driver, who nudged the animals forward until the chain drew taunt. As the team heaved into their collars, one ox slipped on the pavestones.

Calgacus suddenly bolted through the jubilance seconds before a dreadful crack penetrated the air. He grabbed Boudica and leaped into the crowd with her. The cheering stopped as the column fell and settled where her mother had been standing.

When her mother climbed onto the haunch of the fallen horse statue, the walls shivered from the thunderous joy.

"Today, we take back what belongs to us and purge this city of all that is unsacred. All that defiles our gods! To Andraste! To Camulos! To Epona!" Her mother's voice carried over the throng.

Column after column fell, releasing its own lonesome cracking sound and then crumbled, each in its own turn, until only the square sanctum remained.

Screams from those trapped inside rose through the temple's crumbling thatch roof. It matched the same destruction inside Rhianna's soul until all that remained of her was her flesh.

Chapter 36

CAMPFIRES BURNING AROUND THE TEMPLE lit the lone rectangular structure with a treacherous glow made brighter by the darkening shadows surrounding it. The smell of roasting food mixed with the odors of thick smoke, ale, wine, sweat, and urine drifted over the boisterous celebration sweeping around the temple's plaza. Drunken brawls broke out with the night bugs. Laughter followed. No shrieks of terror lifted through the temple's roof.

However, terror pulsed from the solitary structure like smoke from the fires smoldering amid the pillars lying in fragments at the temple's base.

On the steps, her mother and the druid huddled in deep conversation, occasionally pointing at the temple remains or out over the dead city.

Rhianna tore her gaze from the two and watched the drunken celebration before her. She had never witnessed people drunk on raw power, each believing they were free of Rome's control.

And, if they were now free, was it worth all this death and horror? What would happen when the Romans left? Would the united tribes return to being enemies and then turn on themselves . . . again? Was this truly what the gods wanted?

What if Rome returned to retaliate? Julius had assured her all Rome wanted was what was best for her people. Roman peace.

And there had been peace while her father lived. Once he was gone, the Romans had enslaved her people, whipped her mother, and raped the Iceni women. Hadn't she herself become a Roman's slave?

Was her mother right about them and their lies? That Rome's peace came with submission. Had she somehow become drunk, believing that Julius had truly loved her? She avoided the answer tearing at her heart.

Calgacus remained nearby, talking to a group of his men standing by the wagon. They had found the swimming ponds inside one building and now stood about with dripping hair. Other warriors continued to wear Roman blood like a badge of honor.

She climbed from the wagon and found Neeca asleep by a storefront. Rhianna drew the child closer for warmth and closed her own eyes to block out the questions still stabbing at her brain. Faolan snuggled beside her.

Tancorix and his other friends left Calgacus in search of more entertainment than standing there with him. However, they left him with a full mug of ale.

He lifted the liquid to his lips, letting his mind return to the Roman's house and all that Rhianna had refused to take. She was right about the grain and things they would need, but people had a right to take what had been taken from them.

He wanted to give her anything that could make her smile again. He glanced over at the little girl in her arms. He would give her all the children in the world if they would make her that content.

Morrigan appeared out of the darkness with an armload of blankets. "I thought you could use these tonight. There's a chill even with the fires. Best keep them for later." She nodded toward Rhianna. "Who's the child?"

"A slave girl Rhianna found this afternoon. Her mother was killed."

"Oh, a Roman lover." Morrigan nodded toward her sister. "How's she dealing with this?"

He shook out a blanket. The spring dampness was settling in heavy. "As expected. Not pleased. She refuses to take anything other than grain and food."

"We may need those. More join us every day. More mouths to feed." Morrigan scanned the mist settling around the drunken jubilation. "This needs to end soon, or it will be too late to plant. Some of the men are already worrying about winter." She looked at him again. "How long before the Romans find out about the city?"

He shifted his weight against the support pole. "They know."

"What happens now?"

Shrugging, he drank ale and then rested the mug on his arm. "I just hope it's soon, though, while their anger is still hot, while we still have full bellies and ale."

She took his mug and drank. "Mother says tomorrow we burn everything, beginning with that." She motioned with his mug toward the broken temple. "Then, she wants to go to the settlement by the river Thames, where the Romans' supplies are, and burn that as well. No Roman building is to be left standing."

He laughed. "Tell your mother we may burn this city to the ground over the next few days, but we won't be moving anything anywhere for a while, at least a week or more."

"She won't be pleased to hear that." Morrigan turned to leave, handing him his mug. "Keep warm, Calgacus."

He spread a blanket across his sleeping twins who looked like mother and daughter. He wrapped another around his shoulders and then slumped down beside Rhianna. He drew her under his arm and left a kiss on her head.

Faolan shifted his allegiance and snuggled against him. "Keep them safe for me, okay?" He received a lick along his arm before drifting to sleep.

Chapter 37

"LOOK BEFORE YOU! See the destruction of Rome's gods!" Boudica motioned to Churl to release the fire arrow into the temple's thatched roof. "Today we continue the cleansing." The arrow sank into the dry straw. The small flame grew quickly, releasing terrified shrieks from inside. They were the same screams that had pierced Boudica's sleep while Romans had gorged themselves on her women.

She smiled as the scent of smoke swept around her. "They are fools to think they can stand against us, force their gods upon us, and expect us to forget our gods. Never!" yelled from her throat.

The crescendo of cheers drowned the hungry flames. Smoke swept downward and swept around the temple like a large, black snake coiling around its prey.

"We have suffered enough! No more! We cleanse this land for our gods! Give back to our people what was taken!" Something crashed inside the walls and then the flaming roof collapsed inward. Terror screeched from within before suddenly silencing as the acrid stench of burning flesh began mixing with the fragrance of charred wood and burnt straw drifting in the morning air.

She motioned to Myrradin's druids to surround the standing walls with anything that burned. The head druid poured oil over what was brought, as if anointing it like a sacrifice. She lifted a torch, letting its flame snap in the brisk wind, and then waited until every eye observed.

"We burn what remains to the ground to cleanse our lands for our gods who are more powerful than any of their gods!"

She touched the torch to the oil that burst into flame, feeding the next and the next, as it raced around the temple.

Suetonius sat behind his desk, staring at the open flaps of his tent where even the night air drifted in carefully. He flipped his stylus end over end, waiting.

The guards announced that Julius had returned. Alas he stepped into the tent, and the stylus hesitated midair. His clerks scurried away like rats into the corners to disappear. "Well?"

"She took it. There is nothing left but ash."

Suetonius slammed the stylus onto the desktop and then gripped the sides of the desk, wishing it were the bitch's throat. "How many follow her? What did you see?" Julius flinched and then cleared his throat. "At least a hundred-fifty thousand, including families with wagons. The city is destroyed. Annihilated. Nothing stands but the shell of the temple."

"Survivors?"

"We have not located any. Our spies said many died in the temple when it was burned, or they were killed outright."

"Sons of bitches." Suetonius melted back into the chair. Trapped in the temple . . . all those people who had expected his protection. "That bitch will pay for this. By the gods, she will pay for this." He looked up at Julius.

"Her next move?"

"Londinium."

He began drumming his fingertips on the desk. Of course, Londinium. The supply base. "It will be days before they will move," he muttered. But when they do, nothing will be left in their wake."

He rose to pace behind the desk like a trapped animal. "Barbarian shit." He could already picture the black trail the idiots would leave in their tracks.

He halted and looked at his new laticlavius, standing there wearing his new black and white crest and white cloak. "Send messages to all forts between Camulodunum and Londinium to evacuate immediately and move to Londinium. Alert the IInd Augusta to meet me in Londinium. I want that legion there when I arrive."

Julius looked to the clerk hiding behind a curtain. "See the orders are written. I will see them delivered to the cavalry." The clerk evacuated into the adjacent area of the tent.

"Join me." Suetonius waved to follow as he stepped outside.

Fragrances of the first summer flowers greeted them as he walked toward his stable area. Straight tent lines gleamed like naked ribs in the moonlight. The staked palisade appeared like fine lace around the perimeter where guards looked for any movement beyond the deep protective ditch.

The pungent smells of horse and dry grass drew him to Imperious, tearing at the hay bag tied to a corner pole of the makeshift stall.

"By the gods, I would love to go to the thermae right now," Suetonius muttered. He stroked the stallion's neck. "I assure you, Julius, every last one of those bastards will pay for this."

Suetonius brushed the white forelock from the horse's eyes as the stallion nuzzled for its nightly treat. The animal's warm breath tickled the hair on the back of his hand, soothing the desire to do more than just stand there. He wanted to be plunging his gladius into the Britanni bitch. He wanted to hear her beg for mercy.

He closed his eyes to contain himself. Slowly, his breathing relaxed, and he shifted his thoughts to different matters. Procilla. He would never have forgiven himself if she had not left and had been inside that temple.

"You did say your new wife and mother had already departed for the mainland? Am I right?"

"Yes, they should be nearing Rome by now."

"Ah. Good." He combed the silky white mane through his fingers. "I bet you wish you were back in Rome with your new wife.

"Actually, I prefer being here, consul."

"Why is that, tribune?"

Julius glanced at his feet then at the stallion. At last, the consul's gaze found his. "There is nothing between us, consul, other than privilege. She has what she wants now."

"I see." Suetonius gave way to the stallion's prodding and produced a sweet biscuit, hidden beneath his leather cuirass. "And you do not have what you wish?"

"I have . . . what I need for election to the Senate."

"Ah yes, your election. A very costly pursuit. I remember." He did. Like Julius, his wife's family had paid for most of the necessary votes that won his election to the Senate. Suetonius scanned the tribune standing there with his white cloak gleaming in the moonlight but failed to see Julius' shadowed face. "I have sent my reports to the Senate and Nero commending your performance at Mona Insulae. I am sure that will assist you with your election."

"Thank you, consul. Both families will be grateful for your thought."

"You?"

"Of course, consul."

Suetonius chuckled at all the proper answers that were half-truths if that. "Ever see the Britanni celebrate?"

"No."

He had, many nights. "Crazy drunks. Fights everywhere. Women are as wild as the men." He rested his hand on the horse's shoulder, ignoring the continual nudges. "We need to get to Londinium before this bitch does. With the IInd Augusta, the auxiliary cohorts, and the retired soldiers already there, we should be able to contain her."

He stooped for grass and then presented the gift to the eager lips. "Decianus better be there. I expect a full explanation about what happened with this . . . Boadicea? Boudicca? Boudiga? What is the bitch's name?"

"Boudica."

Chapter 38

J ULIUS' HONEYED WORDS HAD BEEN NOTHING more than lies that burned in her belly like hot coals. However, the child within her was real and it was hers . . . a life she would never forsake at any cost. So, along with Tancorix, and other chariot drivers, Rhianna stood like a husked shell beside Calgacus in his chariot as the tribal leaders gathered before the blackened remains of Camulodunum.

For six days, people had set fires to anything they couldn't load in a wagon. Flames roared and dark smoke twisted in the breezes, spreading ash over everything. It silted into clothes, food, and water. Even the temple walls had heaved in over its burned victims as if to bury them.

Drunken brawls erupted each night with equal fury and celebration until no one wanted to move. Even now, they listened like dull stones.

"People!" her mother called out from the rise of the main gate. "The seat of Roman slavery is destroyed!" Cheers erupted from meager, weary voices. Still, she waited for silence and motioned to the druid beside her.

Myrradin lifted the defiled stone head of Claudius from beneath his cloak and held it to the clouds. "Camulos, god of this land," he called out. "This city has been purified for you. It is yours again." He turned to Calgacus' father. "To your people, we give your city back to you."

Diras accepted the token and then looked at the Catuvellauni leader. Together, they threw their fists toward the sky. This time the onlookers roared. Some began to dance. "Andraste! Andraste, great goddess of war, send us proof you are with us! We beg you,"

Myrradin yelled. "Give us a sign that you want these people to cleanse and return this land to you!"

People whose fists and weapons were raised skyward were chanting of victory. "Andraste! Andraste!"

The druid waved his arms, and his huge raven swooped from the forest, silencing the throng. A low gasp of awe rippled through the crowd until the bird landed on the druid's arm. Then insanity erupted even greater.

"Andraste. Camulos. Andraste. Camulos."

Once again, Boudica waited until all quieted. "But Rome remains," she yelled. "Rome continues its greed in Londinium. I say destroy it!"

"Destroy Londinium!"

Calgacus' yell startled Rhianna. His ponies reared and jerked the chariot, wanting to be released just as all those around them.

Boudica stepped onto Morrigan's chariot and thrust her lance-filled hand into the air. "To Londinium! Destroy it!" Diras joined Tancorix, who released his chariot in Morrigan's wake, while the other leaders climbed hurriedly into theirs.

"Hang on!" Calgacus slapped the reins over the backs of his ponies. The chariot bolted away with the others, leaving Rhianna clinging to the rail wishing she were back with Neeca in the wagon. Faolan raced alongside, leading the throng charging away from the blackened hill.

"Dominus, you best be wakin' up."

The sound of Lugh's voice scratched through Julius' brain. He did not know what time it was or where he was. Obviously, the short night had ended, and the early morning began. His brain felt dead and his body numb.

He had managed to see that Suetonius had the reports on his desk. The Britanni numbers had grown. The XXth Valeria and the XIVth Gemina had finally left Mona to join them . . . eventually.

A messenger was now racing with orders for the IInd Augusta to be in Londinium by the end of the week. Julius wondered if the legion could arrive by then.

Oddly enough, the Augusta's legate and his laticlavius traveled among the consul's staff. It would be up to the camp prefect to fulfill Suetonius' order, and the man had better, or he would face Suetonius' wrath.

That was beyond Julius' concern. His job was done. He straightened his stiff back and loosened his shoulders. The consul's words echoed in his brain. "These Britanni women are, you know . . ."

Oh, he knew quite well how Rhianna was in bed. He dreamed of her every night, ached for her every day, and worried about her constantly.

Where was she in all this? Was she with the fool who had kidnapped her? Had she given up that he would find her? His guts twisted with thoughts of what would happen if he did not find her before Suetonius released his fury on the Brittani.

Julius walked outside so the morning air could clear his head. The camp was in preparation for leaving. Men were filling the protective ditch outside the wall. Gear and supplies were being loaded on wagons. The tents would not come down until the order was given, but stakes had been removed. Suetonius appeared from his tent. His white tunic with broad purple stripes rose up his thighs as he stretched to greet the dawn. Obviously, Morpheus had granted him a most wonderful night of sleep. "Ah, good day, Julius. I hope you slept well."

"Yes, consul." The lie flowed from his lips like the sweetest wine.

Guards at the main gate came to attention and then allowed a scout through at a full gallop. The rider pulled the lathered horse to a halt in front of the officers' tents and saluted. "Report on the Brittani's movements."

"Report, soldier."

"The Britanni are moving, killing all who remain faithful to Rome, and burning everything along the way. They are nearing Caesaromagus."

The joy of the new day evaporated from Suetonius' face. "By the gods, I will see them destroyed." The look in his eyes pierced Julius' spine. "Has the fort been alerted?"

"Yes, they move toward Londinium."

The consul blinked, ending the threat. "Good. Take a cavalry guard and alert Londinium and assess its defenses. I want a full report when I arrive." He started to step away but stopped. "Find Decianus. I want to talk to that greedy little catamite."

Chapter 39

CALGACUS LET AERIE DRINK from the river Blackwater while the parade of people moved past. They had destroyed Rome's capital, Rome's temple, and now Rome's villas. Along the way, anyone who failed to join the revolt was determined to be a Roman lover and was executed. Now, they moved to destroy Rome's port town that fed the legions . . . Londinium.

His thoughts drifted to the day before when another Roman fort was burned to the ground. Orders to evacuate must have arrived, because little was found inside, which only proved the Romans knew what was being done to their precious settlements. He wondered if Roman spies moved among the tribes. They would be sorry if they did.

Everyone had gathered around Boudica that day at what remained of the guard's station, where Myrradin and Diras stood along with the other tribal leaders: the Catuvellauni, Durotriges, Silures, Dobunni, Coritani, Belgae, and Atrebates. Many even had come from Ordovices in revenge of the massacre on that island. Warriors had defied Cartimandua and had come to fight and destroy the Roman invaders. The throng grew every day, seething with hatred that grew more lethal with each breath.

A boy ran up beside him, causing Aerie to jerk his head from the grass. The boy staggered to a halt. "The fort's gone," he gasped. "We burned it to the ground. All of it."

The older boys had been given the responsibility to burn everything and see that nothing remained.

Calgacus smirked. They must have done well because black soot covered the boy's entire body, making his proud smile brilliant. "Well done, Loren. I am sure there will be more to burn."

"Can I go with you into Londinium? Can I?"

He pretended to consider the offer. Thoughts of Seric stung his memory. "Can you follow orders?"

"I can. I promise. I can."

"I'll speak to the elders."

The jubilant boy darted into the stream of people, not knowing that his orders would be to continue to guard the women and children.

A huge thundercloud pillowed up in the skies beyond the trees. Calgacus sniffed. A hint of rain rose in the dust. Rain.

Normally, he would be thrilled with the possibility. It would be good for the crops. However, rain slogged everything down to a crawl. More than anything, he now wanted this over with and to go back to make a home for Rhianna before winter set in.

His thoughts shifted yet again. Since Camulodunum, Rhianna had drifted even further from him. Yes, she cared for him and Neeca with the same attentiveness and concern of a good woman, but she had become lifeless.

He couldn't get her to laugh. She ate little, didn't sleep, and fought something in her dreams. By Brig, if it took a lifetime, he'd do whatever he must to heal her from whatever had destroyed her.

The sun broke through the pillowy clouds and blazed across the distant grove of trees to the north. The fragrance of damp soil and fresh water drifted in the air, taunting him to get away from it all. Come. He smiled and accepted the invitation.

Rhianna poked the ox to keep it moving and to remind herself to do the same. She didn't want to go another step, but she had no choice. Where would she go? What would she do if the Romans came?

Nights gave her no respite. Vultures with faces of her mother and the druid came the moment she closed her eyes. They plagued her, turning dreams into nightmares. They clawed for her baby.

Julius would appear with his soft smile, sending the creatures away. He would take her in his arms, make her body sing, and convince her again that he loved her, that he wanted her with him and planned to take her away to Rome.

"Rhianna, just trust me. I'll take care of you until I can free you and marry you. You have my heart, Rhianna, I love you." Lies. He was married now.

She had believed his Roman words, but somehow, she had to forget them. How could she? He would be there whenever she looked at his child.

She began swinging the prod through the ankle-high grass. Calgacus wanted what she had once wanted: a simple hut, land to farm, horses and cattle . . . and a family. She ran her hand over her belly, feeling the growing soul, knowing that she loved it more than life.

She should tell him that she carried a Roman child, but the words froze in her throat, especially after seeing what was being done to anything Roman.

If he rejected the babe, Myrradin would exclaim to everyone that the child belonged to Andraste. Then nothing and no one would stop the druid from sacrificing her and the baby to the goddess.

Yells echoed over the burgeoning throng of people, drawing her attention toward the distant rise where smoke blackened the southern horizon.

"What are they doing now?" Neeca asked.

Rhianna looked up at the girl riding on the grain bags in the wagon. "Likely burning another fort or home of some poor Roman."

"Another one?" The girl's newfound kitten, named Id, scampered over the bags piled in the wagon bed to her.

"I hope they looked for grain before they burned it," Rhianna said with a sigh.

Neeca frowned. "They didn't the last time."

So very true. Her complaints to Calgacus about not searching for supplies before they burned everything went unheeded. "The number of bags of grain from Camulodunum shrink daily," she had complained. He had simply shrugged, promising he'd speak to the leaders again. The crowd before her shifted across the landscape.

Her mother must have motioned to halt for the night so everyone could bask in the glow of the burning buildings. Rhianna scanned the hill for a place to camp. She didn't want down by the river where most would set up camp. She wanted away from the drunken celebrations that happened nightly.

"How about here?" she asked Neeca. The girl nodded. "I think it's good."

The oxen must have agreed because they came to an instant standstill. Rhianna leaned against wheel. She just stood there, watching the sun linger like a bloody red dot behind the drifting smoke. *Why couldn't the Romans just leave? They never would. They conquered.*

Yet, if they did leave, the tribes would go back to fighting like before. Horrid memories returned of her father leaving each summer to reclaim whatever had been taken from the Iceni. The fear of him never returning still sickened her. Clashes between tribes were accepted. *Didn't animals fight for their territory?* he would say.

If the Romans left, Julius would go with them, back to his new wife. That thought cut deeper than it should.

Beyond her, people made camps—some to eat and rest, others to begin their revelry. She gathered wood from the wagon and dropped it where she had kicked the ground clear for a fire pit.

Calgacus dismounted and walked toward her. A strange boyishness danced in his blue eyes. A taunting grin appeared beneath his mustache and almost made her smile until she noticed Morrigan's pendant pinned to the woolen cape covering his shoulder.

Her heart sank to the pit of her stomach because she knew Julius still wore hers. Or did he? Had his new wife claimed it by now as a part of her jewelry?

Calgacus drew her into his arms and kissed the top of her head. "Rhianna, I want you to come with me."

She backed away. Had the druid commanded her to the leaders' campsite? "No, I won't go near the leaders' tents." "Not there." His gaze danced over her. "Let Neeca and Faolan take care of the wagon for now."

She struggled out of his grip. "She can't. She's too young."

"I'm not too young!" Neeca scurried from around the wagon. "I can take care of everything. I can."

He let go and plucked two blankets from the wagon. "Besides, Morrigan is staying here tonight."

Before Rhianna could argue, he tossed her onto the stallion and then swung up behind her. "Faolan, stay and guard." His arm entrapped her waist as the dog sat, its ears wilting.

Chapter 40

RHIANNA'S BODY RELAXED with the rocking motion of the easy canter. A subtle scent of male pulsed from Calgacus, making her feel safe. She let herself melt against his chest the farther they rode from the encampment.

The fragrance of rain lingered in the evening air. The clean fragrance of a river drifted to her. With it came an evening dampness and the sounds of night creatures breaking into a symphony. All caressed her with a peace she had forgotten possible.

He drew to a halt in a thicket of trees hemming a lulling inlet and slid off the stallion, taking her with him. Something, a fish probably, plopped in the nearby river.

He tied Aerie to a sapling. "All day, I've thought about being alone with you."

His mustache caressed her face as he gently pressed his mouth onto hers. The delicious essence of ale played through her mouth, stirring her dead soul.

He pulled away, sucking life force from her. "I'll get us something to eat," he said and winked at her before disappearing into the thickening darkness.

She stood there stunned. His kiss had ventured deep but seeing Morrigan's pendant piercing his cloak brought back memories. She should never have given away her only possession. The Roman didn't deserve it. He was that to her now—a Roman who lied. However, a small part of her heart still denied that fact.

Calgacus deserved her loyalty. All she needed to know was that he would accept her child. Nothing more. She couldn't just she let him think the child was his, even though they had been together enough times.

But what if the child carried Julius' features instead of hers? Then Calgacus would know she had lied to him, and that lie would shatter his heart, which did not deserve to be broken. He deserved to know the truth.

By the time he returned, she had spread the blankets, lit a meager flame with her flint stone, and ground two straight sticks into the dirt to roast whatever he brought back. He appeared with two rabbits and soon, fat dripped into the playful flames.

She relished the void of boisterous laughter and revelry. No press of people. They were alone with only the river, trees, and fireflies darting about in the growing darkness. Calgacus lazily turned the rabbits.

He suddenly stood and placed the half-cooked meal on a tree limb. "It's time."

The peaceful moment shattered without logic. "They're not done."

"I don't mean the meat." He suddenly scooped her into his arms and bolted toward the riverbank. Her scream filled the looming darkness when he leaped from the edge and splashed into the current.

He surfaced with a proud smile. "I couldn't wait another moment, not since I've waited for this all day."

A giggle rippled from her lips as she treaded water. "Have you?"

"I have." He scrambled out of his clothes and then tossed them to the riverbank.

She swam out of reach, feeling the drag of her gown. Scrambling free of it, she threw the fabric onto his pile and then drove away when he swam toward her.

All her life she had enjoyed swimming. The feel of the water seemed to wash away whatever tormented her. The leather band binding her braid drifted downstream, and she let her hair float around her.

Calgacus appeared beside her like a large otter lolling along. He reached for her, but she dodged his attempt and stuck out her tongue. The lazy delight in his eyes sparked into playful determination.

He slowly sank beneath the surface. The feel of his hands gliding around her ankles left no question of his intention to pull her deeper. Instead, he lifted her from the water and launched her across the water like a lance. His laugh followed. She dove into the water and glided out of his reach.

Long-forgotten joy rippled through her. She swam farther out and then surfaced to kick water at his face.

His gaze sparked with retaliation as he sank beneath the surface like a heavy pot. Before he could surface, she darted over him, too quickly for him to grab her, and swam deep enough to feel the underwater plants brush against her breasts.

His feet and legs kicked in circles as he searched for her. She swam a safe distance away before rising to the surface for air. When he found her behind him, his gaze danced with mirth.

"You always were a little fish. But I will catch you, my love."

"Never!"

He stopped when she laughed—the sound foreign even to her. Then, as he came at her, she plunged deep into the water again, curling around like an otter. When he grabbed for her, he missed, and missed again.

Then his fingers clutched her ankle and pulled her back through the water. Before she could kick free, he lifted her, gasping for air. "I said I'd catch you, little fish. Now I'm going to keep you."

"Not for long, you won't." She squirmed, enjoying the crush of his hard body against hers.

Water lapped against their necks and drew her hair behind her. His floated against her collarbone like long, lazy ropes. His taunting smile trickled through her.

"I won't let you get away from me ever again."

The sound of his voice seeped deep into her heart, deep into her soul. She needed him surrounding her, carrying her, and never letting go.

Something changed the instant Calgacus drew Rhianna's body to his. Moonlight revealed a glimmer in her eyes that he had never seen. It was deep and hot with desire.

He scanned her face covered with water diamonds and felt her arms glide around his neck and then her legs encircled his hips. The distance that had kept them apart evaporated the moment she slid over him, joining their bodies. An exquisite groan ground from his chest.

They were one . . . one body, one desire, one need—hot and starving. They feasted, melting with one movement.

The water thrashed until they spent themselves, each crying out in that magic moment. He couldn't tell if it was tears streaming down her cheeks or river water, but it didn't matter. Whatever had kept them apart had shattered.

Happiness that Rhianna thought she would never know again flooded through her as Calgacus carried her from the water to a smoldering fire.

The river had washed the past away and left joy blossoming within her, spring fresh and new. There was no doubt, now, that she belonged to this man—no doubt in her soul that she wanted to be with him and no other.

Calgacus placed her on the blanket and settled his dripping body down beside her. His hands cupped her breasts, streaking lightning through her. Gasping, she drew Calgacus' lips to hers and languished as he pinned her beneath him with his hard body.

"I will forever love you, Rhianna of the Iceni." He kissed her yet again.

She wrapped her legs around his waist, inviting him. This time he was strong, demanding, and possessive, not tender and careful as if she were a fragile flower. Forgotten joy opened her soul as she looked into the deep blue gaze above her. "I will love you for an eternity, Calgacus of the Trinovante."

Lightning flickered between the tied tent flaps that released thunderous explosions outside Julius' tent like a war of its own. He grabbed for Rhianna's necklace and found it dangling between his shoulder blades.

Trashing winds pummeled the leather walls. He tried to remember what woke him. The storm? No, he had been dreaming of Rhianna. She had been beside him, so close that he could smell her violet fragrance. He could feel her flesh in his hands. He was capturing the sound of her desire with his mouth, and then jolted awake.

He slumped back to his pillow and stared at the undulating leather above him. Images returned of taking her to his villa, showing her the vineyards, the fields of waving grain, and the stable of horses. He even heard their children chasing each other and laughing as they stood in the doorway. He still wanted the life that he had promised her. His hand fisted beneath his head. He wanted her here with him now. He needed to tell her he loved her, that he needed her. That his soul belonged to her.

Not to Domitia. It never could.

The image of his wife appeared as a lemur, a ghost, as if to remind him of what he had agreed to. Why had he ever gone through with the charade of marrying her? Insanity? Stupidity? Weakness? Domitia could never give him what Rhianna already had—a reason to live.

He rolled to his side with a groan. Like all of his friends, he had accepted whoever was arranged for him to marry because that was expected.

What was even more chilling was that he had no idea that becoming a soldier meant nothing more than becoming a pawn for some officer. Wasn't he now simply Suetonius' messenger boy? Wasn't Suetonius Nero's pawn in all this?

Julius could hear his uncle's lectures. The legions promised a good future, election to the Senate, prestige for his father's name, and a fine house in Rome. Yet all that now seemed pointless when he could stay with Rhianna and their children.

He cradled her pendant in his hand, hearing her oath. *As long as you wear this, my soul will be yours.* Yet he could feel clearly that he was losing her.

Every day, she drifted farther and farther from him. If that happened, then nothing would matter any longer. Rome could do as it wished with him.

He rose beneath a thick rumble of thunder, walked to his armor to retrieve his dagger, and then went to the desk where the flame in the oil lamp flickered in the stirring air. "Venus, goddess of love and life, bring Rhianna back to me. I beg you." He sliced the blade across his palm and let blood drip onto the flame. "I give you all the glory and want nothing more in return if you will grant me this plea."

Chapter 41

JULIUS DREW HIS GUARD TO A HALT to study the burgeoning supply port pulsing with the stench of hungry commerce. New warehouses had sprung up along the pier during the four months since he'd arrived. A fleet of Roman galleys bobbed like corks along docks of the thick, wide river.

Like Camulodunum, Londinium possessed few or no surrounding walls and lacked guards and a protective ditch. There was no doubt that Boudica would swoop down on this filthy hovel like a volcano, spewing her hatred like lava and smoke, annihilating everyone and everything in her path.

Lugh kicked his horse alongside Julius. "Hasna' changed a bit since I be here. It's still filthy."

Julius scanned his slave, whose audacity never wavered, and then refocused on the Roman fortress to the west—the supply headquarters where Decianus should be. Facing the little fat bastard sang in his veins.

"Horatio," Julius called out. "Take half the guard and bring all the available men to the fort. They had better be there before the consul arrives."

"Yes, tribune." The soldier saluted and then pulled back to gather his group.

"Gio, take two men and find out how much time until the Britanni get here. I want to know everything." Three soldiers saluted before breaking away at a gallop.

"Marcus and the rest—with me." *Decianus is mine!*

He nudged the stallion into an easy lope down the mucky hill to enter a muddy street filled with garbage, waste, and every sort of human life possible.

A prostitute stepped from a squatter's hut. "Soldiers, come, rest yourselves on this." She pulled up the hem of her gown to display her thick thighs and bushy crotch.

"I would not touch that Britanni bitch with my hands, much less with my cock," one soldier muttered.

"All of 'em here are like that. Filthy and bitchy," a second added.

Lugh smiled at her. "Ah, she just be needin' a bit of caressin', lads."

"There are more important things to think about," Julius snapped, ending the comments. "I want the procurator."

A cart crumbled before them, blocking the narrow roadway. They worked their horses around it and then continued the slow crawl through the stench pit. The horses balked, shied, or flinched every step of the way to the timbered walls of the fort.

"Who goes?" the guard demanded from the pathetic gate of the filthy city behind it.

"Consul's laticlavius," Marcus answered. "Special message for the procurator."

"Not here, tribune."

I knew it. That little pissant is running. Fury exploded through Julius, stirring the horse beneath him, and it bumped Marcus' horse.

"Decianus Catus left? When?"

The guard shrugged. "Leavin' now on the Venus. Last I seen him, he seemed in a hurry." He leaned down. "Open the gate." He looked back. "See for yourself, tribune."

Julius raised a hand to halt the others from entering. "Has the IInd Augusta arrived?"

The guard looked at the other men in the guard station. They all shook heads or shrugged. "No, tribune."

By the gods! The IInd had failed to arrive. Julius pictured Suetonius' forthcoming tirade. A cold sweat broke across his neck.

From his cuirass, he pulled Suetonius' letter and handed it to Marcus to give to the guard. The guard read the parchment, scanning the official seal.

Julius adjusted his restless horse to direct his next words to the guards. "Get all available men here before sunset, before the consul arrives. Understood? If any of us want skin left on our backsides, they had better be here."

"Yes, tribune." The guards saluted.

Julius turned his horse toward the docks. Lugh moved his horse close again "You wouldna' want to be going there," he said in Iceni. "I'll be showin' you a quicker way, dominus. Tis tricky. Plenty of back alleys filled with Britanni spies about."

Julius nodded and let the slave lead the way. What private time he had been blessed with had been spent learning Rhianna's language. It came easier now.

"I want Decianus squirming before the consul," he muttered.

Marcus smirked. "That would be better than any match at the games."

Chaos and congestion increased the closer they came to the wharf. The stench of rotting fish added to the dissonance of filthy children running everywhere, blocking the narrow streets, and scaring horses. Women with work-worn hair hanging about their faces peered curiously from shop windows. Ragged beggars squatting against walls lifted calloused hands for an offering.

A massive array of warehouses lined the dock area like grotesque monsters ready to feast on bales of wool, crates of barking dogs destined for Rome, and groups of chained Britanni captives going to Napoli. Rhianna was not among any of them.

Relief surged through him. He halted before a sundried sailor leaning against a wall. "You there, where is the galley leaving for Gesoriacum?"

The man shrugged.

Boudica's revolt had obviously reached the port. "By orders of Rome, answer me, or I will have your tongue ripped out."

"By orders of Rome, is it?" The man huffed. "I expect you are planning to get your imperial ass back to Rome before Boudica arrives?"

Julius motioned to Marcus, who began to dismount.

The sailor nodded toward the galleys. "Third galley down. The Venus."

The wooden image of the goddess thrashed against the ropes holding it to the busy dock. Sailors and crewmen carried cargo aboard and scurried about like busy ants. The smell of pitch cut through the stench.

He and Marcus dismounted, leaving their horses with Lugh and the guards. They climbed the dancing gangplank, stopping three sailors from exiting for more goods. "The procurator. Is he on board?" Julius asked.

One of the sailors pointed to a short, middle-aged man with a ledger, standing on the deck. "Ask him."

The weather-baked man watched them cross the deck. "You the captain?" Julius asked.

"I am. Why?"

"The procurator, Decianus Catus . . . is he on board?"

"Could be. Who's askin'?"

Julius licked his lips to quell the mounting frustration. "The consul of Rome."

"You don't look like no consul of Rome to me." Clenching his fists to keep them off the man's throat, he glared at the man. "Look, you son of a bitch, is the procurator on board or not? Answer me."

The captain smirked. "Yeah, he's in his cabin." He motioned to a nearby sailor. "Tell that other Roman filth that one of his kind is looking for him."

Moments later, Decianus strode through the doorway. "Well, Julius, you are laticlavius now. Very impressive." His grin oozed into a smirk. "Found your slave girl yet?"

Julius felt the hair on his neck rise. "Whether I have or not is none of your business." He swallowed to make his next words distinct. "Suetonius expects you at the Principia. He arrives tonight."

Decianus shook his head and smiled. "I do not give a damn what Suetonius expects. I answer to Nero, not the ass you kiss now. Fuck the consul's orders."

Julius motioned to Marcus and the other guards waiting on the docks to join him.

"You order them near me, and I will see Nero hears about it, as well as any other charges I can drum up. I will see you ruined, Agricola."

Every muscle screamed to order his men to drag this cocksucker back to the fort. However, although it irked Julius, the procurator was right. There was no way Julius could touch this man.

Yet, if he did not find a way to get this fool back to the fort, he would be the one facing Suetonius. The blood in Julius' veins turned to ice.

"I am sure Nero will be impressed to hear in Suetonius' report of how you created this revolt, refused his orders, and fled with your tail between your legs."

Sweat broke across Decianus' brow. The fool crossed his fat arms over his chest. "Nero sent me to collect taxes. I have, and I am taking them back to Rome, you little prick."

"I hope you do expect an audit of that report."

Decianus huffed. "Oh, I am truly frightened." The crew began releasing lines to the pier.

There had to be a way to stop Decianus. Julius had caved once before and let this bastard rape women.

He glared down on the captain. "This galley does not depart until either the procurator goes with me or the consul releases it. Is that clear?"

"What?" The weathered man turned scarlet. "I am to leave immediately. A storm is coming in."

"You heard me. This galley does not move until the consul grants you permission to leave." He looked to Decianus. "He arrives tonight."

Decianus' gaggle of guards gathered behind him, spawning a new confidence in the man. "I will ruin you, Agricola, if you try to stop this galley. I will see that you never make the Senate . . . if Nero lets you live that long."

"Guards, stand to the lines and kill any man who tries to release this galley."

The six remaining guards saluted and then went to the lines stretching to the dock. Two stood by the gangway. Julius looked at Decianus. "By the time the consul is through with you, I doubt you will be able to do anything more than shit your pants."

Horatio reported to the galley with the soldiers from Caesaromagus and a few retired soldiers. By then, the captain had ordered Decianus off his galley where his Gallic guard remained and departed with it.

As the blare of cornicens drifted in the air, Decianus was fuming in the consul's living quarters in the Praetoria, surrounded by the guards.

Julius started toward the gate. Dread consumed every step as Suetonius loped into view, ahead of his cavalry. The thought of Decianus facing Suetonius should be something Julius would enjoy watching. However, the IInd Augusta had still not arrived. The number of soldiers Horatio had found amounted to nothing if they were to save Londinium. And Boudica's assault was within a day's time of arriving. None of which the consul wanted to hear.

"Open the gates for the Consul Suetonius Paulinus," Julius ordered.

The wooden gate creaked open in time for the thunder of hooves and the jingle of metal to pass below.

Chapter 42

SUETONIUS GRIPPED EACH END of the armrests and rose halfway out of his chair on the dais. "Decianus Catus refused my orders and left me to deal with his mess?"

"Yes. He stated that he reports to Rome, not you. And to fuck us both," Julius stated clearly.

"Fuck us both, is it? We will see who fucks whom." He would see that asshole of a procurator ruined. "Where is this prick?"

"He is under guard in the Praetoria."

"Well done, tribune." He stared at Julius, impressed that the boy he had once known had become what appeared to be a real soldier. Suetonius washed his mind of the thought and drove it back to reality.

Suetonius settled back in his chair. "I will deal with him later. Where is the IInd Augusta?"

"They have not arrived, consul. And there is no word of when they will arrive."

Without the IInd Augusta, there was no hope of defending this piss pot of a city. "Any word from the camp prefect?"

Julius snapped his fingers for the clerk to come forward. "Any messages from the IInd Augusta?"

The clerk scrambled to hold the scrolls in his arms. "N-nothing from the IInd. I checked. Like the tribune said, not even from the camp prefect. I-I—"

Suetonius' choices of facing the bitch here in Londinium were dropping like fall leaves in a windstorm. "I want Larrentus and that damn laticlavius of his in here, now!" Julius looked to one of the guards who disappeared with the order.

Suetonius slashed his hands through his hair and stood, wanting someone or something, anything to kick. Instead, he strode across the hall to the table covered with a map of Londinium. "How many soldiers do we have now?"

"Hundred-forty from Caesaromagus. Forty retired who are in no condition to fight."

"Where is the bitch?"

"Thirty miles away. They sacked Caesaromagus two days ago and are moving slowly."

"In this mud, I doubt they will make five miles." He could easily imagine the Britanni celebrating like drunken fools in the storm thrashing outside. "Any word from your uncle?"

"Nothing, consul."

Suetonius closed his eyes and leaned against the map table. The thought of leaving another settlement for the bitch to destroy burned in his veins like liquid fire.

Oh, he was going to enjoy dealing with the imperial prick now. First, he had to see to the fools living in this filth. "Alert every citizen to evacuate south to the Regni lands. Send the king word to attend to them."

"Yes, consul."

The Augusta's legate entered the hall with his pampered laticlavius. "Consul? You called for us."

Suetonius wheeled on the man. "Your camp prefect has refused my order to bring your legion."

The legate's face turned white with panic. "C-Consul!" the legate squeaked. "I . . I did not know. I mean. The . . . the tribe there . . . the Durotriges are restless because of the attack on Mona . . . the druids. Maybe that is why?"

"You. Do not. Know?"

"Consul, I have not received any reports." His tribune murmured something to the legate. "Yes. Possibly the report was destroyed with Camulodunum."

Suetonius forced himself to breathe and glared at the fool whom Nero had appointed as leader to this legion. "Get the legion to Verulamium. I do not care how you do it. But do it. Is that clear?"

"Yes. Yes, I will . . . I will send the report now."

"And Larrentus, they better be in Verulamium when I arrive. Now, get out of my sight!" He turned to Julius. "Get that prick of a procurator in here."

"Yes, consul."

The following morning the threat of Boudica had spread through Londinium like a disease. The camp prefect had ordered the fort's gates closed to the angry mobs yelling and throwing stones and torches over the walls, demanding that the soldiers save their filthy squalor from Boudica's approaching horde.

As Lugh had predicted, wagons and carts jammed the bridge in their desperate escape south to the Regni lands. Fights erupted throughout the night, leaving defenseless women and children huddled in dark shadows. Why they failed to get out, flee anywhere, rather than stay in the city, Julius wondered.

Decianus was being escorted toward the docks under guard in order to leave for Rome. Unfortunately, Julius had not been spared from the confrontation between both imperial appointees. Still, he relished the yelling that echoed inside the closed chamber.

Ultimately, Suetonius had ordered a messenger to accompany Decianus to Rome on the next galley. Julius was then ordered to write a full explanation of all that the little prick had done to start this revolt.

He had spent most of the night crafting that report as ordered with every detail he could remember. Every detail, with the exception of Rhianna.

His bandaged hand throbbed with every word written, a small pain to endure if the goddess granted Rhianna safety and returned her to him after the uprising was squelched.

He followed Suetonius out of the Principia ahead of clerks carrying bags of official business to load in the wagons. Behind them, smoke billowed into the morning sky from the unimportant documents being torched. Slaves checked the ropes of the supply wagons carrying personal belongings and what little treasury Decianus had left behind.

One guard held Imperious to let the consul mount. Julius vaulted into his saddle, followed by the guards mounting their horses. The soldiers formed under the echoing orders from the centurions and the calls of the cornicens.

Suetonius motioned Julius closer. "Those remaining here are fully aware of what will happen if they do not leave?"

"Yes, consul. It has been posted and yelled by the crier."

"It is time we go as well." Suetonius motioned to the cornicen to sound the call. The parade of soldiers drew to attention. He wheeled Imperious to face the formations and yelled the formal questions before every march. "Are you ready?"

"We are ready."

He yelled out again. "Are you ready?"

"We are ready."

Restless to flee, Imperious reared beneath him. "Are. You. Ready?"

"We are ready!"

Julius remembered issuing those same three questions the day of the assault as well as the reverberating sound of the men's voices echoing their answers.

His throat closed as every moment of that day, from the thrill of command and the horror that followed, flooded into his mind. The memories blinded him as Suetonius charged toward the north gate in an eager lope.

Julius kicked his horse into a lope and followed through the north gate toward Verulamium. The men behind him moved in his wake.

A man charged from the mudslinging crowd. "You Roman shit, you are supposed to protect us! Now, you run like dogs with their tails up their asses! Damn Rome and all her taxes!"

The cavalry guards rode forward, surrounding both him and Suetonius. Soldiers in the Ist cohort raced between them, shoving the crowd back, frightening everyone from the roadway while the column moved through.

"Sacrifice a town to save a province," Suetonius muttered as they left.

Julius could not believe the words that just fell from Suetonius' lips. Words that Rome would never forgive or forget. Gaius Suetonius Paulinus, this decorated Roman consul—appointed by Nero and the Senate of Rome, assigned to establish control of the province of Britannia—was fleeing from a woman.

Chapter 43

RHIANNA ENJOYED THE SOUNDS of the disgruntled animals and the constant creak of the wagon instead of the angry mass ahead of her. The animals reminded her of home. The home she wanted again.

She glanced back at Aerie tied to the rear of the wagon. The horse tried to amble along while feasting on bits of grain. Faolan rode like a king on the wagon seat next to Neeca. Calgacus walked beside her as she prodded the oxen to keep moving.

She bumped him with her hip, making him dance to avoid stepping in a fresh pile of manure. "I don't know how you stand it back here," he grumbled.

"It's easier avoiding this shit than that." She pointed the ox prod toward the mass before them. "Much easier to deal with."

She basked in the new sense of joy that Calgacus had given her. Even though he deserved to know about the babe, she couldn't crush the new sprout of happiness thrumming between them now. Soon. She would tell him soon.

Cheering and war cries drifted toward them on the wind. "Something's happened," he said and went back for Aerie. "Let's go see. Neeca, take over."

Before Rhianna could refuse, Calgacus had claimed Aerie, swept her up before him, and then nudged the horse into a gallop. They rode through the crowd until halting by his father's chariot.

Warriors were dragging an old man before Boudica. His legs sprawled beneath his yellow toga. White fear radiated in the man's eyes as he resisted. His wife raced from their small, white-plastered villa. "Please, leave us be. We are too old to do you harm."

Diras and the other leaders looked at each and then to her mother. She pointed her lance at the elderly couple. "You are no longer our people. See how you dress. You have become Roman. Kill them."

Rhianna jerked the reins away from Calgacus and attempted to turn the horse to escape this horror. Instead, Aerie reared.

A deafening yell from the crowd resounded after one of the warriors lifted the old man's head in the air, leaving his body twitching in the dirt. The stench of blood and shit filled the air.

She slid to the ground and then ran back toward the wagons. Tears blinded each step. Calgacus followed on foot, grabbed her, and wheeled her around. "Rhianna, stop!"

"No!" She gasped and then pointed at the joyous crowd. "You wanted to know why I stay back here? That's why! That man didn't deserve to be murdered." She jerked from his grip. "Don't ever take me up there again. Ever."

He wrapped her in his arms. "I didn't know, Rhianna. I didn't know."

"I hate this. All of it." She jerked away and stood there, searching for somewhere to go to get away from the butchery. There was no place. "When will the killing stop? It's all so senseless."

He came to stand behind her, his strength like a shielding wall. She faced him. "Calgacus, I want to go away now . . . make a home for us anywhere." Hot tears poured down her face. "Where we can raise our children in peace. Where they will never know the sight of blood and hatred like that."

His thumbs brushed her cheeks. "It will be over soon, my love, and we'll have all that. I promise." He kissed her forehead. "As soon as this is over. As soon as every Roman is gone."

"Calgacus, please. I want to go now."

"I can't leave my father and our people. You know that." She felt like a dying plant rooted in poisonous ground.

She couldn't leave her father's people, nor would he. If they did, they would never be welcomed anywhere. Where could they go to live in peace and know their children were safe?

There was no place. Even if she went to Julius, she'd be nothing but a slave to him now, her child a bastard in his eyes.

"Rhianna, please, can we talk about this after Londinium?"

She glared up at her pleading husband. "After Londinium . . . what happens after that? Another Roman city. More senseless killing. When will it ever end, Calgacus? When?"

Calgacus rode Aerie through the mass gathering on the distant hillside overlooking the port town the Romans called Londinium. The leaders had divided this town into parcels, each tribe drawing their section by lot to avoid the chaos that happened in Camulodunum. His father had drawn the sector of the Roman's fort.

"Take anything you want. Burn everything to the ground," Myrradin had ordered the night before. "But bring all captives to the wharf. The gods await them." Already Calgacus pitied those who failed to flee.

The sound of drums, cheers, and war cries silenced in his mind to Rhianna saying she wanted a home for their children. That had sent his heart soaring to the gods. He'd dreamed of her belly swollen with his child.

She was right. The murderous insanity had spread like a disease starving for more blood, power, and revenge. It had started in Camulodunum and had grown into a thirst for Roman blood.

He wanted her to remain with the wagons and not go near the river settlement, to wait for him to come back for her. In truth, he no longer wanted any part of the looting and drinking that would ensue as surely as the sun rose each day. He wanted nothing else but to get this revolt over with and make plans for a future and a family with her.

"About time you joined us," Tancorix said. "Thought you'd decided to stay with the women."

Calgacus accepted his sword, Cadaryn, and shield from his father's chariot driver. "And leave you all the fun?"

Morrigan drove her mother's chariot along the ridge overlooking an array of rambling hovels clustered together like filthy pots.

From the back of the chariot, Boudica yelled over the restless crowd. "The Romans flee like hares before the hounds! Londinium is ours!"

An explosion of cheers answered in waves as Morrigan continued along the rise.

"The Romans fled?" Calgacus asked.

Diras nodded, while his driver steadied the team. "A scout brought the news that they run north."

A dangerous thrill tingled through Calgacus. He released his own ecstatic war cry with all the others.

A captive ray of sunshine broke from stormy clouds and blazed down on Boudica. A blustery wind swept her auburn hair up like hungry flames. She pointed her black lance toward her next victim. "Destroy it!"

Chariots, riders, and warriors broke from the ridge like a burst dam. His father's chariot led their warriors to the timbered fort that was theirs to destroy.

As they approached, nothing greeted them. Nothing stood in their way or even challenged them. Nothing, but the smoke billowing up from the heart of the enclosure. They rode through the unmanned gates. No weapons fired. Unlike the rambling filthy streets beyond the walls, the roadways were straight and direct. Everything around them was simple, efficient, clean, empty, and eerie.

"Where are they?" Cyric asked as chariot and horses ambled alone, unchallenged.

"Gone," Calgacus said, coughing from the smoke. "Just make sure those damn walls burn completely down. I want to plow this ground come fall."

The warriors spread through the fort, while he, Cyric, and Tancorix followed his father down the main avenue toward the largest building burning in the center of the fort. The smell of roasting grain hung in the air with the ashes. Calgacus grimaced. The Romans had torched what grain they had left behind. Rhianna would not like hearing that.

Eventually, the men gathered with Diras outside the main gate. Smoke billowed all around them from the fires now engulfing the fort and the filthy city.

Calgacus dreaded trying to explain to Rhianna that they had found little more than iron skillets, a small knife, rusted spearheads, and baubles from a horse harness. No food. No blankets. Nothing to feed anyone.

His father pointed his lance toward a tall warehouse close to the wharf. "We are done here and can go our own way. Remember, all those fools who stayed are to be taken to the druid."

Like released children, the warriors disappeared into the huts, stores, and mud-daubed homes to toss items into the street before setting the structure to flame.

Calgacus and his father's guards remained with Diras and worked their way through the prisoners being herded to the wharf, while others looted and burned. The damp breezes from the river drove the smoke inland, clearing the air as they neared the docks.

Orvic bolted from a nearby warehouse and stumbled into his father's chariot. "By all the gods and fathers of the land, he's gone mad!" The warrior stabbed his sword in the direction of the building before vomiting.

Shocked, Diras nodded toward the warehouse doorway. "Calgacus. Tancorix. With me. The rest, take the captives to the druids."

With the first step inside the warehouse, everyone froze. Sunlight, slicing between the wall slats, beamed onto massive bolts of wool piled along one wall and six nude women hanging from ropes tied to heavy crossbeams.

Their hair straggled over bleeding jaws stuffed with their own breasts. Thick blood oozed over their flesh and down their long, slender legs to drip from their toes into a common pool below. The creak of the turning ropes added to the cheers further down the docks.

"Cut them down!" his father yelled.

"Leave them."

Everyone turned to the deep, deadly voice from the shadows, where a large man, covered with blood appeared, his stance daring any to challenge him. "I did to them what the Romans did to my wife and daughter."

Smoke seeped into the cavernous building like snakes, swirling round the bodies like spirits hungry for souls. The darkening shadows closed around them like death's fingers. Calgacus wanted to be free of the place but wouldn't leave his father's side. Not with this man here.

"Da, leave it with him. Let's go."

Chapter 44

SIMMERING FURY, Boudica's constant companion, fed her, kept her alive, and reminded her of the horrors Rome had inflicted on her people. A victorious laugh coiled up through her as she watched smoke swirl from the burning bridge, the burning fort, and the burning warehouses.

"Go back to Rome or die at our feet!" she yelled up to the Roman gods.

Myrradin joined her on the wooden dock, vacant of Roman galleys. "Yes! And all who bow to the Roman yoke!" he cried. Joy radiated on his face with the same rich pleasure.

He scanned the whimpering captives, cowering along the edges of a large ditch embedded with wooden spikes implanted in the mud and the sharpened ends pointing upright.

"Sacrifices to Andraste!" he yelled as he swept his lance over their heads. "The goddess has shown me her desires. She wants this soil cleansed of all who invaded her land. She wants the Roman gods defiled because they have dishonored her." The lance rose skyward. "Andraste! We now cleanse your lands with their blood." Chants of the goddess' name filled the air.

A messenger struggled through the leaders standing with Boudica on the dock. "Boudica, legions come to join the Roman consul."

She turned to the intruder. "We destroyed the Hispana. They cannot come."

"And the Augusta won't move from their fort," the leader of the Durotriges said with a smirk. "Because we threatened its very presence if they try."

The messenger shook his head. "No, from the West Country."

She studied the man. "How many?"

"Two legions, the Gemina and Valeria."

Diras laughed. "That means we still outnumber them ten to one."

"And it will be a full moon before they arrive," the Durotriges' leader added. The other leaders' faces relit with renewed confidence.

Boudica's guts froze. They had to keep moving. "When this sacrifice is over, we must pursue the head of the snake before it joins with his body," she said to the glowing faces surrounding her.

They sobered.

"The men deserve the chance to celebrate this victory," one leader blustered. "They need rest."

The others agreed with eager nods.

An invisible wall rose between her and the leaders. "Don't you understand what that means? You want to celebrate and get drunk with victory while Rome prepares. We cannot allow this to happen."

"Boudica," Diras said, "let the Romans gather. Let them think they can face us. Our victory will be all the sweeter."

Before she could argue that many were already whispering of going home while there was still time to plant for the winter, the druid raised his arms to the sky.

"We honor you, gods of the Britanni!" he announced. "We give you these sacrifices to purify this land to show you that we honor and respect you."

He scanned the line of prisoners huddled like frightened sheep and pointed to one of the captive men. "Bring him to me."

His attendants dragged the man forward and held him while Myrradin sliced off the man's testicles. Screams pierced the air while he hoisted his prize to the sun. "Andraste, great goddess of war!" His voice penetrated the thickening silence as blood raced down his arm. "We thank you for your victories and offer you the enemy!"

Two attendants tossed the man onto the nearest spike. Myrradin focused on the movements of the screaming sacrifice, reading the movements like an omen.

Satisfied, he straightened and then pointed to a young, pregnant girl to be brought forward. She instantly began pleading as he yanked her tunic from her lithe body and eyed the unborn child with pleasure. "Andraste, I give them to you!"

He dangled the girl by the armpits over the corner spike and then released her. Her screams pierced the air while she danced upright on the spike.

Vomit climbed up Boudica's throat. She read the attention of those watching. Horror, joy, and delight feasted on the druid. Doubt cut through her for the first time.

Chapter 45

WINDED HORSES SHIFTED RESTLESSLY as everyone looked at the black smoke rising like thunderclouds behind them—smoke from Londinium. Pity for Rhianna's people ate into Julius' conscience. They all must be fools to think they could force Rome to give up the province now. Once Boudica's revolt was destroyed, Suetonius would show absolutely no mercy to any of the tribes.

"Looks like they have reached Londinium," Julius said as Suetonius studied the same view.

"And if any fool remains in that shithole, they will be sacrificed to Andraste," Suetonius added and then swung Imperious around to Marcus. "Decurio, put the men into a forced march. Bring them to Verulamium by morning. We will await you there. Send scouts to follow the bitch's movements. The rest, with me."

They loped over the slow, lazy hills covered with a multitude of summer flowers dancing in the passing pastures. Hawks circled in the sky. Here and there, a covey of quail shot skyward to swoop down into the tall waving grass. It was almost easy to forget what they had left behind.

Suetonius signaled a halt on a knoll that granted everyone a view of the Britannia's most Roman of cities in the province—Verulamium. A slow-moving river ran along white-plastered buildings that lined the straight streets leading directly into the market area and forum.

Julius closed his eyes to another nightmare—another town with no defenses. By the gods, how many more settlements could Suetonius afford to lose?

A sigh escaped from the consul's lips. "Julius, I expect news of Hispania when we arrive. Let us go find out, shall we?" He released the stallion into a gallop.

Julius followed as Suetonius led everyone through streets filled with children running about like happy puppies beside the lathered horses as if there was no possible threat nearby. Loaded carts of goods stopped at the intersections to let them pass. Scents of fresh-baked bread and sizzling meat floated through the air with the inevitable stench of garbage.

He and his guards followed Suetonius to a newly built white-washed building in the forum area. A short rotund man appeared through a doorway skirted with huge potted plants at either side of the entry. "Suetonius! Welcome, my friend."

"Corvius! I cannot believe you are still here." Suetonius dismounted, and the two men pounded each other's backs. "Of course, I am!" Corvius spouted. "How could I not? I am proud to say Verulamium is becoming quite a city because of you." He glanced curiously at Julius.

"This is Valerius' nephew, Gnaeus Julius Agricola, my present laticlavius. Agricola, this is Corvius Alba, the best engineer in Britannia—Rome, for that matter."

"Julius, join us." Suetonius slid an arm over his friend's shoulders and then led him into the building. "Tell me, Corvius, this is the new thermae?"

"That it is, my friend. It will be my honor to show it to you. It is complete. However, the caldarium is not working. Not hot enough, but it will be before I'm through with it." He chuckled. "I will see it cooks your balls."

"Well, I'm glad I came now and not later!"

Julius followed both laughing men into the freshly painted changing room that reminded him of the baths in Camulodunum where he had nearly passed out.

They began undressing. Lugh drew close. "You'll be wantin' another pretty purple sash in case I need to cart your bandy ass off the field if 'n you're hurt. Am I right?" Lugh asked in Iceni.

When they had left Londinium, Lugh had used the officer's sash to tie bedding together, and it broke.

"Yes," Julius answered, also in Iceni.

Lugh held out a palm. "Want it stolen or paid for, dominus?"

Disgruntled and still not sure he trusted his new slave with his coin bag, Julius handed Lugh six denarii.

Meanwhile, slaves scurried to remove armor, tucking the articles into the niches along the walls or hanging them on wall hooks. Julius pulled his white tunic over his head and handed it to the closest slave.

"We will see this cleaned if that is what you wish, dominus," the slave said in Iceni.

Stunned to hear another speak Rhianna's language, Julius answered in the same. "I do." A sense of accomplishment trickled through him. Would she be happy that he was using her language now?

"What is this I hear about Camulodunum?" Corvius directed them into a steam-filled room. "And now Londinium?"

"You heard right," Suetonius answered, submitting to the slaves sponging the day's sweat from his body.

Worry blazed as hot as the steam on Corvius' face. "Do you think the bitch will bring her horde this far?"

"Most likely." Suetonius released a long sigh as he settled on the warm bench. "Ahhhh. I have waited all day for this moment."

Julius sat down an arm's reach from the consul, whom he could barely see through the thick steam.

"Surely, you will not let anything happen here?" Corvius' voice swelled like a toad. "Surely, you will protect my city?"

Suetonius claimed a towel from a slave to wipe his face. "Depends. If the legions arrive in the next few days, there is a chance, yes. If they fail to arrive, no."

"Suetonius, you must stop them!" the engineer stood up to face the consul. "You cannot let them have my—"

"Corvius, last I checked—today as a matter of fact—the city has no defenses. So, if the legions fail to arrive, there is no choice but to evacuate."

"But—"

Julius began to relax and feel the tension melt from his body. Muscles relaxed.

"Agricola, find out if there is word of your uncle or the legions. If not, spread word to prepare to evacuate. And, unless there are important reports to tell me, do not bother me until I finish here."

"Yes, consul." Julius jerked to attention, saluted, and dragged his body up to leave.

At the moment, he did not give a damn about whether the city was doomed to the same fate as the others. Every ounce of his body wanted to stay, relax, enjoy a massage, and actually feel clean again.

Once in the changing room, he realized that he had nothing wear now since the slave had taken his tunic and Lugh was out shopping. He would have to walk half-naked through the streets if . . .

An attendant touched his arm. "Is it true? Boudica is coming . . . here?"

"Yes."

With the purple sash dangling on his finger, Lugh appeared in the changing room with a clean tunic laying across his arm. "Thought you might be needin' these."

Suetonius leaned back against the plaster wall, feeling the warmth suck the tension from his body. "There is no other alternative,

Corvius. Unless the legions arrive, I have to let the bitch have your city."

The engineer paced the hot room. "I should have seen to those damn walls." He stopped. "I never figured anyone would challenge Rome—here of all places."

Suetonius' thoughts drifted behind closed eyelids. A different heat simmered beneath his skin—the desire to destroy this bitch and her horde of fools. He wanted to laugh at her folly but doing so was becoming more difficult with each day.

The bitch had seized the advantage, had she not? What was more, thanks to Decianus, he now faced an embarrassment beyond even his own imaginings—losing to a woman.

If that happened, he would never be able to show his face in Rome again. The fact festered beneath his skin. Sons of Dis and Jupiter, he had not come out of retirement to allow a woman to ruin his military career that he had given blood and sweat to achieve. By the gods, no. He could not let that happen.

A slave rinsed the pouring sweat from his body, and then he headed for the tepid pool and dove in. The cool water soothed his skin as he swam, while his mind continued to burn.

Could he protect Verulamium even if the legions came? Not without defensive walls. The nearest fort was of little use. It was barely bigger than a marching camp, and it was situated too far north. There were barely enough soldiers to dig the walls in time unless the two legions arrived.

He could already hear the Senate grilling him over this over-sight. He had not ordered the city built, yet the blame would still fall to him. And Nero would have his head for it.

He swam another length of the pool. There had to be an acceptable site to confront this bitch. He knew the maps better than his own hands now. He had seen no such place between Londinium and Verulamium; he had no choice but to continue north to meet up with Valerius.

And when he found this magical place, he would punish this revolt, and whomever remained would know Rome's wrath. Never again will any of those fools ever dare challenge his authority ever again.

Corvius paced along the pool's edge. "You have to do something, Suetonius. You cannot just let them have Verulamium."

Suetonius lifted himself out of the water and sat. "I suggest you start praying the legions arrive." He scooped the water up over his face. "Once the fools have sacrificed what animals and people they find, they will drink and eat until all is gone. Then, they fight and kill each other—the less I will have to kill. So, I say you have possibly have less than a week."

Corvius stopped. "How do you know this?"

Suetonius looked at the engineer. "I was invited to such a celebration once by the Gallic auxiliary. They drink wine straight, Corvius. They do not water it down—ever. Oh, the pain they endure the next day. Then, if the bitch queen can manage to get them to move, they will begin a very slow march here."

"That is hardly enough time."

Julius appeared in the doorway. "Consul, news of the XXth Valeria and the XIVth Gemina. They will be in Manduessedum in about four days."

Suetonius grimaced. Another city to feed the bitch. "Send a messenger. We will meet there."

The morning sun greeted everyone with another cloudless sky. Panic filled the air. Suetonius' orders to evacuate Verulamium raced through the streets like the fires that had destroyed the other cities. Children no longer played but clung to parents packing carts and animals.

Julius appeared in the consul's atrium where a young boy pointed to the nearby triclinium. "He's in there." Fear poured from the urchin's face.

Julius nodded to gods as he passed the lararium and went into the dining area.

Suetonius bit into a peach, motioned for him to recline, and then wiped fresh juice from his chin. He looked at the young boy. "Are your people waiting for you?"

The boy nodded briskly. "Then go." He fled the room.

Suetonius adjusted the cushions under his arm. "Any news?"

"Nothing more, consul." Julius helped himself to a piece of cheese and dry bread on the center table and then rested back on his lounger.

"Any word on the bitch's movements?"

"Camped this side of Londinium. Barely moving."

"I figured. Their fatal mistake. She should have her brood on my tail to see that we do not meet up with the legions." He smirked. "One mistake I will not make. Any word of the IInd?"

"Nothing."

Julius reached for a peach as a knock resounded on the atrium door. The door slave opened it to one angry Marcus storming toward the triclinium and halted, waiting to be recognized.

Suetonius bit into the fruit. "Yes, decurio?"

"Consul, the men are setting up camp by the south gate."

"Good work, decurio. We leave midday."

Marcus sagged as if another burden had just fallen on his shoulders. "I will go stop the camp preparations and get them ready to march."

"I suggest that you do, decurio."

He looked to Julius. "And, Julius, I want scouts sent to watch for your uncle."

<h1 style="text-align:center">Chapter 46</h1>

"CAN I GO HELP THE OTHERS?" Neeca asked with hope blazing in her eyes. Rhianna looked up from her mending. The girl had grown since Camulodunum and finally smiled, maybe because she had friends now. "Yes, go. Be careful."

Neeca skipped into the evening shadows that blanketed the half-filled grain wagon. Rhianna laid the bone needle on Calgacus' breeches. He had left to join the leaders who were fuming about her mother's wishes to pursue the Roman consul. To her mother's dismay, they were determined to remain in Londinium to continue to scour what little remained of the port city, even though it had mostly burned to the ground. She rested a hand on Faolan's soft fur while the dog slept beside her. "At least you stayed with me." She picked up the needle and worked loose a knot in the wool thread. Faolan raised his head and growled. She followed the dog's glare to the shadows beyond the firelight. A spear of ice cut through her heart at the sight of the druid.

"May I join you?" Myrradin squatted by the fire and eyed Faolan carefully. Spots of dried blood from the sacrifices still lingered on his tunic and cloak. "Your grain cakes fill the air with delightful aromas, Rhianna. You have a gift for such things."

She waved at the food. "They are ready if you would like one."

Why wasn't he with the leaders, plotting his next sacrifice to Andraste? Had he already found one? Her child? She couldn't breathe. Her fingers sank into the dog's fur as her hand fisted.

The druid tore his gaze from the dog and settled it on her. "Thank you, but no. Food is too precious now. I come for another reason." He picked up a burning stick and poked at the glowing coals. "Faolan, isn't that the dog's name?"

"Yes."

Busy little flames erupted in the fire pit. She should remove the cakes to keep them from burning, but she couldn't move. Faolan was all that protected her from this man.

An eternity seemed to pass before he spoke again—to the fire. "Many notice that you do not share their determination to destroy Rome."

"I'm not like my mother and my sister. I do not enjoy death and destruction. Everyone knows that."

His obsidian gaze shifted from the fire and focused on her. "Could it be from losing your tribune?"

She kept her fist in Faolan's fur, not letting it move to her baby. "If you mean my master, no. I do not miss him."

He looked into the busy flames again, his face hidden in the shadows. "You have not had your blood flow since your return from your master's care. When you came to the hill fort two months ago, you assured everyone that you did not carry the Roman's child." He studied her. "Are you still certain?"

How could he know about her monthly flow?

"I forgot."

Myrradin's eyes gleamed with hungry greed. "Then, you must be with child."

That was what had brought him. He wanted her baby to add to his bloody victory. Memories returned of her father's long-standing suspicion of the druid. Now her own distrust morphed into pure hatred.

Faolan felt her fury and sat up, his ears flat against his skull. A snarl curled his lips. She wanted to let the dog rip the druid apart. "Faolan, down."

The dog slunk to the ground but remained taut as a bowstring. "If I carry a child, then it belongs to my husband."

Myrradin shifted his attention between the growling dog and her. "He knows?"

"How could he, if I didn't know?"

The druid rose, brushing his tunic free of leaves and dirt. "I am sure this news will bring a welcomed distraction to the death and destruction that surrounds everyone." The slow smile stretched his thin lips. "Remember, Rhianna, this child will bear the features of his parents, and we will all know."

Her heart clamored to a halt as he disappeared into the dark shadows. She had no choice now but to tell Calgacus. Should she lie as she had to the druid? No. It was not a lie. The child was hers.

However, if Calgacus didn't believe her and would not accept her child, then she had no choice but to flee, even if it meant going to the Romans.

"Modron, mother goddess of us all, I beg you to give the babe my features and the Roman's heart. Protect it. Please." She dropped a grain cake into the fire and smelled the nutty fragrance of her sacrifice as it drifted to the stars.

Faolan's tail brushed the dirt the moment Neeca stepped into view. "I-Is everything all right?"

"Yes." Rhianna moved back from the fire.

Neeca patted the dog's furry head. "I don't like that druid. He's mean."

"Yes, he is." Rhianna put the needle in her pouch. He was more than mean. Words failed to describe Myrradin.

"Is he right?" Hope sparkled in Neeca's face. "Are you going to have a baby?"

"I think so, yes."

The girl cradled the dog's face. "She's going to have a baby. A real baby." Faolan licked her chin. The girl giggled and hugged Rhianna. "I will help you. I can. I promise."

<h1 style="text-align:center">Chapter 47</h1>

RHIANNA BARELY FINISHED MAKING more grain cakes and removed the griddle when Calgacus strolled into the camp carrying an armload of wood. He squatted to place the wood on the coals. The firelight lit his face and made his mustache gleam golden.

Images of Julius flickered in her mind: lean, brown eyes, and brown hair. Calgacus was solid, had blue eyes, and golden hair. Both men were different in every feature.

"We follow the Romans tomorrow," he muttered.

She clutched his wrist. "I don't want to. I want to leave, Calgacus, and find a place to live. To stay."

His arm encircled her shoulders. "I want that, too. But Romans remain in our lands, and they must be destroyed." He claimed one of the grain cakes and chomped it down as if attacking it. "There will be no peace until then."

"I don't care anymore." Tears spilled down her cheeks. "I can't deal with this any longer."

He drew her to him. "Is something the matter?"

She had to say it. She had to. "I'm . . . I'm pregnant."

"You're what?" He lifted her chin to look at her. "Pregnant?"

She nodded, fear making her tremble.

He scooped her up and whirled her around. A triumphant war cry bellowed from his lungs. He set her carefully on her feet and cradled her face in his palms. "You carry our child!" Tears gleamed in his eyes like rippling water. He bent to kiss her.

Men brandishing weapons burst from the darkness. They halted, confused. He faced them. "Rhianna carries my child! Our child."

The fright melted into jubilation. Men pounded him on the back, offering congratulations. Women appeared, curious of the commotion, and then encircled her, assuring her all would be well, that there would be time to prepare after they defeated Rome. More people appeared in the fire light, and laughter rippled like breezes in the tree limbs.

Neeca climbed out of the wagon and stood beside Rhianna while Faolan wagged his tail as if all the commotion happened for his benefit. She just stood there, letting their attentions wash over her.

The night was sleepless, and the morning was rising on a black fire pit. Nearby, Tancorix and Calgacus lay sprawled in the bushes. Only Neeca remained, holding her water bucket after a trip to the river.

"Do you need anything?" she asked. Rhianna climbed from the tent space next to the wagon, feeling more exhausted than ever before.

"A drink, yes. Thank you."

Calgacus stirred awake, wiping his face with his palm. He shook his head and groaned. Finally, he focused on her standing by the wagon wheel.

"Do you need anything? I'll get it," he said. "Just tell me."

Tancorix stirred to life with a serious groan. "You can get me a drink."

"Get your own." Calgacus pulled to his feet and staggered to Rhianna. "I mean it."

Glee danced through her. Her child was safe. The mother goddess was with her. "Fortunately, I have Neeca," Rhianna said as Neeca handed her a cup brimming with water.

Calgacus slouched against the wagon and looked out at the stirring encampment. While the sun rose over the trees, everyone eased gently into the day.

"Rhianna, you can't stay back here any longer. I don't want you here."

Panic roared to life. "No, I won't stay with my mother. No, Calgacus. You can't expect me to stay with her."

"Stay with my parents, then."

She crossed her arms and stiffened. "I prefer it back here, so why can't I stay?"

He drove his hands through his uncombed hair. "I don't want you that far from me. And you have to walk . . . back here."

Neeca dropped the bucket. "I can drive the oxen. I can."

Calgacus studied the girl. "I know you can, Neeca. But, well, I just want you both with me." He cast that devilish grin that taunted Rhianna. "You know, we have to tell them before everyone else does."

Rhianna refused to unlock her arms as he came toward her.

"Fine. We can tell them. But I don't want to stay there."

He kissed her cheek.

"I'll get the chariot. You're not walking."

The chariot moved through the blanket of people milling around blackened campfires that dotted the hills. Many climbed out of makeshift tents, stretching to greet the dawn even though it was midday. Some had never made it to a tent but lay sprawled in their drunken stupors. Wine gourds lay inches from open palms.

They passed a naked couple still asleep and wrapped in each other's arms. A man marched past with fury written on his face. Calgacus called out to him, but the man failed to respond. Occasionally, a stench of vomit mixed with the odors of manure and urine.

It was so much cleaner back with the herds, Rhianna thought as Morrigan drew Skye to a halt.

"What's this I hear?" her sister asked when Calgacus stopped the ponies. "My sister is to bear a child, and I'm not told first?" Her gray eyes twinkled like polished silver. "I have to find this out through gossip?"

She wore a Roman's mail coat over her short brown tunic. The days training in the sun had bronzed her skin, and the sword she fought with had honed her body into a weapon. All the warriors respected her now that more Roman heads dangled off her mother's chariot.

"Rhianna just told me last night." Calgacus snapped the reins over the ponies' backs. They lurched the chariot forward.

Skye followed along. "Has mother heard yet? She will not be happy if she hears it through gossip."

"We'll make sure that doesn't happen. Hold on." The ponies jumped into a gallop.

A cold chill steeled inside Rhianna. Her mother had to know, as well as Diras and Marleth. They would expect her to be excited and happy about the news.

She wanted to be that happy about her child. Yet the memory of Myrradin's cryptic smile threatened that hope. The tents grew thicker the closer they came to the leaders' camp. The tall blue tent in the center nearest the council fire was her mother's. No doubt, Myrradin already had told her the news.

Panic squirmed through her the moment her mother stepped from her tent. The lacerations covering her were now scars that appeared like white worms clinging to her tan flesh. Her auburn hair still gleamed like fire and swept down her back to her knees.

Gray eyes sparked with sharp curiosity. "Son of the Trinovante, welcome. Rhianna, it is good to see you. What brings you both?" her mother asked.

Calgacus halted the chariot inside the bare earth that encircled the main campfire. "Boudica, leader of the Iceni. We feel you should hear the news from your children, rather than through gossip. Rhianna carries our child."

Joy flooded through Boudica. How long had it been since that emotion had stirred? The scars had rooted deep into her soul until all she felt was her hatred.

A smile eased gently on her lips as she studied her daughter who resembled her father in so many unseen ways. Both had carried the spirits of gentleness and calm, something much needed, but so fragile in these violent times. That was a rare strength few had. It had served Prasutagus well. He'd be proud of his daughter.

Boudica's pleasure vanished the instant Rhianna's gaze met hers like a trapped animal ready to fight for its life or protect the life she carried. Was this truly Calgacus' child or the Roman's? The answer came quietly.

Boudica studied Diras' son who was bursting with pride. He remains innocent. How do you destroy such a precious thing? She could not. She would leave this to the gods to answer. "Is this true, daughter? You carry a child?"

"It is."

"You bring a promise of the future for all of us. A child. Born without the threat of Rome." Boudica scanned the gathering crowd, realizing that this could renew everyone's determination to rid their lands of Rome. "We must thank the gods for this promise. A child— a promise of rebirth for our future."

The last edges of sleep followed Calgacus' father from his neighboring tent. "What is this I hear? A child?"

"It's true, Da," Calgacus said. "We come with the news that the gods have blessed us."

"Glorious day!" The chief of the Trinovante enfolded his son in an embrace, beaming with equal pride. "Come! We must celebrate!"

Her daughter's attention froze on the druid carrying a goblet of wine as he stepped through the rejoicing onlookers. His hatred of Rome nearly matched her own, but it was not welcomed here. Not with her daughter carrying a promise that could bring the future for everyone. Boudica's hands coiled at her sides.

Myrradin raised a goblet to the sky. "Andraste, may you watch over this gift to your people." He lowered the cup and drank, red wine trickling like blood from the corner of his mouth. He wiped the traces from his lips and then handed the goblet to Calgacus, who drank. He handed it to Rhianna. She drank, eyes closed, only a sip and then handed it back to her husband.

Boudica drew close to the restless chariot and opened her hand for the cup. She drank before handing it to Marleth, who had joined them.

Boundless pride beamed from Calgacus' mother as she handed the cup to Diras. He handed the cup back to Boudica. She lifted it to the sky and announced, "Tomorrow, we continue to cleanse Romans from the lives of our children!"

Leaders looked to each other and down to their feet. Diras walked closer to Calgacus' chariot. "Boudica, Suetonius lounges in his Roman city. There are no reports of his legions coming any time soon. We will trap him there."

Boudica's arm dropped, pouring the remaining wine at her feet. "The body of the snake comes to join the head, does it not?"

"Yes but, Boudica, my people are tired," the Dobunni leader interrupted. Rumbles of agreement stiffened his resolve. "We choose to rest or go home."

She faced the wine bloated man. "Yes, we are all tired. So, flee. Go home. Leave the rest of us to keep the head of this snake from its body."

"Boudica, we need a few days. Our swords need sharpening. Arrows need to be made," Diras pleaded with open arms. "Even if the snake does rejoin with its head, we have nothing to fear. We outnumber the Romans tenfold."

Chapter 48

RHIANNA REMAINED IN THE LEADERS' CAMP simply because Diras and Marleth had begged her to stay with them. Calgacus' mother was different from her own in so many ways. She had lost two sons to Rome, yet she remained kind and gentle. However, the fear of losing her only remaining son lurked heavily in her gaze.

While Rhianna sat outside Diras' tent, Calgacus sharpened Cadaryn in long, slow swipes. When he looked at her, joy followed. She quickly discovered how that sustained her; how it helped her endure being here. He had also become quieter than before, as if a new determination had settled over him.

She and Calgacus had instantly become the promise of what life could be without the Romans. People came to touch them, to offer gifts, wanting nothing more than a kind word or a smile in return.

That afternoon, one of the women presented her with a gift of wool fabric. "For your babe. It'll be needin' something to wear and 'tis a blessin' for sure."

As another night drew over the sky, Rhianna longed for the soft lowing of the oxen instead of the rasping of swords being sharpened, people arguing, and crackling fires.

The Dobunni leader was right. A keen sense of exhaustion spread over the entire throng like a wet blanket. People were tired, their gazes flat and their voices weary. They longed for the same things she did—a home and knowledge that they would survive the coming winter.

Boudica continued to walk among everyone, encouraging them. "Yes, we grow tired. Our bodies ache from battle and victory. Yes, we want to go home to our fields. If we stop now, the Romans will come back stronger, feasting on their vengeance. We must destroy them quickly. All of them. And run them to the waters where they came from while we still can."

A warrior burst into the campsite. "They flee Verulamium!"

Leaders gathered as Boudica walked to the man. "The Romans? Flee? Their new city?" she asked.

The bonfire distorted the warrior's features in the flickering glow. "Yes. Gone north. Their legions approach."

"How far away are they?" Calgacus asked as he joined the circle.

"Three days."

Boudica nodded. "As I said, the head of the snake flees to join the body."

"Let him," one of the leaders barked. "We will destroy them all like stink bugs." Laughter rippled and cheered.

"Who remains in the city?" Boudica asked.

"No one." The scout opened his empty palms. "The city is ours."

The day quickly grew hot as if brewing up another storm. Suetonius hoped he was wrong and motioned to walk the lathered horses. All those behind him slowed as they continued toward Manduessedum. He was glad to be free of Verulamium. It was a suffocating trap.

The reports galled him that the Britanni horde had killed thousands of people in Londinium. However, they had been warned, just as he had warned Verulamium. The people there, at least, had the sense to believe him and had vacated the city.

He scanned the passing area as Imperious ambled along, nervously swishing his tail at the miserable heat. No one doubted that the Britanni frothed with determination to force Rome from the province. If that happened, would Nero retaliate? Likely. On the other hand, would he simply toss the province aside like trash?

If Nero ignored such defeat, other provinces would revolt. That would be disastrous for the entire empire and to himself as well. Especially himself.

His only choice was to defeat this bitch. To do that, he needed his legions. He needed their presence. A dust cloud blew over everyone as a Roman scout galloped along the vanguard behind him. The soldier drew to a halt.

"The Britanni have reached Verulamium," the rider gasped.

"As I figured," Suetonius sighed and patted the stallion's neck. "Any word from the IInd?"

"Nothing, consul."

That was the other thorn in his side. The IInd Augusta had failed to move a single soldier from their fort, which left him with ten thousand soldiers to confront two hundred thousand Britanni. Jupiter's balls, the Augusta's camp prefect would pay for refusing his repeated orders to bring the men.

He motioned to the nearest centurion. "Rest the men. Tribune, decurio, join me."

The horns sang out, and the meager column sagged to a halt. The urge to charge down the road flooded over Suetonius. He gave Imperious his head, and the stallion lunged into a gallop. The tug of his white cape fluttered behind him, granting him a moment of freedom from the looming responsibilities.

Every lurching stride of the horse steeled his determination to keep the province and his reputation intact.

Yes. Every Britanni will eat the ash and shit for every city they have destroyed. They will rebuild everything with their sweat and blood. When I am through with them, all Britanni will fear revolting against Rome as the slaves had after Spartacus' revolt. They will pay. I will see to that.

He drew Imperious to a sliding halt and blinked at the vista before him.

What the fuck? There had been no order to halt! Julius drew his galloping horse to a stop, barely avoiding a collision with Imperious' haunches.

Behind him, Marcus drove his horse off the stone road to avoid slamming into either him or the white stallion. The guards then fell in disarray and confusion behind them. Unaware of the near collision, Suetonius scanned the vista down to the river Anker, sparkling blue as it cut through the flat ground. He wheeled Imperious around and studied the deep valley running between two forested hills that came together at a higher rise. A hawk floated beneath the canopy of clouds above it all. Its screech pierced the silence.

"Agricola, with me."

Julius kneed his horse into a slow canter behind the consul and tried to see what had captured the man's attention.

All he saw were two tree-covered hills running almost parallel to each other, behind which rose a third hill lined with a forest of trees. Between them stretched valley that poured out to a vast river plain. It was not until Julius turned his horse to view the river that he understood exactly why the consul was smiling.

"This is it, Julius. We meet this bitch here."

Chapter 49

RHIANNA GROANED AS THUNDER RUMBLED, threatening even more rain. Were the gods trying to wash them back to their villages? Three children had died during the night from the continual dampness. Adults coughed as they walked. Some with festering wounds limped along or rode in wagons. The plundered prizes were being left behind, creating space for someone to ride or simply lighten the load on the exhausted animals as they approached Verulamium.

When a vagrant sunbeam burst from the restless gray clouds, her mother waved everyone to a halt on the hill overlooking the doomed city. It poured down on the distant vista where no cattle or sheep grazed in the fields. No wagons were seen moving in and out of the gates. No smoke drifted to the sky.

Shields and swords dropped to warriors' sides. Lances butted into the mud. Lightning streaked through the darkening clouds like a curse, followed by another rumble of angry thunder. A storm wind twisted the treetops about like toys.

"Where are they?" Rhianna asked.

Calgacus held the anxious ponies in line with the other drivers. "Ran off, I guess."

Boudica waved her lance. As if released from a tether, people flooded down the hill in search of shelter instead of victory.

He held the ponies back until Rhianna's grain wagon approached. "Let Coolan drive, and you stay under the canvas, my love. I'll find us a safe place for the night and come back for you."

He smiled and kissed the top of her head as she stepped from his chariot. Even it held little of its previous gleam now and looked more worn than the wagons.

Rain began to fall. Rhianna tugged Neeca beneath the oil tarp to keep the girl dry. When Calgacus found them by the city gate, the fat drops of rain quickly morphed to a downpour as if a bucket had been tipped over. Rather than looting, everyone had disappeared into vacated buildings and homes for protection.

He took the prod from Neeca's friend. "Go, you're among your people, Coolan."

Rhianna peeked from beneath the oil tarp covering the grain. The battle paint from the rituals the night before ran down Calgacus' arms like blue blood, and his long hair lay like bronze snakes over his shoulders.

"Coolan, your parents are near where we're staying!" he yelled over the rumbles of thunder. "I'll show you. Now, get in the wagon."

The boy shook his head and kept walking while the lashing storm thrashed. Somewhere in the midst of the empty street, the wagon jolted to a halt before one of the doorways along a narrow alley.

Calgacus pointed at another building three doors away. "Coolan, your parents are there."

As the boy headed in that direction, Calgacus came to the end of the wagon and lifted the canvas. "Tancorix kept this place for us," he said as Rhianna and Neeca crawled from the wagon bed. "And he'd better have a fire going when we get inside."

They raced through the downpour for the open doorway, yet they were drenched by the time they entered the small hut. The forlorn kitten, Id, jumped from Neeca's arms and bolted for a warm corner. Faolan shed enough rain for a river.

Rhianna pulled from Calgacus' protection and surveyed the room, which was wondrous after nearly three months of campfires and tents. A bucket rested on the end of a bench, full of fresh water.

Wood lay in a pile near a fire crackling in a large black nook in the wall, its smoke disappearing up a tunnel.

She had grown up on floors of hard-packed dirt, a fire pit burning in the center of the round hut, and various food containers lining the floors along the daub-and-waddled walls. Here, the floor was limestone slabs, and the pots, jars, and canisters lined the many shelves on the white, plastered walls. She could easily enjoy making a home here, and she could see Calgacus returning from the fields or from hunting and coming through the door each day. Neeca would be busy taking care of her child crawling about the floor.

Rhianna walked to a sack left on the large table in the center of the room. "I think Tancorix left this." She held up a wine pouch full of ale and dry biscuits.

A sparkle lit in Calgacus' blue eyes, hot and hungry; it warmed the room. "Neeca, you want to take Coolan's parents some wood?" He motioned to the stack of kindling.

"If you want me to." The girl filled her arms. The storm had lulled when the girl hurried out the door. Thankfully, the storm erupted with a new rage after she left, stranding her with Coolan's family for the night.

Peace permeated through Rhianna as she stirred against the rock-hard body lying beside her. No part of her wanted to leave the bed ever again. An actual bed . . not blankets spread on the ground or a wagon bed.

Calgacus' arm tightened around her waist as he grumbled with satisfaction. Rhianna gasped awake. Images of Julius and Calgacus had appeared in her dreams—one lean and agile like a stallion, the other huge and strong like a bull. Both wore her pendant on a chain around their necks or pinned at their shoulders. They waited, their gazes piercing her.

"Choose!" a voice bellowed.

How could she? The choice was already made. Julius had decided that for her by joining with another. He had lied, just like all Romans lied.

Calgacus had fought for her, rescued her, and wanted her at his side—he was her soulmate. In that moment, the image of Julius simply vanished.

Calgacus rose up on one arm, worry blazing in his eyes. "Rhianna, what is it?"

She brushed his mustache aside with her hand and smiled. "Nothing. It was nothing. Really." Another lie. The dream was everything and very real.

He lay back, drawing her to him, which she welcomed. Yet, the instant she closed her eyes, Julius returned, smiling at the bundle in his arms. The smile lifted to her, and with it came knowledge that could never be erased.

She would see him every time she gazed at his child. That fact sent needles into her soul; one day, Calgacus might realize the truth. Would he hate her, or would he understand the child was hers and love it as he did her?

Julius gasped awake. "Rhianna."

His insides mirrored the tent walls thrashing in the storm. He drew his pillow to his face to inhale the tiny bit of her fragrance of violet. Like the pillow, he knew he was losing her.

He cradled the back of his neck with his scarred hand, leaving it there. His and Lugh's discussion over dinner echoed in his mind. "The Iceni would be skinnin' your Roman arse if you set foot near her now."

Again, his brain searched for options. What Lugh said was true. With the insanity exploding around Boudica, the consul needed every soldier who could handle a gladius to stop her, and he would kill everyone who had joined her.

His hand slid from his neck only to claim Rhianna's pendant. Her promise whispered in his ear as clearly as the day she made it. Yet, he knew he was losing her. The void grew wider each day.

He kissed the metal and slumped back on the cot. Did she love this man, or had she stayed with him just to survive? Had she married him because her people expected it of her, as he had Domitia, or because she chose him?

A small oil lamp still burned, its sputtering flame reflected on his dagger's sheath, lying on his desk. He rose from the cot and unsheathed the knife. He closed his eyes. "Venus, goddess of love, I continue to beg you, bring Rhianna back to me. I beg you for nothing more." He drew the sharp blade across the scar, shooting pain through his arm. Once again, blood dripped into the flame, as he whispered, "That is all I ask."

Chapter 50

FOR TWO DAYS, RAIN FELL WITH A FURY. All that time, Rhianna had enjoyed every moment in their little house. She cooked meals and washed clothing. Calgacus mended harnesses and sharpened weapons. During the nights, they talked about where they would live when all this ended.

He told her his father had planned to give him the area west of the main hill fort outside Camulodunum. The land was rich with forests and fields ripe for harvest, cattle, and sheep.

They agreed that if her child were a boy, he would learn to fish, hunt, and fight as Calgacus had. If the babe were a girl, she would grow up as Rhianna had, learning herbs, cooking, and weaving, unlike Morrigan, who had become a warrioress. They both laughed at this fact, even though he said her sister was lethal with her swords.

They both wanted a home like the one now burning with the rest of the Romans' newly built city. Warriors raced about like ants with golden torches, touching rooftops, and stuffing anything burnable against the plastered walls. Familiar black smoke now shrouded a third Roman city.

Rhianna sat on the back of the wagon with Neeca, who swung her legs and taunted Id with a string. She had driven the wagon to a distant ridge well before dawn to avoid Myrradin's sacrifices of the captives who hadn't fled. Fortunately, only a few had remained.

She recognized her mother's ponies approaching at a crisp trot. Boudica's auburn hair gleamed like a flame stolen from those that burned the city as she drove her chariot up the hill.

Rhianna's heart slammed in her chest. "Neeca, do you know where Coolan and his friends went?"

"Looking for truffles."

"Do you think you could find some?"

Excitement blossomed on the girl's face. "I can. I'll find lots of them."

She raced down the hill before Boudica stopped beside the wagon and tied the ponies to the wagon wheel. "It's a good day, Rhianna."

"I suppose." Rhianna tried to swallow as her mother leaned against the space Neeca had vacated. The usual bitterness didn't surround her. There was even a flicker of concern in her eyes. How strange to see that expression again. It allowed Rhianna to breathe.

"Can you believe it is almost over?" Boudica asked with a smile. "Before long, we will go home."

"Home?"

"Yes. Home. Something we all yearn for." Her mother brushed dust and grains from the wagon bed and then gazed over the vista. "Soon, all this will be our land again. What we sow will be ours and no one else's."

Rhianna's doubt drifted with the meandering river. Would Rome return with more legions to take everything back? If so, this was merely the beginning of horrors to come.

"If Rome doesn't return, I welcome it, mother. But have we become like the Romans when this is over when we do return home?"

"What do you mean?"

She pointed to the distant wagon struggling through the mud with plunder piled inside. "Have we become like the Romans who take without regard to whom it belonged? Will we ever be satisfied with the simple things once the Romans are gone?"

"It would be easier to stop the wind from blowing than to deprive them of their revenge."

Her mother's voice held a soft tone to it, gentle possibly. It brought back memories of everyone before things had changed and become hard, determined to destroy.

"Do you think Calgacus will accept this child?" her mother asked.

Rhianna looked down at her hands, knowing the true reason of the visit. Oddly enough, the question didn't stun her. "I hope he does."

"Why should he?"

She looked up and met the steely gaze. "Because it is my child."

Boudica turned away and watched as three men struggled to get a huge jar of wine into a wagon.

"Why did you tell the druid?" Rhianna asked. Boudica shook her head. "I didn't."

"Then how did he know?"

Boudica bent down for a blade of grass and then twirled it between her fingers. "Druids seem to know most everything, even people's thoughts." Her iron gaze met Rhianna's, but without its usual bite. "Why did you decide to keep the Roman's child, Rhianna?"

"As I said, this is my child, mother." She placed her hands over the baby. "And I trust that Calgacus will accept it."

Their gazes shifted as rooftops collapsed into the growing inferno and cheers carried up the hill.

"Rhianna, the child is doomed." Her mother's scarred hand rested on Rhianna's knee. "Let the druid have it when the time comes."

The words stung like hornets. "Myrradin will never touch my child!" Rhianna snarled.

"Then take this." Sighing heavily, Boudica pulled a small package from beneath her belt and turned to Rhianna. "You must rid yourself of the child. The pain will be sharp, but it will end. It will be as gentle breezes compared to the pain of watching your child suffer at the hands of the others."

Tears gleamed in the iron gaze. "An unending pain I do not wish upon you, daughter. You will have another one day; one you can cherish as I do you."

Chapter 51

THE LAST OF THE GRAIN SACKS were opened as the line for food grew. Rhianna poured the granules into a woman's bowl. "I'm sorry. I wish I could give you more."

The woman smiled and pressed a hand to Rhianna's belly. "May the mother goddess bless your child for what you share." Rhianna sprinkled a few more grains into the bowl.

The next cup appeared, and she filled it. When she turned back for another scoop, she noticed the blankets, kitchen utensils, and the blue-and-white ceramic bowl that Calgacus had taken from the villa outside Camulodunum now outnumbered the few remaining bags of grain in the wagon.

A tiny cradle carved by one of the Trinovante men sat among the bags with the other baby gifts. He said he'd made it because he had grown tired of the destruction.

She poured a scoop into another bowl and then looked over the endless line of people. Dirt and blood stained what was once vibrant hues of their clothing. Now, it was a parade of a dull and threadbare existence. Their weary faces and trudging footsteps displayed their exhaustion.

Three months ago, every step had been defiant and determined. Now, people fought over who rode in slow chariots or wagons. Children didn't chase each other. Horses ambled instead of pranced. The dwindling herds of goats and sheep were used for milk instead of meat. Warriors no longer brandished weapons but caressed the leaves or stalks of the few remaining crops and talked of harvesting, of seeds, of plows—anything but war.

She envied those who had left, already back at their homes. Each day the sun rose on another barren campsite. Yet, her mother continued encouraging everyone. "The Roman scourge will grow stronger and hungrier. Their taxes will be even more. They will take whatever is harvested, leaving us to starve. We continue because Rome grows tired, too."

As the sun set, Boudica walked past Rhianna's wagon outside the leaders' area and toward her own tent when another leader stopped her.

"My people want to go home," he said.

"Then go." Boudica's iron gaze cut into his. "But remember this as you do. The head of the snake flees. We outnumber the Romans."

She scanned all those drawn to her words. "We will prevail. We will run Rome back across the waters." She nonchalantly waved the man to leave. "So, go. Tuck your tails between your asses and run if you fear them, while we who remain save the future for your children."

The leaders grumbled among themselves as Myrradin stepped close. He lifted his arms to the heavens in a grand display. "I beseech you, Andraste. Do you wish us to return to our home and crops, or must we continue to purge your lands of Roman filth?"

Out of nowhere, his raven floated through the air and dove for his sleeve like a black arrow. "You see! The goddess is with us!" he yelled to the cheering crowd. "She demands that we rid her land of all things Roman. Free it from their gods!"

Rhianna groaned. Unfortunately, no one realized the bird was simply the druid's pet. Since Camulodunum, people believed that Andraste had granted him the bird because it brought the goddess' power and wisdom. The druid's searing gaze fell on her as if he had read her mind. Her child shifted for the first time inside her womb.

The thrill of feeling a life within her drew her hands to her belly to assure the babe, which was more real now than ever before, that she would protect it with her life.

Myrradin looked away as Calgacus stepped beside Diras and Marleth, standing before their tent. "We all know that harvesting is hardest when it is almost complete," Calgacus said calmly. "The days seem longer, while they are shorter. Our bodies ache as they do now."

A long, weary sigh issued from his lips as he joined Rhianna on the wagon and wrapped his arm about her waist. "We have planted seeds to destroy Rome. The harvest is ready to be gleaned."

She leaned into his protection. He looked down at her and smiled. It faded as he scanned everyone and continued. "And now we reap what we have sown, so that we may live."

Chapter 52

THE THROBBING CUT IN JULIUS' PALM stung from salty sweat as he wiped his forehead with his arm. Smoke from the burning brush piles caught in a down draft of wind and swept around him like coils of a snake, making his flesh more miserable.

Suetonius' order to remove the scrub brush and trees from the two hills had quickly become a contest between the soldiers and the cavalry.

Now the twin hills were nude, except for the grass hiding the sharpened trunks of recently cut trees left standing mid-calf.

The last tree cracked and fell seconds before Marcus' last bundle of grass fell on their fire, granting the soldiers a victory over the cavalry. They all looked to the white-crested centurion standing on the rear vista that joined the two hills for the final decision.

The centurion pretended to study the hills and then pointed his vitus stick to Julius. Roars of victory exploded over the hill as rebuttal resonated from the cavalry.

Furious, Marcus began peeling off his filthy tunic while storming down his hill toward the river. His friend's action only made Julius' sweat-soaked tunic more miserable.

He dropped the sickle and raced to catch up with Marcus. "Where are you going, decurio?"

"To get rid of this official sweat, tribune." Julius sniffed. "You need to."

Marcus returned the sniff. "As you do, my friend."

They neared the riverbank already lined with naked men plunging or throwing each other into the crisp water.

"You cheated on that hill," Marcus grumped and shoved Julius into the river. The cool water felt glorious; however, Marcus was going to pay for that move.

Julius burst from the surface, in search of his friend. "Looking for me, tribune?" Marcus asked from behind as he treaded water.

"Definitely, decurio. Your ass is mine now."

"I can whip your ass after a twenty mile march any day, tribune."

"On the bank, now, and we will see."

They both clambered out of the water and stopped on a stretch of grass perfect for a wrestling match.

Men fled the river and surrounded them as he and Marcus circled each other, arms spread and eyes dancing. In the background, Lugh was already collecting bets as more men came to watch and cheer. A centurion broke through the mass to break up the fight, but instantly became the referee. Julius grappled, slapping Marcus' hands away like insults.

Then Marcus lunged, grabbed Julius around the waist, and threw him. Stumbling, he drew upright and slammed Marcus into the grass, heaving to pin Marcus' chest to the dirt.

His throbbing hand slipped. Marcus rolled and jumped to his feet to the cavalry's cheers, leaving Julius also lurching to his feet. Again, they circled.

Once again, it seemed they were in the sands of the gymnasium back home.

Straining every weary muscle, Julius worked free from Marcus' grip and then wheeled onto the man's back to flip him over and pin him. Marcus rose like a lion, carrying him upward. As he started to slam him to the ground, Julius jerked free.

The soldiers and cavalry either roared or booed every move.

"Get free, decurio!"

"Slam his ass back in the dirt, tribune!"

They circled and then collided, chest against chest, grunting and panting. Their legs slid in the grass, struggling for any toehold.

Marcus landed on him like a concrete slab, crushing all breath from Julius' lungs.

Sucking air, he worked one pinioned leg free and then rolled to bring Marcus under him.

"Tribune!"

The order jerked both his and Marcus' attention up to the young soldier. Julius expected Marcus to roll and claim the win. Instead, they both climbed to their feet.

"What is it, Lucus?" Julius asked, brushing grass from his chest.

"The consul wants you . . .," the young soldier pointed at Marcus, " . . . and him in his tent. Now."

"Received," Julius said. He glanced at Marcus as they both snatched their filthy tunics from the ground and headed for the river.

"You know I had your ass."

"Never have; never will."

Suetonius smirked at the two officers dripping river water from their wet hair as they stood before him. Their helmets were tucked neatly beneath their arms as they saluted.

"Who won?" he asked from his desk chair as a slave filled his cup.

"I did," they both answered.

He chuckled. "Well, I commend you both on clearing the hills. Well done." He toasted them with his cup of wine. "Join me."

Both soldiers sat on the wood bench across from the desk. "Tribune, what happened to your hand?" Suetonius asked.

Julius looked at the bandage, turning it over on his leg, flexing it. "Nothing serious, consul. It is my shield hand."

"Good. I hope you do not have to use it." Suetonius drank and then set the cup on the desk. "How are the supplies?"

"Meager. Men are searching for whatever is available."

A slave handed Julius a cup of wine. "There is a village not far from here. Otherwise, about a day's worth of grain is left."

Suetonius nodded. "With any luck, the men should be able to find more there. And, no doubt, the forest is filled with deer or boar."

Noise outside drew everyone's attention. A guard stepped inside. "Report on the legions for the consul. The XXth Valeria and the XIVth Gemina arrive tomorrow."

Tears almost rose to his eyes. Suetonius cleared his throat before speaking. The reason for ordering the tribune and decurio had evaporated instantly. He looked at the delight mirrored in the officers before him. "See we are ready to receive them."

"Yes, consul," both answered.

Chapter 53

TWO HAWKS FLOATED IN AN AZURE SKY cushioned with white puffy clouds as Suetonius led the official group away from the newly built camp. He loped along the road curving into the thick forest, the same forest that had cloaked the rise behind the twin hills.

His hand shot skyward as he drew Imperious to a halt to listen to the cadenced sound of marching feet that greeted his ears. It was more melodious than the birds singing in the trees. Glints of silver sparkled through the greenery.

Jupiter Optimus Maximus, they are here! His legions had arrived, and none too soon. Suetonius swallowed the sudden lump in his throat as the constant vice around his chest eased.

To be certain he was not wrong, he kicked Imperious into a gallop and rounded the turn to witness Valerius striding before the two gold eagles carried by silver wolf-skins that caped soldiers. The red standards of both legions rippled in the morning breeze as they strode with the power of Rome.

The column appeared like a long diamond bracelet sparkling with ruby red tunics, shields, and capes as if pulled from an emerald-green pouch. Valerius' white crest bobbed with each stride until he lifted his fist upward. "Halt!" he commanded.

Cornicens blared the order, and the approaching line came to an echoing halt so sudden that it stopped Suetonius' heartbeat. These men were the very weapons he needed to destroy the bitch and her horde. The soldiers were his muscle, and his officers the nerves.

"A glorious sight, is it not?" he said aloud to whomever rode near him and then swung from Imperious to clasp Valerius in his arms. "About fucking time you got here."

"Damn mountains. If I ever see any again, it will be Mount Olympus from a distance. I swear the gods tried to wash us back to Mona, too."

Valerius looked like a worn shoe. "Suetonius, we got here as fast as I could push the men. Any harder, and they would not have feet."

Suetonius' laughter burst free like a cork from a fermented bottle. "Well, you are here, my friend. At the perfect moment."

The officers rode forward and dismounted, handing off the reins to nearby soldiers. Curious smiles lurked beneath their red crests as they strode forward.

"Lubrius! Cicerio! It is good to see you. How are the druids?"

"Gone, consul," the stout, blond-haired legate answered. "Tribune Cordus remained with the Xth cohort to see that our time was not wasted."

"Excellent, Lubrius. Excellent." However, he may well need those men who had remained behind.

The officer's dark brown eyes searched his. "Are the reports true, consul? Two cities lost?"

"Three. Now that you are here, they will pay for every life taken."

Suetonius motioned to Julius. "Tribune, see the men back to the fort."

With both legions fed and settled in their tents, Julius placed his helmet on the small table. For a second, he studied the laticlavius' black and white crest made of stiffened horsehair and the white cape of command. He never dreamed he would wear such a crest, at least so soon. Nor had he expected it to carry such demands as it did. No heavier than the black one, this one settled on his head like a boulder.

Yet, a trickle of pride ran through him. He glanced at his bandaged hand. Had the gods willed this? Were they watching?

Lugh removed the white cape, hemmed with dirt now, as Julius' uncle stepped through the tent flaps and dropped onto the bench, dangling his arms off his knees.

"Uncle," Julius said as Lugh continued to remove the armor.

"Nephew."

The weight of his uncle's gaze bore down heavier than the crest. "You look tired. Go rest. We can talk tomorrow," Julius stated, not wanting to talk to the man.

"Is that an order, tribune?"

"No." Julius took a goblet of wine from Lugh, who offered a second one to his uncle.

"Leave us," he said in Iceni. Lugh nodded and walked outside.

"Still learning that shit Britanni talk, I see." Valerius emptied the goblet. "That little bastard should be learning Latin."

"Knows it better than you do." Julius sagged into his desk chair. "Knowing Iceni has already come in handy. Our scouts caught two of their warriors. They never expected me to understand what they said."

"What did you find out?"

"Nothing that we did not already know."

"Where are the prisoners now?"

Julius stretched back in his chair. The presence of his uncle was bothersome. The man had not come simply to be greeted with open arms by his nephew. "They were sent to the IXth."

"After what the Hispana experienced, I am sure they were well taken care of." His uncle sat up and twisted, popping his back. With a long sigh, a smirk appeared on the man's face. "Know where that girl slave of yours is?"

He rubbed the burning wound across his palm. "Somewhere with her people."

"Best be forgetting her and concentrating on your wife. Heard anything from your wife?"

Julius shook his head. If he got anything from Domitia now, it would be divorce papers from her father. "More wine?"

Valerius offered his cup. Julius poured.

The centurion stretched back with a sigh. "I cannot believe Suetonius let the bitch get this far."

"Better to lose a city than a province," Julius recited the consul's words and toasted his uncle.

"But three!" Valerius set the goblet on the desk. "And did I hear him right? Postumus refused a direct order?"

"And I do believe the camp prefect will be dead or without balls before Suetonius leaves here," Julius assured him as he swirled his wine.

"I completely agree there." Valerius' rough hands smacked his ruddy knees. "Well, we will make sure everything is in order for tomorrow." His uncle stood. "Suetonius wants us drilling. The men are not going to like it." He stopped at the tent flaps. "So, you know, he told me he is glad that he made you his laticlavius. You must not have screwed up too much. That will be to your advantage when you run for the Senate."

Julius climbed the steps to the south guard station as thunder rumbled like war drums and the sky released another heavy downpour for the second day in a row. He leaned back against one of the support poles and pulled Rhianna's pendant into view. A burst of laughter broke from below in the nearest row of tents. Yelling turned into threats.

"Heard you were up here."

Julius turned. "Marcus?"

Marcus drew his red cape around him as the leather canopy tore at its ties. "You must be desperate to come out in this shit. How is your hand?"

"Better." Julius ran his thumb over the scar that continually throbbed as if to remind him of his oath.

Marcus nodded at Rhianna's pendant resting on the bandage. "How are you going to explain that to your new wife?"

"Did already." Julius smirked. "I am certain a divorce awaits me when Rhianna and I go back to Rome." He dropped the pendant under his cuirass.

Thunder cracked overhead, releasing sheets of rain, blanketing everything from view.

"Reports are they outnumber us three to one. True?" Julius nodded.

"At least three-to-one odds."

"Explains why he has us drilling so hard."

Lightning cut through the black clouds, releasing an explosion of thunder.

Marcus growled, "Enough of this shit. I will be in my tent, warm and dry if you want to join me."

Julius leaned back against the support pole as Marcus disappeared down the steps. He imagined Rhianna warm and dry in his tent, smiling, coming to him. He could feel her sliding the necklace over his head again and whispering, "As long as you wear this…"

He lifted the Iceni pendant to his lips and kissed it. "Rhianna, be safe. I will find you."

Chapter 54

THE RIVER TOW'S BANKS HAD FLOODED from the recent storms. The mud on either side of the road forced riders and chariots to use the Roman roadway. Riding with Marleth on her wagon, Rhianna looked back at the long drab snake of people following the leaders' chariots. It strung out in a single column with no end in sight.

The blatant desire to end this rode on faces like masks. All anyone overheard was talk of going home and surviving the winter. There had been one good change that had happened since joining her mother's revolt. The young people of all the tribes now walked together, holding hands, laughing, talking, and working together. She hoped that continued.

Calgacus rode close to his father's chariot, handed Diras two rabbits, and then dropped two more into her wagon bed, carrying the two remaining bags of grain.

"I'll find more." He wheeled Aerie away.

A warm sense of contentment trickled through her. When this ended, Calgacus had assured her that he would adopt Neeca, allowing hope to blossom for the child she carried.

Her mother motioned to stop on a rise by the busy river where a wide filled-in ditch encircled row of black dots from dead campfires. Rhianna recognized everything. Roman tents. Roman fire pits. A Roman fort. She recognized it all as if it had remained in existence.

As everyone spread out over the damp ground for the night, the leaders stopped where the poke holes of officers' tents had been. She wondered if Julius had slept exactly where her wagon stopped. She could see it. Right here.

She could envision his personal trunks stacked along the tent wall, his desk centered right there on the wood flooring, even the flame of the oil lamp. And his cot would be over there—where their child was conceived. She reached to touch the stanchion that had held his armor and helmet.

"Good place for tonight."

She jerked her hand away at the sound of Calgacus' voice as he tied Aerie to the wagon wheels and walked to her, smiling. "At least it's drier here than most."

Tents and wagons had begun sprawling both in and out of the ring of dirt, showing nothing resembling the Romans' pristine design. Calgacus' mother had warriors setting her tent where Decianus' tent would have been, which meant their tent would set up beside it.

Rhianna didn't want to be any closer to Julius' tent area than possible. "No, we can't stay here. Not here. Down by the river. It will be better there."

He frowned. "Rhianna, it's a bog down there."

"Don't be silly, Rhianna." Marleth grinned as she pulled blankets from her wagon. "This is as good a place." The woman motioned to Orvic and another warrior. "Help her set her tent. I can do the rest here."

"No."

All afternoon, the druid priests had collected wood for the sacrifices before the leaders' tents, and now they chanted and danced around a wooden pyre. Myrradin expected everyone to gather for the gods' protection from all of the gods one last time before they brought victory over the Romans.

Fury raged in Rhianna as she stabbed the needle into a hole in Neeca's dress. "I'm not going."

Calgacus stopped sharpening his gladius. "Rhianna, please. Everyone expects us to be there."

She shook her head in defiance. She couldn't endure that as well as the images of Julius surrounding her. "Go. You and all the other warriors. But I can't."

He reached to draw her close, but she jerked out of his reach.

"Rhianna, tomorrow it's over. We go home. Isn't that what you want?"

She looked at her fire, trying to block the images of Julius sitting at his desk, listening. "It's what I've wanted all along." She looked at her husband. "But will it be over tomorrow? Will it, Calgacus?"

"It will be. I promise."

Tancorix appeared by the wagon, somber and serious. "Calgacus, Myrradin wants Aerie and Skye."

Calgacus wheeled to face the warrior. "Why? What for?" The man shuffled his feet, uncomfortable with his answer.

"He says the goddess wants all things that submitted to Rome given to her."

Rhianna dropped the needle. "No! Not Aerie. Not Skye." The stallions were the last of her father's things. They had not submitted to the Romans. Like her, they had no choice in the matter.

She jolted to her feet and grabbed Calgacus' arm. "It's not Andraste who wants them. It's Myrradin. He wants them to make a grand show. Neither Aerie nor Skye submitted to Rome. They had no choice. We had a choice. Don't let him do this. Please, Calgacus, don't let this happen."

Two priests appeared behind Tancorix. The shorter, more muscular druid stiffened with arrogance. "They allowed the Romans to ride them."

"No, they didn't." Rhianna wheeled on the apprentice. "No more than we did. Are you going to sacrifice every man who built their temple? Every man who raised crops that the Romans claimed as taxes? Every woman who was raped by them?"

The other lifted his pointy chin. "Andraste has spoken. She wants the horses."

Rhianna's mind raced to save her father's stallions. Yet who dared to go up against Myrradin's power now? Everyone believed he had a direct connection to the gods. He was their voice and their speaker.

The priests began untying Aerie's rope to lead him away. She grabbed for the lead line. The stallion reared. "Liars! All of you. Andraste doesn't want any of this." Calgacus jerked her away.

"Calgacus, I was there. So were you. You know both stallions fought the instant they heard the whistle."

"Yes. Rhianna, we were there." Tears lingered in his eyes; his voice cold enough to freeze her. "Don't do this."

Blood rushed to her head, dizzying her with hatred. She wanted to cut their hearts out for the goddess. A much better sacrifice.

"Will my mother let you sacrifice the Iceni women for letting the soldiers ride us?"

Both priests glared at her and then her belly. "The goddess has spoken."

She turned, ready to beg, but Calgacus had claimed his helmet, shield, all of Aerie's trappings, and had started toward the river.

Rhianna raced through the tall reeds and found him on the bank of the river, his arms filled with his armor and weapons. "Gods of our people," his voice raised to the night sky. "If you wish all that the Romans have touched, take these as well."

"NO!" He needed those weapons to protect her and her child. The gods couldn't take him from her. Not now. Not ever. Please!

Before she could stop him, he hoisted everything into the river. The Roman gladius sank into the black liquid. His helmet! Bridles! Saddle! Shield! Roman metal-ringed cloth! It all disappeared from view. All but Cadaryn.

He just stood there like a statue as the river passed. She wanted to dive in and retrieve everything and give everything back, so nothing would happen to him.

The night air filled with a horse's scream. His arm trembled. Seconds passed as another scream drifted on the air. A cheer from the crowds resounded in the darkness as tears drizzled down his cheeks.

She clutched his iron hard arm. "Calgacus, let's leave now. Go north, like you said."

"We leave when this is over."

Chapter 55

SWEAT POURED BETWEEN JULIUS' SHOULDERS as he stood before Suetonius' tent to direct the review of the legions. He had attended parade processions before, but always with the rest of the men, not as the one responsible for it. If one thing went wrong, the men would see it as a slight to the gods.

The guards outside the consul's tent jerked to attention as Suetonius appeared.

"Attention!" was barked.

The tribunes and legates braced, eyes riveted straight ahead, as the consul strode from his tent toward the reviewing field.

Julius stepped in behind him and all the rest of the officers followed according to rank. In step, they strode to the parade field. The cornicens announced their arrival. The men jerked stiffer in attention, eyes straight and blank.

Suetonius led them past the standards of the legions, various cavalry, and auxiliary units, before the field gleaming with polished armor, standing in perfect squares. Each soldier held a red shield before him and a glinting blackened pilum at his side.

Cornicens played as the officers climbed the steps of the platform that released the scent of freshly hewn lumber. Julius halted behind the consul, placing his hands behind his back, while the other officers and tribunes took up positions to his rear.

"Salute to Rome!" roared Julius.

Cornicens blared the order. The soldiers' right arms rose together, pointing a bit above their shoulders with palms vertical, fingers straight up. The sound of ten thousand men in one voice thundered through the air.

"People of Rome, we salute you!"

Arms snapped back to sides in one motion. Suetonius nodded and drew a breath to speak. "It is an honor to view such fine soldiers as I see before me. I apologize for this honor ceremony being late, but you are aware of the reasons. Be assured your deeds and efforts for Rome are not forgotten. Be assured those reports have reached the emperor. Each and every one of you brings pride and honor to Jupiter himself. To Rome. To the province of Britannia. And to your families. It is my honor to be in your presence." No one moved a muscle, but the air seemed to relax.

Julius motioned to a clerk, holding a gold chest, to step forward and open a box. The clerk removed a scroll and presented it to Julius. "Tiberius Cicerio Poetovio," he yelled out.

Another clerk handed the consul a rolled, embroidered flag as the centurion of the IInd cohort strode forward from the front line and then dropped to one knee before Suetonius.

"For outstanding service during the western battles, I award you this banner of recognition," the consul said. "Stand and receive."

The centurion stood, fighting a smile, and accepted the rolled flag. Another name was called. And another. Many of the men receiving the awards were from his IXth and Xth cohorts that Julius had recommended.

The last scroll was removed from the box and was handed to Suetonius. "Gnaeus Julius Agricola."

Stunned into absolute ice, Julius forced himself to step in front of the consul and drop to one knee, his heart thundering like a drum.

Suetonius' voice continued to carry out to the men. "For outstanding service during the assault at Mona, for taking charge of the VIIIth and the IXth cohorts and bringing victory to all, I award you this banner."

The consul unfolded a red fabric fringed with gold before everyone. On the small flag blazed an embroidered gold boar with the letters of the legion he fought his first battle with: Legio XXth Valeria.

Suetonius handed him the small banner. "Well done, Julius."

"Gratitude, consul." He rose, spun sharply about, and stepped back behind Suetonius, struggling to keep from looking at the rolled fabric clasped in his palm.

Suetonius slowly scanned the men. The air drew crisp. "I stand before you with a challenge. As you know, some of the tribes of Britannia believe they can break the might of Rome. They believe they can make us run. They believe we fear them. They believe their gods are greater than our gods!"

The silver lines snarled as they listened. "I ask you—do we accept this challenge?"

"Yes!" The answer was deafening.

The consul nodded as he waited until the men quieted. "I promise you that you will see these fools break before you. They will feel your steel, your courage . . . and flee. These glories are yours! Take this victory! And all will be yours! By the power of Rome . . . this I promise!"

The men cheered and lashed out with their pilums. The roar was thunderous.

Suetonius pointed to the right and yelled over the rumble pounding the ground.

"Are you ready?"

"We are ready!"

Suetonius yelled to the center. "Are you ready?"

"We are ready!"

Then Suetonius turned to the left and then swept his hand cross the field.

"Are! You! Ready?"

"We! Are! Ready!"

Even the plank where the officers stood vibrated with the answer.

"Then go and prepare for victory!"

Suetonius scanned the faces of the officers and centurions gathered in his tent. Valerius stood to his right. Julius stood to his left. Each stiff and upright as any statue.

It was obvious the recognition had had its effect on Julius. Rome had recognized him. Something few ever received so soon, even for a lifetime of service.

As Val had said after the review, "Now, maybe the stupid little fool will get his thoughts off this Britanni bitch and get them back on the matters of his family and Rome."

Suetonius cleared his throat and mind of Val's comment and focused it on what was before him. "Tomorrow, we finally meet these Britanni bastards. I believe, as do the gods, that the odds are in our favor even though they outnumber us.

"However, if that is not the case and Rome loses the province, we all will face death and humiliation either here or in Rome."

The centurions, resting on one knee, grumbled and looked to one another. The tribunes sighed heavily, knowing every order rested on them.

"Like Hades that's going to happen tomorrow," Val announced.

"Right now," Suetonius continued, "the Britanni are celebrating their victory. They drink, cheer, dance, and think that just by their numbers they have destroyed Rome."

"May Bacchus curse their brains," someone said from the back. Chuckles rippled, and Suetonius smiled at the remark.

"I totally agree, and I am certain their gods will so bless them." He pointed back at the wall map behind him. "I commend you all for clearing the hills as ordered. Well done. I am pleased that a few of you had the energy to cheer on the tribune and decurio in their wrestling match." More chuckles rippled the tent while Julius and Marcus shot glances at each other, their mouths twitching with defiant smiles.

Pointing at the back map, Suetonius drew his finger along the defile between the hills. "This throat is what makes our battle plan perfect. The horde will start with their usual assault of chariots. They will race through here and race back over the hills to come at us again. This is where the hidden stumps will surprise them as their ponies stumble and their lovely chariots break apart. Those who make it through will leave their chariots and join the mass of warriors who will charge through here with everything they have."

"Let them come."

Suetonius smiled at the interruption. "Yes, let them come." He ran his finger along the plain sandwiched between the forest and the rise behind the twin hills. "We will be here, waiting. Not one man is to flinch or fart until ordered. Is that clear?"

Heads nodded.

"What you remember at the Isle of Mona will be child's play in comparison. The ground will tremble when they charge, their war cries thunderous. I want all standards to the rear. I do not want any one of the bastards coming close to one eagle. The scorpions and ballistae will be released on the chariots and as the fools flood into the defile. Nevertheless, that will not deter their advance. It will only slow them down."

He looked directly at the group of centurions in charge of the firing weapons. "I will rely totally on your judgment. Fire at will."

The weathered faces nodded assent.

"Tribunes, you have your assigned cohorts. You know where they will be. At the start, however, you will not stand with them. You will remain with me and the laticlavius here on the rise. When ordered to advance into a single pointed wedge, you will break away to your cohorts."

The tribunes settled with the order.

One centurion frowned.

"What is it, centurio?"

"A single wedge, consul?"

"Yes. In order to advance in line forward until we clear the defile, and then swiftly move into a single line, each forming their own wedge. And you will proceed to mow them down like grass."

He looked to Marcus. "The cavalry will ride over the twin hills until we clear the defile, and then advance to the flanks." Suetonius smiled. "You will keep the fools from surrounding us and drive them back to the center."

Marcus nodded. "Consider it done, consul."

"It is up to the rest of you to stay together, listen for orders, and not stop until you hear the order to halt." Suetonius placed both hands at his waist and looked into the eyes of the men before him. "And that will only happen when every one of these bastards is dead."

Chapter 56

D AWN SEEPED INTO THE BLACK SKY as Rhianna made a small fire beneath the dense canopy of overhanging branches. Faolan had found them by the river where Calgacus sat cross-legged with Cadaryn lying across his thighs.

Relinquishing Aerie had enraged her, but it had devastated him. He had stared either at the scurrying river or his father's sword all night.

She had endured nightmares of Julius coming for her, calling her name. When he found her, she was standing alone amid the carnage of a bloody battlefield. Then, as he reached for her, Calgacus rose from the slaughtered, his battle cry ringing in her ears.

An invisible force surrounded her while both men circled—Julius stalwart and calculating, Calgacus roaring in a full war lust. A bundle moved at her feet, and she had screamed herself awake.

Calgacus never heard her. Nor had he moved while she built the fire and prepared possibly their last meal together. The grain cakes had been made with her tears. "Calgacus, it's ready."

He didn't move.

She went to him and touched his shoulder. "Please. Eat. Talk to me. Move. You're scaring me."

He looked up at her as if she were a stranger and then took a grain cake, set it on the blade of the sword, and pulled her down beside him. "You were right about Myrradin."

As much as she relished hearing what she had known, she didn't want to. "Father never trusted him. He doesn't care what the gods want. He'll destroy anything for power. You. Me. Anything."

Calgacus rested his hand on the baby and nodded. "I'll see he never hurts you or our child."

She touched his serious, dark face to feel reality, to feel flesh. Pressing his mustache aside, she drew his mouth to hers. Their bodies ignited in a desperate need to be one.

Time halted as their souls danced, never to be separated even in death. Still, the fear of losing him tore through her. What they had now had become so much more than just protecting the child. Who would love her? How would she live without him? She didn't want answers.

She looked up at the man staring at the canopy of trees brushing in the morning air. "Please, Calgacus. Let's leave now. Go north. Go anywhere, but not stay here."

He shook his head. "I can't, Rhianna."

He claimed one of their cups filled with river water and stirred the blue powder with his finger. Naked to the gods, he stood to present the cup to the rosy dawn.

"To all the gods, I beg you to protect Rhianna, daughter of Prasutagus, daughter of the Iceni and the mother of our child. Keep them alive as I fight to bring you glory and care for all that is yours."

He looked to her. "Will you cover me with your protection?"

She had never drawn with the sacred paint. Her hands trembled as she accepted the bowl and then lifted it the morning sky. "Gods of our ancestors, I beg you to return Calgacus, son of Diras, son of the Trinovante, to me alive that we may share a life that honors you."

After dipping her finger in the paint, she drew identical circles over his heart, and then her fingers claimed a life of their own, directing where and how she painted wavy streaks—over his bulging arm muscles, down his hands, his back, and across his broad shoulders. More blue designs flowed around his thighs and belly.

With the last of the paint, she drew a long blue stain down her forehead to her chin.

"I go with you. May the gods protect you, Calgacus, son of the Trinovante, and bring you back to me," she whispered. His gaze broke from the sun bleeding across the sky.

His sword dropped from his hands, and he yanked her to him. His lips fell on hers. She melted into his arms and feasted on his strength flowing into her.

He released her and reclaimed Cadaryn, lying in the grass. His hard gaze returned. "Rhianna, stay with the wagon. I'll come for you."

Faolan rose, his black tail wagging. "Stay. Guard."

Julius held his scarred palm forward and silently repeated his plea to Venus to protect Rhianna. He and the other officers knelt with Suetonius in the consul's tent as dawn was dedicated to the gods.

With the white wool cape covering his head, Suetonius raised both palms upward and began the ritual plea to the gods at the first glow of Apollo's chariot. "Jupiter Optimus Maximus, may you find our sacrifice favorable . . ."

Finishing the familiar litany, he stepped back from the lararium and knelt close to Julius, palm out, his bowed head covered. The priest broke the neck of a hawk and then drained its blood onto a candle. The odor of burning blood rose thick and malevolent as he inspected the bird's entrails. "Omens are excellent, consul. You will be victorious this day."

All rose with Suetonius and recited, "Hail Jupiter. Hail Rome. We will bring you victory."

The consul turned to face everyone. "Now go and see that we do."

As the officers and centurions solemnly left, Julius waited beside Suetonius staring at the rising sun. "I pray we bring the bitch nothing but destruction," he muttered.

"The men will."

Suetonius jerked as if he had forgotten Julius stood nearby. "It will not be easy, Julius. None of this will be." He released a heavy sigh. "But we have a very good chance if the men execute as planned." A façade of confidence settled over the man. "Now come, let us see that they do."

Chapter 57

WHILE FAOLAN BOUNDED BACK AND FORTH in the empty wagon, Rhianna followed Marleth's wagon that led the rest of the women and children filling the various wagons spilling onto the river plain. Some cheered. Others rode in silence, carrying the same worry as Rhianna. Their men were out there. Would they come back?

Warriors raced chariots back and forth before the two hills, their war cries flooding the plain. Drums thundered. Horns blared their deep-throated cries. Massive clots of men brandished weapons at the distant rise behind the twin hills. It was all an insanity meant to strike fear in the enemy's gods and empower their own.

A lanky youth with a sling in one hand and a full pouch of river rocks bouncing at his waist ran toward Marleth's wagon. Like Calgacus, his body displayed the blue war paint. "The foxes are trapped in their hole!" he yelled.

Rhianna's heart slammed against her ribs.

"Where?"

"There." He swung his arm behind him, toward the barren hills cloaked by a forest behind them where Roman soldiers stood in straight rows of perfect squares like polished silver statues ornamented with red crests, glittering pilums, and large red shields. At either end, cavalry sat on horses nodding heads and stamping at biting flies.

Behind this, specks of gold and silver and dots of white, red, and black crests decorated two lines of men, also on horseback. They, too, waited like statues.

Between her and the soldiers, frenzied warriors raced before women and children standing on wagon seats, screaming and yelling. "Destroy Rome! Kill them! Kill them all!"

Morrigan drew the lathered ponies to a halt by the wagon.

"Rhianna, with me!" Boudica called out from her chariot's platform.

Fury screamed up Rhianna's spine. "I want no part of this, mother. I want it over and to go home."

The iron gaze pierced her like a spear. "You will ride with me, daughter of the Iceni, and show your loyalties, or die by your loyalties."

"I—"

"Rhianna." Calgacus walked toward the wagon. "Go with her."

She wanted him to carry her away. Nothing more. "No, I want to wait here, with the wagon, for you."

His gaze hit her like a fist. "Do as I ask, Rhianna. Go with your mother." He shifted his attention to Morrigan. "Then bring her back here."

Morrigan's ponies pawed the ground. "I will. Then, Tancorix and I will join you with the others."

Rhianna forced herself to step up beside her mother and clasped the front of the chariot as Morrigan gave the ponies their freedom, and they bolted across the river plain. The wind tore at her hair, streaming it out behind her like a flag.

Morrigan made a wide sweep before the line of wagons and warriors and then stopped in the center of the roaring mass. The rest of the chariots gathered on either side.

With Calgacus in Guntar's chariot next to her, Tancorix drew Diras' chariot beside him. Calgacus' gaze was blind to all but duty, as were his warriors, gathered on foot behind the chariots.

Rhianna tightened her grip on the leather wall of her mother's chariot as Boudica's voice cut through the insanity, calming the roars.

"See and know Rome's compassion!" Boudica ripped away her tunic, displaying the white scars covering her flesh. Rhianna's skin crawled as Morrigan walked the chariot before the two growling lines, allowing people to observe what awaited them if they failed.

"Rome knows no compassion. To you or your daughters! To your sons! They only know greed! They want what is ours. They want to destroy us."

She waited a few strides. Boudica thrust the black lance skyward. "But they will fail this day!"

The ponies broke into a trot, jerking the chariot faster between the lines. "Today, we gain our revenge! Today, we take back what is ours! Today, we finally cleanse our lands of Roman filth! TODAY!"

Everyone roared as she passed. Weapons brandished in the air. Swords pounded on shields. All silenced as Morrigan stopped the chariot before the leaders again.

"Follow me to victory! Follow me and DESTROY ROME!" Boudica yelled.

"Stop. Let me out! Now!" Rhianna ordered.

Morrigan's ponies reared long enough for her to jump free of the chariot seconds before they bolted into a full run toward the valley.

Horns bellowed. Drums thundered again. Anger frothed. Hatred pummeled the air.

It was like watching a cat playing with its next victim, Julius thought. Beautiful and deadly. Crazed Britanni warriors raced chariots across the river plain like the twisting tentacles of a venomous hydra. The thundering chariots, bellowing war cries, pounding drums, and blasting horns threatened to control his heartbeat.

The endless swarm of warriors expanded like a deep breath, only to withdraw to breathe again. Standing between this heaving insanity stood Rome's quiet, solid strength.

All along the back rise, the XXth Valeria stretched beside the XIVth Gemina's soldiers, both legions glinting in their armor, bejeweled with red crests gleaming like rubies.

Each soldier had planted his shield before him and held two pila at his right side, each waiting in perfect squares. At the right front corner of each stood the centurions, displaying their significant black and white crests, starting with his uncle's white crest with the XIVth's I[st] cohort, and ending with Fabius' black crest with the Xth cohort of the XXth Valeria.

In the center of each gleaming square rose its identifying red banner, its signum, held by the signifier. With the sway of his banner, he relayed orders to the centurion. All relayed by the cornicens to the center soldier, the optio, who not only heard the order but was responsible to see that no soldier fled from the fight.

Behind the optio stood the cohort's cornicens, ready with their golden horns, each fixated to the sounds that would replay the consul's cornicens and drums that stretched in a short line before Imperious.

Behind Suetonius' cornicens, the black crests of the tribunes and the red-crested legates sat on still horses. At the consul's command, they would dash away to their assigned positions.

Outside the lines of sparkling soldiers stood the auxiliary with their multitude of colors: forest greens, leather browns, and mustard yellows. Some were on horseback, some on foot, and all holding curving bows, lethal arrows, strange swords, and a variety of shields.

Julius found Marcus' red and black crest at the far–left end of the formation. His friend held his horse before his cavalry unit identical to the cavalry unit at the other end. All that moved were the restlessly swishing tails of the horses.

Scattered about the grassy ridge were the ballistae and scorpions. Behind each were baskets of huge arrows capable of penetrating the guts of three men or tearing apart any chariot. Their arrow points sparkled dangerously in the mid-day sun. Behind each ballista rose mountainous piles of stones, ready to obliterate anything it hailed on.

Before him stretched ten thousand men awaiting that one order that would bring them all to life, from that one man beside Julius—Gaius Suetonius Paulinus, imperial consul of Rome. A gluttonous chuckle rippled from the throat of that man.

Humor? Julius studied the consul for some explanation, as the sun blazed down on his white crest, white cape, and white horse as if he were turning into a god.

Following the consul's gaze, Julius found the answer. The venomous hydra was drawing its wagons along the riverbank, creating a wall that would lock in its warriors, allowing no one to escape. They had created their own trap!

Chapter 58

JULIUS' GAZE TRAVELED WITH THE RIDER whose golden hair lashed from Boudica's chariot racing back and forth before her throng. Rhianna! She lives!

Joy surged through him to his horse. The animal reared slightly and twisted, bumping into Imperious. Suetonius glared at the disruptive movement that was not to happen.

However, the flood of chariots flooding into the defile and over the twin hills jerked his attention back.

"Ballistae! Tormenta!"

Drums thundered. The cornicens raised their golden horns and sounded the order. Rows of siege engines immediately began firing. Arrows screamed as they were released from the scorpions. The swinging ballistae threw the stones like muted thumps of drums as they launched rocks like an avalanche.

A scorpion bolt slammed into a chariot, lifting it from the ground, rolling it over and twisting the ponies onto each other. Another shot into a driver's belly and the warrior behind him, yanking both off a second chariot.

The ponies raced onto the nearest hill, where they tripped on the hidden stumps. More chariots attempted to veer around and found it impossible. They were only to be caught in the oncoming stampede of warriors as they retreated down the hillsides.

The siege engines continued blasting missiles onto the gush of warriors that poured into the defile like flash flood. Here and there, lances reached the soldiers who simply lifted their shields, and the weapons merely bounced and bumbled to the ground.

Calgacus staggered to a halt as a huge arrow cut through the Dobunni leader and his driver's chariot, lifting it into the air. Rocks rained down like hail, slamming into everyone and everything as they charged toward the Romans just standing there like statues. Just standing there!

On the side hills, chariots flipped and smashed into each other or they slammed over some invisible object that tripped the ponies' legs out from under them, and they lay there screaming in their harnesses.

A chariot raced down the slope to avoid the collision covering the hills. One of the Roman arrows shot into the warrior and driver, ripping them into the air.

His father's chariot bolted back out to the river plain and almost tipped as Tancorix drove the ponies along the steepest slope of the hill. Boudica's chariot continued to race back and forth before the Romans, up one side of a hill and down the other.

The warriors close to the Roman lines launched their lances. Red rose to shield the soldiers, letting the weapons simply bounce away. The shields peeled apart, and the Romans' narrow-throated pila flew into the air.

One came at Calgacus. He lifted his shield and felt the point slide through it, stopping inches from his face. He tossed it aside and then shoved the man next to him away for more room to use Cadaryn.

The effort did little good. The press of warriors became too thick to move anywhere but forward. The hills on either side held them close like sides of a bowl.

More pila shot from the middle formation. One plunged into Morrigan's stomach, ripping her from the chariot. Another instantly dropped one of Boudica's ponies. The other animal twisted with the chariot, tossing the Iceni queen from view.

He scanned all those with him. Tancorix and his father had found him. They were shoulder-to-shoulder, barely able to lift new-found shields from the press of warriors.

Drums thundered. The clarion sound of the Roman horns filled the air. The entire length of silver statues stirred to life.

Calgacus jerked his attention toward the rise as the center formation started forward, followed by the formations at its sides. They came slow and steady, beating the sides of their gladii against their shields with each step.

A fury welled inside him. Not only were the Romans tyrants, but they hid behind their shields like cowards, never standing alone to fight man to man. Cowards before their own gods.

May Andraste see and hear. The Romans are mine!

His war cry bellowed from his soul, rallying all nearby as together they charged forward.

"To victory!" Suetonius called out.

"To victory!" the tribunes echoed. They broke from the command position and galloped after their assigned cohorts, already moving forward into the wedge formation. Julius' horse reared to join them, as he wanted to do.

He silently cursed the command that kept him rooted next to the consul and away from Rhianna. He stroked the animal's neck as his gaze swept the wall of wagons for her, but there was no trace of golden hair.

A war cry sounded. For a second, he thought he had heard that somewhere before, but it was drowned out by the warriors charging. The sound of their full-throated yell drove them forward and onto the Roman shields.

A group of soldiers broke through the rear of the advancing line and then started up the hill with a captive. Four of the consul's guards raced down and dismounted to claim whatever the soldiers were dragging with them. A woman.

"Is that who I think it is?" Suetonius asked with glee dancing in his eyes.

Julius nodded. "Yes. The Iceni queen."

"So that's her. The bitch who thought she could destroy me. Nero will enjoy my little prize. Will he not?" His laugh was worse than his smile.

The soldiers shoved Boudica before Imperious.

"The first centurio sends his regards. We bring you the female Britanni leader," one of the guards announced.

She stood to her full height, revealing the scars that coated her body. They shoved her to her knees, and Suetonius rode closer, admiring the nude woman. "I must say, Decianus did his work well."

"Die, you filthy Roman!" Her spit floated through the air to Suetonius.

He lifted the edge of his cloak to remove the insult that fell on his arm. "Make sure she observes what happens to all those who challenge the might of Rome."

Boudica twisted from the view as the guards jerked her to her feet, gripping her chin in the direction of the valley before her. Her heart wilted as sharp whistles cut the air, ordering soldiers in the front of the formation to shift positions with the second line, keeping the destruction fresh enough to eat through her warriors now pressed tightly into the juncture of the hills.

Diras' words rang in Boudica's ears. *Even if the snake does rejoin with its head, we have nothing to fear. We outnumber the Romans ten fold.*

Now her people charged as if by numbers alone they could stampede over the Romans. Yet her warriors could do little more than shove their knives into shields, while the enemy's gladii stabbed into exposed flesh.

As the formation pressed forward, the rear lines feasted on what the front lines fed them. Bodies were crushed beneath hobnailed boots, stabbed, and left to die.

The Roman consul, the head of the snake, laughed gloriously and then spewed his poison.

"Exquisite is it not?"

Chapter 59

WATCHING FROM HER WAGON, Rhianna tightened the shawl around her shoulders as if she were cold. Yet the day was warm and clear. The women watching from their wagons lining the river's edge suddenly fell silent as the warriors raced out of the defile like wet rats.

"What's wrong?" Neeca screamed. "What's wrong?" Id scrambled off the wagon and disappeared in the underbrush. "I don't know. I don't know." All she did know was that wasn't supposed to happen.

Women began bolting toward the river, as she should. As Neeca should. But she had said she'd wait for Calgacus in the wagon.

She peeled the girl's arms from her waist. "Neeca, go. Go check on the oxen. Take Faolan with you. He'll protect you."

The girl jumped from the wagon and raced toward the river with all the others. Faolan followed at her heels.

"I told them you should be the sacrifice."

The malicious voice wheeled Rhianna around to Myrradin, who was walking toward the wagon. A knife gleamed in his right hand. "No one will stop me now."

She tried to back away, but the wagon bench cut into her knees, dropping her to the seat.

"I know you carry the Roman's child. It belongs to Andraste." His eyes gleamed with a murderous gaze. "Now your blood must be spilled so that Romans will die! Now!"

She leaped into the empty wagon bed.

"My child has nothing to do with this!" She grappled for Calgacus' knife at her waist and jumped from the end of the wagon.

Myrradin followed. "Andraste demands it!"

She turned to run for the water, but his sharp fingers clutched her arm and swung her around. His blade gleamed high over his shoulder, ready to plunge into the babe.

Faolan suddenly ripped into the druid's neck. Myrradin howled as man and dog fell and rolled. Rhianna backed closer toward the river as the druid drove his blade into dog's side.

"Consul, the tribune to the VIth and VIIth cohorts is down!"

Suetonius studied the gasping young soldier and then looked at Julius. "Take Liberius' place."

A prayer answered. Julius saluted and then jabbed both heels into the horse's sides. His horse sprang into action, much slower than his heart.

The vice around his chest eased with every stride closer to his cohorts and to the Britanni wagons, where Rhianna had to be. The rear of the VIth and VIIth drew closer to the mouth of the defile where the thunder of weapons and war cries made thinking impossible.

The sound of Suetonius' drums and his cornicens barely carried over the thunderous roar of battle. Immediately, the wedged line opened as it strode onto the river plain like a saw blade of cohorts. Cavalry engulfed each end, protecting the formation and routing those trying to surround the soldiers.

Calgacus couldn't breathe. He couldn't move. He couldn't lift Cadaryn an inch from his body, much less swing it. The press of warriors kept pushing him forward, as the Romans continued plunging their blades beyond the shield wall, slamming each man like a stone.

Those in front of him heaved to turn and flee but couldn't. They were caught with nowhere to go. Fighting was impossible. It was like being fed to the silver line. Helpless fear chilled his hot veins, something he had never felt in a battle.

The hungry red wall came closer until he could see eyes glaring over each shield. Teeth snarled from the depths of the silver helmets.

He focused on the Roman directly before him. Gazes locked. He lifted Cadaryn as a shrill whistle blew. The Romans disappeared and another set of eyes appeared, fresh and eager.

The press of warriors behind him drove him closer to the red shields. He shoved the man beside him away for room to fight. However, the man was slammed back at him like a toy. A warrior in front suddenly fell, and a red shield slammed into Calgacus' face with the force of a bull. The metal cracked his cheek, knocking him dizzy.

Cadaryn refused to lift high enough to bear down onto the glaring eyes. He couldn't lift it. Pain exploded in his side. Another pierced his shoulder. A third cut into his thigh. Another shield struck, knocking him on top of fallen warriors. Hard feet stomped on his guts. Feet kicked. Gladius blades stabbed into the warriors around him. The torture passed, only to have more trample over him. The edge of a shield smashed down on his back as if to break it. More feet. *Rhianna! I'm sorry. Rhiann—*

"Andraste will not be denied." Myrradin tossed Faolan aside and staggered to his feet. His face twisted with demonic rage as he lifted his knife, dripping with the dog's blood.

"The goddess doesn't want my child!" Rhianna backed into a rear wagon wheel and gripped the knife until the hilt cut into her palm. "You want my child!"

"She will not be—"

A flash of growling, black fur landed once again on the druid's back, heaving him onto Rhianna's knife.

Myrradin's beady eyes widened as both dog and man fell. Growls melted into whimpers as Faolan lay in the grass. She dropped beside the dog as life twitched from the man sprawled nearby. "Faolan, don't die. Calgacus wants you to be there. Faolan."

The delicate pink tongue licked her hand. She tried lifting him to the wagon, but the dog cried out in pain.

She instantly let go. "Stay. Guard. I need you, Faolan. Please."

His tail struck the ground twice as if to agree and then wilted into the grass.

She dragged her shawl off the wagon bed and wrapped it around his body, tying it tight to stop the blood, enduring the whimpers of pain. Yet the blood poured through it, spawning like a disease.

"Wait, Faolan," she whispered as she stroked the furry cheek. "Wait. Calgacus will come for us. He'll take care of you. I promise. Hold on. Please hold on."

She felt the delicate wetness of the dog's tongue lick her hand one more time. It was hot and white as it fell over the white fangs.

"Faolan, please. No!"

A blood-covered warrior raced past her toward the river. "Go! Run! Romans are coming!"

She froze as bloody warriors raced around the wagons to get to the river. Soldiers covered with gore swarmed in as angry hornets with swords ready to clutch hair or slice necks. One soldier stabbed Marleth. Another, Neeca's friend. A woman, another girl, a boy . . . it didn't matter. They just slaughtered.

Rhianna rolled under her wagon, drew her knees tight, and covered her head with her arms, trying to block it all from her mind. *Please, Andraste, stop this madness. Stop this . . .*

Her wagon fell on its side.

"Look what we have here."

The deep voice broke through the invisible barrier that surrounded her. Every muscle in her body tightened as a hard hand grasped a handful of her hair and lifted her inches from the grass.

Her scream locked in her throat as did her entire body that rolled whichever way the hand jerked.

"She's locked up tight."

"Then we need to unlock her, now don't we?"

She kicked as the soldier settled between her legs and shifted to find a way inside her.

"Love it when they—"

"Get away from her!"

The sound of that voice echoed of another moment. Then she felt a familiar touch lift her in his arms.

"Rhianna? Talk to me. Rhianna, are you all right?"

She stared up at the man with soft, brown eyes, wearing a Roman helmet with a black and white crest.

"J-Julius?"

A smile appeared beneath the cheek guards, the one she remembered from somewhere.

"Yes. Praise Venus in all her glory, you are safe!" Ever so gently, he placed her onto a horse and then vaulted up behind her.

The horse lurched its way over a sea of bodies staring at the sky or faces covered with sprawled arms. Slaves and soldiers plunged daggers into backs and slit throats as they plundered knives, swords, helmets—anything they could find. Flies and crows were already feasting on blue painted flesh.

Thoughts of Calgacus lying among them tore at her. He had to be among them, or he would have already come for her. Her heart shattered.

The horse worked past a warrior lying face down with arms sprawled out. Cadaryn no longer filled his hand. His golden hair tangled in the gore and blood across his back. *Calgacus!* Pain ripped through her.

She had to go to him. She tried to lurch off the horse, but Julius held her to his chest. "Rhianna. No, Rhianna!"

"He needs me." She tore at his arm clamped around her. "Let me go."

"Never again, Rhianna."

Chapter 60

THE SNAKE'S VOICE ECHOED in Boudica's brain. *Exquisite is it not?* No, it wasn't. It was unimaginable. None of this would have happened if the leaders had listened. None of that mattered now. She had failed Prasutagus. She had failed her people.

Images of Morrigan being jerked from the chariot by the Roman arrow flashed in her mind, along with those of the Romans cutting everyone down like a harvest of wheat. She let the guards drag her toward their fort. Every scar burned with each step. She did have one thing left. Her pride. Though tears tore from her heart, no Roman would ever hear her cry or make her beg for mercy. Nor would she allow the Romans to defeat her.

The soldiers stopped, letting Boudica collapse to the ground. They laughed as they made bets that the consul would send her to Rome for his triumph with all the bounty of her people. Another gambled she would be entertainment in their death games, once their emperor was through with her.

How could Andraste allow this? Their gods were no greater than . . . Something soft brushed her leg. How strange she should feel something so delicate after months of feeling nothing but hardness.

The caress drew her attention to a young yew tree, still wearing winterberries on its branches.

The ropes jerked her upward. "On your feet, bitch."

As she struggled to her feet, she cleansed the gentle plant of its nettles and dried berries with her hand. She tossed them into her mouth before the guards could do anything. The bitter taste flooded her mouth as she swallowed what the gods had offered her. Immortality.

"Stand up!"

Boudica heard the order. By the time the guards had dragged her to the Roman leader, she could no longer walk, much less stand. Nor could she think. Prasutagus was there. He had forgiven her.

Her body trembled as if she were standing in a snowstorm. The thick smell of leather sucked her breath away, leaving her nauseated. The gods were coming for her. She felt her spirit start to break free.

"Make her stand."

The guards cupped their arms under her armpits and lifted. She smiled until the face of the scowling snake head appeared before her. She tried hawking spit again, even though her throat remained dry and her jaw didn't understand.

He slapped her, splitting the side of her mouth. There was no pain. Just the taste of her own blood. She would have gasped, but her lungs burned for air. She sagged onto the arms holding her upright.

She didn't feel the hand slap her again. How can a snake slap someone? With its tail? She wanted to laugh but couldn't.

Hands grabbed her fist, peeling open her fingers. An uneaten berry fell. She wouldn't need it.

"Get the medic in here. Now!"

"I'll protect you. We'll build our own home like this. I'll take you away from this, Rhianna. We'll go north. I promise. I have to get Aerie. We have to leave now. Now."

It was dark—midnight dark. Wild terror and screaming horses wailed in Calgacus' brain as he tried to move his arm. Like a foreign object, it failed to move from the rancid mud. When he gasped, urine sucked into his nostrils. He snorted and finally flopped over onto his back.

Gasping, he opened his eyes to the distant shadow of black trees. It was too late to plow fields. Find Rhianna and go away. Build her a house with a fire pit like the one in . . . he couldn't remember.

Pain pierced through his body as he moved his leg. Flapping noises and furious caws surrounded him the moment he heaved over a body.

"Tancorix?"

No response.

"Tancorix."

Another body sprawled nearby. All dead. All staring at the darkness. All bloody and dead. What happened? Then he remembered the line of Roman soldiers. He remembered the feel of the shields smashing everyone backward. Memories returned in flashes.

Rhianna. He needed to find her. His son. Yes. She was right. They should have left. They would go now. Before the Romans came back.

Pain seared through his body as he rolled onto his stomach and pulled himself toward the trees, toward the river where the wagons were.

His arm gave way and dropped him face first into a puddle of bloody urine. Darkness filled with growls and ripping flesh. Wolves. He had to get away. He had to find Rhianna.

His mind blurred with pain as he slid across body after body toward the sweet smell of the river. His mind floated with memories of swimming with Rhianna and hearing her laugh. It drove him on until he slipped into the cool water. How easy it would be to let the water gods have him.

So easy. Luring. No pain. Simply drift away.

He had to find Rhianna before the Roman did.

Chapter 61

DRESSED IN HIS BLACK MOURNING TOGA and red boots, Suetonius gazed at all before him, as did all the other officers with him on the reviewing platform. How many of these funeral rites had he attended? Too many. But this was a victorious moment. The bitch was dead. And her warriors with her. A long pile of broken chariots, swords, black lances, round shields, harness decorations, and anything the Britanni owned that their dead could no longer use, stretched before the platform.

Beyond this, the cornicens formed another line, their horns ready to call the attention of the gods. Rigid lines of cohorts—in full parade dress, polished and perfect—covered the parade field in perfect formations. In front of each cohort stood the eight hundred soldiers who had died destroying the Britanni revolt. Each had been washed and dressed by their brothers, and each was propped up with a pole for the last time.

Drawing the black wool over his head, Suetonius lifted his arms to the sky. "Together we stand one last time with our brothers who gave their lives for Rome. We honor them. We honor their sacrifice. May the gods accept their souls this day." He slowly lowered his arms and nodded to Julius, who yelled, "Attende!"

The cornicens sounded the order, and the snap of armor and men, stiffening to attention, echoed over the field.

Clutching the wool beneath his chin with one hand to keep his head covered, Suetonius stepped from the reviewing stand and walked to the Ist cohort.

The first row of men stepped forward with Valerius and reverently untied their brothers to carefully lay the bodies onto a pyre saturated with oil-drenched wood. Once in place, Suetonius nodded to the dead before walking to the IInd cohort and then the next.

He returned to the official platform and lifted his arms to the sky. "In honor of Rome. In honor of you who bless our great Empire, we send our brothers to your care." Then he began a litany of names of each slain brother, and with the announcement, a pyre exploded to life, releasing the stench of burning flesh into the air.

As flames finished their tasks, Suetonius promised himself he would have Decianus' balls for this. He nodded to Julius to dismiss everyone.

"Exiti!"

The first centurion of each unit stepped forward to lead the men away in perfect rows, leaving only assigned men to guard the fallen. One by one, the cohorts passed the reviewing stand and the pile of booty. Once the Xth cohort passed, the tribunes strode from the reviewing stand. Julius followed and then Suetonius.

Each step felt heavy as he left the parade field. Eight hundred men had died for Rome, and thousands of Britanni had been left to the vultures searching for one last morsel of flesh that the wolves had not eaten.

After the funeral rites had been performed, his uncle strode beside Julius. He could feel the fury pulsing off the man, angry because Rhianna was alive and not dead as the others. She remained alive in his tent because she was his slave and under the protection of Roman law.

"That little cunt of yours better stay in that tent is all I can say," Valerius growled.

Julius stopped outside his tent and faced the polished centurion.

"Just make sure the men know that no one touches my slave. Is that order clear, centurio?"

"As clear as a trumpet, tribune." His uncle's fist hit his chest in mock salute.

Julius relished his small victory. The guards opened the tent flaps for him to step inside. He placed his helmet on the small desk and found Rhianna sitting lifeless on his cot.

Lugh stepped to his side to remove Julius' cape. "She dunna' moved a muscle."

"Go. Help with the wounded." Julius waved a dismissive hand and then sat next to the lifeless being staring at the rug.

"Rhianna." He brushed loose strands of hair from her face. "Rhianna, you are safe now. Here with me." He pulled her pendant from his chest. "Look. I still have it. I still love you."

An eternity seemed to pass until her gaze left the pendant and flashed up at him. "Neeca! Where is she? I have to find her!" She suddenly bolted toward the tent flaps.

He caught her by the waist. "Do not go out there. You know what will happen."

She fought his grip on her, clawing at his arm.

"Where is she?"

"Who? Who is Neeca?"

She wheeled to face him, her eyes wide with panic. "I have to find her, before the druid does."

She fought like a strange banshee.

"Rhianna, I will find her."

Rhianna almost jerked free of his grip. "I have to find Neeca!" She looked up at him as a calmness floated over her. "Faolan is with her." A small smile appeared. "Yes. He'll take care of her." Her brow wrinkled with anger. "But the druid wants my baby. I won't let him have my baby."

"Baby? You are pregnant?"

Rhianna looked up at him; his gaze was deeper than any river. "The druid wants to offer my baby as a Roman sacrifice to the goddess. Don't let them sacrifice my baby! Please?"

"Your baby. The father?" Was the baby his or this Britanni who kidnapped her?

Tears streamed down Rhianna's face. "Yours. Please understand. It's my baby. I can't let Myrradin have it. Please."

Joy beyond joy surged through Julius as he cupped her face with both hands, brushing the river of tears away with his thumbs. "Rhianna, nothing will happen to our child. Nothing."

She stared at him, the haze in her eyes evaporating. "J-Julius?"

"Yes, my love. Our child is safe as long as you stay here."

Chapter 62

Six months later . . .

ENVY BURNED THROUGH SUETONIUS as he watched two lovely wenches pleasuring Valerius on the other side of Cartimanuda's tent. There were times rank did not have privileges. He raised his goblet for more wine and smiled at the girl filling it. "She is lovely, is she not?" The Brigante queen whimpered close to his ear. "Do you want her?" she asked.

He drew away from the queen lying beside him on her large couch. "She pales compared to you." A total but functional lie.

However, after the mess with the Iceni bitch, he had the responsibility to see that this queen profited from her loyalty to Rome by keeping her tribe where they belonged . . . on Brigante land. Had the entire tribe sided with Boudica, Rome might well have lost the entire province. Not that Nero cared either way.

The intention of his visit was to reward her for her loyalty—not her husband's. Spies had reported that Venutius and his band of warriors had assisted the Iceni bitch. Yet the fool was smart enough to leave before the final confrontation. Now it was Suetonius' task to see that Cartimandua remained wealthy and in favor with Rome.

Nevertheless, rewarding the woman came at too high a price, as usual. He knew she expected him to fuck her. The idea was sickening. Getting drunk would help, but he would never get drunk with the Britanni, no matter how loyal they seemed to be.

Cartimandua drew his chin toward her. "You think too much."

April showers added a thick humidity as if the tent were a caldarium. "A leader does, as you well know." His fingers grazed along her arm as she snuggled closer, her limp breasts pressing against his side. She lifted her chin for a kiss.

He smiled and smoothed wayward strands of black hair from her face, coated with enough makeup for three Roman women. Even his wife back in Rome would never appear like this, even around her slaves.

"You make me long for home," he whispered.

Cartimandua held out an empty cup to be filled. "I would, one day, love to see this city called Rome," she cooed as she resumed her position against him. "I hear it is beyond imagination."

"It is." He lifted his cup for more wine. Maybe getting drunk was the answer.

"I hear an Egyptian queen was granted a parade through Rome for her loyalty."

"I will see that you do as well." Not likely, especially for felines like her. He drank.

Cartimandua toasted him. "Well, I have something that may influence Caesar's thoughts."

"And what would that be?" he asked, forcing a smile.

"A Britanni. One you failed to kill."

That did interest him. He sat up. "A Britanni warrior?"

"Yes. He almost died, but he is strong now, perfect for your killing games." Cartimandua snapped her fingers. Two warriors appeared in the double doorway. "Bring the prisoner."

Four warriors dragged their captive in chains through the opening. His body was a mass of bulging muscles. Golden hair streamed over both broad shoulders. A full mustache draped over a snarl mean enough for the arenas.

Suetonius admired what stood before him. Nero would relish owning this gladiator.

Cartimandua waved her cup at the captive. "He hates everything Roman. He says one of your tribunes keeps his woman as a slave. Calls her Rhianna."

Valerius tossed the two girls off his body and sat up. "Yes, my nephew fucks her." He strolled around the man lurching at the chain. "Your name . . . so I can tell your woman that you live."

A sharp blue glare fell on Valerius. "Tell her Calgacus will come for her."

"For your whelp, too?"

The warrior stilled. "The babe lives?"

Valerius chortled. "I knew it was a Britanni bastard all along."

"What have you done with them?"

"Nothing yet."

Calgacus lurched against the guards barely controlling him. "I will kill you and your nephew for touching either of them."

He drew back to strike the insolence from the bastard's face.

"Valerius!" Suetonius snapped. "Not tonight. We will discuss this gift later. Take him away."

Valerius paced outside the prisoner's hut, waiting for the auxiliary soldier from Gaul to join him. He would be arranging this without Suetonius. Fortunately, the consul was willing to turn his attention elsewhere.

The blond guard appeared in the torch light. "I like it here. The women are willing."

Valerius led the auxiliary guard farther from the captive's hut. "I want you to do something, but it will take a smart man to do it."

The man huffed. "Of course. What can I do for you, centurio? That Britanni is in there?"

Valerius nodded toward the hut. "Yes."

"Do you think you can convince the fool that you are his friend and that you will help him escape to find his woman?"

"Escape, yes. Find his woman, I don't know."

"She lives behind the tavern of the fort in Londinium."

"I've seen her," the guard said with a smile. "She is the tribune's female slave?"

"Yes." Valerius lifted a bag of coins. "There is double if you kill all three of them after that bastard in there thinks he has gotten away with his little family."

A dangerous smile eased across the guard's mouth as he plucked the bag from Valerius' palm. "Three?"

"There is a whelp between them."

"I will need others to help me."

"Fine." Valerius placed the bag in the man's hand. "But you pay them."

Chapter 63

JULIUS STROLLED TOWARD THE SOUTHERN GATE, enduring the oblivion of the thick fog suffocating the fort. The smells from river Thames lay heavy in the air. The consul's orders to finish the reports had kept him in the Principia long enough. He could not think, much less concentrate. So, he walked the fort to release the frustration of being kept from Rhianna for another night.

"Halt! Password?" the duty guard ordered. Metal chinked as three other guards gathered under burning torches that sizzled in the dampness.

"Venus Victorious." Julius climbed the steps to the guard's station.

The tension melted. "Ah, tribune. All is secure."

"Good." He rested against the corner pole. "Nasty night for guard duty."

"Could cut this fog with a knife, I think."

"I agree," he said and scanned the black shadows of Londinium that lay in ruins. Torches burned in the burgeoning village like small yellow spots. Even in the misty darkness, he knew exactly where the tavern was that housed Rhianna and his son.

He had rented an apartment in the back of the tavern and wished every night he could be there with her. However, he was expected to live in the Praetoria with Suetonius, to be at his immediate call.

Fortunately, his orders back to Rome were due any day, and he would finally be taking his new family home. He smiled to himself, but it melted as the last conversation with his uncle echoed in his mind. *You have a proper wife in Rome waiting for you.*

Did he? He wanted to laugh.

Not one letter had arrived from Domitia, much less a notice of divorce from her father. It did not matter. He was taking Rhianna and his son back to Rome. He would deal with that then. He no longer cared what his uncle or his mother thought. Rhianna and Gnaeus were his life now.

He laid a hand on the guard's shoulder. "Stay vigilant, comrade." He climbed down to continue his walk.

Regardless of the fact that Rome had granted the XXth Valeria the title of Victrix and the XIVth Gemina the title of Martia Victrix, Suetonius had ordered the legions to remain under tents instead of relishing warm winter quarters. And it was the legions' orders to make certain that those who survived their little revolt continued rebuilding whatever they had destroyed.

If this was part of Suetonius' plan to make the legions temperamental and mean, it was working. He was not certain, now, who was worse—Suetonius or Decianus Catus. Julius passed more guards and recited the password.

Decianus Catus had disappeared, and his replacement had finally arrived from Rome. Julius Classicianus seemed a reasonable man But now both the consul and new procurator were caught in their own war—a war Julius no longer cared about.

Suetonius complained that the procurator was too lenient. The Britanni needed to learn what the supporters of Spartacus had to learn: Do not mess with Rome.

Classicianus disagreed and admitted to Julius that he had requested that Suetonius be replaced as soon as possible . . . before he created yet another revolt. Julius totally agreed. Anger was once again stirring a dangerous pot.

He strolled by the stable area where horses stamped and tore at the fragrant hay. He stopped in the intersection of roadways to pull Rhianna's pendant from beneath his cuirass.

As long as you wear this . . .

He kissed it and then dropped it back where it would always be, near his heart, and continued his walk. What he had paid the tavern keeper had been a wasted expense. Rhianna mended things for the soldiers now, and they looked after her when he could not. As did Lugh. Julius smirked.

Lugh had managed to make Rhianna laugh, something she needed. Until Gnaeus was born, Julius had worried constantly about the sadness that claimed her. Since the birth of Gnaeus, she had changed back to the woman he once knew, the woman he had fallen in love with.

Both Lugh and Rhianna conversed constantly in Iceni. He gave up trying to understand their jokes and taunts, enjoying what time he had to hold his son.

Gnaeus. Gnaeus Julius Agricola.

At one point, he wondered if the boy was truly his or the Britanni's. Yet the moment Gnaeus clutched his finger in his tiny fist, the doubt vanished. Now, all he wanted was to raise his son as he had been raised.

The granary buildings loomed before him. He could not see the long rectangular walls, but he smelled the grain. The guard started and then grabbed for his gladius. "Halt! Password!"

"Venus Victorious, Scripio."

"Oh, sorry, tribune. I could not see you."

Julius stopped at the steps to the granary porch where the soldier stood. "All is well?"

"Not even the mice are about tonight."

"Good." He leaned against the railing. "So you know, a new shipment arrived from the mainland today."

The guard rested against the building, propping his foot on the lower rail. "Men will appreciate the change in rations and wine. That is for sure."

"I am sure they will. Stay vigilant." The guard saluted.

With his first step away, Julius' mind returned to Rhianna pointing out that Gnaeus had his nose, his eyebrows, his lips, even the same chin.

He had rebutted that the babe had his mother's blonde hair and her blue eyes. She assured him that all babies had blue eyes at first.

To his delight, for the three months since Gnaeus was born, they had remained her cornflower blue.

Rhianna returned to the low stool at the end of the cot, picked up another torn cape, and tried to match the frayed edges. "Gnaeus, I can't fix this," she told the babe. "I'll tell Cletius he needs a new one."

Her son lay on the cot, kicking his feet. Their son. Yes.

Their son. Calgacus would . . .

She cut off the words when a sliver of cold stabbed her heart. *Calgacus is dead . . . dead like everyone else. Morrigan is with Mergith. My parents are together. I have no one left but Julius who had assured me there was no chance Calgacus lived, because every man left on the bloody field had been executed.*

He also explained that he had been unable to think straight after the first attack when she was kidnapped. And because of the attack that nearly killed him, he had let his uncle and mother talk him into the wedding ceremony he wished he had not endured.

And Lugh had convinced her that what Julius said was true.

She sagged against the slat wall, warm from the burning brazier, and listened to the male laughter seeping into her new home. The narrow room contained everything she needed: one cot, one table, a stool by a burning brazier, and a braided rug made from scraps. Two dresses that Lugh had found hung on the door beside a brown cloak.

She resumed the mending. When the soldiers brought their tunics and cloaks, they also brought small handmade toys for Gnaeus, which, apparently, had become a competition between them. Who could make one larger, more decorated, and softer?

She never imagined that the soldiers who had devastated her people could act this way over a child. Nor could she have imagined her people wanting to—

A large man, covered with a black cape, barged through the door, and reached for Gnaeus. The baby screamed, shooting fear through her. She charged the demon, the druid, whoever he was.

"Give—"

"Rhianna!"

Her heart slammed into her throat.

"Calgacus? You're alive?"

The familiarity flowed through her the instant his palm cupped her cheek.

"I'm taking you and our son away from here."

He started for the door.

"We need to go. I'll explain everything later."

Chapter 64

R HIANNA RACED INTO THE FOG-FILLED ALLEY after her son as Calgacus led her toward a small stable where two riders approached with the horses. "I smell Romans prowling. Let's go," one said. "I do, too," Calgacus said as he handed her Gnaeus and then lifted her up onto the horse.

"I . . . I thought you were dead," she said.

"Almost was. You kept me alive." He vaulted up behind her. "Hold on." He kicked the horse into a gallop.

The thick fog brushed her face as they rode through the dark cloud. "Where are we going?"

"As far from this Roman stench as possible."

A guard appeared in the doorway of the Principia where Julius tried to focus on another grain report. "Tribune, Decurio Marcus needs to speak with you. Urgently . . . a matter regarding a disturbance in the settlement."

Marcus charged past the guard. "Julius, I mean, tribune, you need to come. Now!"

"Why? What is it?" The frantic look on his friend's face brought Julius to his feet.

"It is Rhianna."

His heart choked his throat. "Rhianna. What is—?"

"There is no time. You have to come."

"Inform the prefect that he has the fort!" he yelled to the guard as he raced toward the gate, spouted the password, and charged into the settlement.

Julius bolted into the alleyway leading to Rhianna's doorway that lay open. The cot was empty. The room yawned lifelessly.

His insides collapsed as he faced the curious crowd gathering in the alley. "Fifty denarii for anyone who can tell me where they are. A hundred!" He pulled a sack of coins from his belt. "I want a name!"

A Britanni woman shuffled forward. "We, I mean, I . . . I saw them leavin'." Her dry, mousy-brown hair hung over her disheveled clothing. "Carryin' a babe." A shard of straw fell from her skirt.

"We? Tell me who!" Julius ordered.

A man stepped beside her. "I was with her. Two of 'em were mainlanders. The othern' was a big man with yellow hair. He was the one carryin' the boy."

"She called him Calgacus," the woman said. "Somethun' like that."

Julius looked at Marcus. "He is supposed to be dead." That failed to matter now. All that did matter was finding Rhianna and Gnaeus and killing Calgacus this time.

A soldier shoved his way through the clot of people. "Tribune, we found which way they went. They left on horseback. However, there will be no finding a trail in this shit. Not tonight."

"I am going after them." He started down the alley.

Marcus grabbed him by the arm and swung him around. "Julius. Attempt anything in this fog, and you are a dead man."

Julius tore his arm from the iron grip. "They are getting away, Marcus. I have to go after them."

"Not in this." A fist cut through the air and slammed into Julius' jaw.

Chapter 65

SOMETHING ABOUT THE TWO STRANGERS reminded Rhianna of the druid. Maybe it was their cold gazes. Maybe they were too quiet, but their presence bothered her. During the few stops to rest the horses, Calgacus had told her how they had helped him escape from the Brigante queen. They had told him that, after Rome killed their families back in Gaul, they hated Romans as much as he did. If so, then why were they on Britanni lands, she wondered.

Calgacus halted the winded horse beside a river stream to let the animal drink. "We camp here and leave before dawn. No one will follow us in this fog."

"As good as any place to make camp," one said.

Calgacus lowered her from the horse as Gnaeus fretted in her arms. She sat on a log to nurse him and watched the men settle for the night. One of the strangers left for wood, and the other cleared space for a small fire.

Calgacus finished the makeshift tent and then sat beside her, brushing his fingers through Gnaeus' hair as the babe ate. "He has your face and your eyes." He held the little hand. "And heart."

Rhianna managed to breathe as Gnaeus' tiny hand clutched Calgacus' finger, instantly melting the man. He beamed. "I said we'd have a son. Remember?"

"Yes. A son." Tears trailed down her cheeks.

He kissed the little hand. "Colin. Son of Calgacus. Son of the Trinovante. Do you like that?"

"Yes. Colin. Son of the Iceni."

Calgacus adjusted the blanket over Colin's tiny feet and remembered plucking the sleeping boy from the cot and holding his son in his arms for the first time. In that moment, he was complete again . . . healed completely.

He studied the sleeping child that had Rhianna's face and blue eyes, golden hair exactly like his, a strong grip, and a loud voice when hungry. There was nothing Roman about Colin.

He would be forever grateful to Ivan and Evart for killing the Brigante guards and helping him escape the same night Cartimandua had presented him as a gift to the Romans.

He slumped back in the blankets. He'd expected to see Rhianna panic because he knew she had been told he was dead, killed like everyone else.

There hadn't been time to explain anything to her while they were getting away from the settlement. But now she knew he planned to get them as far north as possible and away from Rome's clutches.

The gurgling sound of the nearby river brought back memories of the night Colin was conceived. He remembered every moment of bonding together and Rhianna saying she loved him. He'd thought nothing else could be more perfect, until now. He had a son—Colin, son of Calgacus, son the Trinovante, and son of the Iceni.

Rhianna shifted in her sleep, drawing the child ever closer to her. If the gods willed it, there would come a day when he would lead a mass so great that Rome would tremble and flee.

He had begun to understand why the Romans had won over the numbers that came against them. It would never happen again.

"Colin, this I promise you. You will never see another Roman."

Shadows thickened as flames in the fire pit burned down. It needed more wood to keep Colin warm. In addition, he needed to piss.

Calgacus eased from the makeshift tent and found his way through the stubborn fog to the riverbank. A long sigh had barely escaped when Rhianna screamed. Then Colin wailed.

He bolted back to the small camp as Evart released Rhianna and reached for Colin. Calgacus kicked him out of the tent, knocking him back into Ivan who stumbled backward into the glowing fire pit and fell. Flames ignited on his shirt, sending the man into frantic screams.

Holding a bloody knife in his hand, Evart rose to his feet. Calgacus charged, took Evart to the ground, broke the man's grip on the knife, and slashed it across the man's neck. He lurched to his feet for Ivan, but the fire had claimed him.

Colin's screams cut through his blood rage. He bolted back into the makeshift tent and fell beside his wailing son.

"Rhianna!

He clutched her lifeless body in his arms, lifting her from a pool of blood. Her head flopped back, exposing a gash across her throat.

"NO-O-O!"

The roar bellowed from the depths of his soul, as he rocked her and his wailing son in his arms.

Not now. Not now, Rhianna. Not now.

The babe's desperate screams finally broke through the pain shredding his heart. His son. Their son. Lived. He lived.

"Rhianna, Colin is alive. Our son is alive."

Tears bathed his words as he spoke to her dead gaze.

"Before all the gods, I promise, Rhianna, I'll protect him with my life."

Chapter 66

"I AM SORRY TO HEAR ABOUT YOUR SLAVE, Julius." With a façade of compassion, Suetonius looked down at Julius from the dais and sipped his wine. "Taken by one of her own, right?" Gulping his red fury, Julius nodded. He needed to leave now. He needed men to go find Rhianna before they got any farther. Marcus had his cavalry ready to leave. Yet, without the consul's approval, not one man would leave the fort.

He should have gone last night. However, Marcus had halted any chance of that. His head still thundered from being knocked out by one he had thought was his friend. At least, Marcus had the gall to be there when he came to and had endured his wrath while attempting to rationalize his actions.

A slave refilled Suetonius' goblet. The man turned his attention back to where Julius stood. "I am glad you maintained the sense to not go after them in that fog."

"Consul, I need—"

"You are a good officer, Julius. I have made certain that Rome is fully aware of your competence throughout this unfortunate event."

Suetonius presented a letter. "These are your orders to return to Rome, a well-deserved reward, and it comes at a most appropriate time as well."

Sons of Dis. His orders. Julius staggered as he read the parchment. Released from duty. He could have taken Rhianna and Gnaeus home. He could have. If this had not happened. The written words seeped through his disbelief. He was free. He no longer needed to follow anybody's orders. Hope swelled in his guts as he faced Suetonius. "According to this, I am no longer tribune. I am now a civilian of Rome."

Suetonius smirked. "Good observation, Julius."

It was official then. Now, according to Roman law, Rhianna and Gnaeus were his property. As a citizen, he had a right to find them and kill the person who stole them. Moreover, as a citizen, the military had to assist in any wrongs inflicted upon him.

He would need a scouting group to find the trail. Plenty of men were willing to help; Marcus being one of them. He would still need the consul's permission. If not, he would go alone.

He braced with the new resolve humming through him. "Then, as a citizen, I am requesting the assistance of a scouting group to find my slaves and the man who—"

"Denied."

Red fury beyond reason boiled his blood. "I am a citizen of Rome. What belongs to me has been stolen by a fucking Britanni. I demand that you allow men to assist in finding my slave."

Suetonius shifted in the chair and looked away as if considering the demand. He handed the goblet to a nearby slave. "As consul, I have the responsibility to protect all citizens and soldiers. Considering Britanni sentiment toward Rome at this time, the action that you demand, as a citizen, would be irresponsible. Nor will I order good soldiers to accompany you on a retaliatory mission just for a few Britanni slaves. Rome does not need another uprising from these fools."

He leaned forward in his chair, forearms on his thighs, hands clasped. "Besides, you are too valuable of a soldier and citizen to lose. Rome needs men like you. Shall I continue?" Every sinew in Julius' body coiled. No one gave a fucking damn about Rhianna or Gnaeus.

The consul continued. "A galley leaves for Rome today, this afternoon in fact. I think it would be best for you to be on it. Any further questions?"

Oh, he had plenty of questions, but he already knew the answers. However, he was not leaving without Rhianna and his son. He nodded a lie.

"Good then. Go. And may the gods speed your journey home."

Julius stormed back to the Praetoria. Fuck the orders. Rome had dictated enough of his life. He did not care what his uncle or his mother thought.

He would find Rhianna and Gnaeus. Lugh knew the land and the languages. Together they would find where the bastard had taken Rhianna.

Anger seared through Julius as he stormed into his quarters and plowed into Lugh carrying out one of his personal trunks. "What are you doing? You were supposed to get the horses."

"Following my orders." The sound of his uncle's voice wheeled Julius about.

"I will order them out when I am damn good and ready. Now leave, centurio."

His uncle smiled. "You are no longer laticlavius, you stupid little shit. And, since you are a citizen of Rome and need protection, I am ordered to see that you leave on that galley."

"Get the horses, Lugh. We are leaving now." Julius refocused on the hulk of his uncle blocking the door. "And nothing you say or do will stop me."

Valerius leaned on the doorframe. "Have you lost your mind, Julius, over this Britanni bitch and her whelp that is not even yours?"

"Watch me." Julius charged him, wanting to shove the insult down his uncle's throat.

Valerius smashed him against the nearest wall and pinned him there. "Get some sense, boy. You have a wife and a career to think about. Your mother has sacrificed enough to keep the name of Agricola respected in Rome. Do this, and it is all ruined."

Julius braced against the wall to heave his uncle aside, but it was like trying to lift an aqueduct. "I do not give a damn what Rome wants," ground from his throat.

Smashing his head against his uncle's forehead stunned the man long enough to shove him backward. His uncle staggered and then rose like a bull.

Julius swung at the blood-red face, only to be thrown on the bed, smashing it. They rolled to the floor.

Suddenly, Julius was flipped to his stomach with his uncle sprawling over him like a blanket. "I have been ordered to see you on that galley," his uncle hissed into his ear. "And I follow orders, as any soldier who has a brain left in his skull. You are going back to Rome if I have to drag you there like a slave."

"No!"

Suddenly, the weight disappeared. Julius sprang to his feet only to be met by his uncle's elbow slamming against the side of his head and everything went black.

First, it was the odor. Dank. Musty. Fishy. Next came the pain stabbing through Julius' brain as he shifted on a hard surface.

Groaning, he raised a hand to wipe away his confusion, but his wrist, unusually heavy, barely reached his face. He jerked at the restraint. No give. He looked down at the ropes encircling both of his wrists and bound to the curving hull of a galley.

Panic cleared his mind in an instant.

Above him, voices talked and laughed while things were scraped across the upper deck. He scanned the small cabin where his trunks and armor filled a corner. The cry of sea gulls finalized what was happening. *You are going back if I have to drag you there like a slave.*

Terror clutched every muscle, every thought, and every nerve. His uncle and Suetonius were forcing him leave without Rhianna. Without Gnaeus.

Julius yanked at the ropes that simply shifted like snakes and continued to hold him on the narrow cot. "Lugh! Get in here!"

The door opened and a guard appeared.

"Get my slave, damn you. That is an order!"

The guard shook his head. "Orders are to keep your man away until we cross."

Overhead, lines thudded to the deck along with orders to get under way. The galley shifted free in the water.

"No!" He thrashed for some element of freedom and searched the small cabin for some weak spot. Nothing.

"Do not do this to me. By the gods, please," he pleaded as Rhianna's pendant moved across his chest. He grasped it until blood dripped onto the wooden floor tilting with the waves.

With each drop of blood, the vow seared into his soul.

I will come back. I will find you and our son. I will return.

Fini

Historical Note

The historian Cornelius Tacitus wrote gloriously of his father-in-law, Gnaeus Julius Agricola. He stated that Julius was present in Britannia during Boudica's revolt and did, in fact, act as the second-in-command, or tribune laticlavius, to Suetonius Paulinus the assigned consul/governor to Britannia when Boudica decided to run Rome to the sea.

Julius may well have been present when Decianus Catus, the procurator who arrived soon after the death of Prasutagus, demanded payment of taxes, and ended up having Boudica flogged and their daughters raped.

Boudicca. Boudeaca. Boudica. Boadicca. How to spell her name or even say it, no one really knows. Celts did not write. However, in his book *Boudica*, Graham Webster explained why he believes the Iceni queen's name was spelled as I have it in my story. "Thus, this romantic Victorian poet helped to perpetuate this error, which remains with us, since most people know her as Queen Boadicea, her actual name is Boudica." Throughout the years of researching this fantastic lady, I have noticed that even the History Channel has come to agree with Mr. Webster.

Boudica was not alone in her hatred for Rome. Many tribal leaders throughout Britannia despised Rome's taxes, its demand for young men to join the legions, and the confiscation of lands for retired soldiers. However, their greatest threat was to the many Britanni gods, such as Andraste and Camulos. The murder of the druid priests on the Isle of Mona did little to assure the Britanni that Rome would respect their gods as long as the Britanni honored Rome's gods as well.

Suetonius Paulinus was in Wales and had been ordered to destroy the druid stronghold on the Isle of Anglesey/Isle of Mona. It was there where he received word of Boudica's revolt and that the IXth Hispana was almost annihilated as they came to Camulodunum's aid.

Today, if you dig in the dirt beneath Colchester/Camulodunum, you will find fifteen inches of ash left by Boudica and her Britanni followers. Colchester's History Museum sits on the original foundation of the Temple Claudius where people were burned alive inside the sanctum. During my visit there, I actually stepped into the lower vault filled with the only remains left of this fire. In the case in London/Londinium, Tacitus says Roman women *were* found naked, mutilated, and dangling in a warehouse, and that more bodies were sacrificed on stakes and beheaded by the river Thames. I walked along Watling Street where Boudica led her people out of this burning settlement to follow Suetonius to St. Albans/Verulamium, the third and final city she destroyed.

Tacitus did quote Suetonius as having said that he had to "sacrifice a city to save a province."

The camp prefect of the IInd Augusta truly did refuse Suetonius' orders and later fell on his sword, leaving Suetonius only the XXth Valeria and the XIVth Gemina to meet him in the area of Mancetter, which is presumed to be the place of the final battle. This site has not been located with any certainty, but Tacitus places it around the river Anker.

Reports say 240,000 Britanni faced 10,000 Romans that day. Was it any wonder that Boudica and the leaders thought they held the advantage? Yet the Britanni lost against Rome's legions for the same reason all the barbarians did. They fought individually, man on man, against Rome's trained fighting machine.

As for Morrigan and Rhianna, their names are as Britanni as I could find because there is no record of their names. Yet Tacitus wrote that both daughters were raped. However, what if one was not? What if she fell in love with a Roman officer and he with her?

For me, this may explain why Gnaeus Julius Agricola returned to Britannia in AD 71 as legate/commander and again, from AD 73-84, as consul/governor of seven campaigns in Britannia.

- What could possibly bring him back to this island that offered him little prestige or wealth in the eyes of Rome?
- What could drive him to conquer more of this island than any other consul?
- What could drive him to confront Calgacus, the leader of the Calédonie/Scottish tribes, in one final battle at Mons Graupius?

Perhaps Gnaeus Julius Agricola returned looking for his son and seeking revenge against the man who tried to destroy his life.

In addition, who was this man called Calgacus, who actually did lead the Caledonian tribes against the might of Rome twenty-four years later?

- Was he a warrior who escaped Boudica's revolt and went north?
- Could he have loved a Roman's child as his own?
- And what became of the boy named Colin, half Roman/half Iceni?

Find out in the coming books of my Agricola Series Red Fury—a story of a father's love. But which one?

THE CHRYSALIS

JF RIDGLEY

343

Just when the caterpillar thought the world was coming to an end, she turned into a butterfly

Chapter 1

MORRIGAN SHRANK AWAY from the Roman slaver's filthy hand reaching for her. The short chain to her slave collar allowed him to clutch her hair and yank her close. "I look forward to fucking you like we did last night." The stench of his foul breath hit like a fist.

"Look forward to it, little princess."

Images of that horrid night seared through Morrigan—soldiers raping all the women of the Iceni as their men watched. Hatred boiled in her veins. She sank her teeth into the Roman's fat cheek.

"You little bitch!" He backhanded her, knocking Morrigan into the woman chained behind to her. Stars swarmed in her glare as she struggled to stand. Still, she managed to ram her knee into his groin. The Roman doubled over in pain.

The master slaver, the one named Silvio, the bastard who planned to sell them in Rome, charged his horse between them. "Leave the bitch alone, Ruisco. I don't want her ruined like you did the last—"

A lance sang through the air and jerked Silvio from his horse. Another pierced the Roman's back, throwing him toward Morrigan. She moved aside and let him fall to the mud at her feet just as an explosion of war cries burst from the thick bushes and undergrowth lining the road. Livid glares of angry warriors flooded into view.

Diras! Calgacus! Joyous tears sprang to Morrigan's eyes. She had never seen a more beautiful sight as Trinovante swords gleamed in the midday sun while the tribe's warriors slaughtered all those who were not chained.

One of the men behind her was cut free, allowing him to search Silvio's body for the key to the slave collars. Once freed, he shoved the key into her palm. "Free the rest. I have some killing to do."

The feel of metal falling from her neck would never be forgotten. Morrigan tossed the key to the woman beside her, fell to her knees, and snatched the knife from the Roman's belt to plunge it into his chest.

"Die, you bastard. Die!"

All the pain the Romans had done to her people rose to a boil in her soul. Memories returned of holding Mergith—the man she loved more than life itself—as his blood poured onto the ground. Seeing them lash her mother after they had insulted her father's funeral. And then the killing, the raping. Selling the Iceni as slaves. She wanted the Romans dead, all dead.

Shoving vagrant strands of auburn hair from her blood splotched face, Morrigan scanned the grove for another worthy of her wrath. There were none. The other Iceni women were purging the same horrors onto those who thought they could break them.

"Never." Morrigan lifted the knife to drive it into the body yet again when a hand gripped her wrist. Her heart froze. The image of a Roman shifted into the bloody warrior who had been Mergith's friend came into view.

He let go of her wrist. "I think he's dead enough," Tancorix said and offered a hand to help her up. "We need to leave before the Roman patrol arrives. Besides, your mother calls for you."

Her mother!

Morrigan belted the knife and turned to scan for her mother's wagon. It lay overturned. The funeral gifts, claimed for taxes, scattered the ground. Her mother wasn't there. "Where is she?"

"Over there." Tancorix pointed his bloody sword toward another wagon slipping over the sharp ridge.

Groans greeted Morrigan as she scrambled onto her wagon and sank beside what was left of her mother, the Iceni queen, Boudica.

The Roman's whip had competently torn her regal body until she was barely recognizable and barely alive.

"Mother, Diras came. We're no longer slaves. They freed us." The glorious news failed to stir the Iceni queen. Fear sliced through Morrigan. "Mother, answer me?"

"M…Mor…Morrigan," whispered from Boudica's torn mouth. Her hand rose, searching for something.

Morrigan clutched it, feeling the fragile strength in her mother's grip. "I'm here, Mother. I'm here."

"The . . . Romans?"

"Dead. All of them. Dead."

Boudica nodded. "G-Good. They die." A faint smile appeared and then faded. "Rhiann . . . Rhianna?"

Morrigan could never tell her mother that her sister had been taken by a Roman tribune and that she wasn't among them. "I don't know where she is."

Marleth, the stout Trinovante queen sitting beside Boudica, swiped a wet rag over Boudica's forehead. "Never fear, dear friend. Calgacus will find her. You must live until then."

Morrigan noticed Tancorix strolling victoriously beside the wagon. "I pity any Roman who faces Calgacus right now," he said.

"Kill all the Roman bastards," she retorted.

Tancorix shrugged. "We will. In time."

Diras, the chief of the Trinovante, and his son Calgacus pushed through the lumbering crowd following the wagons, leaving the blood bath behind. Both were as big, blond, and blood covered as Tancorix. Triumph radiated in their gazes.

"How is she?" Calgacus' deep concern surrounded Morrigan like thick fur. Mergith had once said that Calgacus was one of the best warriors in either the Iceni or Trinovante tribes. He also worshipped Rhianna, something no Roman would ever do.

"Boudica lives," Marleth said to the concerned gazes.

"But we need to get her to the hill fort as quickly as possible."

Calgacus turned to his father. "I'll let everyone know to hurry. Tancorix! With me."

Morrigan started from the wagon as both warriors turned to leave. Diras stopped her. "Stay. Your mother needs you. We'll see to your people."

Gratitude blurred Morrigan's vision as she lay a hand on the chief's forearm. "May all the gods see your strength and bless your people."

Boudica nodded. "An. . . Andraste sees. She is with. . . us."

Jubilance over the Romans' defeat sang in the air as the Iceni people moved quickly toward the Trinovante hill fort. Songs, laughter they thought would never live again, and cheers rang in the air until they passed Boudica's lifeless body. All silenced into whispers.

"I'm glad Boudica spit in the bastard's face. He deserved it."

"All Romans do is take and leave us nothing."

"I'd like to shove Rome's taxes up their bloody asses."

"Send 'em back where they belong, I say."

Morrigan listened to their hatred and agreed. Over the many years, her father had had little choice other than to either barter with the Romans or be destroyed by them. Then Rome returned his co-operation by rejecting his will and demanding payments for taxes they did not owe. What was to stop these invaders from taking anything they wanted, taxing as much as they wanted, and destroying all that was sacred from every tribe? Nothing.

Morrigan lifted her face to the afternoon sun. "Andraste, help me. From now on, I will kill every Roman I see." She drew the Roman's knife and cut a blood offering to the goddess in her palm.

She climbed down and walked, feeling life begin to surge inside her bones. It felt glorious. Again, she lifted her face to the goddess and stumbled on a grass mound.

Tancorix grabbed her arm before she fell. "You won't kill an ant, much less a Roman, if you can't walk," he said with a hardy laugh.

She swung to claw his face, but the warrior clutched her wrist and then the other, letting her thrash just as the Romans had. Terror whipped through her. As before, she slammed her knee into his groin, seeing the same pain cut through the warrior as it had the Roman.

Tancorix's smirk vanished as he tossed her away. Meager satisfaction stirred as she stumbled into a nest of warriors. A sword hilt brushed her hand. She snatched the weapon away and swung it at Tancorix, still cursing in pain.

Cheers rose as people circled. "Get him, Morrigan!"

Suddenly alert, Tancorix stepped back and slid his sword from its sheath, welcoming her threat. Morrigan swung the heavy blade where she could. His head. His legs. His narrow waist. However, the warrior merely blocked her attempts or stepped back enough to feel the passing breeze.

Seconds later, his sword slammed against hers, shooting pain through her entire body. He closed the distance between them and reached for the sword. In that instant, the iron became heavy, very heavy. Heavy like her heart. She couldn't carry both.

Before there was the possibility of his flesh against hers, she jerked away, only to feel him come with her and wrench the sword from her grip. Burning tears burst from her glare directed at the warrior. Hatred seared every nerve.

Calgacus broke through the cheering crowd. "What going on?"

"Nothing really." Tancorix chuckled as he stepped back, handing the sword back to its owner. "Our little princess got a little upset because she didn't have a rag to wipe her tears."

The same words spoken by the Roman hit hard. Morrigan charged, determined to claw the smirk off the warrior's face. Calgacus' arm swept around her waist, lifting her from the earth. She kicked and tore at her captor as powerless as she had been with the Romans. The fact struck sharp as any arrow.

"Wait, Morrigan. Owww!" Calgacus set her on her feet but held her to his chest as she thrashed. "Tancorix, apologize before she tears my arm off."

"No. Let her thrash until she realizes she will never be able to kill Romans. We would all be safer with her sitting at her loom."

His words froze her with fury. "I can kill Romans! And I'll start with him." She jerked for her freedom. "Calgacus, let me go!"

"Morrigan. Stop." Calgacus jerked her around to face him. "Your mother needs you. She—"

"She doesn't need me. She has your mother." Morrigan glared at Tancorix. "And I will kill any man who thinks he can destroy me, including you."

"Go ahead. Try."

Calgacus kept his grip on her shoulders. "Morrigan, you can't just grab a sword and think you can kill a man."

Halting, she turned her venom on her captor. "Then teach me."

A smirk rose on Calgacus' lips as he relaxed his grip. "Morrigan. Let us take care of the Romans. It's too much for a woman."

"Too much for a woman?" She stepped away, glaring at both men. "If you won't teach me, then I'll find someone who will teach me to kill any Roman . . . or any man."

Grinning, Tancorix propped both hands on his hips. "Fine. If you want to learn to fight, be outside your sleeping hut before dawn kisses the skies." He waited for her answer. So did Calgacus.

"I'll be there," she snarled.

Tancorix beamed like a victor. "And you'll do everything I say."

"All but fuck you."

"All but that." Tancorix nodded. "You heard her, Calgacus."

"Oh yes. We all heard."

Chapter 2

ORRIGAN WALKED THROUGH THE DOORWAY of the simple straw hut Diras had given her and her mother. It was comfortable and clean, but bare. They had bed mats, stools, and blankets, at least, to keep the spring chill away. Three Iceni women appeared early and assured her that they would care for her mother. Knowing that, she stepped outside into the growing bits of dawn.

Later that night, like the rest of the women, she had scrubbed in the river until her flesh was raw in hopes that the horrors would float away with the current and that their lives would return to normal. Yet, the disgust remained, festering like an infection beneath her skin. Would she ever be free of the horrors of their hands, their voices, their bodies?

While birds chirped in the distant trees or the thatched rooftops, she paced. A rooster crowed from somewhere in the village. Sheep bleated piteously to be taken to the pasturelands. Would Tancorix come, or did he consider her time wasted?

She remembered the smirk eating on his face when he offered to train her, thinking she would never be strong enough to kill a Roman. His task was to prove that to her. Anger warmed her. She could kill Romans, or she would die trying. She wanted revenge. The thought tasted sweet in her mouth.

Was Tancorix coming? She didn't think he would miss another chance to humiliate her. Part of her wanted him to come, but another dreaded what she was attempting. To fight meant having male flesh touch her, hear their growls, and feel their pummeling fists again.

Even knowing that, she welcomed the challenge, because she needed to hear their cries of pain instead of her own. Whatever

Tancorix demanded of her, she would do. Anything but lay with him or any man. That part of her would forever remain with Mergith.

"Greetings, warrior."

Morrigan's heart thundered in her chest from the words stated behind her. She wheeled. "I'm not a warrior . . . not yet."

"No?" Tancorix walked close enough for her to smell him, soap made with pine. "Do you think you can become such?"

"We'll see, won't we?"

A gleam flickered in his gaze. "Warriors never doubt."

"Then, yes. I'm a warrior."

The rosy dawn bloomed in the sky as he smiled. "Good. Then, keep up with me." He turned and broke into an easy stride.

Morrigan stood there, dumbstruck. She expected him to do anything but run off.

Tancorix turned and ran backward. "You coming, little princess?" An eternity passed with the morning sunlight, and now every muscle in Morrigan's body rebelled against any attempt to move. They had run until her legs gave out and she had collapsed. Then, Tancorix ordered her to lift logs until her arms couldn't bend. And they ran again.

Now, he tossed a stone at her, expecting her to toss it back. It landed in her palms, slipped free, and thudded to the ground. All she could do was stare at it.

Tancorix waited, grinning as if he'd done nothing all day. "Pick it up."

She couldn't force her arms to move. "I can't."

"Pick it up and throw it back or I will not see you tomorrow."

She couldn't bend. Her hands seemed frozen. Her legs had solidified into wood. Her body begged to be left alone.

"Guess you don't want to kill Romans after all?"

His ridicule grilled through her. Ignoring the agony slashing across her shoulders, ignoring the pain searing through her blistered and bleeding palms, ignoring it all, she launched the stone at the smirking warrior, wanting it to smash his face.

He caught it.

"Good. Now, go wash. You stink." She couldn't even snarl at his back as he walked away.

Fourteen days now. Fourteen. It was getting easier to face the man coughing to let her know he was waiting for her to step from the hut. At least, she didn't have to listen to the rooster's crow before she could breathe.

Releasing a painful groan, Morrigan eased her legs off the bed mats and managed to stand. Her right arm cramped, shooting pain to her fingers as she rubbed her thighs. Stiffness in her shoulders eased as she moved them, and her legs loosened enough to put one foot in front of the other so she could struggle into her knee-length tunic and braid her hair.

A grin slid over her lips as her body began to submit. She was healing. She felt it deep in the marrow of her bones. She wasn't the delicate creature Mergith had known, but she knew he would like what he saw. The image of his smile floated across her memories, softening her heart. This was for him. And he was pleased. Knowing that, her body eased into a stride that took her outside.

Tancorix stood there as hard and tanned as polished oak. His ever-present smirk barely hid beneath his brown mustache dangling on either side of his wide mouth. His green eyes gleamed with pleasure at seeing her. Unlike Calgacus, he stood her height, so she could glare directly into his gaze.

This man, this warrior, her constant tormentor, had proven to be unbreakable, driving, and loyal, granting little mercy even for himself. It was getting harder to hate him.

His gaze studied her from her head to her feet. "So, killing Romans isn't as important now as combing your hair?"

She granted him a smile. "A warrior needs to appear lovely when killing the bastards, don't you think?"

Tancorix's chuckle was reward enough. "Let's go, if you think you are up to it."

"I have been every day, haven't I?" Morrigan asked. She'd never admit that the muscles in her legs trembled at the thought. She started into an easy jog.

Tancorix followed. "This slow enough for you?"

"You want faster, fine."

Against her body's wishes, she bolted along a busy stream bubbling down the hill. They raced past the pasturelands filled with cattle, past the thick line of trees, and toward a small group of men by a pond who were tossing stones or each other into the water.

She halted. "What are they doing here?"

He stopped with her. "You afraid of a few men?"

Yes. She was afraid. Her heart pummeled her ribs like fists. All she saw were men just standing there, chuckling between themselves as if this were a game and she was the prize. It was like being with the Romans again.

With every breath, she wanted to run back to the hut and hide. Dread flooded into every particle of her aching body. She couldn't do this. "We would all be safer with her sitting at her loom," echoed in her brain. Maybe she should go back with the women and weave wool.

"Morrigan, face these men as you will Romans one day."

Mergith? He was there with her. A calmness settled through her, enough to study each man. Two were short and strong like an ox. The other two were taller and likely agile as Tancorix.

"They are just men, Morrigan. Just men, not monsters."

"Thought you wanted to learn to fight . . . men?" Tancorix asked.

"Still want us to help you?" one asked and then glanced around at his friends for approval. They laughed and nodded.

Tancorix looked directly into her eyes. "Well?" he asked. That taunt. That same irritating smile trickled across his lips.

Mergith wanted this for her. He was there with her. She could do this. "Yes."

Tancorix waved everyone around the two of them.

"Let's see."

Vomit rose at the thought of them touching her, gripping her. Sweat covered Morrigan's skin as the feeling of cold claws cut through her guts. One of the men grabbed for her. She slapped his arm aside. Another grabbed from behind. She whirled to kick him, only he shoved her into another who grabbed her shoulders, spinning her into the next man who heaved her backward. The ground claimed her—hard. Her mind screamed to run, to flee. Tears burned her eyes.

The circle of men stood there, gloating. "Aw, look. She's crying."

She closed her hands into fists as if clinging to some form of invisible strength and willed her heart to quiet. She rose slowly, brushed grass from her legs, and tried to swallow.

One of the ox-like men with a gloating smirk asked.

"Ready to go again, little princess?"

"Don't call me that."

He laughed. "What are you going to do if I do, little princess?"

"Make you regret it."

All the warriors chortled except for Tancorix, who stood outside the circle like a hawk on a tree limb.

One grabbed for her again. She clutched his wrist, yanked, and flung him across the circle. He stumbled into one of the men.

"Very graceful, Orc!" Tancorix yelled.

Orc wheeled and lunged like a lion. Without thinking, she dove between his legs and clutched his balls as he slammed to the earth behind her. Triumph poured through her as he lay there, curled in pain.

Orc growled and struggled to his feet. "Little bitch! I'll show you."

Morrigan lurched to her feet, her heart thundering in her dry throat. At least, he didn't call her "little princess." A smile emerged on her lips. Her small victory melted like morning dew while they circled.

Orc charged. She sidestepped, bending under his arm, and spinning to his side. He came up empty and wheeled around.

"Still waiting," slipped from her mouth.

The observers' gazes shifted to something behind her. Morrigan spun and kicked the tall man's knee. He collapsed with a thunderous roar of pain.

Taking a stance foreign to her, but a stance, for anyone else to try something, she realized, she was actually starting to enjoy this. She was clueless of what she was doing and how she was doing it. How long could she keep this up? She let her instincts tell her as she watched their every move.

Anger roared behind her as Orc charged again. The sight of his bloated image coming at her froze her in place. Tancorix launched himself at the man's legs, taking both to the grass. Hands grappled for a solid hold. Then, Tancorix flipped Orc on his belly and yanked the man's arm across his back. The warrior submitted.

"Been a while since I really had someone try to best me," Tancorix said as he let go and stood.

"I didn't try to whip your ass," Orc snarled as he got up, rubbing his shoulder. "I wanted hers."

"I know. But I want something to play with later." Tancorix dusted himself off. "We're done here."

Orc stopped. "We get to play with her again?"

"If you want your balls ripped off," poured from Morrigan's lips.

"Be ready, little princess." The men meandered away, taunting Orc.

Tancorix sighed and turned to her. "That's fighting, Morrigan. And for a girl, you handled yourself well . . ., like a girl."

She scanned every inch of the man before her. He was wrong. She hadn't fought like a girl. However, she had fought and, oddly enough, some of her fear had been shed like a snake's skin.

"That's all it takes to fight a Roman? I just have to fight like a girl?"

Tancorix stared at her and then laughter reeled from him until his legs crumpled and he lay there rolling in his laughter.

A triumphant smile bloomed on Morrigan's lips as she watched.

Chapter 3

Again, her body balked like a mule. Her hands simply could not grip the sword, and her arms refused to lift it. "I can't. I can't do any more," she gasped. She had blocked Tancorix's sword every time he had come for her. Sweat poured not only off her, but this time it covered his body as well.

Tancorix squatted to rest the sword across his thighs. Normally, he slid it into its sheath. "You're finally showing promise," he gasped.

The last month had been grueling. Each day the warriors joined them, intent on showing her a new move and how to use a sword, a knife a lance, or any weapon. Orc still tried to take her down and had twice. He came up taunting her with his nickname for her: "Little Princess." It no longer stung because she had nicknamed him "Ox." and it had stuck.

"You still want me to bring him?" a voice yelled a short distance away.

They both looked up at a boy leading a bay horse toward them.

"Yes," Tancorix answered as he stood, wincing with the effort.

Her insides caved as Morrigan studied the lumbering animal meandering behind the boy. Not again. Another horse to vault onto. This was for Mergith, she reminded herself. For his death. And her people.

She had repeated this mantra to herself each time she had to force herself to do more than she dreamed she could. If vaulting onto another horse helped her kill even one Roman, she'd find a way to leap onto the animal until nightfall. Determination solidified through her, sizzling like a hammered blade plunged into cold water.

The misery lasted until the poor creature sidestepped after she had slammed into the animal's side instead of landing on its back. Pulling her body from the dirt, Morrigan planted her foot behind her to try again.

"You ever pull my hair again; I'll whip your ass proper."

Morrigan turned as a boy stumbled back against a nearby hut. His assailant had drawn her bucket back, daring him to return.

"I'll pull your hair any time I want to." The boy charged the girl, missing the bucket by inches. The girl screamed as he gripped her shredding braid and yanked her down to the dirt.

Morrigan bolted toward them and threw the boy aside. "Stop this, now!"

The boy swung a fist at Morrigan's chin. Without thought, she shoved him face-first into the dirt. "You heard me. I said stop this. Now."

He rolled over, tears gleaming in his eyes. "She hit me with that bucket."

Morrigan planted her feet between the snarling children. "Looks to me like you needed it. Don't ever do that again to any girl on this hill fort."

Defiance shot the boy to his feet. "I ain't takin' no shit off no girl for doing nothin' to her."

"If you do anything like this again, you'll deal with me. Or him." Morrigan motioned to Tancorix, watching the whole thing with a smirk. "Do you understand me?"

For a long moment, the boy's fists opened and closed until he turned and raced from sight.

Morrigan turned to the girl. "Did he hurt you?"

"No. Just made me dumped all the water is all." The girl turned to Tancorix and waved her empty bucket toward Morrigan. "I'm gonna be a warrior like her one day."

Morrigan and Tancorix stood together as the girl swaggered back to the stream. "I think your plan of becoming a warrior has started something," Tancorix said.

"I hope so." She wanted all the women to feel strong, not only physically, but mentally. If any woman wanted to learn to defend herself as she had, then it would be worth every pain she had endured.

Chapter 4

TANCORIX FINALLY PINNED MORRIGAN to the ground. He got up and let her climb to her feet. "Want to try again?" She brushed dirt and grass from her leggings. It didn't matter that he had bested her, but after two months of working with the warrior, she was finally making him work for it. To her surprise, she was starting to like the challenge of the hard contact.

She shook her head at him. "I think you need a break."

"Me? Hardly." However, it was obvious Tancorix appreciated the offer.

She slumped down on a stump hidden in the tall grass and watched smoke drift from the village toward the clouds—good smoke, happy smoke. Smoke that fed bellies and made weapons.

Each day more people came with news of Rome's latest insult. More taxes. More land taken from them. More sons forced into Rome's legions. The Trinovante hill fort now brimmed with angry warriors from every tribe who wanted Roman blood as much as she did.

Roman scouts were seen almost daily, meandering on the horizon, watching. Boys tending the herds would stop them to idly chat while another snuck back to the hill fort with the news. Once informed, somehow the village got quiet. The hammering of weapon making stopped.

So far, The Romans never came close enough to . . .

Tancorix yanked her into the grass, clamping his hand over her mouth. He shook his head to be quiet. He jerked his chin toward the ridge where two horses appeared and then eased his hand from her lips.

Silver on their bridles glinted in the morning sun as riders in their gleaming metal shirts, red capes, and silver helmets continued forward. Roman scouts.

Panic flooded through Morrigan while the scouts scanned the busy hill fort. Her body was flooded with horrid memories.

The herders must not have spotted them. Perhaps a warning not arrived in time because the sound of the smiths making weapons still rang in the air. By Rome's decree, no tribe was to have or make weapons; now these scouts would report this back to their leader.

"What are they doing here?" she whispered.

"Likely they heard rumors of your mother's plans to drive them back to the mainland."

She gripped his arm. "But they can't know we are making weapons for that. What do we do?"

"Kill them." He studied both riders. "I'll distract them. You go bring Calgacus and the others."

You go bring Calgacus and the others. By the time she got back with Calgacus, Tancorix could be dead or taken as prisoner. Cold anger swelled deep. He didn't believe she could fight, even now.

Morrigan shook her head. "I have a better idea."

"A better idea?"

"Yes. Where is your lance?"

Tancorix nodded toward the distant rock where they had left the swords and lances.

"Think you can get to your lance after I lure them away?" Morrigan asked.

He glared at her as if insulted. "Yes. Why?"

"Give me your knife and see."

"What? My knife?" Tancorix loved his knife.

She opened her hand for the weapon. "I need it to kill a Roman."

Tancorix withdrew the weapon from his belt. "Are you sure you want to do this?"

"Yes." She had to.

"Then, make sure I get it back."

Morrigan hid the knife in her knee-high boot and then rose from the grass to amble innocently away from Tancorix and the hill fort. She brushed grass from her breasts and belly, and then lazily swung her braid over her shoulder. She undid it to comb each auburn strand out the length of her arm, letting it filter through her fingers in the sunlight.

When the scouts noticed her, she halted, truly frozen. She felt their hungry gaze as if it were a lance piercing her body. A strange new feeling coiled inside her. This was different. "This is for you, Mergith," she whispered. Her hand stopped at the length of her hair, letting the last of the strands fall.

Every moment of those soldiers' scrutiny was an eternity. The desire to scream and flee to the hill fort charred through her insides.

"Well, what have we here?"

She made herself meet their gazes fully before bolting toward the clump of willow trees. The scouts raced their horses after her, cutting off her escape into the trees.

"It's been too long since I had a nice piece of Britanni cunny," the squatty Roman smirked.

Seeing Tancorix slithering like a snake toward his lance steadied her. Morrigan studied the soldier who was a little bigger than Orc but not as thick. Yet she knew he was equally as strong. That morning, she had managed to get a knife to Orc's throat. This time, her cut would be real.

Backing up toward the trees and away from Tancorix, she said with as much authority as her mother would have said, "Go back to the Roman hole you climbed out of this morning!"

Ignoring her comment, both scouts slid from their horses, leaving them to graze. "You look familiar. Have I fucked you before?" the tall soldier asked.

Suddenly, she recognized them as well. Every moment in their tent flashed before her. This time, her hatred destroyed her fear. This time, she needed to hurt them as they had her. She braced her feet, ready for whatever.

They ambled toward her, unbuckling their sword belts as she continued to back toward the trees. "Yeah, you're that Iceni bitch that bit me on the hand." The short one rubbed his hand with the memory.

One of the horses lifted his head from the grass as Tancorix claimed his lance. She inhaled and slowly let it out, returning her gaze to the soldiers. She eased his knife from her boot.

"Think that's gonna stop me?" The short scout laughed and grabbed for her arm.

She slapped his hand away. "Yes."

"Well, I promise, your mate won't like it when we get through with you this time," the tall Roman chortled.

"He'll kill you if you try."

"Really? I don't smell any filthy Britanni warriors around here other than you."

A sneer coiled across her lips. "If he doesn't kill you, then I will."

The short one crossed his arms and set a wide stance.

"Kill both of us?"

"Yes."

He looked at his friend. "She really believes she can."

"Guess we'll have to teach her that she can't."

"Absolutely."

Every muscle in her body coiled, ready to run, but it was too late for that. The hair on her neck rose. Sweat coated her palms. She pictured the knife slamming into the short scout's chest as it had the slaver. It steadied her.

One grabbed her wrist and yanked her back to the moment. She let herself fall, as Tancorix had taught her. The urge to cut the air with her knife burned through her. However, Tancorix had taken the weapon too many times when she had.

The Roman lunged to fall on her. She thrust her knife straight for his neck, but he jerked aside for the blade to miss its mark. However, blood appeared from the tiny slice on his neck. She heaved him aside and sprang to her feet.

"You filthy little cunt!" He grabbed for her knife.

She clutched his wrist and tossed him aside with her leg. Once free, she lunged to her feet. The tall Roman charged for her. She wheeled and drove the blade into his flank. Warm blood poured over her hand as she jerked the knife free and slammed it into his crotch. He collapsed, taking her down with him to the grass. Still, she managed to yank the blade free to drive it beneath his jaw. Once. Twice. She was driving for a third time when a hand caught her wrist.

The other Roman.

She swung about, ready to drive the knife into the other scout, but again, found Tancorix grinning down at her.

"I want my knife back."

She swiveled away, searching for the second scout. "Where is the other one?"

Tancorix stepped aside for her to see the Roman lying face down in the tall grass and wearing a lance in his back.

Joy surged through Morrigan. "You actually can hit a target!"

Tancorix started to snarl, but his scout moved. Her elation melted. "The bastard lives!"

Tancorix reached for his knife. "Not for long. Give me my knife."

She pulled if from his reach. "No."

Morrigan walked to the scout and jerked the lance from his back. His cry of pain was music. She handed the lance to Tancorix. "This is yours, I believe."

He took it to lean on while she kicked the soldier over and knelt at his side. He was the one she remembered most. He was the one who haunted her dreams. Calmly, even slowly, she cut through his loincloth and clutched his limp penis.

"This is for all of the Iceni women you raped, you filthy piece of shit!"

She sliced the organ from his body, silencing his curses by shoving it into his mouth. She stood and faced Tancorix while the soldier gagged on his blood as she had his semen.

The smile that filled Tancorix's face was one of pride. He dipped his fingers into the Roman's blood and spread it across her forehead, down the bridge of her nose, and across both cheeks. "Well done, warrior. And know that I'll gladly fight at your side."

Warrior. Tancorix said he would gladly fight at her side—the oath shared by all warriors. Tears swelled in her eyes. She cleared her throat of the tears and said, "As I will fight at yours."

She nodded at the dead soldiers. "What do we do with them?"

Tancorix scanned the dead Romans and shrugged. "Take the bastards back to Diras. I figure he'll feed them to the pigs and give the horses to Myrradin to decide if Andraste wants them." He started toward the horses still grazing in the grass.

She stopped him with a touch to his arm.

"Here's your knife."

Tancorix's gaze lingered on the weapon and then rose.

"Keep it. I think it likes you."

Chapter 5

A PROCESSION BEGAN FOLLOWING THEM as she and Tancorix led the Romans' horses burdened with the dead scouts through the hill fort. Questions shot like arrows. Proud glances danced between her and Tancorix as they strode toward the main hut where Diras and Calgacus appeared in the doorway. Boudica followed with Marleth steadying her.

A smile lurked beneath Diras' thick golden mustache.

"You come with Roman gifts?"

Tancorix handed the reins of his horse to the Trinovante chief. "Dead Roman gifts."

Morrigan presented the reins of the other horse to her mother. "And I bring you Roman blood."

Boudica's smile twisted the scars crossing her cheeks as she accepted the gift. "I see you wear the marks of a warrior."

"As well as my oath to fight at her side," Tancorix announced, loud enough for the gathering to hear.

Murmurs rippled.

"How did the daughter of the Iceni earn such an oath from you, Tancorix?" Diras asked.

"The daughter of the Iceni confronted both Roman scouts alone and drew the last of their life's blood with her own hands," Tancorix said. "Before my eyes and the eyes of Andraste."

Amazement flickered between the warriors clustering close, while Diras examined the scout who had taken Tancorix's lance. He pointed to the wound. "And this?"

Tancorix nodded. "My lance, but her idea. A plan Morrigan made and executed."

Diras smiled at Morrigan. "The Trinovante accept your gifts, warrior!" he announced for all to hear. "And we thank you for protecting us this day."

"As do the Iceni. May Andraste be proud!" Boudica said. Pride in her mother's gaze drew tears to Morrigan's eyes. However, she left them to burn even as Mergith's smile bloomed in her heart.

Diras waved his arms, startling the horses. "Tonight, we welcome another sword, the sword of Morrigan of the Iceni, to defeat Rome!" Diras yelled. "As proof that, soon, we shall finally be free from its yoke."

Boudica stood to her full height, pulling away from Marleth. "Come, daughter of Prasutagus, daughter of the

Iceni. Your people wish to honor you. You have done well."

Morrigan's heart thundered in her chest as the warriors gathered behind her. Each wore a cocky smile as they mercilessly taunted Tancorix for granting her the victory, and yet they waited for her to lead them into the main hall.

Fini

Acknowledgements

There are so many to thank. God for starters. My family and friends who have all persevered with my dream all these years. All the Roman living historians who have been so generous with their time and knowledge. All my writer friends who continue to encourage me to keep improving. RWA and the Historical Novel Society for all they do to help everyone who writes. All those professionals: Cathy Helms of AvalonGraphics.org for the cover and Lisa DeSpain of Book2bestseller.com for your patience and expertise, and Patrick, Yvonne at Urated.com

Love you all.

And you, dear reader, for taking the time to enjoy my story. After all, that's what this is all about.

You.

About the Author

I love the ancient world. Even after years of researching and many trips to the sites of my stories, I am still fascinated by what I find for my next story. I love bringing this world to life in my award-winning stories of power, greed, violence, and love.

Be sure to stop by my website to discover more about my stories and to also sign up for my newsletter so you never miss what's coming next. Be assured that I do not share your address or send an excessive barrage of information. Please be sure to sign up for my newsletter at www.jfridgley.com.